MOON LORD:
THE FALL OF
KING ARTHUR

THE RUIN OF STONEHENGE

BY

J.P. REEDMAN

To Helen
With thanks
Hope you enjoy!

[signature]
(J P Reedman)

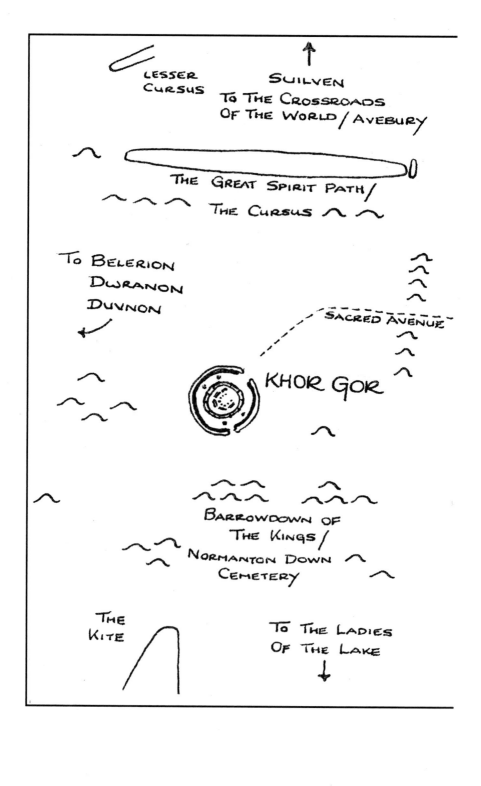

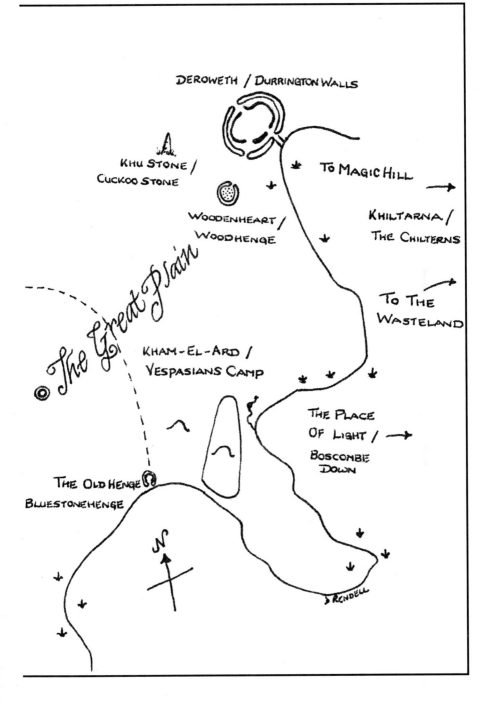

PROLOGUE
THE VISION

The last storm of winter shrieked across the Great Plain, blowing clouds of snow on its boreal breath and painting the stones of the ancestral temple of Khor Ghor with glittering patterns. Icy flakes crept into worn carvings and under lintels and made a frosty beard on the great Stone of Summer with its bowed head and glowering mouth.

In the heart of the circle the old man stood alone, listening to the roar and shriek of the storm. His face was leathery, brown from the elements, hawk-like in profile; his free-falling hair, once as black as the birds beneath the capstones of the circle, was now a dull slate-grey, sullen and harsh as the stones themselves. He wore a calfskin tunic, fringed with bones and tusks, and a hat of beaver skin protected his head from the blast of the wind. In his hands he carried his seeing stone, a lump of rounded quartz bequeathed to him in youth by his long-dead mentor, Buan-ann, the Old Woman of the tribe in distant Faraon, where the holy mountain God of Bronze rose to heaven, the dark spikes of its summit visible all the way to the Isle of Ibherna. He raised the quartz to his eyes and breathed heavily upon it, his breath fogging the age-polished surface.

He was the Merlin, high priest of Khor Ghor, the Dance-of-Ancestors... and an old man with fear in his heart.

"What can you tell me, spirits?" he murmured to the seeing-stone, to the sky, to the thin dark bluestones rising round him like a ring of watchers, frozen tribesmen from some ancient time. "What do you see? Why have I felt fear in my heart from Solstice onwards?"

The wind howled louder, rising and ululating, filled with malice and the voices of the long dead who did not sleep easy in their barrows. With shaking fingers, Merlin slipped a handful of chosen berries beneath his tongue in order to commune with the spirit-world. Within minutes his vision blurred, dimmed, streaking away into nothingness. Dizziness overwhelmed him and he thudded to his knees in the snow, back resting against the Stone of Adoration, the focal stone of Khor Ghor, standing alone before the colossal arch of the Door into Winter, with its enormous capstone, attached by sturdy mortise and tenon joints, thrust up almost into the lowering snow-cloud.

In his age-spotted hands the seeing stone grew hot and Merlin fancied could see figures stirring in its heart, playing out some secret, sacred dance... No, not figures, not of men, at least... The image was of the Sun, a wheel of blood, dying over the altar of Khor Ghor as He did every Midwinter on the Shortest Day.

But this time, in Merlin's vision, Bhel Sunface did not rise again, as He had risen since the world was forged.

Instead His light became dim, obscured, a weak thing on the verge of extinction. The Sun in Merlin's seeing-stone was eclipsed by a Moon as black as jet.

CHAPTER ONE
YNYS YRCH

The King was dead.

Loth of Ynys Yrch lay upon a bier of woven branches in the cult-house, his body puffed with putrefaction, rancid and purple after a week of death. Seashells covered his eyes, hiding their hideous fixed stare, while his jaw was bound shut with a strip of sinew to keep his mouth from opening in the endless rictus scream of the dead.

Well might Loth have screamed, his tormented voice echoing in spirit realms both above and below, for he had died not only horribly but ignobly, not on the field of battle or leading his men in the hunt but when he was lounging around his roundhouse with his warriors, drunk and stinking, a captive woman from a coastal tribe upon his knee. One moment he had been dandling the slattern with one hand and slurping from his big, ceremonial beaker with the other; the next he had clutched his throat and toppled to the ground, foaming and retching, the mead spewing from his mouth in a bile-filled fountain. The slave –woman ran off screeching while Loth continued to writhe in the rushes, his face livid and his tongue thrusting from his mouth.

His men gathered round trying to rouse him, but he was past the aid of men; his throat rattled and he passed into the shadowy arms of She-Who-Guards, the protectress of the Dead and ancestral bones.

It was not just the Death-Spirit who roamed that night. Sinister as the Watcher herself, Loth's wife, Morigau of Belerion, had stolen in to his hut and claimed his corpse, carrying it with the aid of her sons and attendants to the great cult-house that sat in decaying splendour between the two ancient stones circles, Ring of Moon and Wheel of Sun, that stood on a long peninsula between two lochs, one saltwater, the other fresh. Morigau was priestess there, by her own appointment after the mysterious deaths of her rivals, and it was her right to claim the body as Loth's wife, but men made the sign of evil as they saw her pass in her cloak of raven crow-feathers, with her followers carrying Loth's corpse high on their shoulders and the terns and sea-eagles wheeling hungrily above.

In the cult house with its red-painted walls and four jagged stones standing sentinel at the door, Morigau set about performing rites over Loth's body but she did not speak the words to assist the dead man's spirit upon its journey into the West. Instead she cursed Loth, uttering dreadful chants to bind his spirit between the Lands of the Living and the realm of the Everliving Ones for eternity. A terrible punishment, the worst one could wish upon the newly dead.

She had hated her husband.

3

"Yes, Loth…" She trailed her index finger over the putrescent cheek of the dead man. The long nail would have drawn blood had there been any left to bleed. "I have my revenge at last. You beat me and humiliated me once too often—I, who am a priestess and of royal house, not some drab to warm your bed! Even worse, you maltreated my beloved boy, my beautiful one, who shall be king after you… and who knows what else he might be one day."

The sound of footsteps in the long, tomb-like passage leading to the inner sanctum of the cult house drew her from the reeking bier of her dead husband. Lips curved in a snarl, she groped for the honed flint dagger she always carried concealed in her robes… She knew that unrest grew in the tribe, and that with Loth's demise she and her four sons were in some danger. She was not loved on Ynys Yrch and rumours had quickly spread about the possibility that henbane-root had poisoned Loth's last beaker of mead; these harsh whispers were followed by hostile questions about the parentage of Morigau's boys, Agravaen, Gharith, Ga'haris, and, especially her eldest son, Mordraed who was potentially Loth's heir.

Morigau's lip curled contemptuously, giving her small, heart-shaped face an ugly, petulant look. Agravaen was obviously Loth's get, a surly boy, with not much of Morigau's blood in him: pimply, heavy-featured and a dullard, but strong of limb and single minded. Arrow fodder, maybe, but one who would do as he was told without thinking. Gharith and Ga'haris? Well, most men of the tribes had brown hair and eyes, as did both boys; and who could say for absolute certain who a child's father was, unless men came to locking their women away from all other male contacts?

She did not care overmuch what happened to those three anyway, legitimate or not. None of them could compare to Mordraed, her firstborn, her best… the one who deserved the world, and she would give him that if she could.

She breathed a sigh of relief as she recognised his familiar shadow in the corridor and re-sheathed her secret dagger. Moments later Mordraed strode under the arched door-lintel with its painted red diamonds and lozenges. Her other sons followed on his heels, a pack of eager puppies. Mordraed always led them, caring for his younger brothers in a way that Morigau, their mother, could not bring herself to. She had not wanted such a gaggle of children, only the one who would bring her desires to fruition, but they had come and she had whelped them like a bitch, and farmed them out to whatever village woman would suckle and tend them. Had her will been her own she would have exposed them, giving them to the spirits in return for greater gifts of power for herself but they were princes after all and Loth would have none of it.

"Mother, it is bad news, I fear." Mordraed crossed the room without glancing at his mother, making the required bow at the sacred shrine at the far end—a dresser similar to that seen in the local homes but larger and more finely crafted, filled with holy objects both on its shelves and under its stone slabs—strange little figurines of blobbed stone with crude eyes pecked on them and fine polished axe heads that were too good to be of use to any but denizens of the spirit-world.

"Tell me…"

Mordraed turned on his heel, folding his arms. He taut as a bowstring, every muscle quivering with rage. "The Boneman and Cludd rally the people against us. They cast blame on you not only for father's death but for the poor catch of fish and failed harvest of the past few years."

Morigau stood in silence, staring at her eldest son with her feral dark eyes. Despite the urgency of his words, the terrible truth he was imparting, she could not help but feel a surge of pride and of a fierce, almost unnatural love at the sight of him. *I wrought this… .* she thought. *Me…*

Her son. Surely a man-god blessed by the spirits, born of a coupling of sister and brother, in an act taboo and yet sacred, marking his special-ness.

In the dim light of the burning tallow cups that ringed Loth's bier he stood proudly alert, holding a short, composite bow with an arrow on the string. Dark and beautiful, he was like a hero from an old legend—hair the colour of jet fell in loose waves down his back, framing a high-planed face with a nose as straight as a blade and a mouth shapely if stern. Yet none could mistake his male beauty for effeminacy. Although not overly tall, his body was hard and lean, the muscles beneath his jet-studded leather jerkin perfectly developed from years spent mastering the art of the bow.

He was a deadly archer who seldom missed his mark.

And if any still believed him weak, fooled by the deceptive beauty of his face, his eyes would have told the truth. Deep as the sea, fathomless, they were a rare dark blue, so dark they appeared almost black, fringed by long lashes that he lowered to conceal his true emotions.

They were ice-cold eyes, which could at a moment's notice become blank and pitiless, wholly without compassion.

Death eyes.

Morigau, daughter of Y'gerna and half-sister to Ardhu Pendraec, Stone Lord of Prydn, loved Mordraed's eyes most of all.

"Mother!" Mordraed's voice rose, sharp and irritable. When she stared at him with such devouring intensity it made him uncomfortable. "Have you not heard a word I said? Ack-olon thinks it too dangerous for us to stay on Ynys Yrch; he counsels that we flee for the mainland… ."

Morigau hissed like a serpent, eyes igniting with anger. "How dare he suggest such a thing without consulting me first? What of your birthright? You should rule after Loth!"

Mordraed's lip curled. "It would seem many do not believe Loth was my father… . Cludd, his sister's son, in particular. He has petitioned the Boneman to be instated by Mother-right and men rally to his cause."

"The traitors… the traitors…" Morigau cried, and she spat at Loth's fat, decaying body. The tallow-filled lamps that lit the chamber swirled, and

5

suddenly the sinew supporting the dead king's chin snapped and his jaw sprang open as if to utter a horrible mocking laugh from whatever underworld his spirit was trapped in.

The two youngest boys screamed, flinging their arms round Mordraed, whose lightning hands brought his bow to the draw in an instant. He'd kill Loth again, by the Moon he would, if the hateful old bastard were to return from the dead. Like Morigau, he had despised Loth, and the feeling had been mutual; Loth had suspected the boy might not be his from the day he was born and Mordraed had heard the rumours too … snide comments from other boys, whispers behind the hands of gossiping women. He had cared little, for Loth had been harsh and cruel, taunting him and aiming blows whenever he passed by. He wanted no blood-claim on the foul old man… just to inherit his chieftaincy over these storm-tossed isles as Morigau had promised since he was a tiny child, when she had given him a little bronze dagger and told him whenever he was angry to stick it into an effigy made of bones and straw that looked a little like Loth.

The tallow cups fluttered again and a swirl of salty sea-wind rushed down the passage. Someone else was coming, brought into the cult-house on the storm…

Torches flared and suddenly the whole chamber was brightly illuminated, shadows fleeing backwards in a mad umbrous rush toward Loth's bier. Cludd, the son of Loth's sister Clotagh, marched sternly into the chamber surrounded by upwards of a dozen men, some carrying fire-brands, other bearing unsheathed daggers and menacing clubs lined with spines of flint. The shaman known as the Boneman strode at Cludd's side, a scrawny elder with a cloud-grey beard to his waist and a necklace of men's finger bones jangling against his bony chest. He was the guardian of the crematory hearth in the Temple of the Moon, and was acclaimed oldest man in the tribe, having lived nearly three Moon-Years… over fifty Sun-Turnings. He had staunchly opposed Morigau becoming a priestess from the moment she arrived on Ynys Yrch, a new bride with her belly already swelling—and was the only one of her rivals to live to confront her, for he would not treat with her in any wise.

Morigau's face was thunder-hued, her eyes sparking. "You have no right to come here! The spirits will curse you!"

"It is not the true men of Ynys Yrch who will be cursed," said the Boneman. "You are the one who is blighted. Your taint has scared the fish from our shores and caused the crops to wither. And so you must go, renouncing all ties to this island."

"And if I refuse?" She glared at him, gaze black with fury.

"You die, and your brood of bastards with you."

Cludd, a heavy set man who resembled his uncle Loth, circled round Mordraed, looking him up and down. The youth's fingers were still on his bowstring, his eyes murderous.

6

"You..." Cludd walked in front of him, arms folded over his broad chest which, Mordraed noted, bore two round sun-discs of sheet-gold—an assertion of power and authority, objects that proclaimed his wealth and lineage. "Put down that bow and you may live. I am not a harsh man... I have no real quarrel with you, Mordraed, despite the fact you are the scion of that she-bitch, Morigau. But you are to go from this place and never return... along with those surly whelps." He gestured to the cowering younger boys and scowling Agravaen. "Gods only know who their fathers might be but I have no doubt they are not spawned of my uncle, Loth. No more than you are."

"You dishonour me!" Mordraed snarled.

"No, that bitch has dishonoured you" Cludd jabbed a finger in Morigau's direction. "Now go, and take her with you... or you will all be burnt in the Bonefire by the next dawn."

Mordraed looked mutinous and would have drawn his dagger, but Morigau, standing nearby, began to waver. If someone, anyone had come to her defence she would have fought her ground. But she would not risk Mordraed in some hopeless battle, he was too important... even if he would not be King of Ynys Yrch after Loth. "We will go," she cried, thrusting herself between Mordraed and the stocky figure of Cludd. "But this will not be forgotten, Cludd, mark my words."

Morigau exited the cult-house, her face almost demonic with despair and rage. The young boys scampered after her, wailing in terror as fat Agravaen pinched and swatted at them, taking out his own frustrations at losing his princely position in the tribe. Mordraed saw him jab his fingernails into Gharith's arm, drawing blood, and the older youth slapped his chunky hand away, then twisted the fingers back until he yowled like a wildcat. "Stop your foolishness," he warned Agravaen, "or you'll never wield dagger or bow again, I promise you, brother."

Agravaen scowled at him and pulled himself free, cradling his wounded hand, but he did as bade and ceased to torment Gharith and Ga'haris—he knew his older brother made no idle threats.

Huddled close together the outcast family hurried down the old path that led to the seashore. Crofters in huts stared out of their doorways, calling curses and spitting—Morigau had been hated indeed, well known for her evil dealings and bloody rites, and now that she had been toppled from power they were not afraid to show their dislike.

Half way to the shingle spit that faced the nearest point of the mainland they saw two men waving at them, beckoning them on from atop a dune of sand. Morigau's two loyal companions La'morak and Ack-olon. Not only her protectors, but her lovers of many long years.

"Where have you been?" shrieked Morigau angrily as the little band neared the waiting men. She struck out with her fists, pummelling one and then the other. "You should have been at the temple, guarding us! Guarding my sons! No, you were off hiding, while that oaf Cludd threw us out like shite into the midden!"

A muscle twitched in Ack-olon's cheek but he managed to keep his composure. He was too afraid of Morigau, of her poisons and sharp knives, to answer her wrath with anger of his own. "We were helping, Lady; we had not abandoned you. We could do nothing at the temple in your defence—except die needlessly. So we stole away when tempers flared high and prepared a boat to take us to safety on the mainland. The boys will have to help paddle—they can do that, can they not?"

He gave Mordraed a mean, piggy-eyed look; Ack-olon had been Morigau's lover since they were little more than children and it irked him the way she fussed about the boy, treating him like he was already a little king, better than his brothers, better than him and La'morak, who were of high status clans themselves. Ack-olon was also privy to the truth—that Mordraed was the child of a broken taboo, cursed, for he had been there that night when Morigau, masked as the raven, had seduced her own drink-addled half-brother.

Mordraed noticed the look and stiffened, his eyes turning black with fury. He hated the two men who were always sniffing about his mother, hated the sly jokes they shared, their wandering hands when they thought he could not see. How he wished Cludd had finished the two warriors, but he was certain that they had been, as Morigau had accused them, in hiding... or at best, preparing the boat to save their own skins should the worst happen.

"Of course I will help." He cast a frosty smile in Ack-olon's direction. "It would be rude of me not to help an old man."

Ack-olon's teeth gritted; a vein throbbed on his temple but he forced himself to turn away. At his side La'morak choked back a laugh.

"Old *men...*" Mordraed added.

La'morak's smile curdled like milk.

Mordraed carried on to the seashore, grinning, enjoying their almost palpable dislike.

*****

A boat lay on the shingle, carved from a great log, long and slippery as a sea serpent. The wind was blowing fiercely, as it often did on those bleak treeless isles, and the waters beyond were choppy and wild. Clouds of spume blew past the faces of the refugees.

La'morak looked worried. "The tide is not good. The wind is up. It is a fierce crossing even for experienced sailors."

"We have done it before, we shall do it again," Morigau stated flatly.

"Maybe wait till dawn and see if the wind dies."

Morigau stared over her shoulder, head on one side, listening. A little bead of sweat appeared on her brow to be licked away by the wind. "Are you deaf? Can you not hear? They proclaim Cludd as new king in the Circles of Sun and Moon. They are deep in their beakers and their anger rises. They will come looking for us, and if we are not gone they will tear us all limb from limb!"

"The boat it is then." Mordraed shoved Gharith and Ga'haris into the log-boat, and beckoned impatiently for Agravaen to join them. The loutish boy thudded clumsily into the craft, almost tipping it over before the party had even set off. Mordraed squashed himself in just across from him and grabbed a paddle made of driftwood, while Morigau sat with her back pressed against her favourite child and the youngest two crushed between her knees. Her two servants pushed the log-boat out to sea and began to paddle with all their strength against the fierce riptides. Mordraed joined them with his own paddle, amused to see how swiftly they tired, their brows lathered and dripping, while he was still fresh and keen, not even breaking into a sweat.

The wind blew and the craft skirled, tipping dangerously to one side. The youngest boys screamed and were violently sick, spewing over the side. Agravaen moaned horribly and slumped to one side, vomiting, his shifting weight threatening to spill them all into the cold, deadly embrace of the sea, where Mahn-ann waited with his scaly green face and hair full of fishes.

"Agravaen, control yourself!" Mordraed slapped the younger lad with an open hand, making him leap back howling from the side of the log-boat. "You had your man-rites a Moon ago—act like it, or I will smack your arse like a baby's!"

The boy glared mutinously at his brother and pressed his fingers to his red, stinging face but he obeyed, moving not an inch. Not one, for he knew Mordraed made no idle threats.

Finally, beyond all hope, the exiles spied land, grey and hazy in the approaching dawn. Seabirds were just waking, wheeling over the waves and the misted green shores. The boat ground onto a pebbly spit and its occupants tumbled out, the older men exhausted from constant paddling, the little boys worn out by fear, Agravaen still holding his churning belly and slapped cheek. Morigau and Mordraed, however, seemed untouched by the perilous crossing, eager to go on.

"We cannot linger here," said Morigau. "These lands are ruled by Loth's kinsmen, sons of his brother Urienz, who was killed by my kinsman Ardhu. They have no love of me or my blood. News spreads fast, and I fear we won't be safe long here either."

La'morak clambered up, unsteady, his face grey and stubbled in the murky dawn-light. "What is your plan, lady? Where is safe for the likes of us?"

She smiled; a smile that did not reach her green-brown eyes "We will be safe with my brother, the Foe-hammer, the Stone Lord. My dear brother in the south. How would you like that, my boys?" She turned to the youngest of her children, gesturing them close. "We will travel to the great temple of Khor Ghor and meet with Ardhu Pendraec!"

"My uncle!" Mordraed yelped in surprise. "Have you gone mad? From the

9

time I was a babe you told tales of how much you hate him! Why would you go to him for help?"

She sighed and, unexpectedly, threw her arms around Mordraed's waist, making him flush with embarrassment. Agravaen made a disgusted noise, eager to score against the brother who had shamed him on the sea-crossing. "I do it for *you*, my beautiful son. For you."

"For me?" He shook her too familiar hands from him. "How exactly? I would be gladder if you raised a war-band to take back Ynys Yrch... my birthright."

"There is better for you than that harsh place of pigs and the wind!" Ignoring his obvious reluctance, she coiled a hand in his hair, ran lips like dried leaves along his cheekbone. "Mordraed, soon I will tell you... tell you all. But not now, not before your brothers. Not until we are away and safe from the savage kin of Loth."

*****

Mordraed brooded for the next few days as they travelled through wild, wide lands fringed by mountains with heads cloaked in grey cloud and criss-crossed by thundering streams, swollen from winter rains and melting snow. Frigid rain pelted the refugees, sometimes turning to snow when they crested the highest hilltops—great flat flakes that slapped into their eyes and melted on their lashes. The wind was sharp as a blade, but fortunately their seal-skin capes and boots helped protect against both water and wind. The younger boys, less afraid now that Ynys Yrch was far behind them, started to laugh and play childish games, casting snowballs at each other and their brothers and catching snowflakes on their tongues.

Eventually the fierce mountains diminished and the great glens that gaped between their adamant feet fell away, and the lands around them became tamer, less stony and remote. Standing stones lined rills and ridges—territorial markers of the various northern tribes who lived in these regions: Painted Folk and Khaledoni mostly, both known as head-hunters and not the type of folk who would give the former queen of Ynys Yrch succour.

By a dark little wood of pine the travellers found the remains of an abandoned round house, roof shorn away by time and wind, an open pit gaping before its door where some Ancestor's long interred skull had been wrest from its long sleep when the hut's owner had decided, for whatever reason, to take all his own and flee.

Ack-olon and La'morak set about making a fire in the long-cold hearth and putting down skins for their mistress and her sons to sit on. Morigau ate a piece of dried fish from her pack, giving nothing to the boys who watched her hungrily, and when she finished gestured for Mordraed to come to her.

She stroked his face, still smooth, a pretty youth's face but with a hardness beneath the glamour. "Your eyes are haunted. Can you not trust me?"

"No," he said, pursing his lips. "I cannot. You told me from the time I could walk that I would be king after Loth… and now you act as if I should smile at the loss of a kingdom. Smile… and go to the house of an uncle who is an enemy of my house, and beg him for scraps!"

"It is time for us to talk," said Morigau, and her lips curved into a crooked, almost sinister smile that made Mordraed feel vaguely uneasy. He knew his mother dealt in dark things; he had seen the blood on her hands, smelt the scent of death on her robes. But she was a priestess, she served the Blue-Faced One most of all, and the Dark Moon, and it was not for him to question.

"Then let us talk," he said gruffly. "Be out with it."

"Not here." Morigau took the sleeve of his jerkin and drew him from the hut toward the trees that surrounded it. "What I must tell you is not for the ears of your brothers. In fact, they must never know."

Intrigued though vaguely apprehensive also, Mordraed let Morigau lead him in the direction of the grove. Ack-olon and La'morak were huddled together in the hut's door, staring after them and nudging each other, faces smug with some private knowledge. He did not like that at all, and longed to slash away those smug grins with his dagger…

Morigau picked her way between the trees, which swayed and creaked in the rising wind. Dead branches lay denuded on the forest floor, bark bleached silver-white like old bones. Fleshy mushrooms clustered in the damp, spores puffing up in a yellowish cloud as Morigau's feet passed, filling the night with vapours and strange earthy scents.

Where the grove ended, a worn path wound out into grassland long stripped of trees in some ancient clearance. Morigau strode out into the sea of grass, her long black hair streaming like a banner in the breeze. She walked so confidently Mordraed wondered if she had been here before; on her travels throughout the isle of Prydn before she finally settled down as priestess and wife to Loth of Ynys Yrch. Wondered if the empty hut and its rifled door-step grave could have had anything to do with her visit…

Up ahead he could see the pinnacles of two stones, weather-pitted oolitic fangs that jutted from a cobbled surface still red from old burning. A huge recumbent stone weighing many tons rested between the knife-like flankers; it was streaked with quartz, but a thousand exposed and brutal winter's nights had cracked it, the cold splitting the great megalith so that its dark inner core lay open to the elements.

Morigau hastened to the recumbent stone and lithely vaulted onto it, sitting between the flanking stones as a queen would sit upon a throne. The Moon was behind her left shoulder, her face shadowed, her head a silhouette against the blazing stars.

Morigau loved drama and effect; Mordraed knew she was using her theatre on him now, to awe him, to make him fear. He made a soft snarling noise, hating such mummery. "Mother, it is too cold for these games. Say what you must and let us return to the fire!"

He moved another step closer. He was standing on the cobbles now, loose and jumbled and filled with ash and charcoal. Objects crunched noisily beneath his ankle-high cowhide boots; glancing down, he started in surprise, for the things half-hidden in the gloom were white and rolling, fragile as eggs fallen from the nest of some giant bird. But suddenly, one tumbled toward him, pivoting as it struck against his foot, and he realised these frail objects were not eggs at all but the domed crania of neonates, newborn children.

He scowled and his spine prickled. "Why must death always go with you?" he spat at his mother, and he gave the nest of skulls a great kick. They disintegrated in a puff of white dust.

"Death is always with us." Her eyes gleamed, feral. "Look!" She reached forward and grabbed his arm, fingers digging like tiny knives into his flesh. "Is this not the bow-hardened arm that wields death?"

"Maybe... but you will not let me use it!" he spat at her. "Mother, you promised I was to be king... but you made us leave Ynys Yrch without a fight, stealing away like cowards in the night! I would have fought... fought to the death! For my honour...and yours."

"Throwing your life away would be stupid, Mordraed. Yes, I once saw you as a ruler on Ynys Yrch, a rival for my brother in his high hill of Kham-El-Ard. But I have seen... better things for you. My mind is never quiet, my son; it works night and day, devising, foreseeing. You will be a king, Mordraed, that is true... but you will be king of more than just a lonely, wind-scored isle. You will be master of all Prydn."

Mordraed's lip quirked. "Your brother would have something to say about that, I'm sure. Are your wits addled, woman? What are you thinking? That he will somehow see me as his heir? He has a son, does he not? He does not need a sister's son for inheritance; many tribes do not follow Mother-right any more."

Morigau licked her lips; they looked black, dry as dead worms in the shaky starlight. "I want him dead, Mordraed. Dead, so that all that I lost through him is restored to me—through you. The boy, of course, must die too. The woman, the White Queen, will become your woman, as she is Sovereignty and men will respect what she is, even if they have no love of you."

Mordraed's heart pounded. "This is madness! No one would follow me, a usurper!"

"No, Mordraed." She reached out and caressed his silky cheek, her fingers now oddly gentle. "They wouldn't. But you would not be a usurper. Mordraed, Ardhu Pendraec's young son is not his eldest. The eldest is... you. Know that you are Ardhu's son, so true heir to all he owns."

Mordraed jumped back as if she had struck him. The spot where her fingers had caressed him burned like fire. Cold waves of sickness and terror ran through him. "He cannot be... I knew my fire was not Loth... but Ardhu! He... he is your brother!"

"So he is, my son. The sacred blood of kingship flows doubly in you from our Ancestors in deepest Belerion."

Mordraed fought the waves of nausea that washed over him. His head spun. " You tell me I come from a union that was taboo! I am a creature born of great wrong!"

"Then turn that cursed birthing into a great right..." She reached down and caught his arms, drawing him towards her, pulling him near until he was almost lying across the great cracked block of the down-lying stone. She was stronger than a woman ought to be, strong as a war-goddess. "Look... look, Mordraed, see the Moon behind us, see her beautiful white skull? Near nineteen Sun turnings has the Moon's cycle, and you were conceived when the cycle was on its turn, so you shall come to your full power as it ends. Then shall great sacrifices be made, and Ardhu, my brother, will be amongst them. The Moon is your mother, my boy, not the Sun that rules Ardhu, and she will eclipse his Sun as in the days of old—and her shadows will not pass away. The very stones of Khor Ghor will tremble and fall before your hand, Mordraed, my one of Great Judgement, my son of the Dark Moon."

He knew not what to answer, but lay as one frozen, the horror of her words sweeping over him, the cold of the stone eating through his clothes, grasping at his beating heart as if to still it. Morigau reached under her cloak and drew out an obsidian blade set into a hilt of horn and raised it, its edge winking dully. She kissed it and then with a sudden downward motion slashed Mordraed's left cheek. He screamed in shock and pain and blood pattered, black in the moonlight, onto the great block on which he lay.

Morigau skirled the flowing blood into patterns with her fingers. "It is done. You are sworn by the shedding of your royal blood to the dark Mother that rules the Moon. I am sorry about your beautiful face, Mordraed, but that is your sacrifice... to the one whose spirit will guide you... and to me. Come, I will make it better, so it will not look uncomely."

She drew him towards her; he was whimpering like a child, hating himself, hating Morigau both at once. Morigau took her dagger again and refined the cut across his cheekbone, before taking blue powders from her belt pouch and rubbing them into the wound. "There..." she said happily, as if well satisfied. "You have nothing to worry about. A nice tattoo to mark you. You do swear to me, don't you, Mordraed? Swear to follow the Moon that helped make you... follow me, your mother, your priestess, who only wishes the best for you... for both of us."

"Have I any other choice?" he said.

"No, you do not," she replied.

CHAPTER TWO
THE HALL OF THE STONE LORD

The youth ran along the crest of the chalk ridge, bent low to the ground, seeking animal spoor to follow. Frosty leaves crumbled beneath his feet, but his soft deerskin shoes made no noise upon them so light of foot was he. He was like a spirit, a pale ghost in the mist, fast moving and insubstantial in his tunic of white aurochs' hide and grey wolf-skin cloak, a tribute-gift to his father from a distant Northern king.

He was gifted and he was touched by the spirits.

He was Amhar, son of Ardhu Pendraec and his White Queen, Fynavir.

Amhar had been born amid great fear. He had nearly killed his mother at the birthing, and Ardhu had ridden to Khor Ghor during her long travail and treated with the spirits to let them both live. The King had slashed his own flesh to give the Stones blood, to show them his suffering and willingness to sacrifice. And on a clear sunrise, after five bitter days, when the Ladies of the Lake crowded round the sacred pool moaning and chanting, the child finally slid forth into the waiting hands of Nin-Aeifa and Mhor-gan of the Korrig-han. "It is a man-child!" Nin-Aeifa had cried, lifting the red and purple infant up by his feet to drain the choking fluids from his lungs. The baby's mouth cleared and he started to scream, and Mhor-gan had taken her ceremonial dagger of finest flaked flint and slashed the cord that bound him to Fynavir, freeing him into the mortal world. He had then been swiftly carried to Khor Ghor in a robe of soft red fox-skin and presented to the five trilithons, where the ancestors watched with ancient eyes—the Portal-of-Ghosts, Throne of Kings, the Western Guardian, the House of the North Wind and the Arch of the Eastern Sky. The afterbirth had been burned before the Stone of Adoration as an offering and Merlin had anointed the child with animal fat, writing sacred, protective marks upon his skin while Nin-Aeifa sang strange women's songs in a high, trilling voice, driving off any evil spirits that might seek to snatch the young life away.

Amhar his father had called him, the child-name that would fool malign beings into passing him by, and then he was carried in his fox-skin back to Kham-El-Ard, his shrill cries tearing into the twilight. Face wan and strained from the fear and elation of the day, Ardhu had called out to his sister, Mhor-gan, in the women's birthing house, "Does my wife yet live?' and when she told him yes, Fynavir would survive to raise her child, he and his chief man An'kelet, as drained and stark-faced as his lord, fell into each others arms and embraced with gladness, though Ardhu had no idea of the true reason for his friend's relief.

After his harsh entrance to the world, Amhar had thrived well enough, drank milk and grew large with a lusty wail, but he was a strange one, as was quickly noted by the folk of Kham-El-Ard. He resembled neither father nor mother. Although his eyes were green like Fynavir's and of similar shape, they were a darker shade than hers, a deep rich leaf green with hints of gold, like sunlight dappling a forest glade. Dark, rich red hair grew down his back; in shadow it almost took on a purplish hue, like wild foxgloves. He was taken to having strange fancies and dreams, and on rare occasions he would become very still and far away, as if entering another world... and he would fall to the ground and shake for a moment or two and sometimes utter a strange, unworldly cry as he fell. One of the healer-priests from Deroweth had examined him and suggested that maybe they try to cut a roundel from Amhar's skull to let any possible evil spirits out... but Fynavir had screamed in horror and Ardhu had grabbed the priest and flung him out the door of the Great Hall at Kham-El-Ard.

"Get the Merlin before we even talk of such a matter, priest!" he shouted after him, and sure enough the Merlin soon came, stalking on his spindly legs up the crooked hill, his jaw-topped staff in hand and the bronze-bound skull of his totem-bird shining on his breast. He had gazed into Amhar's eyes, drawn his finger from nose to chin and told the boy to follow its path, and asked questions of the little lad that none could hear. And when he was done, he sat back and sighed. "He bears a mark, your son—a mark of the Otherworld. He would doubtless make a good priest were he not the Son of a King. When the spells come upon him, just leave him and watch he does not choke and he will return to you after he had travelled in other realms."

And so Amhar became known as one touched by the gods, and besides his strange turns, he also began to walk strange paths, daring to walk where others would not... out to the Spirit-Path that stretched across the fields alongside Khor Ghor, bounding the lands of the Living and the Dead, or to the barrow-downs of old Kings, white-capped and shining, where the wind was full of a thousand dead voices. Fynavir sobbed and railed at her son when she heard of his exploits, but he merely hugged her and knew no fear, and no harm came to him.

But his strangeness marked him, and because of this, even at sixteen summers he had not yet become a man. He had a child's dagger and a youth's slight bow, and still wore two braids in his hair which would be cut off and burned in a bone-fire when he underwent the manhood rites. The Merlin said often that thought he might make a better priest than heir to the chieftaincy of the West... but Fynavir had never quickened with child again, and Ardhu had refused to think of his son as anything but a warrior who would follow him and continue the line of the kings of old. However, the uncertainty surrounding his path in life had delayed his time of passage beyond that of the youths born in the same year.

Amhar was not angry or resentful as other boys in his predicament might have been. Briefly he wondered why he had to endure what most saw as shame... but soon decided the Ancestors must have some deep design for him. He had suspected the Old Ones' had favoured him since he was very small and had seen lights that no one else could see glowing amongst the barrows of the plain. Mother had hated those lights, and wept and cried and tried to cover his eyes. She was used to them now, though; she had come to realise her fey son would not change, nor would the Old Ones leave him be.

Amhar gazed ahead into the twilight as he walked through the valley of the Lakes, with the burial ground of kings on his right, hidden from view by a high crest of land, and the curves of the shining river Abona on his left, with the farms of men and the Hill of Ogg the Eloquent in the distance beyond. He could see the river was frozen, the spring coming late this year; white tendrils coiled from a layer of thick ice, and the trees overhanging it were rimed with hoar frost. He curled his toes, wondering if he could spare an hour or two to tie a pair of long, flat bones to his shoes and skate on the surface as he had done when he was younger. But no, the wind was picking up, tossing his hair and reddening his cheeks, and he knew he must not stay out much longer. His intention had been to catch a hare, to make its pelt into a hand-warmer for Fynavir, or even a deer that could bring much cheer to Ardhu the Stone Lord's table, but he had found no spoor from either beast in that wintry desolation.

He was just about to turn and head home, when he heard a noise, a vague murmur of voices, the words carried away on the shrieking breeze. Cautious even though the lands were at peace beneath his father's rule, he quickly dived into a bush and stared down toward the Deadlands where the great chiefs and kings lay sleeping in their earthen barrows, silent under a blanket of snow. Were they tossing and turning, trying to wake and speak with him?

His heart began to hammer, a dull thud against his ribs.

But no... the voices were not those of the Old Ones with their grinning fleshless mouths and dry sepulchral whispers that rasped from throats long vanished. A party of wanderers travelled along the downs, heads bowed as they pressed on into the wind.

Trying to capture a better look, he peered through gaps in the ice-rimed bush, pushing aside annoying fronds with cold fingers. What manner of men were these? Who dared to walk in those empty lands where spirits dwelt? As the party drew nearer he could see there were seven in the group - an auspicious number. Two were men in their late prime, bearded and dark-eyed with fatigue, with huge fur cloaks, mangy from wear and weather, dangling from their shoulders. They were guarding a small dark-haired woman wrapped in the sleek hide of a beast unfamiliar to Amhar; she held herself with pride, like his mother, the Queen. A chunky beardless youth with shoulders like a bull marched at her heels followed by two little boys staggering with exhaustion; Amhar guessed she must be their mother, but he was surprised by her lack of concern for them... she did not even glance aside when one tripped on a tree root, fell heavily and started to howl, his voice rising up into the twilight like the tremulous cry of a ghost. Instead it was the final member of the band, bringing up the rear, who strode over to pluck the child from his snowy bed, dust him off, and set him back on the path. A younger man, an adult by his weapons, but not much older than Amhar himself. He had long black hair, the front strands pulled away from his forehead and bound with a spray of feathers from some white seabird, and his cheekbones were sharp as knife-blades through obvious recent deprivation. Despite his thinness he moved with grace, like a wildcat; and he was clearly aware of all that took place around him; Amhar could see him scanning the horizons even as he righted the fallen lad.

Amhar leaned forward a bit further, trying to get a better view of the strangers as they passed beneath the ridge; and underneath him, a branch suddenly cracked. The young man below startled like a frightened horse, and with lightning speed fitted an arrow to the string of his bow. He gazed up to the top of the ridge, and Amhar, darting back into the safety of the foliage, saw the stranger's face clearly for the first time.

He nearly tumbled over with shock. The newcomer resembled his father, the King, and his aunt Mhor-gan—long-headed, with high cheekbones, narrow jaw, and even, defined features, though Amhar thought the cast of youth's face was far prettier than Ardhu's... indeed even prettier than Mhor-gan, who was a woman. But unlike his kinfolk the stranger's eyes were a deep blue, mirroring the fading sky as they swept the landscape, searching. There was something in those fathomless, unreadable eyes that made Amhar both fearful and elated at once.

Here, in the form of this dark stranger, was the beginning of his adventure, his quest—he knew it as surely as he knew the Spirits guided him. He wanted to shout out, to hail the youth with Ardhu Pendraec's face... but it was then his courage failed him, the fear overcoming the coil of excitement in his belly.

Before he dared speak to these newcomers, he must tell his father of their arrival and find out who they were and why they came to Kham-El-Ard, for he was sure that must be their destination. Shouldering his child's bow, he glanced once more to where the dark man stood with arrow to the string, and then burst from his hiding place and fled along the ridge into the gathering night.

*****

"She has come." The Merlin stood behind Ardhu Pendraec, high king of Prydn, Stone Lord and master of the Great Trilithon. "As we knew she would. With the boy."

Ardhu sat on a fallen tree within the darkness of the wood behind Kham-El-Ard, down by the Sacred Pool, where, many Sun-Turnings ago, Nin-Aeifa, the Lady of the Lake, had gifted him the sword Caladvolc. Brown from years of riding in the sun, his face was grim, his youth fled, although in his green-dark eyes were vestiges of the young warrior he once was, full of fire, the conqueror of many and scourge to those who threatened Prydn's shores. A short beard that left his cheeks clean hid a small scar he had acquired from a sea-raider, and the first traces of grey glittered amidst his dark hair.

"Why, Merlin?" he questioned, sighing. "So many years have gone by and we heard nothing. Sometimes I almost fancied both she and her whelp were dead; life is harsh in the North."

"Morigau is harsher." Merlin's eyes were narrowed, his lips thin lines. "Her life there only strengthened her; tempered her will like strong metal. Hatred of you and all you stand for has kept her wrath ablaze when others' inner fires would have died to embers."

"What should I do?" The King grasped the hem of the High Priest's deerskin robe, shiny with the fats that he rubbed in to keep it supple, and clattering with attached bones of animals and men. "Guide me, my mentor. All these years I have ruled well... and yet this woman and her brood bring me fear as no enemy from over the sea ever has! I do not want her at Kham-El-Ard." He struck his fists against the tree trunk, showering rotten shards of bark. "By Bhel Sunface, she already has come too near... Amhar spotted her party coming across the downs, and her brat drew his bow upon him. Gods, what if he had fired..."

"It is no use pondering what might have happened," Merlin interrupted. "That leads to madness. No harm came to Amhar." He began to pace, stroking his thin grey beard, fine as mist around his narrow, age-beaten face. "We must deal with the problem at hand... what to do with your sister and her children, if they have come to stay, which is what I expect. Her sons, if raised away from her influence, may yet grow to be doughty and loyal men who may serve your cause... Remember, the blood of U'thyr your father runs in their veins as much as Morigau's. It is better they grow to manhood under our tutelage than under hers."

Ardhu stared up at Merlin, eyes darkened by tree-shadows. "But what about... him... Mordraed? He... he is already a man; is it too late."

Merlin's breath hissed between his teeth; he glanced away as crows cawed, as though laughing, in the swaying canopy of branches above. "I do not know, my friend. Only the spirits know and often they mock at us men, and try to deceive. Now come, let us go and prepare for the arrivals and make what we can of this unexpected meeting."

*****

Mordraed stared up at the Great Hall of Kham-El-Ard, high on its crooked hill. He felt over-awed, though he forced a look of cold indifference onto his features. Nowhere in his travels with his mother had he ever seen a building like the one that rose above him, stoutly made of huge felled oaks that had been carved and polished. It shone in the sun like an earthly abode of the gods; he half- expected Bhel himself to burst through the lintelled doorway and burn all of Ardhu's enemies to ash.

18

But that was a foolish thought. He sneered inwardly at himself for his flight of childish fancy. Bhel did not walk amongst men. And the only one who would burst from those doors would be his mother's foe... *his* foe... his uncle Ardhu Pendraec. His uncle... and his father...

A knot of hatred mingled with revulsion curled below his breastbone. Why should Ardhu have such an abode, when he had committed such an unnatural crime with his sister? Even when Mordraed had been deemed Loth's heir, nothing on the Ynys Yrch could have matched the opulence of Kham-El-Ard; the monuments of the Northern Isles had been the greatest structures of their time, the very source of the religion of the Stones, but they had been decaying these last five hundred years till they were mere shells of what they had been. He felt suddenly very mean and poor and insignificant, as if he were some unworldly rustic playing at being a prince. He glared at the people gathered on the hillside, the watchful warriors and gold-decked women who had come down from Ardhu's Great Hall to greet the strangers, believing they were judging him, laughing behind their hands at his ragged clothes and uncouth ways.

Shoulders tense, he began to stride up the hill, following the wide, white path rutted in the chalk, ascending the heaped ramparts with their tall palisades and rows of stakes that could impale a man to the core. Ga'haris and Gharith trotted along behind him, big-eyed, craning their necks in both delight and fear, trying to take in all the sights and sounds of this new, alien place. Agravaen was like some lumbering halfwit, jaw agape, his breath railing noisily through his open mouth. Morigau was pinched-faced, sour, pushing forward between her two protectors, Ack-olon and La'morak, who looked as if they wished they were anywhere else but here.

Someone shifted in the crowd. "Bitch!" a woman yelled, and a rock sailed toward Morigau's head. The missile missed, thudding heavily on the ground near Gharith and Ga'haris; the two little boys clutched each other's hands and started to snivel.

Mordraed cursed and snatched at his bow, but Morigau shot him a warning look through narrowed eyes. "Hold your hand. Let us give them no more cause to hate us."

They entered the Great Hall, passing under the carved lintel where the bleached skull of a Sea-Pirate gazed down from where it had been fixed by a bolt of bronze—a warning to the enemies of Prydn. Inside a mixture of shadows and flickering light made the king's abode seem surreal, a place out of a dream.

The floor was denuded chalk, scraped clean, then strewn with rushes that caught animal dung and the discarded bones from the warriors' feasts. Oak pillars held up the soaring pitch of the roof and were carved with knot-work, sun-wheels and crosses, and on one was the Guardian of the Dead with her owl-eyes and on another a series of cup-marks that told the cycle of the Moon. Incense cups belched pungent herbal smoke, while clay containers full

19

of lit tallow swung from cross-struts that helped support the reed thatching above.

At the far end sat the man Mordraed knew must be the Pendraec—the Terrible Head.

His father.

The King of the Great Trilithon sat on a low seat draped in bearskin, its back and arms made from sharp, many-tined antlers and the scapula of an aurochs. He wore a helm of beaten bronze and Rhon-gom, the Lightning Mace that signified his lordship, lay across his lap, its polished fossil head gleaming in the fluttering light of the tallow cups. In a sheath of horn the long sword Caladvolc hung at his side—the miraculous blade which men said had come from the subterranean lair of a water-spirit.

As Mordraed had feared, the face beneath the elaborate helm was much like his own. Darker, somewhat rougher in its set, but the marks of close kinship were there. It was a kind face, or so it seemed... but Mordraed knew from his mother that the kindness was a sham. This man, this breaker of taboos, was unworthy to sit on the throne of Prydn. He was a usurper, a fraud, damaged and evil beneath the pretence.

He felt his anger rising and forced himself to look away, to study the others hovering behind the Stone Lord's seat of Power. Immediately he saw the White Woman, standing like a cold statue in rare, bleached white linen... the one Morigau had told Mordraed he must take because she was bound to the land, her body the kingdom he must claim. His stomach knotted. She had beauty, but she was old, lines creeping beneath her sea-green eyes, and she was so pale it was as if she were made of snow. Surely she would freeze the flesh of any man who dared to touch her...

His gaze was drawn sharply back to Ardhu as the Stone Lord moved. He had half-risen from his seat and was staring at Morigau, who stood before him, a leaf before the storm. There was no kindness in his face now; it was impassive as a standing stone. "What brings you to my hall, sister?" he asked frostily. "It has been many years since I heard of you, and had hoped to keep it that way. You are a serpent with fangs of honeyed venom."

Morigau hesitated a moment, then dramatically cast herself at his feet, flinging her arms around his ankles. "My brother, my kinsman, I beg you listen to me!" she wailed. "Great evil has befallen me and mine!"

"As well it might. The spirits will not smile on the likes of you."

"Loth... my husband... is dead. I am dishonoured... cast out from Ynys Yrch with my children."

"And this has what to do with me?" Ardhu kicked her away with a swift violent motion; she fell in a heap in the soiled rushes, her black hair hanging in disarray over her eyes.

Mordraed expected her to leap up in anger, casting curses at her brother, but she remained motionless, though two spots of angry colour gleamed on her cheeks. Slowly, she inched forward until she had prostrated herself before

20

Ardhu's seat yet again. "I ask for your help..." she said in a faint voice, "not for me... but for my boys, who have lost their inheritances... who have lost what was rightfully theirs due to lies and slander."

"Lies and slander? Knowing you, those 'lies' were likely to be true." Ardhu gave a cynical laugh and glanced knowingly at the two others who stood near the high seat—a tall, amber-headed man of great presence and a sharp-faced elder leaning on a staff who had a bird-headed talisman about his neck. Mordraed guessed the first was the Ar-moran Prince, An'kelet of the Lake, Ardhu's most loyal companion, and that the greybeard was the Merlin, High Priest of the Stones of Khor Ghor, famed throughout Prydn for his power and his machinations that could raise kings to greatness... or destroy them.

Morigau cast her arms over her face and feigned a few harsh sobs. "My story of woe is not of my doing... and I say this to you, brother—kill me for my past misdeeds towards you if it be your will, but do not toy with me. And do not harm my sons, who are innocent of any wrong-doing."

Mordraed stared at his mother, writhing like a worm amid the dog-shit and chewed pork-bones, and cringed in utter shame. What game did she play? For her sons, indeed! When had she cared about any of them, save him, and she had never debased herself in such a way even in his defence?

Ardhu sat back, toying with the Lightning Mace as if deciding whether to strike her skull with it and release her spirit to the gods. "Let me see these brats of yours," he said slowly. "I will decide whether I can train them to be of use to me and to Prydn—or whether they should be drowned like runtling puppies."

Morigau sprang from the floor and promptly grabbed the collars of Gharith and Ga'haris, thrusting them at their uncle. "My two youngest. Small but sturdy. They will be malleable to your will, lord-brother, I swear it. Whether as slaves or as soldiers, they will do you proud."

Ardhu Pendraec appraised the two boys, huddled together like small brown birds sheltering from the winter gales. His face softened almost imperceptibly. "You two... do you know what it is to obey?" he asked, leaning forward until his gaze was level with theirs.

They nodded in unison. They certainly knew the consequences of disobeying Morigau.

"And do you know what punishments can follow disobedience?"

The boys' eyes slid to their mother, then back to Ardhu. They nodded again, silent and solemn.

"When you are grown would you swear to serve me and no other, joining the Men of the Tribe and maybe my warband if you have the skill?" Ardhu glanced from Gharith to Ga'haris. "That means I would be the one to give you orders, not Morigau. That means you will not see her or listen to her, only to me, your kinsman and king."

"Yes, lord!" piped up Ga'haris, the elder of the two by a year. His brother nodded furiously. Morigau was their dam, but both were old enough to realise they had no place in her world. "We would like that very much!"

"Then so be it." Ardhu clapped his hands. "Now, Ka'hai, come and take these lads and give them pork and bread. They are as skinny as skeletons; my kinswoman obviously never saw fit to feed them properly."

Ardhu's foster brother Ka'hai, comrade at arms and ruler of the stores of the Kham-El-Ard, stepped out from the press of the Stone-Lord's men and ushered the children from the Hall, casting a backwards glare at Morigau. He hated the woman, and his dislike grew even more intense when he saw the obvious neglect of her small sons. He had a pack of children of his own from his two wives and could not imagine such cruelty.

Ardhu turned back to his sister and her remaining sons. His eyes settled on Agravaen, bull- shouldered and bull-headed, full of adolescent gaucheness and half-bridled fury. Ardhu beckoned him forward curtly. "Why do you look at me with such rage, boy? What have I done to you?"

Agravaen was silent; he looked slightly confused, as if he had expected open anger from Ardhu to which he could respond with righteous anger of his own. "I... I don't..." he stammered.

"What is your goal in this short life, boy? Do you wish to be a warrior some day?"

"I am a Man of my Tribe—my rites were held two Moons ago. Of course I wish to be a warrior—that is every right-thinking man's desire, is it not?"

Ardhu smiled ruefully. "So many think, and indeed my own wealth has come from the use of dagger and axe. But never forget, boy, it is the man that tills the land and herds the beasts that puts food into your belly. It is the beekeeper that gets honey for your mead and the grain man who pounds barley into bread... and who also brews the beer. A sword's edge has a much more bitter taste than sweet beer or mead. And often that draught is lethal— the cup of death."

Agravaen stared, trying to digest and understand his uncle's words. Farmers as important as warriors... what madness did his uncle speak! "All I know is that if you let me serve you and give me axe and blade, I will try to kill every enemy that comes against you!" he blustered impetuously. He was not quite sure why such an oath fell from his lips, when he had spent years hearing how his mother hated Pendraec, called him usurper and worse, but suddenly he just wanted to get away from Morigau—from her jibes about his lack of brain and her unflattering comparisons with Mordraed. He saw something... different... in the eyes of his uncle, something kinder and more accepting than what he was used to... and he gravitated towards it.

"Then, go, follow your younger brothers," said Ardhu, gesturing to the door "and remember that our eyes will be upon you at all times, watching how you behave."

Agravaen stomped out of the hall, flushed, embarrassed, and elated all at once. Ka'hai smirked behind his hand at his gauche manner, but managed to hide his laughter with a cough and took the lad out to the cooking hut where his younger siblings were already tearing at slabs of meat like hungry dogs.

Mordraed was left alone, before the high seat of the Stone Lord.

Suddenly the room went quiet and still. A dog whined; the fire-pit made a harsh crackling, spitting noise. Wind skittered over the roofline like the feet of malevolent spirits.

Ardhu's face was solemn; his hand gripped the haft of Rhon-gom until the knuckles were visibly white. "You, boy..." His voice was low, almost a growl. "Come to me. Kneel before your lord."

Mordraed took a step in his direction. His face was blank, a hard slate, his eyes shuttered. Arrogance and rage oozed from him, despite his chill demeanour; the truth was in his stance, in the tautness of his back and shoulders, the defiant tilt of his chin. He did not kneel, but continued to stand, staring down at this man who was both uncle and father.

Ardhu's breath hissed between his teeth; the rage of the Dragon, the Terrible Head. With a sudden rapid motion, he flung Rhon-gom to the ground and lunged forward and grabbed Mordraed by the hair, twisting his head back before he had a chance to react. Ardhu's right hand moved like lightning, unsheathing his dagger Carnwennan, Little White Hilt, with its worn antler pommel on which he had carved a mark for every man he had slain in his eighteen years as Stone Lord of Khor Ghor. He pressed the honed blade to Mordraed's throat, drawing a bead of blood.

Everyone in the Great Hall of Kham-El-Ard gasped in horror, and Morigau cried out, her voice as harsh as a raven's caw and full of uncustomary fear.

"Why do you defy me?" Ardhu said, his tone even but with a hint of menace.

"My brothers did not have to kneel!" Mordraed gasped, starting to struggle but mindful of the sharpened bronze at his throat.

"They are children, or scarcely more so. You are not. You are of age to serve a master and serve him well or perish for your folly. Now... *kneel.*"

Ardhu gave Mordraed's hair a vicious twist, forcing him down upon his knees in the rushes. Dog faeces oozed near his hand, along with a chewed bone, a pile of spittle. He writhed, burning with indignation, wishing he could reach his bow and make an end of this miscreant who tormented and shamed him in front of the people of Kham-El-Ard.

"Mordraed!" He heard Morigau's voice, desperate, strained, and he saw the hem of her tattered skirt flash before his face. "Do as your uncle says! Don't be stupid, boy!" She kicked him, the blow landing on his still unhealed cheek.

Pain and the surprise of Morigau's assault shocked him into stillness. Ardhu Pendraec slowly released his hair, allowing him to rise unsteadily to his knees before staggering to his feet. "You know where we stand then, boy," Ardhu said quietly. "You have the measure of me, and I of you. But it need not be this way. If you turn from your path of anger and serve me well… there is no telling how high you might rise within my warband. I would not reject you out of hand because of who your mother is."

Mordraed stared at him; hot anger dwindled to embers but a deep bitter resentment remained in the pit of his belly, a hard indigestible knot. *Yet you have rejected me as your son… your eldest son… You would not dare acknowledge me for fear of your own life! You will pay for that cowardice, for the lust that made me what I am… by the gods and the spirits, you will pay, 'FATHER'…*

"I do not know what arts of war they have taught you on Ynys Yrch," Ardhu continued, "But in any case you will be under the tutelage of my best warrior, the Lord An'kelet, and he will teach you both the skill of sword and spear, but also the temperance with which you must use them."

At that moment there was a movement from the shadows of the Hall and Mordraed saw a youth step past the pale-tressed figure of Queen Fynavir, who, coming suddenly to life, tried to stay him with her outstretched hand. He gently disentangled her fingers from his cloak and stepped into the ring of firelight before Ardhu's seat of power, clearing his throat. "Harsh words have been spoken today, and maybe they needed to be," he said. "But in the haste of the moment, let us not forget that these newcomers are still kindred of the king, and words of kindness can often soothe the anger in one's soul better than those sharp as arrows. I, for one… will give greeting to my cousin Mordraed."

He walked swiftly towards Mordraed, his long legs carrying him smoothly, confidently as any warrior, despite the fact he wore short child's tunic of dark, plain wool. His long red hair burned upon his shoulders, the two child braids in his forelock that would be sacrificed to the Ancestors, bound with twists of ancient gold. He wore a princely necklace of amber, many strings of it wound over and over around his neck; some of the chunks were so large and clear, one could see bugs and beetles trapped within their hearts, preserved and imprisoned forever in those yellow tears of the Sun.

He halted before Mordraed, appraising him with thoughtful eyes of forest-green. "I saw you the other night," he said, "coming up through the barrow-fields. I nearly shot at you and you at me. Glad am I that it did not come to a war of arrows! Well met, Mordraed son of Loth, son of my aunt Morigau. I am Amhar, son of Ardhu, son of U'thyr… your cousin."

Mordraed stared at this slender youth, still wearing a child's garb but not a child in manner or bearing. Cousin… and brother. He felt a sudden shiver, he did not know why… as if somewhere, some barrow-ghost trod on the plot of land that would one day hold his own bones. Hatred was what he should feel… this boy-man was the one acclaimed as Ardhu's heir, the one who would rule the Five Cantrevs after Pendraec was gone, the one who held the positions that would have, should have been Mordraed's. And yet… .he did not hate.

24

Amhar slipped a friendly arm over his kinsman's shoulder. "Come, you look tired. I am sure you are hungry. I will take you for food and then to lodgings. Tomorrow I will introduce you to my father's foremost warrior, the Lord An'kelet, who will teach you the warrior's craft. I will help you here, cousin; there need be no more battling between your folk and mine."

In silence Mordraed moved toward the door of the Hall with the red-haired Princeling talking as if they had been the best of friends for all their lives. Mordraed briefly glanced over his shoulder and saw Morigau watching him depart, her face intense, twisted, almost demonic in the sullen red light of the guttering fire-pit.

She was smiling, her lips drawn back over her canines. It was the smile of a wolf.

CHAPTER THREE
COUSINS AND BROTHERS

Mordraed dropped into a crouch and circled his opponent, lip curled in a fierce snarl. In his hand he held a fine Ar-moran dagger, its blade a deadly rapier that could pierce a man's heart and kill him instantly before he even realised the blade had touched his flesh. His deerskin cloak was wrapped around his left arm—a makeshift shield. He was stripped to the waist, and his hair pierced by a thick pin carved from a human arm-bone; he had whittled it himself one day, when loitering out amid the barrows, hoping that by robbing it from the mound and setting his own seal on it, he would bind the Old One's spirit to him, fortifying him with the Ancestor's strength and prowess.

Across from him, also armed with a fine Ar-moran blade, was the Lord An'kelet, right-hand man of Ardhu the Terrible Head. Despite encroaching age—he was over forty—he still was near as lithe and supple as the youth he fought, and his looks were still striking as if given him from the gods. He towered over most other men in the settlement, and muscle had not turned to fat as it did in many warriors who enjoyed much pork and mead. If the amber brightness of his hair was a little faded and laughter lines crept like fine-spun spider webs round eyes and mouth, none held it against him or spoke of the changes with disdain. He was, after all, the King's closest companion and the protector of the Queen Fynavir... he had saved her once, years ago, from the rival chief Melwas. If any whispered behind his back, it was only about the unusual fact that he had no wife, no woman at his hearth—his life was dedicated to the Stone Lord and to his Lady. Such dedication seemed strange, even unseemly, to some.

Mordraed was one of them. An'kelet had been set up as his tutor in war-arts, and he hated him nearly as much as he hated his uncle-father. Ardhu treated Mordraed well enough, a kind word of praise here and there... but An'kelet... Mordraed fancied he looked down on him as if he were cow-dung stuck to the sole of his shoe. His did not contemplate for one moment that An'kelet hardly recognised him as anything at all; he was just a duty to be attended to on a daily basis.

"Come on, Mordraed..." An'kelet's lightly-accented voice was sharp with irritation. "You can do better than this—I have seen you! You are lazy, that's what's wrong with you—too much time drinking and gazing at your pretty reflection in the river!"

Mordraed's usual simmering rage ignited and he lunged forward, dagger swinging in a shining arc. "You dare to criticise me... you who have no woman, but dote on the King's wife..."

The next moment he was down on his back with a hard thud, his head banging off the ground. An'kelet was kneeling over him, his blade Arondyt at his neck. "Beware of what comes out of your mouth, Mordraed, lest it bring you to ruin. And control that temper, *boy*, or you'll not live long enough to be a warrior of Ardhu's clan."

"Let me have my bow!" Mordraed panted, struggling to be free of An'kelet's hold. "Then you will see who is a warrior!"

"Enough of this folly!" An'kelet suddenly sheathed Arondyt, slamming the long Ar-moran dagger into its scabbard of horn. He sprang away from his floored opponent, brushing dirt off his long woven tunic with its amber buttons surmounted by golden sun-crosses. "I tire of this sparring... with word and otherwise. Go, and come back when you want to learn and not act like an angry bee!"

He stalked across the dun without a backward glance and Mordraed clambered to his feet, muddy and still angry. He was about to go after An'kelet, casting caution to the wind in his vain attempt to save face, when Amhar son of Ardhu, who had been watching the training within a crowd of half-grown lads, strode briskly to his side and placed a hand on his arm. "Kinsman, be still, fighting like this ill becomes warriors of Kham-El-Ard... We are all Ardhu's men; we must hold together and work out any quarrels between each other with cool heads and wise counsel."

"What do you know?" Mordraed said bitterly. "You are not even a Man of Ardhu's band yet... you are still deemed a boy, a child..."

He shut his mouth with a snap as Amhar gave him a reproachful look and bowed his head. No, he must use caution; it wouldn't do well to insult this boy, his rival... his brother. Amhar was one of the few who did not treat him with suspicion in the high camp upon the Crooked Hill, and that could be useful in the long run. Most useful.

"Forgive me," he murmured, though the words of apology came hard. He leaned over and picked up his discarded tunic and his bow. "I come from the North when men do not have gentle tongues. Let us go from this place for a while, I need to wash the dirt from me."

*****

The two youths wandered down to a spot along the banks of Abona where the river widened just before it reached the great ford. Women were beating clothes on rocks in the current, and a cattleman drove a brace of cows across the water, scoring the unruly beasts with a switch as they rolled their eyes and lowed unhappily. Mordraed plunged into the deepest part of the swell, scrubbing at his bruised and dustied skin with a handful of river grit while the youngest washer-maidens giggled and eyed him with interest... until their mothers slapped them and told them to look to their tasks and not to the newcomer.

Amhar sat on the bank, dangling his legs amidst the weeds. "Would you teach me some of your warrior-arts?" he asked at length. "The bow... I am good with a bow, but I know that you are even better, a true master despite your youth. Or... even the dagger... or war hammer."

Mordraed paused, pushing his wet black hair back from his high forehead. He stared at his young kinsman... oh by the gods what disaster he could wreak on Ardhu's kingdom if he were to grant the young princeling's wishes! His mother would be dancing with glee if she heard Amhar speak to him so; the foolish boy was almost begging to be killed. And yet... and yet...

"It is really not my place," Mordraed said smoothly, gliding up to the bank, the water breaking into bright ripples about him. Caught in the sunlight, he looked like a young water-god risen from Abona's beds, the water-weeds snaggled in his locks, streaming down his golden skin. Across the ford the washer-maidens sighed... except for the few who found him strangely unsettling, as if he was one of the Everliving Ones from the Land of Youth—beautiful but cold and amoral. "You are still deemed a child, ridiculous as that seems, and I would not want to anger my uncle Ardhu the Terrible Head."

Amhar cast down his eyes and sighed. Ever since Mordraed and his brothers had arrived at Kham-El-Ard he had felt restive and unsettled for the first time. He had begun to desire to be like others of his age, and take his place amongst the tribe, his father bestowing him with his first dagger and axe. He was a king's son, yet as a child he had fewer rights than the lowest of Ardhu's men. If he died on the morrow he would not even have his own barrow; he would be cremated by Abona and his burnt bones placed into an urn, which would then be inserted into the side of one of the kingly mounds that dotted Moy Mor, Great Plain.

Mordraed forced a smile; his eyes were like hard darts, belying the smile, but the other youth did not notice. "Look... I see that you are sorrowful. I would not have that so, cousin..." He leaned over, whispering in his ear: "If I promise to give you a lesson in arms, will you do something for me in return?"

Amhar nodded. "What do you wish? If it is within my power, I will give it to you."

"Take me to Khor Ghor, the great temple that lies so near to Kham-El-Ard and yet seems so far from us, like a place within a dream. Four months have I dwelt in the Lord Ardhu's camp, and never seen one of its famous stones! I have heard so much of its grandeur, I want to see it and worship my Ancestors, but I am deemed unworthy by uncle..."

"It is not that..." Amhar interrupted. He looked unhappy, troubled. "No one goes to Khor Ghor, unless the day is right. At the feast days the Merlin and the priests of Deroweth make offering there, and when the Moon goes dark and when the Moon falls still. At high summer when the cuckoo calls and at midwinter when Bhel Sunface dies on the great Altar then not only do the priests go to the Stones, but ordinary men too—to marvel and to worship. But at all other times only the warrior-priests who guard the sanctuary and the ghosts of the Ancestors dwell within its mighty arches."

"But you have been there, have you not?" Mordraed pried. He had heard rumours of the boy's reputation for dwelling half within the realm of Otherness, of how he ran over the Great Plain without fear of the Unseelie, even to the great pale stripe of the Spirit-Path with its slumped chalk banks and crumbling barrow terminal marking the lands of Life and Death.

Amhar shuffled his feet uneasily. "Yes... but..."

"Then surely you can show me, cousin." Mordraed's strong hand fell on Amhar's arm. "We will be quick in what we do and not linger, and if any trouble comes of it, I promise that I, as a Man of the Tribe, shall take the blame, not you."

Mordraed stepped out of the river, shaking water from his hair, and wiped himself dry with a handful of leaves before donning his dark woollen tunic. He felt in his belt for his dagger as, with the young prince at his side, they followed the banks of the winding river toward the sacred stone circle on the Great Plain.

*****

They came to Khor Ghor by the paths that crossed the great Barrowdown of the Kings, near the burial places of the earliest rulers of the Great Trilithon and the West, priest-kings and Tin-Lords of a bygone time when even the mossy and weather-lashed stones were fresh and new. On Feast-days and solstices the Sacred Avenue was used, running up from the Old Henge by Abona to the enormous mounds of the Seven Kings and away through the valley toward the monument, but Amhar had counselled against using such an obvious route, despite the fact its parallel banks offered protection from the malignant supernatural forces that might wander through those Deadlands. It would be too open to the eyes of the warrior-priests who prowled the area, bows in hand, watching for any who dared to break the sanctity of the monument.

Mordraed did not mind walking without the protective banks. Other things he feared more than dead men, or so he thought—the dishonour of never regaining his promised birthright as a chief over men, and earning Morigau's displeasure, of having her behind him like a whip, striking him with her tongue and maybe even with weapons if he did not fulfil her desires. He grimaced as he thought of her. After Ardhu had first accepted him and his brothers into Kham-El-Ard, he had fully expected that Morigau would be sent into exile, with a death-ban on her. But Ardhu Pendraec was too clever to allow that. He wanted to keep her in his sights. However, he would not allow her to reside in Kham-El-Ard walls, so he had ordered her instead to live in the valley, near the House of the Ladies of the Lake, where his other sister, Mhor-gan of the Korrig-han, and the priestess Nin-Aeifa could watch over her activities.

Mordraed had seen her sometimes, on the hillside, dark-hooded, sometimes feathered like the scald-crow, watching him with her hot, deep

29

eyes. He knew what she wanted, knew what she expected him to do. And he would do it... by the Ancestors he would take what was his! And yet... he glanced at the red-haired youth beside him, guileless, his face innocent, almost like an idiot's, though Mordraed was well aware Amhar was no idiot. He was like Mordraed's youngest brothers, still deemed a child by the reckoning of the people. It was dishonourable to slay a child, and warriors might not follow a ruler they thought dishonourable...

He made a frustrated noise and gripped the hilt of his dagger till its pommel bit into his palm. Amhar glanced over at him. "Are you all right, cousin Mordraed? We do not have to continue if you have changed your mind."

"I have not changed my mind." Mordraed stared away into the red-gold light of late afternoon, unable to look his kinsman in the face, fearful that Amhar might read the truth in his own eyes.

Mother will be proud of me... he thought, fingering his blade. Why he should care? He did not know but he did... and he cared for Mordraed, and the status of the bloodline he shared with many kings, as much as he cared for Morigau's wishes.

Up ahead he saw the great cluster of barrows on the South-Western side of the Stones strung out along the skyline. Mist was curling up from the cup of the valley as the Sun slipped down towards His rest and a chill crept into the air. The sky was streaked with fire and birds of prey soared shrieking overhead, seeking for mice and other prey amidst the clustered tumuli, their white chalk summits glowing golden as the long-buried grave-goods interred within.

Despite himself, his heart began to thud. He glanced sideways at Amhar, but the boy seemed totally devoid of fear; indeed, he seemed almost enraptured by the sight of the stones. He strode on ahead unaware of Mordraed's slowing footfall, his long slender legs parting the waving grasses. His gaze was firmly fixed ahead. "The priests, they go to meet the night guards up by the King barrows," he said. "We should have time... just a little time."

The two youths passed the last royal mound with its overgrown ditch and berm, and soon came upon the bank that ringed Khor Ghor, Tomb of Hopes, Throne of Kings... and Ardhu Pendraec's round circle where he gathered his men in the presence of the Ancestors to hold counsel for the good of Prydn. Across the white barricade of the ditch—not high enough to hold out beasts or men but instead holding *in* the powerful entities of air and sky and grave-mound—the grey Stones of Khor Ghor glimmered in the dusk, magic sentinels that coloured with the dwindling light, now greenish, now rose-pink, now warm gold, the hues of the Sun, or nature, of Time itself. Crows chattered and squabbled, soaring in and out of the trilithons, those great mouths that yawned into the gloom like the mouths of long barrows... inhaling the cold mist of the Plain, exhaling ghosts into the growing dusk.

Mordraed paused, sudden waves of cold fear passing over him. What he had meant to do here suddenly seemed too great a thing. No matter what Morigau expected, no matter what he desired for himself...

"Come on, cousin..." Amhar was beckoning him forward. "If you are still up for it! We haven't much time!"

The slight challenge in the boy's voice hardened Mordraed's resolve. "I will see this place," he said tightly and he stepped across the ditch and ran toward the heart of the sanctuary, Amhar at his heels.

Inside the Stones night was gathering. Mordraed stood in the centre of the circle, staring up, awed despite his efforts to feel nothing but contempt for this structure used by his father and his mentor, the Merlin, that axe-face old man whose voice was as harsh as the caws of the crows overhead. The five trilithons of the great crescent, each one representing a Cantrev of the West, huddled in on him, looming like unhappy giants; he felt suddenly smothered, realising for the first time how small and cramped it was inside Khor Ghor, despite the enormous size of the sarsen stones. The smaller bluestones crowded in even closer, eight times a man's set of ten fingers, looking like an army of people in the eerie twilight, frowning watchers, Ancestors of old sleeping in stone—for now.

"Can you feel them, cousin?" Amhar's voice was a respectful whisper. "The Old Ones? They are all around us. This circle is the beginning and ending of all things..."

Breath hissed through Mordraed's teeth. He wanted an ending here above all. His hand clutched his dagger hilt, slimy with cold sweat. He half pulled it from its deerskin sheath, careful to make no sound; but it was as if something, *someone* pulled on his arm, forcing his fingers to slide away... *The Old Ones know what my mother wants me to do here!* he thought wildly. *They try to stop me!*

Primal terror flooded him, despite his earlier confidence that no spirit would bring him fear. He fought the panic but it grew worse; shivers coursed down his body and his teeth chattered. The thought of the unseen and undead from the Not-World all around him, oozing up from the ground, from the pits in the bank, from the ditch, from the very Stones themselves chilled him, revolted him... How he hated this place, its stillness, its silence, the awful weight of years that seemed to deaden the very air within the inner sanctum. If ever he should become the king his mother dreamed of, he would slight this frowning, almost accusing monument... by the Moon Mother he would throw these Stones down and build anew, and drive these skulking, hated Ancestors away!

"Mordraed, are you all right?" He was shaken back to reality by Amhar. The lad was standing near him, his hair a dull dim red like the faded sunset. Hair the hue of old blood.

Mordraed shook his head to clear it, to sweep away images of dead faces, of eyeholes black with reproach. He had a duty; he must do what he knew to be right... for Morigau, and for his own future. "Cousin, this temple amazes me. Before we leave, come closer and show me the features that I must gaze upon and worship. I know little of what is here, being but a rude man of the North."

Amhar approached, trusting. He was mere inches away from Mordraed. He gestured up at the immense trilithons, naming each in turn. "That is Throne of Kings... where the true chief must swear to the Land upon the Sacred Sword-in-the-Stone. That is the Arch of the Eastern Sky, and that the House of the North Wind... and the one in the far West is dedicated to the Guardian, who protects our dead Ancestors. The tallest, Mordraed, is the Door into Winter, Portal-of-Ghosts, where Lord Bhel gives himself up above the Altar."

"What a noble sacrifice he makes each year..." Mordraed's voice was a low, dry hiss, vaguely tremulous. *And so too will you... but only once...* He put what he hoped was a brotherly arm around Amhar's shoulders, suddenly drawing him close against him. So close and tight he could not break free.

Amhar looked surprised and slightly confused.

Mordraed's knife, unseen in the gloom, slipped out of its sheath...

At that moment the blaring of a horn was borne into the ancient circle, carried on the rising breeze. Its sound bounced around the megalithic rings, dull and ominous and eerie. "That horn!" Amhar cried "Do you hear it?" He jerked free of Mordraed's slackening grip and ran to the edge of the Stones.

Mordraed stood panting in the centre of the place he hated, his plan in tatters and the enormity of what he had nearly done, what he had failed to do, washing over him like a dark, sucking tide.

A second later the fateful horn blared again, louder this time and clearer. Amhar turned to Mordraed, his face guileless; obviously he did not realise how close to the Ancestors he had come. "Did you hear the horn, Mordraed? We must go with haste! That is a summons to all men of Kham-El-Ard. Something of great import has happened at my father's dun!"

Without another glance at his kinsman, he dashed out into the twilight, leaping over the ditch and away across the mist-bound rises and burial mounds. Mordraed stood alone for a moment inside the Stones, still shocked by the turn of events. The pillars of the ring seemed even darker now, almost angry; he imagined glowering faces, spiteful eyes, in their sides. This place meant him ill; he sensed it with every fibre of his being. Slamming his dagger home into its sheath, he ran like the wind after the cousin he had nearly killed, and the rising breeze snickered mockingly in the gaunt dark archways behind him.

CHAPTER FOUR
THE CART OF THE DEAD

The cart stood within the central enclosure at Kham-El-Ard, a hefty wooden wain with great round disc-wheels of solid oak. A dispirited pair of oxen was bound to it, their flanks grey and mud- splattered and ribs thrusting through shrivelled skin.

They looked half-dead, flies gathering round their slitted eyes, buzzing noisily as they feasted on oozing encrustations. But they did not look as foul as the man perched in the back, hunched and hooded, the gaunt shell of his body furled in a ragged skin that had patches gnawed out of it and sent out a reek of rotten flesh. Maggots fell from its folds, dripping down onto the burden borne by the strange cart... and that burden was most dreadful of all, worse than the staggering oxen or the emaciated carter.

The wain was filled with the dead... unbarrowed and unprepared for their journey into the Otherworld. Bundled together like piles of mouldering sticks, they sprawled on the bottom of the cart, legs tangled with arms, ribs mixed with finger-bones, skulls and pelvises rolling and rattling as the oxen stamped in their traces.

Around the cart the women of Kham-El-Ard began to keen, throwing their shawls over their faces to hide their eyes from such a hideous sight, which might blight their wombs to barrenness or mark the unborn with abnormalities. The warriors of Ardhu cried out in anger, and blades were raised and axes hefted; starting a war-chant, they circled the ominous carter with his burden of the dead, all the while blowing on the great bronze-bound horns that would summon all men to Kham-El-Ard in time of strife.

Leaving the comforts of his Hall at the first blasts of the horn, Ardhu Pendraec hurried toward the gate of the dun, where he could see people milling and hear the lamentations of the fearful women. An'kelet strode at his side, clutching his great barbed spear, the Balugaisa. The extended spines that could easily rip a man's guts from his body glinted wickedly in the light of the torches that had sprung into life all over the great fort on the crooked hill.

Ardhu felt uneasy. Years had passed without incident of note; he had fought off the odd sea-raider, trounced pugnacious chiefs who had challenged his authority, and had sat in judgement on disputes over stolen land, cattle and women, and meted out punishment for murder or blood-feud. Yet this one wraith-like man, in his unwholesome cart of death, filled him with more trepidation than a hundred bellowing, boasting warriors with sharpened axes, and he was not sure why.

Perhaps it was because he had dreamed so ill these many months, turning in restless sleep—dreamed of plague and famine, of Moons that ran red with blood and a Sun that failed. Of crops that stagnated in fields dry as dust, and rivers that shrank to leave foetid, muddy holes. He had even seen, in darkest nightmare, a circle like Khor Ghor, but not made of stones—it was wrought of human bones, a cage of ribs, a trap of death, with leg-bones for lintels, and skulls perched grinning above the entrance...

"Who are you and why do you come unbidden to Kham-El-Ard, bringing the naked dead with you?" he asked sternly, coming to a halt before the wretched cart. He had dressed in his old bearskin cloak, the preserved head moth-eaten and bare after many years of use, and he carried in his hand the sceptre Rhon-gom, so that this unwholesome stranger might know who it was he dealt with.

The creature in the cart moved forward jerkily, motions resembling a spider dangling on a thread. "I am called Pelahan, and I hail from the East, O High King of Prydn," he rasped. "From the realm of the Maimed King, An-fortas, I come to beg for aid, for our land is dying—men call it the Wasteland and do not cross its borders. Crops fail, beasts die, and men starve. An-fortas himself was once a mighty and just chief and our realm a fair and fertile garden, but he has taken a wound that has crippled him so that he can be no true king and so the land fails and all in it."

Standing at Ardhu's shoulder, An'kelet shifted uneasily. "My friend, I beg you not listen to this ill-starred one. As tragic as his plight might be, what have we to do with those far lands and the sickness that assails it? What help could we give? We are warriors, not magic men."

Ardhu sighed and his fingers caressed the fossil head of Rhon-gom. "It is true... but men call me the King of all kings in Prydn. The protector. What would they call me if I refused to go? I have never baulked from settling disputes or putting down rebels when needed."

"But this is different," An'kelet insisted. "No one has ever come to Kham-El-Ard bearing such a grim burden, and looking half of the Otherworld... yet begging for our aid."

The one called Pelahan cocked his head on one side and thrust back his voluminous hood, revealing a skull-like visage—his nose was gone, devoured by some flesh-eating disease, leaving only a jutting nub; and half his grey cheek had collapsed into his mouth, showing a row of bright white teeth through ragged flesh. The village women shied away, and their terrified wailing, which had dwindled when Ardhu appeared, started up in earnest. "If you do not come, the pestilence will spread," said Pelahan. "From one Cantrev to the other. Have you not noticed changes already, Chief Ardhu? A longer winter, darker nights, summers where the rains fall and the sun seldom shines? Have you not had rivers break their banks and wash villages away, and crops and children that have not thrived? Have your cows not calved dead things and the sows eaten their own sickly farrow? Tell me true that you have not seen these things!"

Ardhu's face paled beneath his tan. The last few years *had* seen poor

34

crops and rain, endless grey skies that brooded like his dark night-time dreams. On the last feast of Bhel there had been no glorious Sunset; the snow had fallen so heavily and the night had been so dismal that some believed Bhel was truly dead and would never rise again. And in the summer past, at Midsummer, the rain had fallen in sullen sheets until there were puddles circling the feet of all the stones in Khor Ghor, reflecting the worried faces of the Merlin and his priests. Word had come from the moors of the far West that the rain had been so severe many farms had been washed away, and the soil was ruined forever for the planting of crops. People began to abandon what had once been rich, fertile uplands, and headed for the valleys and coasts, leaving settlements, stone rows and temples to decay in the incessant rain.

Pelahan noticed Ardhu's expression and smirked, his teeth rigid as standing stones through curtains of livid flesh. "I knew it had come here too."

An'kelet tossed his head angrily. "Still, what has it to do with Ardhu? There have always been bad years; that is the way of things!"

"But the King is the land, and the land is the King," Pelahan whispered. "One fails, so does the other. This blight must be dealt... otherwise, it will not be just the Maimed King's domain that is the Wasteland, but all of Prydn. And when the Land is weak, and under a cloud of shadow, then, too, will the enemies from the coasts come in their darting ships, like serpents of the seas."

"Ardhu, I do not like this wheedling, ill-visaged creature," said An'kelet. "Send him forth and let us burn the evil burden he drags with him!"

Ardhu Pendraec held up Rhon-gom and shook his head. "Peace, my brother. We cannot do that, as much as my heart tells me to. We must hold counsel with the Merlin at Khor Ghor; we must call the men to join in the Round and decide the best course of action. For all I shudder at the sight of this stranger, I fear there may be truth in his words. I have grown a better judge of men as my years have increased and do not feel that he means us harm, unsavoury though his aspect may be."

An'kelet sighed and clutched the Balugaisa tighter in his fist. "It will be as you say, lord. You are the Stone Lord, chief of chiefs of Prydn."

*****

The men of Ardhu's warband gathered in the Stones the next day, his most loyal men through the long years. Foremost amongst them — Hwalchmai, still youthful and handsome; Ka'hai with his face creased in its usual concerned expression; Bohrs who was round as a barrel but strong as an ox; horse-maned Per-Adur whose haughty mien had long been tempered; Betu'or the ever-faithful, quiet and serious; the twins Ba-lin and Bal-ahn, still as one soul... they had even married sisters so alike were they in temperament. Walking at the right-hand of his chief and friend Ardhu, An'kelet led them, an imposing figure wearing a gold headband and a long dyed wool tunic with toggles of jet bound in copper wire.

Ardhu himself carried his shield Wyngurthachar, the Face of Evening, and wore his bronze helm that blazed like the Sun amidst the sombre stones. The breastplate of Heaven gleamed on his leather jerkin amidst its patterning of conical golden studs, and from his shoulders streamed a cloak wrought of a rare sky-blue cloth which had come from far beyond the Isles, beyond even the Narrow Sea and the Middle Lands where Rhin and Rhon flowed, beckoning traders and adventurers—a gift of remembrance and thanks from Prince Palomides of the distant isle of Delos, who had been freed from slavery by Ardhu in his first battle by the Glein.

Merlin stood in the heart of the circle, staff in hand. He looked not only old but weary, as if he seldom slept, and many in the company noted that his staff was not solely for use in his magics, but needed for support. The hands clutching the worn ash-wood were gnarled and rimed with bumps—the painful, inflammatory bone-bend that afflicted most of the tribesfolk as they aged.

"My men, I call you, after many years, to accompany me on a quest." Ardhu took a deep breath. "If it is not considered too ill-starred by the mighty Merlin." He glanced towards his ancient mentor, silent in the shadow of the Stone of Adoration. "It is not, I deem, a quest of arms, but one of strangeness—evil magic might be afoot in lands beyond Kham-El-Ard. You have all seen the foul wain that has been driven to our gates, and its accursed master, who comes from a place in the East known as the Wasteland."

The men murmured; some were restless, especially the younger ones that were relatively new to the warband. They had heard of the deeds of years gone by—the Thirteen battles of Ardhu, beginning by the river Glein and ending under the bleak shadow of Mineth Beddun, the mountain of Graves, where he had shaved the beard of the evil giant Rhyttah and defeated T'orc, the otherworldly boar. They longed to do high deeds themselves… but magic was something to be avoided. That realm was for the shaman, the priests and priestesses, the wisemen and women, even, to a lesser extent, the singers-of-songs. It was not for doughty men whose trust was in good bronze, well-shaped stone, and barbed arrows.

Merlin emerged from the long shadow of the greenish block that was the heart of Khor Ghor. His eyes were black beads rimmed with red; he had been consuming many herbs and mushrooms that would bring him into communion with the spirit world. In his shaking hand he held up his seeing stone of quartz. "Yes, it is time for men to journey across Prydn and even beyond, finding that which all men seek to stave off the blight that comes to our lands."

"And what blight is that?" puffed Bohrs, folding huge arms covered in twisted tattoos. He had grown nearly as wide as he was tall in his older years, his beard hanging down to his waist and plaited into the woven girdle that encompassed his large belly. "Let me know who threatens the great peace brought by the Lord Ardhu and I will go forth and strike his head with my axe, the Foe-Smiter!" He fingered the large dolerite axe, its haft tied with bright strips of beaded wool, which hung at his side.

"It is not men... at least not yet." Merlin's eyes were hooded. "Though they will come in the end, sniffing at our doors like hungry wolves. It is time itself that brings us ill, as time always does... and ending to all things fair and foul. However, we can attempt to hold evil at bay for a while."

"How? We cannot turn back time," said An'kelet solemnly from his position beside his lord. "Every man grows old be he chief or farmer. The only ones who never age further are the blessed dead."

"To fall before the wrath of time is indeed the doom of men," continued Merlin. "But it must not happen before we can ensure the endurance of the peace that Ardhu has wrought. Many years of prosperity have we enjoyed, and if it is to remain so down the long ages, we must buy some more time... but change is coming, I know that, I have seen it..." He stumbled suddenly, eyes rolling, sweat glossing his brow. He leaned against a dark, spotted bluestone, hugging it like a brother. "The Dark Moon... comes... a time of betrayal, many betrayals. The cycle of Lady Moon reaches its end, but it is also the termination of a cycle of three, a holy number of fifty six years mirrored in the shaft-pits around Khor Ghor where the most blessed and ancient Ancestors lie, looking to the Moon. Change is coming. Death is coming. The Wasteland will spread from east to west, but the Chalice of Gold will bring it back... for a while. The lamb will fall to the serpent's venom and men will sorrow, but his sacrifice will reap the weakness in our mightiest foes."

Merlin coughed and pitched forward, hand clutching his throat, the power of his prophecy sapping his strength. Saliva that was black from the herbs he had been chewing bubbled on his lips; his limbs shook as if with ague. Froth appeared at the corners of his mouth. "Hwalchmai, Per-Adur!" Ardhu raced to the old man, catching him as he reeled and went to fall. "He is ill; this affliction assails him often these days... he is so old now, older than most men ever live... the strain of his knowledge is too much, the spirits seek to take him for theirs. You have healing arts, learned in these years of peace; use them now and then let us get him to Deroweth where even more skilled priest-healers will tend him. Once he is settled, we will heed his words and ride for the Wasteland and whatever fate awaits us."

*****

Hwalchmai and Per-Adur, both of whom had learned healing skills at Merlin's own hearth, set about making the old man comfortable, turning him on his side and taking care he did not choke on his own tongue. A crude bier was made from twined skin cloaks, and the company of Ardhu Pendraec bore the ailing shaman to the sacred holding of Deroweth, with its timber cult houses, circular enclosure and metalled pathway that led to the flowing waters of the Holy River, Abona. The temple Woodenheart stood nigh to the side of the Great Henge, ringed by a shallow bank and ditch of its own, a forest of leafless trees guarded by several grey stones like warning fingers.

Ardhu was struck by the silence of the place as he entered the settlement bearing Merlin's limp form on its makeshift bier. Grass sprouted on top of the bank of the henge, marring its stark bone-whiteness, and thin beards of moss dangled from the lintels of Woodenheart, rustling as the chill wind blew. Some of the houses clustered around the site were falling into ruin, uninhabitable, their roofs patched with holes. Burial places had appeared on the periphery, ominous and oppressive, the dead encroaching on the living.

Ardhu shivered, and it wasn't just from the bite of the north-easterly wind. When had this decline begun? He could hardly remember. The festivals of his youth had seen so bright and vibrant... but now not so many came at Midwinter to feast on the young pigs and greet the re-born disc of Bhel Sunface. Men were busy in their own lands—settlements and farming had spread; fewer men herded, and fewer folk wanted to make the long journey on foot from across the Five Cantrevs and beyond.

Merlin was carried to his hut, the dwelling of the High Priest, which was situated on a slope that gave it prominence above the other houses. Two smaller thatched huts stood beside it, where food was cooked to feed the master of the central home. A semi-circular ditch open at the front ran around the dwelling, and a stout trilithon of wood reared up before the door, symbol of the power of its inhabitant.

Seeing Ardhu and the burden he carried brought the priests of Deroweth running from their cult-houses, pale with concern, chanting and burning incense in rounded cups to chase bad spirits away. The mightiest among them laid Merlin down within his hut, laving his face with water that had been poured over the holy ancestor-stones of Khor Ghor and then saved in dark pottery bowls that had been plugged by resins.

After what seemed a long while, the old man coughed and opened bleary eyes. He spat on the floor and struggled to sit up. "What are you all staring at?" he snapped, glaring at Ardhu who crouched beside his pallet, watching him. "What is this... a festival? Get you gone, Ardhu, and seek the Wasteland before its plague and famine comes to our door."

"So you will live then, Merlin." The corner of Ardhu's mouth twitching upwards, though his tone remained serious. "You will live to rebuke me one more day!"

"If I do not live to kick you into action, then my spirit will surely chase you down the long ages," rasped Merlin, eyes narrowing. "Now go!"

*****

The wind whispered in the eaves of Kham-El-Ard as Ardhu made preparations to leave, ordering serving-men to pack food and skins and clean the edges of his weapons, Caladvolc and Carnwennan. Its sad soughing came hard to his ears, bringing memories of youthful days and happier times before the ravages of age and the wear of life had started taking toll on most of those he loved well. He felt his own back spasm, low in the lumbar spine, and bit back a rueful groan. Weakness could not be seen. Not even among his own loyal band. There was always someone who might turn, sensing weakness, like a wolf...

"We don't need to all go to the Wasteland," he announced to his gathered warriors, who sat in a circle in the Hall, discussing all that had happened that day. "A few blades should be enough; I do not think this will be a battle of arms."

Bohrs harrumphed and folded his arms over his great girth. "Not arms? Then what? Sorcery? That needs *more* swords, Ardhu, not fewer."

Ardhu shook his head emphatically. "No. It won't be that kind of fight. If it is a fight at all." His gaze raked over his men, taking in the glint of silver in hair and beards, the lines drawn on once youthful faces. There were new, younger men in the band of course, replacing those who died or were maimed in accident or conflict, but could they be wholly trusted, as he trusted his original band? He did not know; their loyalty had never been put to the test.

"Hwalchmai." He glanced at his cousin, who had defeated and taken the head of the fearsome Green Man of Lud's Hole. "Will you come?"

Hwalchmai rubbed his chin in thought, then nodded slowly. He had gone off adventuring on his own each spring and returned in the autumn for near on ten Sun-turnings, ever since his wife Rhagnell had died in childbirth. It was as if he could not abide to stay long at Kham-El-Ard with the bitter memories of Rhagnell, who was taken, along with her infant, near the Summer Solstice, although women loved his still-handsome face, and he had many lovers and children throughout the western villages.

"And you Bohrs?" Ardhu nodded toward the big man. "You may not have need to use your axe in this quest, my doughty friend, but I would gladly have it ready for service should the need arise."

"I am pleased at the thought of that, lord." A grin split Bohrs' face. "By the Everlasting Sky, I have been idle too long! I need to shift some of this..." He slapped his belly with his big thick hands, making his paunch shake and the younger members of the household laugh.

Hearing the laughter, Ardhu smiled ruefully. Twenty years ago no one would have dared laugh at Bohrs, a warrior as fierce as the wild boar of the woods. Now, to them, he was just fat, blustering Bohrs, a figure of fun to the upcoming warriors of the West who were not old enough to have known his reputation first-hand. Time was the doom of men; turning firm muscle to jelly and strong hands to quavering sticks, and making high deeds recede into the stuff of legend...

Turning from Bohrs, Ardhu nodded toward Per-Adur. "And you my friend...over the recent years your fame has grown not as a warrior, but as a healer. Where once your hand brought death, now it brings life. If this Maimed King needs one to attend to his wounded flesh, I deem that man should be you."

Per-Adur bowed. "I am grateful. I would like one last quest in foreign lands. I would heal this foreign king... but also, if need came, I would fight for you, as before."

"And what of me, Ardhu... lord?" An'kelet cleared his throat; his voice was strange, low and oddly reticent. "Do you require my presence on this journey?"

Ardhu gazed at his right-hand man, standing a head taller than most of the other warriors, still golden-bronze as in his youth but dimmed slightly, a hazy dusty bronze like the sun fading into the West at the end of a long, hot summer's day. An'kelet was staring at the ground, avoiding Ardhu's gaze. *He does not want to come with me!* Ardhu thought with a flash of surprised annoyance. He had imagined they would ride out together, as in the days of their youth.

"I would not force you," he said, somewhat coldly. "There are others who would be glad to join me."

An'kelet glanced up and Ardhu was surprised, again, to see that he looked relieved, almost glad. "Ardhu, friend, I give you my thanks. I have no stomach for riding out on such journeys. Not any more. I will stay at Kham-El-Ard and guard your holdings... and your Queen." He glanced over his shoulder at the silent white figure of Fynavir, who went around the great hall with her women refilling the men's drinking beakers when they were empty. She looked up, as if suddenly aware of his attention, and blushed. Quickly she averted her face, bowing her head so that her thick braid of milk-pale hair swung in front of her visage and hid her flaming cheeks.

She was not swift enough. Ardhu, standing face to face with An'kelet, missed her expression; his friend's broad shoulder blocked his view. However, in the shadows, ignored as the newcomer not yet initiated as a member of the warband, Mordraed saw.

Saw and understood.

He had seen such furtive glances before, passed between Morigau and her many lovers while she still dwelt in the hut of her husband, Loth of Ynys Yrch.

The White Woman was cuckolding his father, the great and mighty Pendraec, the Stone Lord, king of the West. With his chief warrior, no less, the man he trusted above all.

Mordraed could have laughed out loud.

But he did not.

It was a secret he needed to keep... for a while.

Pushing a path through the assembled warriors, he raced out into the growing dusk. Dogs barked at him and women muttered darkly as he stormed through the busy heart of the dun, bowling over small children and sending squawking chickens flapping into the air. He did not care. Like a man possessed, he climbed onto the ramparts of Kham-El-Ard, where newly lit torches flickered in the dusk and danced along them. In the eastern sky the moon was rising, its sickly death-light bathing his face and hair, bleaching it of colour, making him a man white as chalk, white as Death, born of the Old Woman in the Moon with her cruel sickle nose. "Soon, Mother!" he breathed to the rising crescent, holding up his arms to the pallid glow in the sky. "Soon the Sun shall lose its supremacy, and the Moon—and Mordraed son of Ardhu—shall rule over Prydn in its place!"

CHAPTER FIVE
HAWK OF SUMMER

Ardhu awoke in the pre-dawn dark beneath the mound of furs in his cordoned-off bed-space at the rear of Kham-El-Ard's Great Hall. Gasping, he sat upright, trying to focus in the dark. The dream again... the cage of Bones. Death upon the land. A cup of gold. A cup of death... a cup of life. He shuddered; he would not sleep again tonight. The Otherworld was trying to intrude upon his life, through his dreams... he would not let malicious spirits gain any purchase.

Glancing over, he saw Fynavir lying curled in foetal position, like a corpse in a barrow, her breath a light rasp as she slept. She had shown little emotion when he had announced that he was leaving on a great Imram, a Journey, but he had expected no more. It had been long since things had been right between them, even before he defeated T'orc the Boar beneath the thundery peak of Mount Beddun when he was but a callow youth. For a while, when Amhar was born and there was much rejoicing in the tribe, a new warmth had grown between them, but over the intervening years it had faded again. She was quiet and dutiful, and men had not forgotten that she was the daughter of a Great Queen and, it was rumoured, a goddess of Sovereignty, so he would never do her any dishonour, for a great King must have a special Queen, for it was women who were bound with the earth that men walked upon...

But love... he smiled bitterly in the warm fuggy darkness... That was long gone, if it had ever existed in more than youthful fantasies. Gods, the hot-headed foolishness that had driven him to ask Chief Ludegran for her when he had known her all of one night! How green and impetuous he had been, a moonstruck boy! No wonder Merlin had been enraged! Beauty and status was not everything, nor was a dowry of gold and cattle... that was a lesson learned with age.

Leaning over, he took Fynavir's hand and raised it gently to his lips as he had not done for many Moons. He had to wake her, speak with her. An'kelet would not journey with him to An-fortas's domain, but another companion would take the long road to the Wastelands in the East. Fynavir would not be happy to hear his news, but it was her right to know before any other.

Fynavir rolled over and her eyes slowly flickered open; she blinked, confused, almost as if she expected another to be lying beside her, holding her hand. Abruptly she frowned, the corners of her mouth turning down. "What is it, husband? Why do you wake me before the Sun is up?"

"Shortly I leave Kham-El-Ard for the holdings of the Maimed King," he said, "and I have chosen men from my warband to ride out with me. But one place in my company is unfilled... the place that would have been An'kelet's had he desired to ride out with us."

Her face became shuttered, guarded; she yanked the fur about herself and stared off into the darkness. "What of it?"

"I have pondered who might take my chief warrior's place... and can think of but one. Fynavir, the time is come that Amhar is given a man's proper arms and place within the tribe. It is right that he puts aside the name of childhood and take on a new name and responsibilities. It is my will that he is given his manhood rites on the morrow, and then we will ride for the Wastelands of An-fortas."

"No!" Fynavir whirled to face him, eyes wild, a trapped beast's eyes, and she struck at him with balled fists. "You cannot! My son! What if anything should happen to him? He... he is all I have...! And he is your only heir..."

Suddenly, she dropped her hands and began to weep, rocking back and forth.

"Fynavir... his time has come," Ardhu said softly. He wanted to embrace her but feared she would strike out again. "All the boys born in the same year as Amhar are now accounted Men of the Tribe. Some even have wives! If you try to keep him as a boy forever, he will come to hate you. And although none speak ill of him now—none would dare—in years hence tongues might flap more freely."

"But... but what of his special gifts?" she whispered. "They *do* make him different, separate from the rest. The other lads do not speak to the Ancestors... and hear them speak back! They do not see the faces of long-dead warriors in the night!"

Ardhu had no more patience for debate. "No, and the other lads are not the sons of kings, wife. Amhar will not sit here weaving with women like some... some Fir-vhan, a man-woman! Nor will he be sent to Deroweth to don the robes of priesthood. He will become a Man of Kham-El-Ard and a true prince of his people."

"I curse you, Ardhu!" Fynavir rose, flinging a sheepskin around her shoulders, and she ripped aside the hangings that protected their cubicle from prying eyes. "You think to do right, but I know in my heart that your stubbornness, your desire to meddle in things that would be best left alone, will bring doom to us all! You may know about war and the ways of men, but I know about my child and what is best for him! Your decision will bring a day of wickedness to us all. I feel this in my heart!"

Sobs catching in her throat, she ran from the Hall, a pale creature seemingly of mist and ice; she raced into the darkened door of the women's house, where females of the tribe gathered when their monthly Moon-bleed was upon them and where it was forbidden for men to enter. Around Ardhu the men of the war-band stirred, woken by the sound of raised voices, and shifted aside their heaps of sleeping-furs and sheepskins.

Hwalchmai rolled onto his haunches and poked at the fire-pit with a stick, pushing back his sleep- tangled hair with his free hand. "Is anything wrong, cousin?"

"No." Ardhu shook his head. "Nothing is wrong, save a woman's foolish fancies. This will be a day of great rejoicing, not of sorrow. A day we have waited too long to see. Today my son Amhar will become a Man of the Tribe and join the warband of Ardhu Pendraec on his very first quest."

*****

The Sacred Pool below Kham-El-Ard lay silent beneath the canopy of trees. Mist coiled from the surface, especially when the air was cool, for the water of the spring was temperate, heated by some hidden Underworld forge tended by a god or spirit so old his name was forgotten even by the Wise like Merlin. On one side of the pool the warriors of Ardhu clustered together, faces painted with spirals and chevrons and zigzags and wearing ceremonial dress: headdresses of swan and jay and buzzard feathers and necklets of animal teeth—the beaver, the hare, the dog. Long cloaks, ochred familial plaques and shields proclaimed their lineages. The wealthiest wore their gold and bronze—all of it, no decoration spared—crescent collars imported from Ibherna, coiled arm twists and bangles, lip plugs and earlobe extenders, scintillating hair rings, and of course their collections of daggers and axes, some imported from the far shores beyond the Narrow Sea.

Ardhu stood amongst the company, holding Caladvolc unsheathed, its red-hot length glowing in the half-light. He wore the Breastplate of Heaven and a belt buckle made of gold to match, but little other adornment. It would be Amhar's day today, his investiture as true prince of Prydn, and Ardhu would not rob the youth of any glory. It was Amhar's time to shine; too long had he been kept in the twilight.

On the opposite side of the pool Mhor-gan of the Korrig-han, Ardhu's full-blooded sister, waited for the new initiate to make his appearance. Ardhu had not asked her to come; indeed, he did not know how she, away in her thatched cult-house in the cradle of the valley, had learned of her nephew's manhood rites, unless it was true that she could speak with the birds of the trees, the worms and beetles of the earth and the capricious wind itself. She wore her customary green kirtle, the colour of both life and the dead, and over it a cloak made of badger skins, black-and-white striped, the light and the dark. Badgers' teeth, inordinately large and fierce-looking for a beast no bigger than a dog, clattered around her neck in a macabre necklace.

Ardhu gestured to Hwalchmai, resplendent in a diadem of hawk feathers that proclaimed his name—Hawk of the Plain and he lifted a cow-horn bound with bronze and blew upon it, a loud blast that sent birds shrieking from the tree-tops and rustled the leaves of the forest.

The greenery parted and in rode Amhar on a white mare. He wore a robe of the finest and palest linen, as white as the women could get it by bleaching it with urine. A golden band circled his neck but he had no other adornments.

He had his boy's bow slung over his shoulder and a borrowed dagger in a plain leather sheath. His dark red hair was tied back, save for the two braids that would be shorn if he passed his rites.

Ardhu looked at him with a growing sense of pride. Yes, it was time indeed for Amhar to take his place within his people. He would have to prove himself, even though he was a King's son, but unlike Ardhu's own long gone initiation at the great henge of Marthodunu, there would be no chance of death or utter humiliation. Ardhu had outlawed such practices several years back, at least within his own demesne. What would it serve to have young men who need not be enemies fight to the death? Only the enemies of Prydn.

Hwalchmai blew his horn again and Amhar dismounted and knelt before his father on the bed of soft, rotting leaves that carpeted the forest floor.

"Today you come before me, my son and heir, to take your adult name and join us as a Man of the Tribe," said Ardhu. "But you must first prove that you are worthy. What skills have you gained in your years, Amhar son of Ardhu? Show us what you might bring to the People!"

Amhar rose and raised his bow. "I have learned the path of arrowflight, the magic of the hunt," he said, and he suddenly loosed an arrow from the string. It whirred away into the green gloom, a flash of white fletchings. A screech sounded from above and a bird suddenly tumbled from the sky, twirling as it plummeted down, to splash into the heart of the sacred pool. Thin streamers of blood fanned out along the ripples made by the falling body.

"Blood!" Mhor-gan's voice was a harsh whisper. "Blood of the sacrifice, given to the Ancestors this auspicious day!" She knelt on the bank, mud oozing round her ankles, and let her long fingers trail in the blood-tipped waves, her eyes reading destiny in the patterns.

Amhar turned from the pool and held up his bow. "Father, is that the shot of a boy or a Man of the Tribe? Can I lay this weapon down or must I return to my mother's hut for another year?" He spoke the ritual words clearly, without stumbling; he must have practiced long for this day, thought Ardhu with a flash of guilt.

"You may lay that weapon down," answered the Stone Lord.

Amhar took his boy's bow, turned it crossways, and with a violent motion snapped it over his knee. He cast the two pieces to the ground. "It is dead, as is he who was Amhar on this day."

"Show us what else the boy who wishes to join the men round the fires can offer us." Ardhu nodded toward Hwalchmai, who was drawing a bronze rapier from a cowhide sheath. He tossed the weapon to Amhar, who caught it deftly, and then drew a second long dagger from his belt, its hilt of amber pinned with gold studs—his blade the Piercer-of-Pain.

"Fight me, kinsman," he said to Amhar. "Do not hold back your strength. See me as the enemy who would keep you from your place amidst the People."

The seasoned warrior and the youth circled each other, moving in a crouch around the edges of the Sacred Pool. The watching men, excited at the thought of a fight, even if not one liable to cause serious injury, began to chant and stamp their feet. Axes were drawn and their hafts beaten rhythmically against the broad, bronze-bound faces of shields of oak and hide.

Hwalchmai made a sudden lunge forward, stabbing into the murky forest air. Amhar whirled away from him, and then circled round to engage, facing the Hawk of the Plain head on with neither fear nor reluctance. His borrowed weapon snaked out, striking, clattering against the slender, slightly-grooved blade of Piercer-of-Pain.

Hwalchmai looked slightly surprised and drove forward, forcing the youth's arm up and exposing his side, a deadly move which could easily mean death to an enemy.

Amhar glanced down, realising his guard was off. Unexpectedly, he snatched back his blade from the dead-locked position, causing Hwalchmai to stumble forward in surprise, and at the same time grasped Hwalchmai's hair and drove his knee staunchly into his kinsman's stomach. The older man's knees buckled and he fell to the ground, winded, Piercer-of-Pain clattering from his fingers.

"You are quick and deal a fierce blow, young cousin," he said to Amhar, between gasps. "I deem you ready to join the King's warband. Or any other warband you choose!"

Amhar reached out a hand to help him up; Hwalchmai was clutching his tender belly, though grinning "Forgive me for your bruises, kinsman. I hope I have not caused you much pain. But I did as you asked and played the game as if we were indeed foes on the field."

Hwalchmai bowed, wincing a little. "You played it well."

Ardhu approached his son and clasped his wrist, raising his arm aloft. Amhar still held the long rapier given him by Hwalchmai; it shone like a needle of flame as sunlight filtered through the tangle of boughs above and struck the elongated blade. "So now the boy may fight alongside the Men of the Tribe, and leave his mother's hearth. He may eat with the Men and drink with the Men, and take to him a wife or wives of his choosing. Today he will give up the things of childhood and join ventures of the warriors of Ardhu Pendraec, lord of the Great Trilithon, Chief Serpent of Prydn—the Isle of the Mighty!"

The warriors started their chant, and blew upon horns to herald the acceptance of a new warrior into their ranks. Ardhu drew a razor from his belt-pouch and cut the two locks that symbolised childhood from the sides of Amhar's head, and Mhor-gan kindled a small fire on a heap of flints that crackled and turned white with the heat, and she burnt the hair and uttered words over it, offering its essence to the hungry spirits who clustered around that ancient site, the oldest of the old who had chased the great White

Aurochs across a land of pine before any man herded cattle or used the plough, and who had raised three great totems on the Plain, facing the maximum rising of the Moon.

Then Amhar was taken and bathed in the holy Pool, clearing the last vestiges of his old life away, and then he was robed again and given a beaker of fermented milk mixed with blood, a ritual drink more potent even than the golden mead. He drank it in one, and the ornate pot, already a hundred years old, was smashed to release its spirit, and its shards hurled into the spring-head.

Mhor-gan came to him, the only woman present, the only female who would be allowed to witness these rites, as priestess and seer, talker to the gods and spirits. She gestured him to kneel and painted signs of protection on his face with a stick of ochre, and she gazed upon him with both sorrow and tenderness.

"You are a special youth, this is beyond doubt," she said, taking his hands in her own. "But I can tell little more than that. The Ancestors cloud my vision with capricious mist, or perhaps Bhel Brighteye, who burns like the colour of your hair, had blinded me so that I may not look too deep into your Fate."

"I do not wish to know my Fate, aunt." Amhar looked into her eyes, earnest and serious. "It does not matter when or where or how, only that I do my best in the service of Ardhu Pendraec, Stone Lord of Prydn... my Father."

"May the Ancestors guide you, Amhar," Mhor-gan said, and she reached down into the Pool, still discoloured by the life's blood of the bird he had downed, and fumbled in the mud and leaves and accumulated sediments. When she withdrew her hand, she held up a strange stone of a type not local to the area, broken clean in half, with a deep indentation in one side. The stone was a deep red colour, almost the hue of fired clay, though slightly lighter towards the centre. She handed it to him, upended, almost as if she proffered a cup, a cup born of the natural world.

He glanced at her, wondering. "This is a talisman," she said, "left here in the pool by our most distant forbears; its magic is strong. As the days pass you will see it change; no longer red like blood, it will change to the colour of the evening sky before Bhel is gone but before Nud covers heaven with his cloak of stars. Drink from it, and it will surely protect you from all harm, imbuing you with the powers of the Ancestors."

"I thank you, aunt." He kissed her hand and hid the small stone cup inside his tunic.

Ardhu approached; in his hand he held a small wooden box bound with copper rivets. Opening it, he drew out first a fine flanged axe on a polished, hardwood shaft, and then a fine Ar-moran dagger with a gold pointillé hilt that matched his own older weapon. "These shall be your man's weapons from this day forward, Prince of Kham-El-Ard, Khor Ghor and the West. The

47

axe is my gift; it is named Head-of-Thunder. The sword was made for you in distant Ar-morah, on the orders of the Lord An'kelet, and it has waited too long for your hand. Kos'garak, the Triumphant One, is its name."

Amhar took the axe and thrust it through his belt. The sword he raised before his face, examining its gold and bronze beauty. The pins adorning the hilt were no bigger than hairs, arranged in patterns by a master craftsman. "These are worthy weapons. I hope I will bring honour to you with them, Lord."

"And now I will give you one last thing!" Ardhu placed both hands squarely on the youth's shoulders and looked at him with wonder, so different in looks and temperament to either himself or Fynavir... this magical boy who had been born beyond all hope, and who now was a Man to ride out alongside him. "I will give you the name by which you shall be known forever more to the people of Prydn. Amhar the child is no more. From this day forth... you will be the Prince Gal'havad, the Hawk of Summer."

*****

Leaving the Sacred Pool in the trees below Kham-El-Ard, Ardhu went to find the stranger Pelahan and his cart of stinking remains. Gal'havad followed his father, walking on his right as befitted the heir of the Lord of the West, and Bohrs, Hwalchmai and Per-Adur marched close behind.

When they reached Pelahan's wain of death, they saw the grim-featured man atop the cart, leaning over the dead and touching them, stroking their emaciated limbs as if willing them to live again. It was a tragic yet hideous sight, and Ardhu felt his stomach tighten in revulsion. The dead should be taken and disposed of decently, in an honourable way, lest their spirits be trapped on earth forever. "We are ready to go East with you, and see this desolate land of the Maimed King," he said to Pelahan, "but the cart will stay here, Master Pelahan, and the carrion you drag with you shall be burned and given to the river."

He approached the cart and yanked Pelahan away from his grim load. The strange easterner looked as though he might protest, then scowled and turned away. Per-Adur and Bohrs freed the scabrous oxen from their traces, and sent them away with smacks on the rump. Kindling torches, they hurled them amidst the dry stacks of bones, while Hwalchmai added dry tinder to keep the flames alight. Soon a roaring blaze took hold; skulls popped in the conflagration and the wood sides of the cart crumbled and disintegrated with a shower of sparks. Rancid smoke spiralled skyward, rising in a vast black plume over Kham-El-Ard.

When the blaze had died to embers, the women of Kham-El-Ard descended from the huts upon the heights and scooped up the ashes into bucket-shaped urns. They lugged them to the banks of Abona and tipped them into the swell, while chanting words to sooth any spirits angered by being cremated so far from their own ancestral land.

48

Fynavir came down from the long house to oversee the women's death-rites for the strangers. A thick fox pelt hung round her shoulders but she was shivering nonetheless; she looked suddenly aged and frail, her whiteness no longer of virgin snow but scored bone. Blue shadows underscored her eyes and her lips were pale, bitten. An'kelet accompanied her, steadying her with his hand as she navigated the uneven ground in her thin moccasins. The Armoran prince stared into the distance, his face like a slab of carved marble, still unable to meet Ardhu's eyes. Despite being the Gal'havad's trainer in arms, he had not been asked to attend the youth's manhood rites, and he knew Ardhu was angry with him for not joining the quest to the East. Angrier than he had ever been.

He knew too, that he deserved Ardhu's wrath... and more.

"Lady, greet your son, the Prince Gal'havad." Ardhu gestured to the youth at his shoulder. "He is now a Man of the Tribe."

Fynavir glanced up at her husband, her smile sickly. "And so he is, and now the son that was my joy is gone from me and wedded to the tribe. Just see that he is not gone forever, my husband! If he returns not to Kham-El-Ard unharmed from your hateful questing, I swear by the spirits I will curse you."

The gathered people gasped; they knew of Fynavir's heritage, of how her mother Red Mevva, was said to be a goddess, and her strange daughter the same, born of the white chalk, the bones of the earth. A curse from her lips would surely be of terrible potency.

Ardhu's eyes blackened with wrath... but it was Gal'havad who spoke, stepping between them, his arms outstretched: "Put this ill will to rest! I will not be fought over, and though I honour you both I will not be torn in two. If you cannot agree to have peace between you, I will hasten away, alone, to the Isle of Afallan or beyond. I shall not be punished for whatever anger lies between you, nor shall I be the cause of dissension in Kham-El-Ard."

Ardhu's face suddenly lightened and he hugged the slender youth. "Not only a Man this day, but a Wise man as well. My son, you are truly born of two worlds—the world of the warrior and the world of the priest. May this gift serve you well."

Fynavir flushed, she realised her outburst had gone too far. Tears filled her eyes. "His 'gift' may serve him well...or be his doom. May the gods protect him! I leave you now, to go upon your way... but I expect to see my boy returned, unharmed, within the next three months of the Moon."

She turned, her long white braid swinging, and marched back toward the hall of Kham-El-Ard, with An'kelet striding swiftly at her side, her protector, her rock against all storms.

Ardhu glanced at Gal'havad who was watching his mother's departure with a solemn, sad face. "Do not let her words disturb you. Affrighted are the hearts of some women, and never forget that your mother birthed you in

49

much pain and that the spirits nearly took you and her to the Deadlands that day and she fought them and won both her life and yours."

"I will not forget her pain and sacrifice," said Gal'havad. "But I must speak truthfully—I am glad to be free upon the road and see the world beyond Kham-El-Ard with my esteemed father and his noble warriors. But before I go… may I say goodbye to my friend, cousin Mordraed? As he is not yet accepted into your warband, he was not permitted to attend my manhood trials, but I would wish him farewell before we travel East."

Ardhu frowned; a shiver of fear ran down his spine. He knew Gal'havad spent much time with Mordraed, and although keeping them apart would be problematic and bring difficult questions from both Gal'havad and others, he wished the two youths were not so close. Morigau was far away, living in a hovel in the lake valley under her younger sister Mhor-gan's watchful eye, and he had barred her from entering Kham-El-Ard unbidden, but she was still the boy's mother and her stamp was impressed upon his personality. He did not dare trust him.

"No," he said firmly. "If he is not here now, you are not to run after him like some hound yapping at its master's heels. You are a prince and a boy no longer. He is of royal blood, too, but he is below you, as the earth is below the Everlasting Sky. His house is discredited and ruined. Do you understand, Gal'havad?"

The red-haired youth bowed his head. "I do, father," he whispered but there was a rebellious gleam in his eyes.

CHAPTER SIX
JOURNEY TO THE EAST

The company set off at daybreak, turning their horses' heads toward the great Ridgeway track that crossed Prydn, a route of traders and merchants and warriors for a thousand years or more. Pelahan had been given a spare pony; he sat hunched upon it like a black crow, an incongruous figure amidst the bright, decorous figures of the King's chosen men. Excited as a young puppy, Gal'havad kept spurring his mount on to faster pace and rushing on beyond the others, only to be called back to safety by Ardhu or Bohrs.

The band ascended the Ridgeway track near the Sanctuary, the thatched cult-house that guarded the main entrance to Suilven, Temple of the Eye, known by the tin-traders of old as The Crossroads of the World. Lines of standing stones snaked away from its lintelled doorway toward distant Suilven, where chalk banks towered over ditches that dropped down sixty feet toward the realm of the Underworld, creating a raised central platform that held three stone circles made of natural sarsen hauled from the nearby Downs. Gal'havad said wistfully that he would like to see these stone rings, so different from the familiar circle of Khor Ghor, and he stared with longing at a trickle of smoke coming from a fire in the heart of the Sanctuary, but Ardhu shook his head and frowned. "No, we have no time... you will go when there is peace in the land. All men will eventually see Suilven."

The Stone Lord turned his horse upon the Ridgeway and touched his heels to its flanks, driving the beast down the rutted chalk road, past tumuli swamped with trees and lonely pilgrims and merchants heading to and from the Great Temple, who stared and gawked to see a gold-clad lord before them, carrying his weapons of might and war. He knew Gal'havad would need to visit Suilven sometime, but he shuddered at the very thought of taking his son to that place with its dark woman-magic and for him, dark memories... It was there, on the Harvest Feast of Bron Trogran, that he had been seduced by his half-sister, the bitter and venomous Morigau—and begot Mordraed upon her...

The Ridgeway wound East, toward the rising Sun and the accursed lands the travellers sought. It meandered through a flat, fertile valley, then rose gradually onto a high escarpment covered in deep yellow grass that tossed in the wind like a maiden's hair. They stopped to give the animals a rest, staring down at the smoky hills beyond, before faring on with speed, passing along the summit of a line of gentle hills that undulated like a snake, almost resembling a spirit-path, but made by the hands of gods rather than men.

As the day died the sky grew blood red, clouds burning in a great conflagration, and the travellers came to a flat plateau, with only a few bare dead trees upon it, limned against the crimson glow of the sky. A hundred yards to the right of the well-worn track, a long barrow crouched like a waiting beast, its portal stones up thrust like a row of teeth. "Here we shall stop for the night," said Ardhu. "The Ancestors will protect us."

They rode over to the mound, long fallen out of use, the entrance to the small cist-chamber blocked by rubble as if someone had striven to either keep the dead spirits inside or to keep grave-robbers out—perhaps both. A façade of large flat-faced sarsens glowered into the gloom, the ones on either end of the façade taller and more pointed than the rest, giving it the appearances of fangs in an upended jaw. The body of the mound tailed back behind the heavy capstone of the penultimate chamber, its edges full of sharp, half-buried stones that had made their reappearance from the ground as the cairn shifted in partial collapse, heavy with the weight of untold years.

"What is this place called?" Gal'havad tethered his horse to a bush that grew alongside the slumping mound. He stared hard at the blocked entrance, as if willing the packing to fall away and the spirits of the place to rise and greet him.

"The Hill of the Old People is one of its names." Ardhu swung down from his horse. "It is one of the oldest of its kind, or so tales tell. The song-singers recite stories of how once there was an earlier wooden house of the dead below this stone house that lies before us. How chiefs battled over land and cattle at a camp nearby, and men, women and children were killed by arrow fire, with no mercy given. The survivors brought their bones here, when the birds on the high platforms had pecked their flesh and released their spirits, and a wooden death-hut, a new home to replace their ruined ones, was raised over them, and bowls and baskets placed beside them to be used in their next life. They lay here long, undisturbed... And then..." He wandered up to the sarsen façade, tracing the lichenous face with his fingers. "The Men of Metal came to Prydn after their long wanderings from the West, and a Smith, one of the first of his kind in all Prydn, set up his forge here, in the shadow of the great House of the Dead."

"Was he not afraid?" Gal'havad joined his father beneath the glowering stones. "Surely he would know that to build a smithy here was disrespectful to the Old One's spirits!"

"He may have been afraid... at first," replied Ardhu, "for they were not his Ancestors buried in the mound and they may not have been happy. They may have pinched him in his sleep, and brought cold winds to chill him and blow out his fires. But they brought him no real harm. Maybe they too were intrigued by his magic... the magic of smelting copper! And when men in local villages saw the fire-metal he wrought, bright as Bhel's eye, rings and axes and daggers—the villagers warmed to him and thought of him as a wizard as powerful as the village shaman. They brought him offerings here up at the Hill of the Old People, and said the gods had smiled on him, that he breathed Bhel's fiery breath into his works. Eventually they persuaded him to

52

come down to their village and join them there as their own smith—they gave him a fine girl for a wife, a big hut, and many furs and weapons. But in order that he never leave them and take his magic elsewhere… they broke his left knee with a stone axe. They lamed him and he never wandered further."

Hwalchmai, who had joined his cousin and nephew, grinned and shook his head. "A fine story, kinsman. You would have made a fine Teller of Tales, Ardhu, had you not been destined to be King!"

Gal'havad glanced toward the dark passage between the flanking stones. He took a copper bangle from his wrist and placed it on the ground. "An offering to the Smith and to the Old Ones," he said, "for letting us stay unharmed in this place."

Ardhu patted the lad on the shoulder and began kindling a fire near the entrance of the tomb. The wind was rising, screeching through the spindly branches of the trees, making it difficult for the flame to catch. Shadows danced, flickering over the stony faces of the temple-tomb's façade. In the distance a fox yipped, its voice high and eerie. The moon was a pallid crescent soaring through the swaying tangle of boughs, casting a strange bluish light over the ancient structure.

At length the fire caught and held, warming the chilled group of travellers. Ardhu laid a joint of dried beef on the mound's capstone as an offering of his own and then gestured for Bohrs to share out food to the group. The companions ate in silence, except for Pelahan, who took his slab of meat and retreated to the farthest stone, where he gnawed on the joint like some kind of monstrous rat.

"Gods, he is an ill-favoured wight," murmured Hwalchmai, watching him out of the corner of his eye. "I wish he had not come on this quest with us. He is not a fit companion for kings… or any living man! He looks half a corpse!"

Ardhu grunted. "He is a guide… he may be of use yet. And if not, we will be rid of him soon enough. I have no desire to tarry on the road any longer than necessary."

Finishing his meal, Gal'havad got up and stretched his legs. He was intrigued by the strange man Pelahan, sitting with his back towards the others in his maggoty cloak. He approached him slowly, stopping a few feet away in case he was not welcome.

The hooded head swivelled round. "What do you stare at, King's son?"

"You are welcome at our fire," Gal'havad said bravely. "You need not sit outside."

Pelahan pushed back his hood; Gal'havad blinked at the site of his scarred face, the disease that ate at his very skull. "Do you not fear me, boy? Your companions do, I wager, even if they claim not to. Even your noble father, for in me he sees everything that he fears, the ruin of all he has achieved."

"I am not afraid," said Gal'havad. "You are a man, if a man afflicted. You are not dead… I have spoken to the real dead, out in the fields of Khor Ghor."

53

"You are a strange boy, different than the others." Pelahan's eyes were glittering specks against the livid mask of his face. "Maybe in you, a youth pure and innocent... and good... there is yet a chance. Even should your father fail, there may be one to take his place, one who can treat not only with men but with the spirits that surround us."

"My father will not fail!" said Gal'havad, his voice suddenly sharp. He turned from Pelahan, no longer wishing to speak with him.

Abruptly Pelahan leapt from his perch and grabbed the boy's arm. Gal'havad reached instinctively for a weapon, but Pelahan hissed like a striking serpent: "It is not me you need to fear, boy! Can you not hear the noise, feel the earth tremble? Horses are coming up the hill at speed!"

"Father!" Gal'havad raced back over to the fire as the warriors leaped up, daggers drawn, and stood back to back, facing the night and whatever hid in its depths.

"Horses? It cannot be horses!" snarled Per-Adur. "We are still the only tribe to ride the beasts for war... aren't we?"

"Apparently not," muttered Hwalchmai. "Look!"

Over the brow of the hill a party of riders appeared, waving brands as they galloped towards the barrow. They were dark-visaged, burly men, with long braids and long beards, and lattice tattooing over their eyes and on their muscled arms. The horses they rode were inferior to those of Ardhu's warband, short-legged and shaggy, with ugly raw-boned heads and crazed rolling eyes, but they moved at great speed, their heavy hooves churning up turf and mud and spraying it into the air.

Shouting and roaring, the men—ten of them—galloped up and over the far end of the barrow. The red light of the torches cast surreal flickering shadows over their features, making them look even more ferocious. One who seemed to be a leader flung back his shaggy head and howled like a wolf, as he drove his mount along the high ridge of the barrow. As he reined to a halt on the capstone he flung his torch down and drew a massive war-hammer with a haft dipped in pitch. Its head was crude, primitive, made of some rough crimson stone, and must have been nigh on a foot in length from end to end. He brandished it crazily, drunkenly, while his men whooped and cheered.

Ardhu raised Caladvolc; the guttering torchlight glimmered on the honed edge of its blade. "You! Lay down your arms. Know you not who you harry? I am Ardhu Pendraec, the Terrible Head, Lord of the Khor Ghor and the West, and with me are members of my warband, famed throughout Prydn and beyond!"

The big man with the hammer sneered. "I know who you are! We've been following you since you left Suilven!"

Ardhu's face whitened in rage. "And you dare to attack me, the overlord of these territories? You fool!"

"I never swore any oath to you, King of the West," the man sneered. "An

54

old man, put in your high place years ago by the flummery of a wizard! Acclaimed king only because you stole a blade from an Ancestor's barrow! I, Khaw, challenge you for right of lordship... and for that pretty sword and gold lozenge you wear!"

Ardhu's eyes glistened, dark and deadly. "I brought peace to this land before you were spawned in whatever pit you come from. Do not break the Pendraec's peace or you will not live to see another dawn."

"Peace!" Khaw hawked upon the ground. "You have reduced us all to cowering women! Well, no more... it is the time for brave warriors to take what is able to be taken!"

He slammed his heels into his horse's flanks and the beast plunged forward, eyes wild. Ardhu raised Caladvolc and leapt towards his adversary, seeking to drive his blade into the horse's breast. Khaw, however, was too quick, and wrenched the beast's head away, forcing it to spin around in a circle. Caladvolc whistled harmlessly through the cold night air.

"You're not so quick any more, old man!" mocked Khaw. "Come, men, take down these braggarts from afar, these followers of womanish ways. It is no longer the time of the Farmer... it is a return to the age of the Warrior!"

Khaw's men surged towards the small party. Their eyes were alight with bloodlust and excitement. Bohrs loosed a bellow, loud as the call of a wild boar, and launched himself at the attackers, swinging his fine bronze axe. He struck the lead pony's knee, smashing it; screaming in pain, the animal went down on the mound, its legs thrashing and flailing, churning the ground to mud. Its weight struck against one of the stones supporting the capstone, and an awful groaning noise filled the air, stone shrieking against stone, grinding like the teeth of angry Ancestors. The support stone shifted, wrenched out of its bed, and suddenly part of the chamber collapsed with a roar. A gaping crater, a maw into the Un-world, opened in the side of the barrow and the pony and its rider tumbled in, both screaming in terror. The other riders yanked on their reins and tried to retreat as the top of the mound sagged, threatening to cave in completely. Khaw's face purpled with rage and he waved his war-hammer again. "To me, you fools!" he yelled. "Don't let this chance be ruined!"

Ardhu made a dash for the tethered horses, who were dancing in fright, pulling on their hemp leads. He grabbed Gal'havad by the arm, dragging the youth behind him. "Get on, boy!" he said, roughly shoving the youth onto his mare. "Ride, ride for the East with all speed!"

"But we... surely we must fight these traitors!" cried Gal'havad.

"If we must, but only if there is no choice—they outnumber us by many. We must not be stupid and arrogant. Now *ride*!"

"But you are the King... !"

"Just ride, Gal'havad!"

Ardhu struck the flank of Gal'havad's steed with the flat of his sword and the horse thundered away into the darkness. Seeing that the mare had reached the gleaming ribbon of the Ridgeway, he flung himself on his own steed and dashed after, with Hwalchmai and Per-Adur galloping madly at his back, shields raised to protect him from spear-casts or arrows. Bohrs lagged behind, having dragged Pelahan onto his steed; the overburdened animal whinnied and fought the bridle, while both men cursed and pummelled its flanks with their heels. Khaw was thundering towards them, his band closing rank around their treacherous lord, their eyes filling with bloodlust as they saw their quarry within reach.

Suddenly Pelahan whipped his hood back from his face and faced the mob. The moonlight illuminated his skull-like head, made black hollows of his eyes and an unholy cavern of his mouth and ruined cheek. He pointed accusingly at the warriors with skeletal hands and let out the most terrible ear-splitting cry, a high, thin ululation that rose and fell on the wind.

The superstitious men, not expecting to see such a tormented visage, yelled in fear and flung up their hands to make signs against evil. "It is a grave-wight!" one yelped, pulling his horse back with all his strength. "He has come from the barrow and is guarding the Pendraec and his men!"

"Don't be stupid... he is one of them!" snarled Khaw... but the moment's hesitation gave Bohrs and Pelahan the time they needed to escape. Bohrs got his beast under control and made a mad dash for the Ridgeway path. Pelahan bounced behind him on the straw-stuffed matt bound to the horse, clinging with bony talons to Bohrs' belt.

"By the gods, man," Bohrs yelled over his shoulder, "you did well tonight, unsavoury though you may seem. But... promise me one thing... promise you'll never scream like that in my ear again! Nud's Clouds, I nearly shat myself!"

*****

The companions thundered along the Ridgeway under the night sky with its cold unblinking stars, the eyes of dispassionate watching Ancestors. Ardhu called out to Gal'havad, and the youth drew on the reins of his steed and fell back alongside his father. "Do you think they will follow us?" the young man asked. His eyes were bright with both fear and excitement; Ardhu could see the stars mirrored on their surfaces, giving them an unworldly silver sheen, and he shuddered and touched the talismans he wore for safety, though not for himself but for the boy.

"They will follow," he said gruffly. "And look, down at the bottom of the valley. More of them."

Gal'havad stared down from the height of the ridge. In the darkness below he could see a line of flickering torches. "These traitors deserve to die." His voice was gentle, almost a sigh, but there was a cold finality in it that made Ardhu shudder again.

"We will try not to engage them," Ardhu said, "but to outrun them. They are drunk; some will lose interest when the fire of the mead goes cold in their bellies. As for the rest... if we move swiftly we will come to Khiltarna, the

Land Beyond the Hills, an area where chiefs are loyal to me. These brigands would not dare step beyond its border for fear of retribution."

The group galloped on, keeping a close eye on the torches swarming like angry bees at the lip of the hill. They heard some shouts from behind, but then nothing... no further taunts, no hoof beats.

Bohrs laughed. "Fools! All show and no guts!" He hawked over the side of the path toward the flickering torches massed below.

Ardhu looked wary. "Keep your wits about you... and your daggers to hand. Too much confidence is not wise."

He had no sooner spoken than Per-Adur uttered an oath and pointed to the slope on the right. The warriors' gazes were drawn upwards along the top of the ridge, where the stars were dancing over the swell of the ancient land. Six dark shapes loomed there, hard against the stars—mounted men. One moved, ever so slightly—a blade shone out like a tiny sun and then was hidden within a cloak.

"They have gone up and around us," whispered Per-Adur. "They know this land better than we do."

Ardhu took up his reins and pulled Caladvolc from its scabbard. "Ride!" he cried harshly. "Ride for your lives!"

The band shouted out to their horses and they resumed a mad gallop along the track. Their enemies atop the crest of the hill screamed war-cries and hammered their heels into their own mounts' flanks. They flew down the hillside at a frightening, breakneck speed, skidding on the dew-drenched grass. Their horse's eyes were manic, their mouths foaming, their coats lathered as they sought purchase on the unstable ground.

"They are madmen!" shouted Hwalchmai. "They will be on us in a few seconds!"

On the left hand side, over the edge of the Ridgeway, Ardhu caught sight of a great flat-topped hill that rose unexpectedly out of the valley floor. It resembled an enormous barrow, though whether it was the tomb of a once-living man, a monument raised to a mighty Spirit like the Hill of Zhel, or a feature carved purely by the hands of gods when the earth was new, he did not know. Their other assailants were at its foot, milling and waving torches, shouting up to encourage their fellows.

Ardhu glanced at the enemy riders. They screamed and howled like wolves, gnashing their teeth and foaming like creatures gone mad. Their eyes started from their sockets, as wild as their steeds'; he suspected they were either lost in battle-frenzy or had taken potions to make them mad.

He looked back to the bald hill. Through the murk, he could just pick out a small narrow causeway joining its summit to the hillside. If his warriors could make their way across the causeway, they could try and make a stand, barring the hilltop against the men galloping from above and keeping the ones massed below where they were.

It was the only way to avoid a battle against berserkers in the dark.

57

"Men, follow!" he yelled, driving his stallion forward. "Quick, before they suspect!"

He pulled his steed's head around and scrambled up and over the side of the track. Hwalchmai and Bohrs yelled out in alarm at first, for it looked to the unknowing eye as if he was riding off the edge of the valley, casting himself and his mount out into the night sky. But then they spied the flat hill and Ardhu crouched low over his horse's neck, picking his way swiftly but carefully down the sharp slope towards it, and they followed without hesitation.

They heard startled yells on the slope behind them; obviously their assailants had imagined, as they had done with Ardhu, that the men of Kham-El-Ard had made a suicide leap over the trail's edge to their doom on the valley floor far below.

The move down the slope gave them the time they needed. By the time the berserkers had reached the lip of the track themselves Ardhu's men had reached the grassy causeway and were galloping like mad men onto the summit of the barrow-like mound.

Once on top of the hill, they flung themselves from their straw-padded saddles and sprang to defend the causeway. Axes and knives would not aid them here, not unless their enemies forced their way across; this was the territory of the archer, and like all men of both high and low status in Prydn, they had all learned archery from the time they were small boys. They kneeled on the damp soil, drawing back the strings on their short, composite bows, their deadly flint arrows with their long, tearing barbs aimed at the berserkers as they came thundering down the hillside towards the start of the causeway.

Hwalchmai's arrow flew true, striking the foremost in the shoulder. The man screamed and tumbled from his horse, rolling over and over on the ground. He tried to rise and pluck the arrow from his flesh, but he overbalanced and fell backwards on the sheer slope that overlooked the valley. Screaming, he began to slide on the wet, slippery grass, gathering speed as he rolled toward oblivion, toward the massed torches in the cup of the vale. A moment later he was gone, and the lights below swirled as the assembled warriors parted to avoid being crushed by his descending body.

"Well shot," Ardhu murmured to Hwalchmai out of the corner of his mouth.

"I wish Mordraed was with us." Gal'havad held his bow in hands that shook ever so slightly despite his best efforts. "He is the best archer at Kham-El-Ard."

Ardhu glanced at his son, then turned his attention back to the causeway, his face hard as granite. *Yes, Gal'havad, he is that… but could I trust him not to put an arrow through MY heart?*

The remaining enemy horsemen were nearly at the tongue of land that joined the hillside to the mound. Hwalchmai loosed another arrow, followed

58

in quick succession by Ardhu and Gal'havad. The darkness surrounding them made aiming difficult, and this time no rider went down. Per-Adur cursed and fired four arrows in succession; they missed, but struck the earth before the hooves of the assailants' horses, frightening the animals which neighed and reared and crashed into each other, threatening to unseat their masters.

"Come closer and next time those four arrows will be buried in your flesh!" yelled Per-Adur. He had become a healer in his later years, but his youth had been spent in war-like pursuits, which he had never forgotten.

"Per-Adur, Bohrs... look!" Ardhu had crawled to the edge of the platform atop the broad mound. Below, the sea of torches was swaying, surging upward in a fiery tide. "The bastards are trying to climb the hill!"

Bohrs gave an angry roar. Spotting a large stone partly thrust up from the ground he tore it from its bed. Raising it over his head, he cast it with all his strength into the massed enemy. Several torches dimmed and the sea of flames parted.

"Keep throwing!" Ardhu barked. "They might be put off. They may not know how few of us there are!"

Bohrs, Pelahan and Per-Adur rushed around the hilltop, ripping out stones and small shrubs and hurling them down into the valley. They yelled and bellowed, stomping around the barrow-top like wild men, hoping the noise and constant stream of missiles would fool and confuse their foes.

Ardhu, Hwalchmai, and Gal'havad continued to fire arrows toward the causeway—not wildly now, though, for the riders had drawn rein just out of bowshot, and it would not do well to waste their arrows if they could not reach their target. Ardhu and Gal'havad, being of highest rank, had fifteen arrows each in their quivers, while the other men had only ten.

"So now I have you, Pendraec." Khaw loomed out of the shadows, grinning. "Caught like a rat in a trap. I could wait here for days and starve you out, or call for my own archers to pick you off one by one... but the mob will be here soon enough and they will give you no quarter."

"You are a coward as well as a traitor!" Bohrs roared at Khaw. "If you weren't you'd settle this by armed combat, one on one. A man's battle! Not sitting on your horse, watching a few battle many, and with a boy and a sick man in our company!"

"Aye!" Hwalchmai cried. "You're craven! You need your band of drunken oafs to do your bloody deeds! Whatever the outcome of this day, you will live in infamy, and the spirits will curse you as will all true men of Prydn!"

"Be silent!" roared Khaw. "I am no coward! I wrestled a boar when I was younger than the lad you have with you! I have slain a bear! On one night alone I killed ten men who insulted me!"

"Then come forth and do battle with me!" shouted Ardhu. "Your grievance is with me, after all. Swear that you will let my men pass on unmolested and I will fight you in single combat!"

Khaw fell silent. His eyes rested on the unsheathed blade of Caladvolc. He had heard of its powers, of how the Lady of the Lake had guided the Pendraec to it in the Sacred Pool at Kham-El-Ard. He did not want to face its charmed blade.

Suddenly Gal'havad stepped forward, planting himself near the end of the causeway, his legs apart, his hair a bright banner in the wind on the height. "If you will not fight my father, fight me!" he cried. "You think the Stone Lord an old man—more fool you, Man of Contempt!—but if that is true, you would have no honour in fighting him. Fight me instead!"

An unwholesome grin split Khaw's bushy black beard. "From an old one to a boy. But at least your head would look pretty above the door of my hut!"

Ardhu grabbed at Gal'havad's sleeve, trying to draw him back. "No, you little fool, you cannot face him! This man is not a noble warrior; he is a brigand and a murderer. You have not fought to the death... you have not fought at all! I must be the one..."

Gal'havad glanced at his sire, and Ardhu saw his eyes shining silver again, unearthly in his white, intense face. He almost seemed a stranger, suddenly grown up, his youthful naivety fled... and there was something strangely of An'kelet about him too—his composure, his single-mindedness. "It is in the hands of the spirits, father. I feel it is right that I avenge the honour of our house, and cleanse the stains of Khaw's treachery with the shedding of his blood on this holy hill... which shall be known as the Pendraec's hill from now until the end of time."

Khaw had dismounted his horse and was slowly picking his way across the causeway. His men started to follow but Khaw waved them back with his huge stone war-hammer. "No, I do not want you. This glory is all my own," he sneered. "I will return before long, victorious, I am sure."

Reaching the summit of the mound, the rebel tribesman stood in front of the silent Gal'havad, hands on hips, raking him up and down with a mocking gaze. He flexed his brawny arms and tapped the head of his axe against his palm. "Do you fear me yet, boy?" he snarled. "Are you regretting your idle boastfulness?"

"I have no regrets." Gal'havad's voice was measured, almost without emotion. "The spirits have told me what I must do."

His hands moved; a white blur in the shadows. The dagger Kos'garak that he had been given only the day before flashed out and stabbed into Khaw's knee. The bigger man stumbled forward, roaring in agony, blood black in the moonlight. He had not expected such an attack; he had expected formality, the bragging and boasting of two warriors set to face each other in combat in the old-fashioned manner.

"You bastard!" he gasped, clutching at his leg. "You've maimed me. Dishonourable brat, that was not a man's move!"

"Dishonourable? You know all about that!" said Gal'havad. "I fight you

60

as you deserve. You are devious and disloyal... a traitor to the West, and you shall die a traitor's death!"

Gal'havad was calm; he pulled his axe from his belt and strode towards Khaw. The hard edge, newly honed, shone blue, the redness of the bronze leached out by the starlight.

The older man cursed and attempted to hobble away, but his wounded leg buckled under him and he stumbled, lurching heavily to one side. Growling like a maddened beast, he swung out with his massive stone hammer, but its weight unbalanced him and he dropped to a half-crouch on the grass, fumbling with the weapon, trying to aim a good strong blow. Gal'havad took three long strides toward him and slashed down with his axe, striking his opponent's arm and shattering it at the elbow. Khaw's great war-hammer thudded uselessly to the ground, as its owner screamed in pain and sudden, overwhelming fear.

"To the spirits I give this evil man!" cried Gal'havad, raising his weapon. "Upon this dark day, my first blooding, a tribute to you Gods and to the Ancestors in the mounds!" He turned, whirling like a leaf on the wind, wielding his axe Head-of-Thunder two-handed for greater impact. The axe-head smashed between Khaw's eyes, shattering his skull and instantly sending his spirit into Otherness. It drank deep of the traitor's blood and brain, passing his strength into the bronze blade of the axe and into the youth who wielded it.

Gal'havad stood with arms and head thrown back, his face so calm, so collected, it almost frightened Ardhu. Blood from the shattered skull had spattered his tunic and streaked his handsome face like war-paint. Ardhu remember the first man he had killed, a Sea-Pirate on the river Glein, and how he had felt sick and repulsed at the time, hating every moment, despite that the man was an enemy. Gal'havad looked almost... rapturous.

"Come, we must away now!" he said harshly, nodding towards Khaw's remaining men, who suddenly broke rank and fled from the edge of the causeway, galloping back down the Ridgeway as if demons were pursuing them. "We don't know if they will return with reinforcements... or what the men below might do."

"No matter what they try, it is a steep climb up—it will take a while" said Bohrs. "Nonetheless, let us depart at once!"

The companions climbed upon their horses, Pelahan once again riding pillion behind Bohrs. Gal'havad's mount snorted and shifted, fearful of the blood-smell upon her rider; he stroked her neck with his gore-streaked hand and comforted her with soft words that belied the fact he had just brained a man.

Ardhu eyed his son as they galloped along the Ridgeway, leaving the crowds of enemies roaring in anger at the foot of the hill that would forever bear the name of Pendraec. "Are you all right, Amhar... Gal'havad?" he asked.

The youth looked over at him and smiled, teeth white between the streaks of red that criss-crossed his face. "I have never felt better, father. Like you, my role in life is to protect Prydn, and with my axe and dagger I will be as a spirit of vengeance upon the foes of my chief and my land."

*****

As the Sun ascended over the rim of the world, a burning disc that shot hot fire into the waiting heavens, the men of Ardhu crossed the border into the expanse of Khiltarna, the Land Beyond the Hills. Deep green rises, still purple with night-shadows, rolled away toward the horizon like waves. Streams ran between the rills and ruts, shining like strips of molten metal, and mist and low cloud hung white and languorous in the natural hollows of the land.

"We should be safe here," said Pelahan. "I know these lands well, having travelled here many times in my youth. The chieftains here are good men who do not seek to rob or harry travellers... as you said yourself, Lord Ardhu. I would counsel, though, that we abandon the Ridgeway, in case any of Khaw's followers decide to cross the border seeking revenge. We can follow the rivers, of which there are many here: Mymrim, Ghad, Khess and Ver, and in the North the tributaries of Great O-os, Ou'zel, Flyt and Hyz. Our arrival in the Wastelands will be delayed, but at least we will not have another evil encounter! When I deem that all is safe and quiet, I can easily pick up another path near Efyn Phen—the Ychenholt, the Oldest Road, which men say was used thousands of years ago by wanderers coming in from the Drowned Lands of the Dagarlad."

"It sounds a wise plan... so let us go." Ardhu flicked his reins against his horse's neck and urged her forward with the pressure of his knees.

The group left the track and headed down the valley. Finding one river, they crossed at the ford, and then hastened East along its bank, green with reeds and decked with white, waving water-lilies. They stopped to rest at noon, sleeping on their cloaks in the warm sun, and then continued on with renewed vigour.

Dusk was falling when they spied a huge treeless hill looming on the horizon. The ruins of a round barrow crowned its summit. The long scar of a trackway marred its flank and curved up and over its bald head. Pelahan nodded in its direction. "Efyn Phen. From there we can pick up the Ychenholt that will lead us to the Wastelands."

They rode on and joined the path that stretched over the hill and wound into the East. By the time the night was half-through, there was a cloudburst and all were drenched and weary; so they left the track again and bedded down in a coppice, stretching a deerskin that Hwalchmai carried rolled in his pack on a wobbly frame made of tree-limbs. They managed to light a little fire, sputtering and without cheer, and drank some thin beer from a clay flask.

Ardhu glanced at Gal'havad. The youth was rocking on his heels, humming to himself as if he was mad. The rain had rinsed away some of the blood on his face but gore still clotted the edges of his hair and left large blots on his tunic. His teeth were chattering and his eyes bright and unfocussed.

"I knew he was not right!" murmured Ardhu, shaking his head. "No one kills a first time and acts as he did!" He went over to the lad, kneeling at his side, passing his hand before the blank-looking eyes. As he did so, Gal'havad unexpectedly let out one of his eerie cries, the sound that heralded his brief journeys to the Un-world, and he fell upon the ground, twitching and convulsing, mud mingling with the blood on his body and garments.

Ardhu fell to his knees and gathered him up, holding him close until the seizure had passed. The rest of the men glanced away; faintly embarrassed; they had heard of the young prince's affliction but it was not something that was spoken of at Kham-El-Ard, and it was infrequent enough to hide. It had not stopped the boy becoming adept with arms, after all—he had proved that when he slew Khaw as if he had been slaying enemies all his life.

Soon Gal'havad opened his eyes and seemed to come to himself. He did not remember falling, and recalled little of anything that had taken place since the attack at the Hill of the Old People. Reaching into his tunic, he pulled out the small cup-like stone his aunt Mhor-gan of the Korrig-han had given him, a gift from the unfathomable waters of the Sacred Pool. He stroked its rough surface and smiled; as Mhor-gan had predicted, its colour had changed from bold orange-red to a dusky purple. It was a cup of the evening, and he was the Prince of Ardhu's twilight.

"Father, pour me some drink into this cup of healing," he begged. "Then I may return to you all and continue the journey."

"Cup of healing..." Ardhu had not seen his sister's gift to the boy; he was dubious. Years of watching men die despite their amulets, despite their prayers, had robbed his faith in either charms or gods. Yes, he said the right words and made the required offerings, but if there was one thing he knew was true, it was that the Ancestors and Gods were capricious and often had no love of humankind.

"Yes." Gal'havad held it up, "My talisman. It will protect me."

Ardhu made a dismissive noise. "Your dagger-hand will aid you more," he said... but he poured some beer into the cup and helped Gal'havad, who still trembled slightly in the aftermath of his fit, to lift it to his lips. "But you won't believe me, will you? You have always been half of the Not-world, like my sister and the Merlin."

Pelahan came up at that moment; in the ruined leprous mask of his face his eyes were strangely kind. More so than men of the axe like Bohrs, who had turned swiftly from the scene, embarrassed by Gal'havad's perceived weakness. "Are you hale, little lord?" Pelahan said quietly. "I do not forget that you spoke kindly to me in my affliction, and so I support you in yours."

Gal'havad nodded. "I am fine. Such turns are not new to me... I have always been this way. I am not ashamed. It is how the spirits set the fire within my head."

Pelahan gazed at the broken stone that Gal'havad clutched. "The broken cup... the colour of even's sky, a sign of the Otherworld, the mystic's sign. That is you, boy, the mystic-child, but not just a tool to whom the spirits speak but also a warrior with a blade in your hand." His sunken eyes suddenly glazed, and Ardhu, listening to this exchange, felt hairs rise on the back of his neck—was the ill-favoured man, wracked by illness, a seer himself? "Keep your cup at hand... but maybe you will also seek a greater cup of gold that will give healing to all."

"What do you mean?" Gal'havad frowned. "What is this golden cup of which you speak?"

"You may soon learn. But it is not time to speak of it yet. Not until we have seen the Maimed King." Pelahan suddenly shook his head as if to clear it and stalked towards the horses. "Now it is time we move on again. Come on, men of the West, we now ride down Ychenholt toward the great Estuary of Met-Aras, where four rivers meet and the Kingdom of the Wasteland stands."

The warriors of Ardhu clambered up, soggy from the rain, hair hanging in sodden coils on their shoulders and their fur cloaks dripping water. Hwalchmai stamped out the sullen embers of their fire and they mounted and turned their steeds' heads toward the broad track. Soon, as the sky lightened, they began to chatter and joke with each other, even Pelahan. Gal'havad seemed to have completely recovered as if he had never been ill.

Only Ardhu remained quiet and dour, riding at his son's side. He had dreamed of a cup of gold, he who was born of good solid earth and dreamed only of hounds and hall, and who understood not the path of shamans and seers like the Merlin.

A cup locked in a cage of bone. A cup that was entwined with all their destinies.

CHAPTER SEVEN
THE TREACHERY OF MORDRAED

Mordraed lounged in the shadow of the Tor-Stone, a burial marker that pointed toward the line of undulating hills that led to Magic Hill in the East. Casually, he knapped a flint arrowhead, making its barbs as long and sharp as he could, deadly prongs that would rip the innards of any living creature it pierced. He was far from Kham-El-Ard, and was shirking his duties for the day, including his weapons training with An'kelet. He hated to admit it, but he was bored without Amhar... though how it would be between them now that the other youth had become a Man and taken his adult name, he did not know. If Amhar... *Gal'havad now*, he thought with a slight sneer... got above himself he would soon have to find a way to bring him down to earth again.

Suddenly he heard a sound behind him, a whisper in the grasses—light feet, almost as soft as hare-feet, but not so quiet that his keen ears could not discern the noise. Grabbing his bow, he leapt to his feet with an arrow on his string. "Who goes there? Show yourself."

A small dark head bobbed up from the tangle of grass and shrubs that grew in the field behind the Tor-Stone. A frightened child's face appeared through a haze of blowing green strands.

"Ga'haris!" Mordraed cast down his bow and ran forward, grabbing his younger brother by the scruff of the neck and swinging him round. "You little fool, creeping up like that. I might have shot you... and then I would have had to finish you off and bury you beneath the Tor-Stone!" He gestured to the menhir behind him, its shadow a long black finger stretching toward the two brothers.

Ga'haris looked terrified, almost as if he thought his brother might just intend to do away with him for disturbing his afternoon sojourn by the stone. Mordraed shook him lightly, frowning. "Little fool, I spoke in jest... I'm not mother... I would not give you to the stone! But I am wondering why you have come so far to seek me out! You and Gharith hardly pay me mind at all, now that you are wards of Ka'hai the Cook." He spoke the last with sarcasm.

Ga'haris grabbed his sleeve and clung. "I...I come because of Mother."

Mordraed's jaw tightened. "What of her?"

"I was playing late, down by the river. I heard a rustle in the bush, and then there she was, watching me. I was scared that someone would shoot her or spear her, 'cos she is not supposed to come so close to Uncle's fort... but she wasn't scared at all. She stepped right out and grabbed me, just like you did! But it wasn't me she wanted to see anyway... it was you. She's given me a message for you, Mordraed."

65

Mordraed felt his heart begin to pound. "What message was that, Ga'haris?"

"She says that now Ardhu is safely away, she wants to see you. Just for one night. Tonight. She'll meet you on the Prophet's barrow down near the house of the Ladies of the Lake. She says she has a gift for you."

Mordraed's eyes narrowed. Gifts from Morigau were often a two-edged sword. "I will go to her. "But you must tell no one, Ga'haris. Not Gharith, nor any other of your playmates. If you do, Mother would have no hesitation in giving you to the Stone... or the Earth... or the River."

"I promise, Mordraed. I won't tell anyone!" cried Ga'haris, his eyes full of pure terror, and he turned and bounded away like a terrified young deer.

Mordraed slowly followed him, wandering back over the stubbly fields, over a hill crested with the tall barrows of local chiefs and then down toward the Abona, sparkling in the late afternoon sun. He wondered what Morigau could want. He doubted very much it was just a mother missing her favourite son.

*****

Night descended over the fort of Kham-El-Ard. Wood-smoke coiled from holes in thatched roofs, and shrill bone pipes skirled into the gloom, merry and inviting. Warriors strode in and out of the Great Hall of Ardhu, where the Queen sat with Ardhu's chair empty beside her. Despite her earlier anguish at the leave-taking of her son, Gal'havad, Fynavir now smiled and laughed. She wore a wreath of flowers in her hair and had reddened her cheeks with berry juice and wore a fine shift of pale linen, thin and revealing, the firelight passing through its folds to catch on the rounded limbs within. A heavy shower of amber beads sewn in appropriate areas spared her modesty yet drew attention to her full breasts and thighs. Even at her age, she was the most striking woman in all Kham-El-Ard.

Mordraed sat in the shadows of the hall, a beaker balanced on his knee, his narrowed eyes fixed on the Queen. His earlier suspicions were still there, and had increased with every passing day. Since Ardhu had journeyed East, Fynavir and An'kelet had grown more relaxed in each other's presence... and then less careful. Others did not see, or else put evil thoughts from their minds, but Mordraed, searching for the signs, saw everything... the easy looks, the glances, a touch upon an arm, a smile. He had hardly ever seen the frosty bitch smile until she had been left alone with An'kelet... and to think he would have to mate with her when he became King!

Rising, he downed the rest of his mead in one go and made a move towards the open door. An'kelet, Prince of Ar-morah, arriving for the nightly feasting and story-telling, blocked his path. He was a good hand's breadth taller than Mordraed, and the younger man felt a surge of irrational anger, as if the older man were looking down on him not just through his greater height but with arrogance and superiority. He noted that the foreigner was dressed up like some bright bird of prey, just like his whore, Fynavir—white feathers were braided in his amber hair and his tunic of painted leather was fastened with shiny jet buttons decorated with gold sun-crosses. A belt of fibres twined with bronze threads hung from his waist, fastened by a ring of polished shale, and his two famous daggers, Fragarak and Arondyt dangled conspicuously from it in sheaths of finest horn. "You leave the hall early tonight, Lord Mordraed?" he said, falsely polite. "Are you unwell? I note you did not come for your arms practice today."

Some of the nearby men sniggered and glanced up, hoping to see a confrontation.

"I did not want to tax you, my lord," said Mordraed, veiling his eyes with his lashes to hide the anger in them. His voice was measured, calm. "I have thought since the Stone Lord left that you have looked a bit... tired. As if something has kept you up at night."

An'kelet stared at him, stunned into speechlessness, his face blanching beneath his tan.

Mordraed tossed back his hair and suddenly cast him a razor-sharp grin. "And if you must know my business, I am faring out to meet a woman, Lord An'kelet. A woman! I know you might not approve, since you are so bound with honouring one woman only, being of great purity and holiness... our Great Lady, Fynavir of Ibherna!" He bowed exaggeratedly low in the direction of the Queen, the ends of his hair sweeping the rush-strewn floor.

An'kelet's fists clenched impotently, and Fynavir made a small gasping noise which she covered with her hand. The warriors lounging about the hearth, already deep in their beakers, laughed, though not unkindly. This was not news. They knew An'kelet was the Queen's chosen champion and that he looked at no other woman. He had made much of oaths he had sworn to his own mother, a priestess of Ar-morah, which bound him to a chaste priest-like life. They did not see what Mordraed was implying.

Mordraed smiled again, a mocking, knowing smile, enjoying the discomfiture of his father's wife and her lover. Then, with another bow in their direction, he swept from the hall into the new-fallen dusk.

Reaching the main gate of the fort he was challenged by a red-faced, tawny-haired dolt of a guard; Mordraed could tell he was stupid just by the look of him. "Oh, 'tis you, Lord Mordraed," the guard stammered, when he stepped into ring of light cast by the man's torch. "You're king's clan so I can't stop you from faring abroad tonight if that's your will. But I'll be shutting the gates after Moonrise, and no one comes in again till dawn... not even relatives of Lord Ardhu."

"That's fine by me, man," said Mordraed. "I'm going to meet a lady, a fine lady... I won't be back ere dawn... if then."

The guard grinned and winked, making him look even more of a simpleton. "A good night to you then, Lord Mordraed."

A good night indeed... that was to be seen. Lithely Mordraed ran down the slope, passing the outer defences with their fierce, man-killing spikes, and entering the field beyond where the Avenue's banks glowed like two white bones in the thin Moonlight. He was glad to be away from the confinement of Kham-El-Ard, where there was always a smelly pork-chewing warrior to your left or right, and people prying into your business, watching you... even when you were of noble lineage. Freedom had been his when he lived on Ynys Yrch—freedom to run over the lonely isles and steal sea-birds' eggs from nests of the cliff and shoot at strange sea creatures that raised their blunt snouts from the swell. Strangers he shot at as well, those who dared to beach their coracles near Loth's settlement; and sometimes his arrows found their mark. He had taken a life before he was even accounted a man, which had pleased Morigau greatly.

He scowled. Although Kham-El-Ard was a great achievement, its buildings and organisation unmatched in Prydn, he did not enjoy its warm, muggy chambers and close quarters where spying eyes were rife and there was little freedom from those you despised. If... when... he was lord of Prydn he would have it ritually burnt at the feast of the Bhel-fires, a conflagration that would surely please the spirits. And if he had his way, a few of the swaggering young warriors who had shown him disrespect would go into the fire as well—extra offerings to the Ancestors.

Striding across the field, he reached the Old Henge on the banks of Abona, its dark ditch sprouting thorny bushes, the vague reek of charnel coming from its central area, where ashes lay scattered amidst the pits left by missing stones. He could hear the river murmuring, its voice almost a chant; River-Mother was restless again, spring waking her from sleep after growing fat and slow with ice and excess water. Soon she would mate with her consort Borvoh, the Boiler, and run merrily on her way again, the Holy Cleanser who swept away the old on her swells and gave life to the peoples who dwelt near her.

Circling the henge, not wishing to disturb any ancient being that might be trapped behind its bank, he hurried down to the edge of the river itself. Rings widened on the water where fishes jumped, silver flashes in the dark, and the stars were like a thousand tallow-candles mirrored on the surface.

He peered at his own reflection too, the stars above him in a crown of light. Beautiful as one of the Everliving Ones who dwelt across the Plain of Honey. But cold, hard as a sarsen slab and death-eyed, with eyes blue, the colour of mourning.

Suddenly an owl shot out of the shadows, flower-faced and with eyes like golden lamps, and swooped above his head. Mordraed's heart sprang into his mouth and he fitted an arrow to his bowstring in an eye's blink, but he held fire and the bird flapped lazily Westwards, wings passing in silhouette over the circle of the Moon. An owl, the sign of She Who Guards, the Lady of the Barrow and the lunar mysteries... she was his mother as much as Morigau and would not harm him. Or so he hoped.

He followed the flight of the bird down the reedy riverbank, out into the valley where the river widened, becoming flat pools of slow-moving brackish water with lily pads floating languidly on the surface. He could see little of the local landmarks but he knew that the hill of Ogg lay across the river, with its enclosure for cattle and outlying settlements of mean huts, and that above the steep north-eastern lip of the valley, lay the Hallows of the Kings and Queens—the great cemeteries of Khor Ghor, where long barrows, their wooden mortuary huts crumbled and their owners' bones in disarray, jostled against later round barrows, the graves of mighty individuals who bore gold and shale and jet and warrior's weapons for their journey across the Great Plain. Next to them stood the women's tumuli, their small central tumps holding skeletons of high-status females whose bony claws clutched items for use in the After-Life: amber and faience beads, incense cups and awls, pendants shaped like the halberds of their men.

Mordraed did not want to go too near these mounds, nor catch sight of Khor Ghor in the far distance, its stones floating like ghostly heads in the night. He had no wish to linger with the dead like his mother and Amhar... Gal'havad... He mouthed the youth's new name with petty mockery, still hating that the boy at last had man's status in the tribe.

Up ahead he saw the river flare even wider, almost becoming a small, glassy lake, and in the most still, sluggish part of its swell, a thatched hut that teetered on long stilts that raised it above the water level. The cult-house of the Ladies of the Lake... his aunt Mhor-gan, the one they called Khorreg, the elf-woman, and her mistress, the one-eyed hag called Nin-Aeifa, who was said to have guided his accursed father to the sword Caladvolc. He would not be knocking on their door at this late hour!

Retreating from the river-bank and the spindly-legged house, Mordraed hurried in an uphill direction, following an indistinct track through berry bushes and gorse. Oaks and hazel trees towered over him, branches rustling in the wind, and holly hedges bled red berries. Thorns tore at his clothes and hair. He started peering right and left... he knew that there was a barrow-hill of great age and veneration nearby, where a great prophet of the times of King Bolgos rested, separate in death from others as he has been separate in life due to his great wisdom.

He spied the hill first—solitary and grass grown, its deep ditch full of offerings deposited by the local people of the valley. And then... she was there, crouched on the tomb's summit like a marker-stone—Morigau, sister of Ardhu, her hair down, flowing free in black waves to her waist, her cloak of feathers billowing around her, its tattiness hidden by the darkness of the night.

"Mother." He stepped towards her. He did not really know if he felt happy or not to see her.

"My boy!" She sprang down from that hill of the ancient dead and flung her arms around his narrow waist, kissing his face and mouth in a way he thought unseemly. Uncomfortable, he pushed her back an arm's length and frowned.

"Are you not glad to see me?" she said. "It has been such a long time. You have been remiss. I thought you would have sought me out at least once since entering my brother's hall."

"I would not have my head on a spike or be watched more closely than I already am in Kham-El-Ard."

"Does my brother mistreat you?"

"No, he does not. Yet I am well aware of my position in his domain. If I stepped out of line, I would be crushed like an earthworm under Ardhu Pendraec's heel."

"And what of your brothers? I have seen Ga'haris, but not the other two."

"They are fine, happy and well fed." Mordraed spoke with slight maliciousness. "Much more so than on Ynys Yrch. Agravaen loves the Pendraec, despite all the tales you told of his evils; he follows him like a loyal hound and is sure he will be an esteemed warrior in his warband some day. He never speaks of you."

Morigau's black eyes sparkled. "He is a useless boy, worse than Loth ever was... arrow fodder as I said before. But he may prove useful to us yet, as he is so stupid, so gullible."

"Ardhu's son is friend to me." Mordraed decided he would tell Morigau about Gal'havad... but he would keep silent about his failure to slay the young prince within the stones. "That may also prove useful."

Morigau nodded. "I had heard this rumour, and saw the way he greeted you in Kham-El-Ard. Pah, a weak, effeminate-looking boy not fit to rule the West. Fit only to feed the dark earth. Not like you, my Mordraed, my Dark Moon."

"There is more," continued Mordraed. "A discovery much more important to our cause. But I would not speak of it here; it is cold and the night is deepening, and gods know who or what might be lurking in the brush... maybe even those two raddled hags from the Lake."

"You are right." She ran down the barrow's slope, lissom as a girl, and beckoned for him to follow her. "We need to talk where unfriendly ears cannot hear nor eyes see... I also have a gift waiting for you, my son... an important gift to aid you on your road to greatness. I chose it with you alone in mind—Ga'haris should have spoken of it, but pah... the boy is probably as addled as Agravaen! I risked Ardhu's wrath and eluded the mean eyes of my sister Mhor-gan to fare beyond and get it for you. Come and see... but do not be ashamed for me, though I live in a hovel and not the stately abode I am due. Curse my brother and his meanness for keeping me in such a state!"

They walked together down the night-furled valley, Morigau clinging to her son's arm as if he were a lover. She could not stop touching him, his arm, his shoulder; he held his head high and ignored her. Soon a ramshackle hut, small and poorly constructed, came into view, its walls painted with magic symbols to frighten off both spirits and passing men. A pig snorted in a pen, and came snuffling up to the fence as Morigau approached. The animal was a big fat sow, horrid and slug-like, its skin bone-white and dotted with sores. "She is an oracular pig," Morigau explained, poking at the creature with a stick until it squealed and bit at the wood. "I use her in hopes that she will soon tell me of the fall of my brother."

Mordraed entered the hut, bending under the low door-frame. The inside of the hovel smelt foul; rot, sweat and ordure mingled to form a heady stew. La'morak and Ack-olon, Morigau's guards and lovers, were squatting in the corner, so grimy and dishevelled they looked as if they had been rolling in the pen with the oracular pig. A cheerless fire of green wood that spat and hissed burned on a central hearth, and a small, faceless stone idol that Morigau must have brought from Ynys Yrch crouched on a plinth before it. Some wild beast had been killed and blood and tangled innards lay reeking at the foot of the plinth.

Morigau kicked Ack-olon aside and threw down a skin for Mordraed to sit on. She then poured him a drink of honey-mead in a crudely fired beaker. "I stole the honey from Mhor-gan's own beehives. She never knew," she said with satisfaction.

Mordraed tipped back the mead—thank the spirits; at least it was not foul. He was disgusted by the squalor around him, and, despite himself, wished he was back at Kham-El-Ard where the women frequently brushed out the hall with branches and threw dry reeds on the ground. The sullen glowers of Ack-olon and La'morak annoyed him too; it was plain to see they hated him being there. The thoughts of his mother coupling in that sty with the two of them, dirt-caked and grunting, made the gorge rise in his throat.

He fingered the beaker Morigau had given him, fingernail tracing the impressions of wheat around the rim. "Do you want to know what I have found while dwelling with my fa… Ardhu?" he asked.

"Of course," said Morigau. "Tell me any news that might help our cause!"

"My eyes are very keen," he said at length. "and, while in Ardhu's hall, I have seen something no one else has noticed. Or if they have, they have put the thought from their minds and pretended it was other than it was."

"Oh?" Morigau poured a beaker of mead for herself—it was a man's drink, but she was a priestess and normal rules did not apply to her. "And what might that be? I am intrigued, my son."

Mordraed grinned the nastiest grin possible, no light at all in his dark, deep-sea eyes. "You know the Ar-moran, An'kelet of the Great Spear? Ardhu's most loyal friend?"

"Aye." She leaned forward, mouth shining with the thick, sweet mead. Lips too full, too lush, parted over her straight white teeth. "What of him? I have heard that despite his status he takes no woman, that he is loyal only to Ardhu's household only." She laughed. "Are you going to tell me he shares my brother's bed as well... ah, my dear, it would not be the first time a king's shield-brother was something more to him besides!"

Mordraed shook his head fiercely. "No! It is nothing like that! The bronze man... he beds the Queen, the White Woman! And Ardhu Pendraec is too convinced of An'kelet's friendship and the honour of his pasty whore to even notice what is going on within his own dun!"

Morigau's mouth dropped open in surprise and then she started to laugh. Clutching the edge of her cloak in her hands, she strutted around the flickering fire in a victory dance. Ack-olon and La'morak glanced at each other before bursting into laughter themselves.

Morigau ceased her dance and knelt back down beside her son. "What welcome news! If there is one thing that can destroy a man, this is it. His woman a wanton slut... and bedding his closest companion, no less. And Ardhu a king, whose household should be above reproach! How all men in Prydn will laugh at his shame! So tell me, Mordraed, what have you seen, what proof of this treachery have you to show Ardhu?"

Mordraed shifted uncomfortably, unnerved by her hot eyes, her hot breath burning against his neck. "None as yet. I know I have read the signs clearly, though... I am no fool. But as you might imagine, if I were to leap up and denounce them both before the warriors, hatred and anger would be directed at me before them and doubts cast upon my word... because I am *your* son."

Morigau slapped her hands against the dirty, threadbare dress straining over her thin thighs. "Aye... aye, you are right. I would not have you put at risk by denouncing them openly... but, let me think... what about your brother Agravaen? You say he has grown loyal to my brother. Others must see his devotion. If you were to... guide him... let him discover the lovers... well, we all know what he is like, he cannot keep his big mouth shut, and he would doubtless roar the place down in dismay if he is as loyal as you imply."

Mordraed rubbed his chin. "I could probably arrange such a thing. Agravaen is none too clever and would never wonder if I were suddenly to befriend him."

"It is set then," said Morigau. "Oh, how I wish I could be in Kham-El-Ard to see Ardhu's kingdom crumble, his family in ruins... just as my inheritance, my family was ruined by his father, the usurper U'thyr Pendraec!"

She rocked on her heels, face scowling and ugly as she remembered her past... being tossed from her mother's hut when her new man moved in, the beatings when she, a difficult child who heard black barrow-voices in her head, screamed and howled and bit both her foster-dam and her own mother.

Mordraed shivered; she looked like some kind of fell spirit, a death-wailer or the river-watcher who beat men's bloody death-shrouds on rocks in streams, as she teetered back and forth on her grimy, heels. Suddenly she shook her head, and the fierce glare of total hatred vanished from her eyes.

"Your news brings another question to my mind," she said in a heavy, triumphant voice. "If the Ar-moran has been bedding the Queen for a long time... who is to say if the boy men call Prince is in fact Ardhu's get? He does not look like our family. If that doubt could be sewn, and the troublesome bastard removed one way or another... a space would open for the rightful heir. *You*, my son, Mordraed."

Mordraed grunted. He had not even thought of such a thing, which surprised him, for his mind often moved in such directions, even as Morigau's. Secretly he thought his mother was wrong, red hair popped up unexpectedly in many families, but putting the seeds of doubt in men's minds would do no harm.

Morigau continued, "Be that as it may, I had another reason to call you here—not just to see your mother who wishes you only the greatest fame and honour, who worships you as she could no other man." She sidled up to him. "The gift... the gift I spoke of. I am sure you will be pleased. I chose it just for you and risked much to get it... Come with me..."

She guided him round the back of the hut, next to the pig's reeking sty, where a small lean-to of woven branches drooped against the hut's outer wall. Mordraed frowned; what on earth could she be about to show him?

Morigau bent over, staring into the shadowed lean-to. "There you go, Mordraed, your gift... Khyloq, my present to you... your bride!"

"What?" Mordraed pushed Morigau roughly aside. Under the branches, huddled in the corner and shivering uncontrollably, was a girl. Long auburn hair a shade darker than Amhar's fell in sodden, dirty tangles over her torn and sodden tunic. Her ankles and wrists were bound, and the twine on her ankles tied to the supporting posts of the lean-to, which would have come crashing down on her if she struggled for freedom.

"Who is she?" he hissed, and when Morigau just laughed, he grabbed his mother's shoulder and shook her violently, until her head snapped back. "Speak, woman! What is this about?"

"She is Khyloq neq Khunedda, daughter of a powerful chief of the middle-lands. A good lineage, my mother's mother's sister was married into the clan, and for the most part the men descended from the old Tin-Lords. I stole her."

"Stole her?" Mordraed stared at Morigau, incredulous.

She waved her hand as if he was silly and childish for being so shocked. "Stole. Abducted... no matter. Her father would not countenance a match since we lost Ynys Yrch, so La'morak, Ack-olon and I took her by night, in the old way. She will make a good wife to you I am sure. She was not much trouble, not too wilful on the road here. Only bit Ack-olon once."

Mordraed exploded. "How dare you do this evil thing? A match and I am the last to know! Have I no say?"

Her black eyes glittered and suddenly she was not just Morigau, but the death-crone, the queen of the Dark Moon, ruling over him, who was only the

73

Moon's servant. "No, you do not. Never forget, my son, that without me to guide you, you will be just another discarded chief's bastard, doomed to watch the less worthy claim things that should be yours."

Mordraed was almost incandescent with rage but managed to control himself. "And what of the White Woman? Did you not say that I must have her as my own, that she is Sovereignty and will confer rulership of the Land onto me? And if you insist on lumbering me with this girl—I cannot take her back to Kham-El-Ard; I am not even in the King's warband as yet and have no wealth to keep a woman!"

"Khyloq will remain with me," replied Morigau. "She will stay a secret until you are well settled on Kham-El-Ard with Ardhu's golden breastplate on your tunic and the Lightning Mace in your hand. You will marry Fynavir... but once the marriage is consummated Khyloq can be brought forward, as second wife. No one will object; a king can have all the wives he pleases. It is only Ardhu's foolishness that keeps him from taking another besides his white bitch. You will need an heir and quickly; you need to establish yourself before other chiefs decide *they* have right to the domains of the West. Fynavir will not give you sons; I have heard that the birth of her brat tore her womb and that is why she has been barren ever since. Once you have lain with her and all know that you have ploughed that sacred earth, you can do what you like..." She grinned unpleasantly, rubbing her chin. "If you truly despise her... well, that can be dealt with in time... it would be most unfortunate if Fynavir died soon after you assumed the position of Stone Lord, but she is growing old, after all... The problem may even be dealt with for you; once Ardhu knows that she lies on her back for An'kelet of Armorah he may get the guts of a proper man and put her to death!"

"But then I could not claim her... and right of rule through her."

"No." she agreed. "But his actions would make him accursed, although in the right. Either way, you win, my Mordraed."

"You are a creature of much spite," Mordraed muttered, "But I do not doubt you have my interests at heart..."

"I do. And since I am the one of all our clan who has both intellect and courage," she said coldly," I will be coming to Kham-El-Ard as your advisor when my brother is deposed. And replacing that old fool, the Merlin as priest. I will rip his stringy guts out and divine from them in the very heart of Khor Ghor! Now, no more talk... look at the girl... what do you think? Does she stir you?"

She grabbed the girl's arm and yanked her forward so that Mordraed could see her more clearly. Khyloq whimpered and Morigau struck her, and then ripped her tattered, sodden robe away. She shoved her forward, pulling back her hair and exposing her white body. "Do you like her?" she asked. "So pretty at that age, before the sagging that comes from bearing too many brats."

"Mother, stop that!" Mordraed snarled and pushed Morigau out of the way. Taking off his cloak he tossed it to the soaked, shivering girl, whose tears were now mingling with the rain. "If you are determined this thing must be done, then she will be considered one of our clan and it would be dishonourable to abuse her! In fact, if she is to be mine, then I say to you... leave her be. She can contribute to the chores of the household—by the Ancestors, someone needs to clean this shite-hole up—but she will not be beaten or abused, not by you and not by those two miserable miscreants squatting inside your hut. If I hear otherwise, you will answer to me."

Morigau suddenly bowed her head. "I hear you, son. My boy is grown— he speaks like a man and a king now."

"I will take the girl inside," Mordraed continued, his voice still sharp. "What were you thinking of, tying her up outside like a goat or a dog? She might have died of cold, and a charge of murder would be raised against you, not just abduction!"

He guided Khyloq into the hut and sat her down beside the fire. Looking at her in the flicker of the flames, he found her quite comely—a heart-shaped face, light green-amber eyes, and a lithe wiry body with long legs. Reaching out, he touched her breast. She gave a little gasp and tried to draw away. He drew her closer "No." He shook his head. "You are mine. You heard my mother Morigau. That is why you were taken. For me. We are of noble house; do not be fooled by this vile shack. One day you may not live in such squalor but in a chieftain's hut with gold and amber at your throat. I do not take you to dishonour you and then discard you."

Behind him, he could hear Morigau chanting, speaking words of the marriage rite that would bring fertility to the union and bind them together before the Ancestors. She shuffled round the pair, hopping on one foot in the traditional spell-caster's position hurling fragrant herbs into the embers then dousing youth and maiden with sprinklings of oils and powders. She had stripped off her deerskin tunic and wore just a necklace made of spiky bones carved into phallic shapes. Red ochre signs were drawn around her breasts and above the join of her thighs. She danced and writhed, waving a rattle - the noise of which would frighten off any malign spirits who might seek to steal the bride's fertility or the groom's potency.

Kneeling beside the couple, she took a lump of ochre and chalked signs on Khyloq's torso to match her own. Khyloq protested, but feebly; Morigau was wiry and strong. Watching her straddle the girl, Mordraed began to feel the first surges of real desire, the need to touch and explore that white flesh, to quench the fire of his loins in the cave between her legs. He ripped at the ties on his deerskin trousers as Morigau shoved Khyloq's thighs apart with her knee. Khyloq cried out, but now Mordraed stifled her cry with his mouth, pressing his tongue in between her teeth.

Morigau backed away from Khyloq and took her son's hand, guiding it between the girl's legs. "She will welcome you. The gate will be open. Let your union be fruitful and blessed."

Mordraed straddled Khyloq, pressing her down into the fur on the floor. She struggled, pushing up against him but the touch of her skin made him even more excited. Suddenly he noticed his mother's men staring, their faces looming over the mean fire-pit, distorted with lust and eagerness. He pulled his cloak over his back, hiding himself and the lying girl below him. "At least have the decency to turn your ugly faces away!" he ordered "And if you ever look at my wife with eyes that that again, I will blind you with my dagger and feed your eyeballs to the crows!"

Morigau laughed. "I will attend to the needs of my men. They will soon forget pretty new flesh." She wrapped a strand of La'morak's lank hair around her hand and yanked him towards her.

Mordraed turned back to Khyloq, propping himself up on his arms to look down at her. She had ceased to resist and stared back at him with an expression that blended defiance, resignation, and something else, too, something he'd seen in other women's faces when they looked at him. Captive or no, she was not blind to his charms. "I won't hurt you," he said, "as long as you do not bite me or scratch me… much."

"I won't then," she whispered. "Unless you ask me to."

He laughed and dived on her, throwing her deep into the fur, and in the next hour forgot about pleasing his mother, or his hatred of Ardhu, or the treachery of An'kelet and Fynavir. Khyloq, perhaps wisely realising she had no chance of escape and glad at least that he was not a smelly old brute who took pleasure from beatings or humiliation, was less reticent than he had feared. When he was done he collapsed across her, and slept almost immediately, snoring lightly with his face buried in the long red coils of her hair.

And dreamed of red hair, but not that of the chieftain's daughter Khyloq, his captive bride.

The foxglove hair of the friend who was yet his foe… Amhar who was now Gal'havad.

CHAPTER EIGHT
THE MAIMED KING

In their night-time camp beneath a lone pine under strange, unfamiliar eastern skies, Ardhu was woken from sleep by a sound he had not heard for a very long time. He rolled over and stared at the sky, saw wings white against the golden-red orb of the rising sun. Beside him Gal'havad stirred. "What is that sound?" he said sleepily. "It is like the wail of a lost soul seeking its barrow-mound."

Pelahan, cooking a hare on a make-shift spit in a little hollow near the camp, glanced up. "It is a seagull, little lord. We are almost at the Wastelands now. The great waters of the Northern Sea will be spread out before you once we pass the next hill."

The companions rose and broke their fast, then mounted their steeds once more. They fared into the burgeoning light, passing stunted shrubs beaten low by the wind and spare, tall trees of a type unseen in their western home. More gulls appeared, screeching and flapping overhead, squabbling over titbits found amidst the grasses, which were long and tough, yellow under the strengthening sun.

"There's a strange smell in the air" Gal'havad raised his head and took a deep breath in through his nose. He licked his lips. "I can taste something in my mouth also."

"That is salt from the sea, Prince," said Pelahan. "The whole sea is awash with it."

"It tastes like tears," murmured Gal'havad, wiping his mouth on the back of his hand.

Pelahan nodded. "Aye. Some say the saltiness is the tears of the Maedh'an na Marah, the Maidens of the Wave, who have the lower bodies of fish but wish for two legs, so that they can come on shore and couple with their mortal lovers. Instead they must take their men Underwave where they drown."

The trail wound up a shallow slope, cresting a dune made of sand and earth, and once on top Pelahan signalled for a moment's halt. He turned his cadaverous face into the wind and let out a long, painful sigh. Ardhu was sure he saw tears standing in his weary, faded eyes. "The Wastelands lie before you," he said.

The companions looked. Ahead they saw an endless stretch of coastline, sand mingling with rough flinty shore. Sea grasses blew, hissing in the wind, and water streaked in amongst them, making small free-standing islets where birds nested—terns, gulls, plovers. The water beyond was choppy and dark, and the sky above it a flat iron-grey. A northern sea, colder and less kindly than the turquoise waters off the coasts of Belerion in the farthest west, and even more fierce than the Ibhernian Sea, which formed a barrier between Prydn and its sister isle.

"It will not be long now before we reach the Maimed King," said Pelahan. "I pray he still lives. I have been gone long and all his men have abandoned him. He is alone, in his agony and despair."

"Before we meet this King, tell me more of what has happened here," said Ardhu, as the party descended the dune and cantered along the bleak seashore under the threatening sky, with frightened nesting birds bursting up before their horse's hooves.

"King An-fortas ruled the East, the land of Y-khen, for many years; he held this coast as you held the west, keeping back raiders who came across from the Flatlands in their boats seeking land and occasional plunder. But he grew old and he refused to see that he could no longer war as a young man... he fought a Northern Man from the Ice Mountains, huge as a giant with hair the colour of the sun, and though he killed the invader, he took a dagger-wound in the thigh which crippled him. Now you know the law, Terrible Head... a king yourself. A king who is blemished bodily must not be allowed to reign. The King and the Land are united in the eyes of the Spirits, and if one is damaged and failing, so will the other be. But An-fortas was loved by his people and none wished death to him, so he ruled on and did not hand his kingship to his son. His health worsened, and no healer could cure his wound... and then a sickness came, and whole villages perished from the delta right down the coast. At one time the sea-strand was alive with fishermen, but look now, it is empty, a place where the gulls play with dead men's bones. Aye, those plague-touched men did not even get a pyre for their last journey, but lay where they fell, food for birds and crabs."

They travelled on a short way, clambering over dunes, forcing their way through tangled bushes stiff with salt. Suddenly Hwalchmai gave a shout. Rising in his saddle, he peered into the distance, eyes shaded by his hand. "I can see a structure built upon the beach. Birds gather over it, like those that hover over biers where the dead are laid that their spirits may be set free."

"I fear we may be too late," said Pelahan grimly. "Let us ride with haste."

The companions cantered down the beach, splashing through the tidal pools, and soon reached a circular structure wrought of stout timbers like Woodenheart, where the rites of the newly dead were spoken. However, there the similarity ended–unlike Woodenheart, its carefully shaped posts were crammed closely together, forming a tight barricade against both the inward-creeping tides and the intrusion of the outside world. The wood it was carved from was dark, smoothed by the abrading salt and spray, and it held a sombre, almost menacing air. A small v-shaped entrance was the only passage into the interior, the gap so small it was impossible to get a clear view of what lay inside.

The companions dismounted and Pelahan fell to his knees in the sand as if overcome, holding his head and rocking back and forth, gibbering in the strange eastern dialect which held words unknown in the rest of Prydn due to migration from the Lowlands and the far North.

Ardhu approached the timber circle with caution. Bowing before it, he cast down some bluestone chips he had brought from Khor Ghor as an offering to its guardians, whoever they were. Then he squeezed himself through the v-shaped entrance; no mean feat, despite that he was still a slender and wiry-built man.

Inside Ardhu beheld an unsettling sight. A giant tree trunk stood upended, its head buried deep in the sands, burrowing down toward the Underworld. Twisted roots snaked toward the hazy sun, and the marks of axes could be seen preserved upon them where the tree had been hacked from the ground. Upended cinerary urns circled it and clustered around the walls of the enclosure.

On this makeshift altar lay the body of a man, spread-eagled, staring open-eyed at the heavens. He was old but still tall and muscled, with white hair and beard that streamed down the protruding roots of the stump. Fine clothes he wore, a tunic of woven nettle-fibres, a belt held in place with polished bone hooks and a necklace of hundreds of perforated shells that clattered in the sea-breeze. His legs were bare, spread apart. In his right thigh was a great gash, open like a mouth, its lips stained black with putrefaction.

Ardhu went to his side and held his golden armlet in front of the open mouth. The metal fogged; the man still lived.

"Per-Adur!" he shouted. "Come at once. The Maimed King is in here... we must get him out and tend to him. There may not be much time!"

Per-Adur climbed through the narrow gap, puffing and panting as he did so, and rushed to his lord's side. Disgust darkened his face as he smelt the odour of rancid flesh. "I will do what I can," he said, "but this is not a good place, in this house of death. Do you not mark what this circle, lord? The Maimed King has come here to give himself to his gods."

"Well, pray they will not take him yet," said Ardhu, "at least not until I know what ails this land and how it may affect the rest of Prydn."

Between them the two men lifted the supine body of the King. He was heavier than he looked, and his head flopped forward as if he were indeed dead. Carefully they squeezed him through the gap in the timber posts and laid him out on the sandy ground. Hwalchmai, Bohrs and Gal'havad stared, dumb-founded.

Pelahan rose from the ground, wiping his haggard, deathly face, and beckoned to Ardhu's men to follow him. "This way, with the King. We will take him to the old village where the people of the East once lived in joy. Anfortas's hall still stands, though ruinous."

Crossing the salt-marsh with the Maimed King lying over the neck of Per-Adur's horse, the company reached dryer land and a deep stand of tall pines. Inside, amidst the green of the trees, was a shallow ditch with a dilapidated wattle fence spanning it. Passing this ramshackle palisade, the companions entered the remnants of a village. Huts lay tumbled in the pine needles, roofs ripped away by the winds, amidst a sea of animal bones, not from any merry feast but from beasts that seem to have died where they stood and then were left to decay.

The central hut, large and thick-walled, still retained its wattle roof, and it was here Ardhu's men carried An-fortas the Maimed King. They placed him on a bier made of their fur cloaks and saddle blankets and Per-Adur knelt to minister to him, while the others stoked up a fire to warm the dreary place.

"It is bad," said the healer, as he prodded inside An-fortas's wound with a pair of fine bone tweezers. "I have never seen worse. I am surprised he has survived this long. There is only one chance… and that is if I can burn the wound with fire and purify it. However, to do such a thing to one so ill might be worse than letting him go to peaceful rest amongst the Ancestors."

"Peaceful rest?" Pelahan's voice was hoarse. "Feel how he burns already!" He placed his mottled hand on the sick man's brow. "Surely your craft could bring him no more pain that what he suffers now."

"You were told," said Bohrs, a bit gruffly, "that we are warriors, not magic men. Maybe you should have asked the Merlin to come here instead."

"If he dies," said Pelahan, "it is the beginning of the end of all Kings of this Age of Men. For you, too, Ardhu Pendraec." He rocked back onto his heels, suddenly staring at his ruined hands as if they were alien to him. "I have not told you the whole story, men of the West," he murmured breathlessly. "I am not just the servant and messenger of An-fortas. I am his son. The people who pass this accursed place on the long trade-roads into the West, call me the Fisher King, for that is all I can do now, with illness consuming my flesh… fish these coasts to provide some small sustenance for me and my failing sire. Once we were masters over these lands and all in them… this settlement was called Kar-Bonek, and was a mighty centre of trade, where chiefs from the Middle and Low-lands exchanged metals and riches with us… but now my father lies fallen, with a wound that will not heal, and I… am the lord of naught but fish! I should have listened to the shamans and done what needed to be done when his illness unmanned him, but I would not move my hand and take up the flint knife. I loved him too much, and that was my weakness… and so the Spirits struck me down as well. Then fatal illness ravaged our tribe, and pestilence was followed by the Ghort, the hunger, the famine. The Spirits are angry, and the Land withers and is not reborn in spring."

Gal'havad approached An-fortas's bier and gazed into the face of the mortally sick man. Grey and soft it looked, as if already mouldering. "The look of the Otherworld is about him," he said softly. "His spirit seeks to leave the flesh that trammels it."

"I fear you are right," Per-Adur murmured. "But let us get water into him; he probably has not had drink or nourishment for many days."

"Here… you may use my holy cup." Gal'havad took out the twilight-hued stone cup that came from the Sacred Pool and proffered it. "This is the cup bestowed upon me by the Lady Mhor-gan. She is a great magic-woman, a priestess, and the water it came from is blessed above all others, the birth-pool of Abona. Maybe its qualities can revive the Maimed King."

Per-Adur's expression was dubious but he bowed his head in agreement… after all, what harm could it do? Taking the small stone cup from the youth, he filled it with water from his pig's bladder flask and handed it back to Gal'havad. "The cup is yours to use, my Prince."

Gal'havad leaned over the Maimed King, thinking how mighty he must have been in his youth, a golden warrior who could cast spear and shoot bow and fight enemies with his axe. Now he was just a broken shell, his kingship robbed by the wound in his leg. Quietly he mouthed a prayer to Nud Cloudmaker, who, besides being lord of the Milky Way and Snarer of Souls, was a healer-god with a pack of red-eared dogs that licked the wounds of the afflicted until their poisons dissolved. Gal'havad wished such magic dogs would appear now; though even hounds of the Underworld might be hard pressed to heal such an evil wound as that in the thigh of An-fortas.

The water from the little cup trickled onto the parched lips of the King. Gal'havad gently pulled the cracked lower lip down to allow more of the fluid to get into the injured man's mouth. An-fortas made an unexpected gasping noise and began to writhe on the furs, fighting his fever, perhaps fighting his imminent death.

His eyelids flickered, and suddenly he gazed up straight into the face of Gal'havad. "Who is this I see?" he croaked, voice rasping out of his parched throat. "Are you one of the Everliving Ones, come to guide me across the Great Plain to Moy Mell beyond? Are you, with your bright hair like flame, the Peaked Red One?" He spoke an ancient eastern name for Bhel in his Year-End aspect, when he carried his burning light down into the depths of Winter, leading a spiral-trail of spirits behind him.

Gal'havad touched his red hair, pushing it back from his face so that An-fortas could see him clearly. "No, lord. I am just a mortal man. I am Gal'havad of Khor Ghor, son of Ardhu Pendraec the Stone Lord of Prydn, and I am here, with my father and the best of his men, to aid you and your son, the Fisher King."

"Gal'havad." The old man grasped his sleeve with shaking fingers. "Hawk of Summer… a saviour come from the Summerlands, despite your protests that you are just a man… I can see purity and goodness in you, with my failing eyes; maybe you of all men could bear the cup of gold that can restore the world, the cup that was taken away."

"What cup is this, Lord An-fortas?" asked Ardhu uneasily, remembering his dreams, remembering the muttered words of Merlin as he fell deep in trance in Khor Ghor.

An-fortas paused, chest heaving as he struggled to take a normal breath.

"In better times I had a golden mug wrought for me from the finest gold in Ibherna. Many Moons their smiths laboured to make it true and fair—a rimmed beaker, with a handle fastened to it by gold rivets. It was not a cup for a chieftain to hold in his hand to show off to his underlings—it was a sacred holy thing, whereby men could commune with the gods by drinking mead flavoured with henbane, which would open the door of the Un-world to them. It was for communion with the sky, with Bhel himself, and also for libation to the Earth, to the Lady whose womb we all return to. It could never be set down, for its bottom was fashioned in a curve."

"What happened to it?" asked Ardhu. "Is it still here?"

An-fortas shook his head weakly. "When I first was wounded I tried to do magic on myself, even bathing the gash with water mixed with special potions in the cup itself. Nothing worked, and one day in anger, I hurled the cup across my hut and dented both handle and base. I know not how tales of my rash anger spread beyond the East, but a Moon-turn later nine maidens, a sacred number, came riding hence on ponies, beautiful girls… no, priestesses, from the isle of Ibherna. They looked on me with pity but also anger, when they took the cup and saw its damage. It was the metalworkers of that green isle who had wrought it, at my behest, and they told me it had been bathed in the sacred basin that was the Cauldron of Rebirth of their chief-god, Dag. Now, they told me, it must go back to be repaired and re-consecrated… and that with my unhealed wound I was no longer a king and no longer worthy to hold it." Tears of despair leaked from the corners of his dimming eyes. "I fear they were right. Once they had left, my kingdom was laid waste utterly, the plagues coming and the sand rising in great storms to cover all, and I have become the ruined creature that you see."

Bohrs was scratching his beard. "This holy cup…" he said. "If we were to fetch it back for you, fixed and made holy again, could that help? Is that what you think?"

An-fortas sighed. "I do not now think there is any help for me in this world. But there is more to this world than me."

He glanced at Ardhu. "You have been a good lord of men," he said. "All know the name of Ardhu Pendraec. But goodness is not enough. Dark times are coming to us all. The Wasteland is like a growth; it is a blight on Prydn, but beyond that it is also a death of hope… and that in turn makes man's mind a Wasteland as surely as a field that gives forth no corn."

"I do not understand," said Ardhu. "I am not a shaman like the Merlin. What I know is what is bought by sword or by trade."

"Know this…" said An-fortas, "the King is the Land, the Land is the King. When the land is empty of seed it must be filled anew in order for living things to grow—the corn, the barley, and the little apples on the trees. If the old King cannot plant the seed and make it come to fruition, he must feed the soil with the very essence of his life."

A silence fell over the men in the chieftain's hut. "He is raving," murmured Hwalchmai, shaking his head. "His long illness has addled his mind."

"Find the cup." An-fortas's voice sank to a whisper. "Maybe it is the one thing that will save Prydn from the Wasteland. Maybe the glory of the Quest will save a king from the perils of encroaching age..." He took another heaving breath, his lungs rattling. "Do not try to heal me further. I must fight my fate no more. Carry me back to the Holy Circle on the strand and let me go to my Gods with dignity. Would that I had heard them calling me home years ago when first I was wounded, and heeded that call."

"No..." Pelahan the Fisher King's voice was a low groan of misery. "Father... do not ask this... not yet. I have brought them hence to save you..."

"It is his wish," said Ardhu darkly. "And if he speaks truth, then it should have been done long ago. But by the Eye Goddess, I wish the Merlin or some other shaman was here to oversee this act."

The warriors of Ardhu carried the Maimed King back down towards the sea. Behind them the pines rustled, their needles smelling fresh and alive. All around the salt marshes gleamed under the light of a huge Moon that cast a light-trail across the swell of the sea. The Moon's face was tinted oddly red, darker than a harvest moon. Their passing feet crunched on pebbles and then brushed through shifting sands.

Soon they saw the funereal timber circle, the Milky Way of Nud Cloudmaker a misty, boiling streak overhead—his enchanted cloak in which he snared the spirits of men to pass on to his son, Hwynn the White, lord of the Underworld, for judgement before they were sent West.

Ardhu and Hwalchmai gently manoeuvred An-fortas through the entrance to the shrine and laid him back on the natural platform formed by the upside-down tree. Its huge coiled roots thrust up into the night, embracing the limp and failing body of the old man. He stared up at the sky, eyes losing their focus, glazing as they looked into otherness and eternity.

Ardhu's breath emerged a ragged fog before his lips and he loosed his dagger Carnwennan from its sheath. "If I must, I will do this thing as King of Prydn." He rubbed at his thigh, suddenly aching as it often did on chill nights such as this—his thigh, wounded long ago by the tusks of the Boar T'orc, the ravager of Prydn sent to plague him by his sister Morigau. But he was healed, well healed... and not so old or so frail... not yet...

Unexpectedly, Gal'havad came up beside him; his pale face awash with a faint sheen of sweat, his forest-green eyes burning with strange passion. "Father, I will do it, if that would please you more."

Ardhu shook his head violently. "You are too young for such dealings, which are the territory of priest and shaman! I must stand in, as called for, for I am King."

"I will be King after you," argued Gal'havad, "and I am touched by the spirits—the Merlin himself said so and you have noted it yourself. A few days ago I sent a traitor to his death and the torments that will await him in the Un-world; now, showing great mercy, I will send this good chief to the Plain of Honey, as he wishes and as the Great Ones wish."

Ardhu stared at his son—the shining face, the dark red hair like a burnished shield in the dimness, the white cowl of Nud's starry mantle above his slender shoulders. "Do as you will, my son. You are accounted a Man of the Tribe, and you have your own special wisdom... more, in some things than I, or so it would seem."

Gal'havad drew Kos'garak from his belt. Starlight glinted on the three golden rivets holding the hilt in place. Three times he circled the failing Maimed King, the fallen giant lying on the upturned stump in the centre of the funerary wooden ring. Beyond the shrine the waves went thump, thump, thump, beating watery fists against the shore, a solemn drumbeat in the night.

Then he bent over the Maimed King and solemnly cut one wrist with his knife. A thread of redness slid from the gaping cut and trickled into the damp soil at the foot of the trunk. He then proceeded to the other arm and opened the second vein, allowing more blood to feed the earth, the hungry earth that was withering and dying without a whole and hale king to reign over it. The Maimed King did not move, seeming not to feel the cuts, the beginning of his life slipping away.

Gal'havad moved the dagger upwards, letting it rest for a moment beneath the white bearded chin. He hesitated a moment, face taut with the enormity of what he had chosen to do, and then with a sharp and brutal motion, he drew it across the Maimed King's throat, instantly severing the great vein of life. The air went red with spray, and the old man gave one great gasp as his spirit fled upward into the sky, vanishing into the star-spangled cloak of Nud.

Gal'havad sheathed his dagger and knelt down in the sandy soils, heaving with sobs, suddenly overcome by the enormity of the sacrifice. Ardhu went to his side and tried to raise him, but he felt heavy, limp, and the pain that sometimes needled Ardhu's leg shot through him, making him unable to lift him further.

Pelahan appeared at the entrance of the wooden ring; no tears for his father marred his ruined face, but his eyes were without light, black and hopeless. He was the one to wrench Gal'havad to his feet, gaze into his face and shake him lightly to bring him to himself. "Look at me, boy. You did what I could not... you did what had to be done, what should have been done long ago, and I thank you."

Gal'havad turned and brought out his small stone chalice, glittering faintly in the gloom. Gently he filled it with the blood of the fallen king, the holy blood that fed the Land. "By the power within this font of life, I swear I will find the golden cup of King An-fortas," he said quietly," though I may fare to the end of the world and die in the attempt."

"Make no vows of such a nature" Ardhu said sharply, eyes narrowing. "Do not forget who you are..."

But Gal'havad's green eyes were stubborn. He said nothing, but stood with the blood running over his fingers.

"We will bury him, now, in a place no one shall ever find him, giving him back to the earth that it might grow strong again with his sacrifice," said Pelahan. "Will you help me one more time in this, King of the West?"

Ardhu nodded, his face grey and weary. "This one more thing... yes. Then I must be away for Kham-El-Ard, to talk with Merlin and Mhor-gan and see what counsel they can give about the blight on Prydn and on this cup of gold that An-fortas spoke of."

Pelahan stood aside and Per-Adur and Hwalchmai climbed into the ring, making gestures against evil when they saw the dead king lying on the tree stump, the blank surfaces of his eyes reflecting the stars and his blood, now a dark viscous stream, puddling on the ground beneath him.

"It is time to bury my father," said Pelahan. "He will not lie here, though our Ancestors and elders did. His is a different death, his flesh not given to the birds and beings of the air, but to the earth and the marsh, the dark wet places that breed new life."

Ardhu's men lifted the body of An-fortas for the last time and carried it forth on its final journey. His corpse was heavy, stone-like, on their shoulders. They bore him far inland, into a land of marshy pools where terns nested and green tongues of heatless flame flittered over the bog, the malevolent souls of Ancestral ghosts.

A jetty of woven withies thrust out into the marsh at its deepest point, the remnants of an old track like that found crossing the fens of Afallan in the West. A rotted stump of an old idol sat at the end of the jetty, its head split so that one could not tell if it was meant to be a male or female deity... and the body gave no indication, for it was a hermaphrodite, with pendulous wooden breasts and a detachable phallus.

Pelahan walked slowly to the end of the withy pier and beckoned the others forward. He took the body of the Maimed King from them and shut his eyes with gentle fingers. Removing his own deerskin cloak he wrapped An-fortas in it, hiding face and hands and feet, and pinned it fast with his own crutch-headed cloak-pin. He murmured words none could hear, nor wanted to for they were words of new king to the old, of a contrite son to a father had he failed. He then raised the body to a kneeling position on the edge of the jetty and let it fall.

With a thick, slurping splash it hit the murky water. Nesting birds whirred up, affrighted, squawking their anger and terror into the gloom. The wrapped bundle bobbed for a moment on the swell, then spiralled down into Otherness, bubbles bursting as it passed into forever.

Overhead the first glow of dawn touched the sky, red as the blood of An-fortas's final wound.

Red as the blood that still marred Gal'havad's garments and skin, patterning his face like morbid tattooing.

Ardhu glanced wearily toward the morning star, Light-of-Day, just rising in the Eastern sky, a pure white flame. It was the only pure thing he had seen for days. All else seemed rotten, putrescent.

"Come," he said, his voice hoarse, ragged. "Let us collect our horses and set out upon the long road home. And may we never return here to the place, unless its fate is changed and its eternal winter turns to spring."

CHAPTER NINE
THE RITUAL SHAFT

Mist swirled around the Stones of Khor Ghor, exhaled from the ground by spirits of the ancient dead. Above, a reddish, mottled moon was shining amidst a circle of feeble stars. Slowly the Merlin hobbled toward the great ancestral monument, his weary feet dragging as he limped up the Avenue. He leaned heavily on his staff, stopping every now and then and scowling. How he hated the growing frailty of his body! His acolytes had tended him well in Deroweth but they told him he needed to rest, that in his last trance, when he had fallen amid the Stones, a malicious spirit had elf-shot him in the temple, causing his left side to freeze. Whether he would ever recover completely was unknown; many men died from such venomous shot, and those that survived were often left blighted, their faces and limbs forever frozen, words slurring in their throats.

But he was not like other men. He was the Merlin, shaman and High Priest of Khor Ghor! He would not lie abed and be spoon-fed slop by women! He would resume his position until the gods of the Everlasting Sky saw fit to smite him down forever. No, he could not die yet and go to the long house of his Ancestors, not while he felt there was wrong afoot in the lands of his people. Not when he sensed the realm he had struggled to build, with Ardhu as his chosen instrument of power, was shaking, shuddering at its foundation. Destruction and desolation dwelt in the East, where Ardhu was now, but day by day more reports came from West and South and North... crops failures, feuds over land, disease that caused abandonment of settlements. Some messengers came seeking the advice of the Merlin or the war-lords of Ardhu's court, but more often these days the displaced, the starving came to Kham-El-Ard, walking on blistered bare feet, clad in naught but the rude skins of beasts as if they were men from a thousand years ago or more. Their sunken cheeks were as sharp as those of skulls, and hollow eyes looked accusingly at the frail, bent figure of the Merlin, as if saying, "You promised more. We had more. But it could not last... the dream has died."

"The dream will *not* die!" Merlin cried out, to himself, to the ghosts and otherworldly beings that floated in the field between the Dance-of-Ancestors and the great Spirit-Path that divided the Lands of the Living from the Domain of the Dead.

He was nearly at the Stone of Summer, circled by its ring-ditch; beyond its vast bulk, the henge bank was a chalky blur in the moonlight. The Three Watchers, Guardians of the Door, rose like twisted fingers to beckon him into the heart of the Great Sanctuary, cave of the Sun, Womb of Time, and entrance to the worlds of the Unseen.

Out of the corner of his eye he saw something move, flitting amid the Stones. Breath hissing between his teeth, he drew the honed flint dagger he always carried at his waist. And then laughed... for between the Stones hopped a large grey-brown hare, one of the sacred beasts of She-Who-Guards, whose faceless plaque towered on the Western Trilithon. It loped away into the coiling mists, vanishing over the hump of the bank.

He followed the animal's passage with his eyes and suddenly his laughter curdled in his throat. He caught movement again near the northernmost of the Four Stations. This time, it was no animal.

He was certain it was not a guard sent from Deroweth; he had seen the warrior-priests traversing the Great Plain as he had crossed from the Spirit-Path to the Sacred Avenue. It also looked too slight to be a grown male... maybe a boy... or a woman.

His eyes narrowed and his thin fingers gripped his dagger hilt. There was one woman he hated—and feared—above all, the woman who was Ardhu's sister, mother of the bastard Mordraed. She of all women would not fear to come here by night, treating with her dark spirits of chaos and death, her hands skimming through spoil on the bank, seeking bone fragments and tiny ear-bones for her spells and brews. How he wished he could have found a way to dispose of her, without starting a blood-war with her kin. He had whispered fell words to the wind, cast evil curses in the direction of her hovel in the river valley, but like old roots grown tough she did not sicken and die but became harder, tougher. True, her behaviour had been exemplary since Ardhu took in her sons, but Merlin knew she was not the kind to bury her hatreds or give up fighting for what she believed was rightfully hers...

He stalked toward the short, squat station stone, his dagger glinting in the pallid light, ready. He had little strength, but by the gods, he would do his best to stop the she-bitch if indeed it was her.

The figure turned and a hood was thrown back. For a moment, seeing wild black hair and dark eyes, Merlin thought it was indeed Morigau, but he quickly recognised the gentler cast of the features of Mhor-gan, Ardhu's younger sister, one of the Ladies of the Lake.

"By Great Bhel, Mhor-gan, I nearly struck you with my sacred dagger," he said harshly. "I thought you were Morigau."

Her black brows rose. "And what made you think of my wayward sister?"

"Because I know too well that she is not sitting in her hut weaving and making pots like normal women! I cannot read her mind, but I know her thoughts are dark. She did not come to Kham-El-Ard just for the protection of her sons, for whom she cares little."

"She cares for one," said Mhor-gan carefully.

Merlin sighed. "Yes, Mordraed... the child of Ardhu's folly. 'Man of Judgement' is what his name means... I can only guess why Morigau named him so."

"They say he is very skilled at arms," said Mhor-gan, "and that, if the

88

other men concur, Ardhu will allow him into his warband by the Winter Solstice, if not before. He is also... friends... with Gal'havad."

Merlin's face twisted, his eyes pained. "Yes, I have seen how Mordraed has availed himself of young Amhar's good nature. What can I say to make them part? What, even as high priest, can I do? Ardhu once spoke of killing all brats born in the month of Bhel-fires when he knew Morigau was carrying his seed, but it was I who cautioned him against such a rash act. Now I do not know if I was wrong."

"The boy has done no evil... yet," said Mhor-gan. "And may not; it would be unfair to judge him for the shadows that lay upon his birth."

"As you say... but I am still troubled. And I deem you are too, for why else would you wander here alone after Moonrise?"

Mhor-gan pulled her cloak tightly about her and stared at the sky. Her breath was a fog around her pale lips. "Yes, you are correct, Merlin. I *am* troubled. I have hardly slept in weeks; my dreams are evil and unsettling. So I came to pray for guidance at the Stones... and now that you are here, I shall also seek counsel with wise Merlin. I knew in my heart you would be at Khor Ghor tonight... and that you have felt my unease too."

She looked at him, her countenance suddenly grown very white. "Merlin... my bees have gone."

He looked quizzically at her, not understanding. "Gone?"

"Fled away. Flown in a great cloud to the south. I do not know why. And the plants I grow with Nin-Aeifa, she of Great Esteem, they have not sprouted, or if they have, they turn to slime when we harvest them. The Great Lady herself has dreamed and spoken in her dream-state; she told of a far-off mountain that breathes flame straight from a pit where malignant fire-spirits dwell... and with the coming of the flame and smoke there will be a year of no summer, a year when night and day are much the same. A time when Bhel will weaken when he should wax strong."

Merlin tried to laugh. The sound fell dead amidst the pillars of Khor Ghor. "Bad years come... it has happened before in my long life. They pass. As for this dream of Nin-Aiefa's... surely it is but an unsettling dream, or betokens other than it seems."

Mhor-gan glanced at the sky; ragged clouds were covering the Moon, wrapping the stars, making them wink out, one by one. "The worst has not come yet, Merlin. But it is coming, I am sure of it. Have you not noticed? On some nights Bhel's visage is bloody... as it is in Winter. The Sky looks streaked by blood. Even the Moon's face is sometimes tinged with red. It is the beginning... of what could be the end of time."

Merlin hunched over, suddenly looking as old as the Stones themselves, a creature old as the time that Mhor-gan thought might end. "We must fight against this threat if we can."

"But can we?" said Mhor-gan. "It is not a battle for blades and arrows... though they may have their part." She tossed back her head, scenting the air.

89

"I can almost smell ash upon the wind, the scent of crops rotting in the fields. The Land is losing its power, Merlin... can you not feel it in the earth below, the air above?"

Merlin's voice emerged a harsh croak; he despised himself for the feebleness of it. "I can feel it, Lady Mhor-gan. And if it is my counsel you seek, I can tell you nothing... only that I am afraid. There... I have said it. The great Merlin, high priest of Khor Ghor, is full of fear."

"And where is Ardhu, my brother, in this time of peril..." Mhor-gan said softly. "The King who is the Land itself, bound body and blood to earth and stone, who lies with the White Phantom, daughter of Intoxicator?"

"You know where he is, lady. He seeks the Maimed King in the East, to put right what has gone wrong in that domain."

"Do you think he will succeed?"

Merlin stared at the ground; he spat the next word out like venom. It hung between them on the cold night air. "No."

Mhor-gan moved forward, touching the old man's shoulder. "Merlin, we must speak more of this matter... in the presence of Nin-Aeifa. Come with me to our House of the Spirits in the land of the Lakes. It is not good for you to be out here in these cold mists so long; you are not well... I can see the frailty in you."

Merlin pursed his lips, shaking his head. He tried to avoid Nin-Aeifa, the only woman he had ever loved, long ago beneath the apple-blossoms of the Isle of Afallan where the fey King Afalak harvested the sacred fruit for his brother, Hwynn the White Fire, to succour the dead passing West into immortality. They had come together like the clash of swords, the snarl of summer lightning, but had parted at destiny's whim, their individual paths mapped out by the powers that moved the earth and sky. He feared her now, old and strange, with her one blind eye that gazed into Otherness... She was at the Beginning of him, and perhaps she too would have a part in his Ending...

Mhor-gan took Merlin's arm like a solicitous daughter. He could smell the scent of her—Abona's water and wildflowers. "Come," she said, her voice kindly, warm.

He peered into her face, so like her malevolent sister's, yet like Ardhu's too. Dark and light, foul and fair. Shadows coiled in her eyes; he could not read her thoughts there.

A shiver of fear rippled through him; in the Stones, the black-plumaged birds that nested under the lintels let out a harsh cawing and flapped up into the heavens, disturbed by something unseen, perhaps a passing fox that ran between the uprights.

What would be, would be.

Huddling into his cloak, he let himself be led like a sacrificial beast on the long path over the barrow-downs to the House of the Ladies of the Lake.

*****

90

The house within the Lake was lit with tallow cups when Merlin and Mhor-gan arrived. Nin-Aeifa sat cross-legged on a cowskin, eyes closed, deep in meditation, the yellowish light flickering over the sharp planes of her face. Her hair had turned stone-grey over the years, but she had caked it with chalk paste and twisted it into braids that had solidified and fanned out from her head like pale, frozen snakes. A necklace made of faience baubles and hundreds of tiny pink shells from the distant shore swung around her neck, and from her belt, cinched tight at the waist with a clasp of polished antler, dangled perforated lumps of shale, amber and quartz, their surfaces pecked with designs.

"Merlin... it has been long since we have met," she murmured, without even opening her eyes. Her voice was deep, rich as wood smoke... unchanged from what he remembered from his youth.

"Nin-Aeifa..." he breathed her name, could say no more. He felt suddenly dizzy and weak. The herbs she burned in a hearth behind her set up a stink that made his eyes water and his head spin.

Mhor-gan guided him to a small wooden stool near her mistress and helped him to sit comfortably, then brought out a red, handled beaker filled with rich, thick mead. "The last for a while, I fear," she said sorrowfully. "Now that my bees have gone."

Merlin took a draught of the mead; the potent liquor steadied him. Nin-Aeifa opened her eyes and fluidly rose to her feet; in silence, she glided towards him. He could have almost sworn her bare feet did not touch the clay floor.

"Merlin," she said. "You see the world of beyond even as I do."

"It has been my gift and my curse. As it is yours."

"You have seen then the darkness and the cold that is to come, the withering of the land?"

"Seen it? Lady Nin-Aeifa, already there are a trickle of people arriving at the gates of Kham-El-Ard, homeless and starving. I have done more than merely 'seen' it in a dream. It is here, though as yet the trickle has not become a flood."

"Then you will not be angered by what I have to say to you."

He spread out his thin, knotted hands on his skin-clad knees. "I will make no promises on that, Nin-Aeifa. Speak."

She took a deep breath, clutching her quartzes and ambers and stroking them like talismans. "The King is the Land and the Land is the King... Merlin, my brother, my lover—the reign of Ardhu Pendraec is nearly at an end. The hand that was strong begins to grow weak. The Sun that was bright is eclipsed by a dark Moon. The skies grow dim with ash and winter grows long. The White Queen who was the earth that mated with the son of the Sun turns her face away... her favours granted elsewhere. What will save the Land? I do not know if anything will. But, time out of mind such bleak events lead to one thing... the Great Sacrifice. The Greatest Sacrifice of all."

Merlin coughed, mead spewing from his damaged mouth and running into his long grey beard. His eyes were wild. "No! You speak madly, woman, seeress or not! Kham-El-Ard and Khor Ghor are still beacons to men, a hope for peace and for alliances. Ardhu may no longer be young, but he is hale... gods, *no*! He..." the words slurred between his wet and shaking lips, 'he is like a son to me, the son I was denied when I chose my calling. At first, yes, he was only a pawn, a boy born of a union I devised; I was great in ambition then. But as time passed by, he became more to me... no, do not speak to me of the Great Rite and of Ardhu! It will never happen by my hand."

"If you will not, then you must at least step aside and let the Wheel of Fate turn as it will, making no interference. Fate may well play its own hand before these days are over..." Nin-Aiefa's voice was a rasping whisper like the wind in fallen autumn leaves. A haunting sound. Merlin remembered suddenly their first meeting in Afallan, near the Holy Tor of Hwynn son of Nud, where she had held a rapier to his throat. Fair and perilous she had been, and though her beauty had now faded into Winter, she was still perilous... the Lady of the Lake and its dark secrets and woman-magic.

He struggled to his feet despite his weakened left side, ignoring the cries of Mhor-gan, who tried to comfort him, to pull him back down onto the stool. "I will listen no longer to this madness! And if I hear you plot against the lord of Kham-El-Ard, I will send the Stone-Lord's warband to burn this hovel to the ground!"

"You accuse me of speaking madness?" cried Nin-Aeifa. "You refuse to listen, although the signs are there for all with eyes to see! You threaten those whose serve the Immortal King Afalak, and Hwynn son of Nud? You have passed from wisdom, old man... the dictates of your heart have addled your brain!"

"I wish I had never laid eyes on you," he snarled, shaking with rage. "You hard, unnatural bitch. And, you, Mhor-gan of the Korrig-han, you wish me to tear the heart from your own brother... but maybe I should not be surprised... all the spawn of Y'gerna are the same except for Ardhu, who was tempered by my hand."

He stumbled toward the door, desperate to be away. Suddenly, his head lolled forward, and there was a sensation of something dropping away within his skull. Lights scintillated in the corners of his eyes. He had been drugged.

"No!" he howled, falling to his knees, thrashing the air around him with his arms. His staff fell with a clatter, the jawbone on the end snapping and rolling away across the floor.

Mhor-gan hurried to his side. "Merlin, you must heed our words. Do not fight us. We have no wish to harm you, who are a priest of high esteem, one of the greatest of your order."

"You have betrayed me, and betrayed Ardhu and Albu the White..." he gasped, striking out at her with a bunched fist that had no more clout than a falling leaf.

Nin-Aeifa glided over to him and stared down; her visage pinched, twisted with a bitter sorrow. "Mhor-gan, take him to the holy place as planned. All has been made ready for him."

Mhor-gan pulled Merlin to his feet, trying to be gentle. He fought her but she was the stronger, and he found himself being propelled out into the dawn. In the East the Eye of Bhel was just rising, a red ball over the edge of the Great Plain. Bloody light flooded the fields and the swells of the river Abona became a stream of gore.

Merlin was taken up a rise, past many a death-house grown with grass. Skylarks soared overhead and other birds darted and skimmed in the waving grasses; the souls of the dead taking flight on this morning of ill-omen.

Up ahead by a stand of trees he could see a shallow barrow, a cup-like depression that surrounded a hole that gaped like an ebony mouth in the verdant earth. A small wooden shrine shaped like a miniature trilithon marked the crater and protected whatever lay below from the worst excesses of the weather. The place exuded a certain menace, and Merlin's heart banged against his ribcage in sudden frenzy.

He should have known what this place might be, but in his old age he seldom came past the Down of Kings, leaving the land between the barrow-hills and the shores of Abona to the ministrations of the Ladies of the Lake and those from the Deepwood Valley who followed them. He wondered what had been happening here, out of sight and out of mind, and thought again of the feel of Nin-Aeifa's cold blade against his youthful throat.

Mhor-gan was pressing him on toward the mounded ring that circled the black pit, and he could see that her face was drawn and uneasy, as if she hated what she was about to do. "Mhor-gan…" he said, using no formalities of title, speaking to her as an equal and Ardhu's sister. "Think, woman, of what you do! Think of your brother… surely you do not wish to see him die!"

"All men must die, Merlin," she responded, her voice a mere whisper, and she dragged him on until they stood together on the edge of the shadowy crater, staring into the heart of the earth.

Merlin writhed, trying to free himself one more time. Gazing down the shaft, he could see that it descended deep into the bowels of Prydn, reaching toward the Underworld and, perhaps, the realms of the restless dead—those who were the shades of evil men, who sucked marrow from bones and were in constant need of supplication lest they cause havoc amongst the living. The tunnel was at least a hundred feet deep, cut straight into the chalk with picks of antler, and a hemp rope ladder dangled down the side and vanished into its depths. A charnel smell wafted up from the hidden depths, tainting the fresh morning air with the hint of old death.

"Merlin, you must go down," said Mhor-gan. "I beg you not to fight me. I have no wish to bring you harm."

"Are you to kill me too… make of me a sacrifice?" A sudden hopeful light gleamed in his tired old eyes. "Could you do this—and spare Ardhu?"

She looked him up and down in sorrow, the scrawny legs and arms, the mouth that now hung at a crooked angle from being elf-shot. "No, your blood would not suffice. Though you are wisest of the wise, you can not stand in for him, his tanist. Maybe once, many years ago, but not now."

She gave him a gentle push from behind and, hands shaking, he began to climb down the rope ladder. Turgid darkness embraced him and the chalk walls rising on either side sweated water and other noxious substances. After what seemed an eternity of dangling in the darkness, his feet touched a solid surface. He released the rope ladder and it was hastily snatched up by Mhorgan, out of reach. He found himself standing on a packed chalk floor beside a stout post the height of a man; he leaned upon it to steady himself then grimaced as he saw the brown, congealed mess that smeared the wood and the white animal bones strewn at its foot. On the ground beside the post were sleeping furs, baskets of food, jugs of water and mead.

The trap had been waiting for him for some time, it seemed, and he had fallen straight into it.

"I will come back each day to check that you are hale and to bring you food and drink." Hearing Mhor-gan's voice from above, he glanced up and saw her head silhouetted against a tiny circle of brightening sky. "I pray soon this time of evil will pass and a new day dawn, and then you will be freed again to live your last years with the honour you deserve."

He spat at her and hurled a curse, which she deflected with a movement of her hand. Then he crouched amidst the congealed flesh and bones and howled in bleak despair.

CHAPTER TEN
BETRAYAL OF LOVE

Mordraed lounged in the corner of the grounds of Kham-El-Ard, his back against the wattle wall and his legs stretched out before him. Battle-training was nearly over for the day and he was surrounded by a dozen other youths, laughing amongst themselves, showing off bruises they had obtained from mock-fights with the likes of the Lord An'kelet and the twin warriors Ba-lin and Bal-ahn. Agravaen was out on the training ground now, Ba-lin facing him as his opponent—he looked big, red and sweaty, like a trussed pig, though Mordraed uncharitably, his eyes narrowing as his half-brother shuffled and puffed around the marked-off ring, thudding clumsily from side to side on his graceless feet. Agravaen would have looked almost comical, a buffoon to jeer at, except for the obvious power in his bull-neck and muscled shoulders, and the determined expression in his eyes.

He wanted to be a warrior. He wanted to be firmly placed at the Stone Lord's side.

His desire was perfect for Mordraed's plans, for it would cloud Agravaen's already dim thoughts...

Smiling, Mordraed turned his attention to his fellows. His keen gaze drifted past those who were the sons of Ardhu's favourites and sought out those who were... different. A rag-tag of boys who had come from across the Plain in hopes of being one of the chosen men; youths who were clearly unsuitable and would never be picked by Ardhu for his warband—those quick to violence, who loved to kill or torture; those unable to take orders, always angry and restive, their own wants placed before others'; and those who were simple, easily swayed and easily impressed, not knowing their own minds yet... if they ever would. These youths had warmed to Mordraed over the past weeks, clustering around him like moths drawn to flame, impressed by his prowess with weapons, his slick tongue and dark wit, and the kinship he shared with the Stone Lord of Khor Ghor.

Little did they realise how Mordraed despised them, hating their fawning, their crudeness, their stupidity...

But they could be useful.

"How do you find the training?" he asked breezily of one dullard sporting a black eye and with teeth already bashed in during some earlier brawl.

The youth, Wyzelo, wiped his sweaty, flushed face on his arm and sidled over to Mordraed. "Good enough. But I'm tired of all this playing at being a warrior. Why can't we join the Stone Lord's band and fight our enemies for real, bashing in their skulls and winning glory?"

95

"Why indeed?" Mordraed shrugged gracefully. "Haven't you guessed, my friend?"

The thick-head glanced at Mordraed, big pale eyes stupidly bovine in the red platter of his face. "No..."

Mordraed flashed him another smile, full of false ruefulness. "Well, the sons of his first faithful are always going to take precedence over other contenders, are they not? They even rank above me, though I am the King's... nephew. As you know, I have not been inducted into the Stone-Lord's warband as yet. Who knows?—if it pleases my uncle I may never well be. The same goes for you."

"That is not fair!" Wyzelo cried. "I'm as good as any of them, if not better..."

Mordraed raised his hand. "Peace, friend. It would not do well to have the Lord An'kelet or Ba-lin and Bal-ahn overhear your words. You'd be cast out for certain. And I, for one, know your value, and would not see you sent away." He sighed, staring at the sky. "One day I may reclaim all the lands that should be mine. I would need a warband like Ardhu's then. If that should happen, would you be my man, Wyzelo? My main warrior, ready with axe and arrow to defend what is mine by right?"

"I would!" Wyzelo answered enthusiastically. "You seem like a wise and noble master to follow! You are young, whereas the Stone Lord grows o..." He shut his mouth with a resounding snap and reddened, realising he had spoken rashly, and in front of the King's own kinsman.

Mordraed put a hand on his shoulder. "Don't worry, Wyzelo," he said smoothly, "I promise your words shall remain a secret. A slip of the tongue, that is all... Say, since you seem so wise and knowledgeable yourself, maybe you could assist me... Who else in Kham-El-Ard is like you, neglected despite your worth? Who else might seek a place within a fighting band?"

Eager to draw the attention away from the folly of his loose tongue, Wyzelo promptly gestured to several other youths standing on the sidelines while Agravaen blundered around the training ground, swinging his axe at the fleet-footed Ba-lin. "Over there... my companion from the same village, Mor Bethuinn... Kehul, Fial and Belenion. You can see they are well grown and full of courage, but the masters here keep saying we are not ready to join the warband."

"A shame... they look like they have the makings of doughty warriors. Meet with me on the morrow, Wyzelo. In the fields by the Old Henge, where it is more private. Bring your friends. We will talk more then."

"I will, great Mordraed of the Stone Lord's clan," said Wyzelo with enthusiasm, and he hurried away toward his fellows.

Mordraed smirked to himself, watching the rough country youth disappear amid the gaggle of boys. It couldn't have been easier. He had always had a nose for sniffing out dissatisfaction, perhaps because he often felt so dissatisfied himself.

Turning from Wyzelo and the other youths, he set his attention back towards his brother Agravaen. He was hand to hand with Ba-lin now, daggers locked, striving for supremacy. Agravaen's lumpen face was bordering on purple, his eyes slitted and watering, his lips curled back over his strong white teeth. Suddenly Ba-lin's knee shot out, catching him in the groin. Agravaen fell like a stone, clutching his crotch. His mouth worked soundlessly for a moment in his agony, and then he got his breath back and loosed the most awful roar of pain and rage... while the youths packing the training yard fell about howling with mirth.

Ba-lin nudged the curled-up boy with his knee. "In a battle you play to win, young Agravaen. Was my move fair? No. But remember... your opponents wish to keep their lives, so they will do anything to shorten yours..."

"Get up." Mordraed walked over to his brother and dragged him to his feet. "You are making yourself a laughing stock... again."

Agravaen's face was puce, twisted in pain. "It's his fault! He tricked me when I came close to bettering him... A few more blows and I could have killed him!"

"You are training; you are not meant to kill anyone. Especially one of the Stone Lord's prime warriors." Mordraed's tone was derisive. "But come, I must talk to you where the others are not listening."

They walked around the side of the hall of Kham-El-Ard and sat in its shadow, out of the way of dogs and carts and men herding beasts, and women coming up from Mother Abona with pots upon their heads. "I have seen our mother," said Mordraed, noncommittally, his tone level.

Agravaen's eyes narrowed. "Mordraed, let me speak plainly here... I do not care. In fact I hope never to see the bitch again. You... you... she loves but the rest of us were as shite on her shoe, to be wiped off and thrown away as far as possible. She... she is a liar, brother. She told us tales of the wickedness of Ardhu, but look... he has taken us in, housed and fed us, almost as if we were his own sons!"

One of us is... The corner of Mordraed's mouth quirked up; a bitter smile, a cold smile that matched his deep-sea eyes.

"So your loyalty is to Ardhu now," said Mordraed, his voice low. "You want nothing more than to serve him."

"Aye," breathed Agravaen, "that is why I try so hard to become a great warrior. I want nothing more than to ride beside him in his warband. But it seems all I do goes amiss..." He scowled and picking up a lump of dried dung from the ground, hurled it angrily across the fort. It bounced off a wooden post on the ramparts and a dog ran out and began to worry it. "I am like that dog, Mordraed. I only get the shite."

"It doesn't have to be so." Mordraed's voice descended to a bare whisper. "There is much afoot in Kham-El-Ard that our uncle had no idea about. Things that could bring his kingdom crashing down..."

Agravaen made a gasping noise. "Treachery?"

Mordraed turned his head, catching the younger boy's gaze in a long, level, intent stare. "Of the worst kind, Agravaen. The Lord An'kelet... and the White Woman... they are more to each other than they should be. They are lovers, I know it."

Agravaen shook his head. "You must be wrong. An'kelet is his friend, close as a brother! He honours the Lady Fynavir, worships her as a goddess. He would not do such a vile thing."

"Because he is the perfect warrior?" Mordraed sneered. "Grow up, little brother. No man is that perfect! Did you really think he has dwelt all these years without a woman?"

Agravaen leapt to his feet, fists clenched. "If what you say is true, why have you not spoken to Ardhu?"

Mordraed spat on the ground. "What... and end up with my head on a pole outside the gates? You know how it is, brother. He tolerates me, but he trusts me less than you and our brothers because I am older and he thinks I am under Morigau's sway. An'kelet and I have no love for each other and he is a favourite; I would never be believed. However..." He sprang up, leaning in toward the stockier youth. "This might be an ideal opportunity for you. If *you* were the one to reveal the trysts of An'kelet and Fynavir, then surely our uncle would mark your loyalty and reward you by allowing you into his warband."

Agravaen scratched his chin, covered with scraggy, downy black traces of a beard. "Maybe you are right... maybe that would work. But... I have never seen the Queen with An'kelet. How would I manage to catch them? You do understand that I must see their treachery myself and not rely on rumour."

Mordraed draped his arm about his brother's broad, muscular shoulders. "I will help you. My eyes and ears are keener than yours. It is my joy to help you improve your lot; after all, we are kin." His smile was wide, friendly but his eyes diamond-hard.

Agravaen smiled back, the smile as naïve and trusting as a child's.

*****

The messenger came from the East, from where he had been keeping watch over the borders of Ardhu's lands. Smeared with dust and sweat from the long ride, he entered the Hall of Kham-El-Ard and stood before the seat of the Queen. "I bring news, blessed Lady."

Fynavir sat before him, palely shimmering like some spectre, her hands outspread on her lap, fingers splayed like icicles on the woad-stained blue fabric of her dress. Her face looked even whiter than usual; she bit her lip in consternation. "Speak!" she nodded. "Keep nothing back. If you bring ill news of my husband or my son, say it now and do not hide it with gentling words."

The messenger cleared his throat. "The King of the Wasteland has passed into the Land of his Ancestors, despite the best efforts of Ardhu Pendraec and Lord Per-Adur. Even now, the Lord of the West travels home with the Prince Gal'havad at his side. Within three downings of the Sun, he will be back at Kham-El-Ard."

Fynavir released a shuddering sigh. "My son... he is unhurt, praise Bhel. My thanks for your tidings, messenger. Go to the fire-pits and you will be fed and given drink and money of copper rings. I must myself move in haste to prepare for Lord Ardhu and Gal'havad's homecoming."

She left the hall, hurrying out amongst the round huts that belonged to the warriors. The wind lifted her hair, tearing it free of its long plait, and men stared, but she ignored them. Finding the largest hut, surrounded by a wooden palisade and a ditch, she passed the threshold and went inside.

Inside An'kelet, Prince of Ar-morah, lay abed under a pile of skins, still sleeping, for the hour was early. Hearing the noise of an intruder, he sat up at once and reached for his blade, Arondyt. When he saw Fynavir silhouetted in the doorway, he cast the blade down and grinned. He threw off the skins and stepped forth naked, his tall frame still lean and muscled and golden despite his age. He pulled her into the circle of his arms and she leaned heavily against him, pulling his head down to hers, her mouth seeking his with almost desperate urgency.

"Fynavir, why do you come here like this?" Suddenly he drew away from her and reached for his tunic and trews. "It is not safe. The Sun is too high in the sky, all must have seen you. We must not become careless, even though Ardhu is not here. Other eyes than his may be watching. Not all are friends to us and men's tongues often wag when they are idle."

"I have reason." She reached for him again, arms locking around his neck, her white hair falling like a shower of snow over his chest and arms. "A messenger came this morning. Ardhu is on his way back from the Wasteland. In three days he will be home." A sob tore from her throat. "I have missed Gal'havad, but I cannot lie... in the depths of my being I almost hoped this time would never end. For the first time in all these long years, we could be together as we wished, every day... and almost..." her lips trembled, "every night."

He took her by the shoulders, shaking her lightly, gently. "Fynavir, remember what we do is a grave wrong! Ardhu would have every right to kill us both if ever he found out."

She pressed herself against him, shivering. "Why have the gods cursed us so, making the love between us a thing of darkness and treachery?"

"Why, indeed..." he said with sadness, stroking her hair.

"Let us ride out..." she said. "One more time... let us lie together. Just one more time before he comes back, and I must do my duty by him... and you yours."

"Fynavir, I do not think it is safe... We must go about our daily lives, as we always have."

"Please... One hour with you, that is all I ask... that I may think on it during all the lonely nights."

He groaned and pressed her close. "I am a fool... but when could I deny you anything, Fynavir, my love... my doom."

*****

Down by the river Mordraed perched on the grassy bank, dangling his legs in the swell. Agravaen was stomping out into the swell, holding up a long bone harpoon, his face crinkled in concentration as he tried to spear a fish for that night's supper. Other youths milled around the trees that grew along the Abona, drinking from water-skins and chewing strips of dried meat as they blathered about non-existent battles and their prowess in them. Mordraed lazily eyed this young unruly pack ... Wyzelo and his friends, the malcontents, the disobedient, the thick-in-the-head. A slavering band of dogs, all of them, scrabbling to get to the top, but dogs could be trained to be loyal with a few thrown scraps... then these dogs would bark for him.

Rising, he casually sauntered towards them. "How is it with my brothers?"

"Not good!" yelled one he knew was called Belenion... the Henbane. Mordraed wondered if the scrawny, hooked-nosed lad was as venomous as his name. "Not enough mead... no women... nor any war! I came here to be a great warrior and I am sent running about like a little boy with a wooden blade every day while the 'great chiefs' look on and laugh. Tired of it, I am! I want to decorate my hut with the jawbones of my enemies!"

"Your hut?" said Wyzelo. "You don't even have a house of your own yet. We sleep together in one hut like children or beasts."

"It is not as it should be." Mordraed sighed deeply, theatrically. "I do not know how my uncle cannot see the wrong that is being done to you. I would not treat you so, mighty warriors that you are. I fear the men around Ardhu have poisoned his mind. I mean, what is An'kelet but a foreign prince? Loyal he might have seemed over the years, but who is to say treachery does not dwell in his heart and that he does not covet all Ardhu owns? Maybe he has just been biding his time."

"Bloody foreign pig," grunted a skinny gap-toothed boy named Ic'ho. "You should be in Ardhu's circle, Mordraed, and treated with just as much respect as An'kelet. You are of the blood of kings. *His* blood. Why does he ignore you in preference to outsiders?"

Mordraed licked his lips. Now was the moment. He could feel the tension in the air, the dissatisfaction growing into anger and disdain. The moment might pass, he might find he had been presumptuous and incur anger or puzzlement from this fractious band of youths, but he had to speak now or forever hold his tongue. "If I asked it and... if my uncle does not acknowledge your worth... would you be my men, my followers instead? Although I have no land as yet, who knows what the future may hold? After all..." His eyes were shining, his breaths short and shallow, "Prince

100

Gal'havad is Ardhu's only heir; his union with the White Woman has not been blessed. And Gal'havad... he is not hale, he has fits and sees the spirit-world. He is more suited to be a priest than a king! Who knows, his affliction may even shorten his days. If he were to die young and have no heirs of his body... who knows what I might be then?"

"King Mordraed!" shouted out Ic'ho, laughing, obviously drunk. "With us at his side as his chief warriors!"

The rowdy youths hooted and whooped, circling Mordraed. Laughing, they lifted him to their shoulders and raised their axes to him in honour.

Agravaen sloshed his way out of the river, scowling at their antics, and tossed his harpoon on the ground in frustrated anger. "What foolish mummery is this? Mordraed, if any from Kham-El-Ard should hear you, it might not go well for any of us!"

Mordraed laughed scornfully at him. "It is only a harmless game," he mocked. "Why so serious, brother?"

Agravaen's face purpled. "And why so reckless, Mordraed? It was never like you... and I do not like it."

At that moment, the sound of hooves interrupted the brothers' verbal sparring. "Someone rides out from Kham-El-Ard!" cried Wyzelo, pointing east with the haft of his axe. "I see An'kelet of Ar-morah upon his stallion... but he does not ride alone. Another is with him."

Mordraed shaded his eyes with a hand and stared towards Kham-El-Ard. He could see An'kelet's amber hair shining in the sun, and his checked cloak, woven with the lozenge pattern of his high-born clan, streaming out behind him in the wind of his speed. Beside him on a smaller horse rode a figure wrapped in a rust-coloured fur, a voluminous skin hood pulled up to hide the face. He immediately knew there was only one person it could be.

The White Woman, the treacherous Queen.

He knew at once his hour was here and he must seize the chance. Whirling on his heel, he gestured to the band of drunken youths, to red-faced Agravaen with his angry expression. "Follow me!" he cried. "Let us go into the wilds after them."

"But why?" asked Belenion, staggering drunkenly on the river's edge. "I don't care where An'kelet of Ar-morah goes!"

"Do not question!" Mordraed's hand caught the front of the other's woven tunic, almost causing the youth to trip and fall into the river. "That is an important lesson you must learn... if you wish to be accounted in any chief's war-band! Listen, all of you, if you want to rise in esteem, come with me now and bring your weapons. This may be a day for great feats of arms, I promise you all. A day that will go down in the memories of men!"

The youths grabbed their axes and untied the peace-strings that bound their copper daggers into their sheaths. The drink was hot in them, stirring them to act. Agravaen stormed up to Mordraed, huffing and heaving; Mordraed noticed for the first time how tall he had suddenly grown... they were now nearly the same height, almost eye to eye. "What are you planning, brother?" he snapped.

"To root out treachery, if there is any to be found," said Mordraed. "Is that not what you want too—to keep our uncle's domains safe? I told you I would let you have the honour of bringing any evil to his attention."

Agravaen grunted, unable to deny his elder sibling's words. "I would bet on this being a fool's chase. But let us go and see, and if you are wrong, I want you to bring me the best bit of beef at the fire tonight and refill my beaker before your own."

"It will be as you wish," said Mordraed excitedly. "Now let us hasten, in case we lose their trail. But do not let them see you... that is most important." He glanced sternly around the gathered group of young men. "Keep to the bushes, keep to the reeds—use every trick of woodcraft you have ever been taught in order to be silent... and safe. Remember, it is An'kelet of Ar-morah who is our quarry today, and he is the greatest fighter amongst men—or so they say. Luckily, he does not seem to have his spear, the Balugaisa, with him—which must mean the Spirits are smiling upon us."

The youths raced down the river bank, single file, sobering up now that the chase was on. Mordraed grasped Agravaen's arm, and pushed him after the rest. "Hurry up, brother. We are the sons of kings—we must lead these cattle and prod them to do what they must."

The group continued along the Abona, nearly to the dwellings of the Ladies of the Lake, but suddenly, as the river spread out into multiple channels, the trail went dead, the clear passage of the horses veiled by the wetness of the ground. The youths groaned and started complaining bitterly that an afternoon's good drinking had been spoiled by a fool's errand.

"Shut up!" Mordraed cast them a dark glare that made them all fall silent. Flinging himself onto his knees, he scanned the water-logged ground, the patchy grass, searching for signs of hoof prints. At length he found a depression in the soil, recent, an earthworm coiling on the disturbed surface. "Further down the valley, to the north... I think they are heading toward the Great Enclosure."

"The Great Enclosure!" Agravaen's face paled. "That's where they used to take the dead. It's an evil place... why should they go there?"

"That is obvious," said Mordraed, face glowing with self-pride at his deduction. "They think no living man would dare set foot among the place of the dead so it would be ideal for their immoral tryst. Come, let us hurry and catch them."

Bow in hand, he raced toward the North, with his pack of youths running like faithful but ill-trained hounds behind him.

*****

An'kelet and Fynavir rode up to the banks of the Great Enclosure, where up till a Moon's Year ago the dead priests of Khor Ghor had lain on wooden platforms, awaiting the cleansing of the flesh and the freeing of their spirits.

The rite had since fallen out of use as burial customs changed and the dead now went straight to their barrows still clad in flesh.

An'kelet swung down from his horse and let its reins dangle; the animal immediately started to crop the tufted grass. Striding over to Fynavir's mount he lifted up his arms for her to come to him. She put her hands on his shoulders and let him lift him down onto the ground. She stared around—the low encircling bank, the empty pits where wooden excarnation platforms had stood. As she moved her foot, teeth fallen from the rotting bodies of long ago tinkled in the grass.

"I hate this place," she breathed. "I can almost smell the scent of decaying flesh... though they are long gone..."

"It is not a nice place," said An'kelet. "But it is a safe place. No one comes here anymore, and the bank protects from prying eyes."

"The spirits look on." She glanced around the site, bleak and unwelcoming, raked by a chill wind that stirred her hair and her fur cloak. "They will know what we have done."

"But they will not disturb us. Nor will those who have no mortal tongues speak of our joining to others."

He took off his cloak, spread it on the ground. The teeth were shining, pearlescent, in the grass, precious tokens of death and ending. They were not as bright, though, as the warm amber of An'kelet's hair, the rings bound in it shining in the muted sunlight. Fynavir sank to her knees, and pressed her hands to her face. "I begged to be alone with you, I cannot deny it," she said. "But now I feel a great fear in my heart, such as I have not felt before."

"I will chase that fear away." He knelt beside her, freeing her hair, his mouth on her neck against the warm pulse of life. She reached up to touch his face, the mane of amber hair. The pale, cloud-swathed blob of Bhel above suddenly picked out strands of silver; she had not noticed them before.

"Seventeen years we have met in secret," she whispered. "Seventeen years we have betrayed Ardhu. We are growing old, my love. How can we continue as we have in the years to come?"

"That is in the hands of the gods," he murmured. "Do not think of it now." He drew her on to his lap, moving her woven skirts aside, his hand questing up her thigh. She stifled a moan as his fingers touched her and she wrapped her legs around his back, pulling herself in against him. She was shivering, both from the cold of the wind and from excitement... and from fear too; no matter his comforting words, a sense of doom and despair and melancholy lay on her like a shroud.

He reached out and unfastened the jet toggles on the front of her kirtle, and pushed her back onto his cloak. His hands were ice-cold as he caressed her. It was always like this, when they could escape from Kham-El-Ard alone... a union in haste, brief rutting like beasts on the ground, then quickly up and back to the fort on the Crooked Hill, with leaves and grass brushed from clothes and smiles of falseness on their lips. That was the price they had to pay for their forbidden love, being forever false and forever fearful...

An'kelet knelt above her and pressed her legs apart, and she felt him slide inside her. Her fear vanished in a shower of pleasure and she writhed against him, drawing him closer. She gazed up into his face, her pupils dilated with her desire... and suddenly she let out a terrible scream.

"An'kelet, someone is here... behind you, on the bank!"

He pulled away from her, cursing, and snatched up Fragarak from where he had tossed it aside on the fur. To his dismay he could see a familiar figure on the bank of the Great Enclosure, staring at him with a shocked, snarling, angry face.

Agravaen son of Morigau.

Their eyes met and held for a moment. Then, Agravaen pulled his war hammer from his belt and rushed towards him uttering a blood-curdling howl, "Traitor! Traitor!"

An'kelet was not afraid—he'd trained this clumsy, over-eager boy, knew Agravaen's only advantage in any battle was his brute strength. But he was also concerned as to what he should do. Killing the lad was his first instinct. But Agravaen was Ardhu's nephew and had been taken under his protection; the Stone Lord's wrath would be terrible... but the boy could not be allowed to tell anyone in the tribe what he had seen.

Dagger in hand, An'kelet stalked Agravaen, who eyed him with both rage and terror. The youth swung his axe from side to side, seeking an opportunity to strike an arm or a leg, shattering the bone and making a cripple of his older, more skilled opponent. An'kelet circled him at a distance, attempting to find a place from where he could dart like a serpent and strike with his honed Ar-moran blade, the hot bronze cutting into kidney, heart or lung, or biting through the great vein in the neck. He would try to make the death quick, because his quarry was Ardhu's nephew and he would not have his friend's kinsman suffer overlong.

Suddenly he heard Fynavir cry out behind him. He whirled on his heel just in time to see Mordraed leap over the embankment and circle her throat with his arm, pressing on her windpipe and felling her immediately. The northern Prince dragged her along the ground, his dagger pressed to her neck, his eyes glittering like hard stars. His beautiful face took on an almost demonic look as he grinned at An'kelet, his expression victorious...

"Let her go!" An'kelet felt the first surge of the battle-fury, the Warp-Spasm, come upon him. His head swam, his voice thickened and deepened. He had never trusted this dark, quick-tongued youth from Ynys Yrch, not for one moment since he had arrived. He should have been sent from Kham-El-Ard with his accursed dam—if not sent to the spirit-world. Mordraed was touched by evil like his mother; he was the snake that bit a man's ankle in the grass; he was the disloyal dog that savaged its master's hand. He was the Darkness to oppose Ardhu's Light...

"Let her go?" Mordraed's fingers reached up to stroke Fynavir's face;

even as she struggled to breathe, she recoiled from his touch as if stung. "A traitor to the Stone Lord? No, An'kelet of Ar-morah, you and she shall both answer to Ardhu Pendraec and to the spirits you have offended with your lust and your deceit."

An'kelet gave a cry and rushed forward, dagger upraised. He would kill this arrogant youth and then he would take Fynavir, whether she willed it or not, and flee with her to Ar-morah. Many of his kinsmen still dwelt on the long tongue of land that jutted into the Narrow Sea and they would shelter him and show him loyalty. Even in recent years he had traded with them, bringing in daggers with gold pointillé hilts, fancy, prestigious pots with handles and rounded brass helms in continental style. He would have the priestesses of his mother Ailin's order break Fynavir's marriage bonds and he would wed her himself as he should have done years ago, before he brought Ardhu to the Dun of Ludegran, her foster-father.

An'kelet's mad headlong rush brought him within feet of Mordraed. The younger man roughly thrust Fynavir from him and struck out with the flat of his bow, catching An'kelet across the upper face with a whip-like motion. It was a dishonourable battle-move but highly effective, momentarily blinding him, making him see only stars and swirling blots of light. Tears of pain streaming down his cheeks, An'kelet staggered back from his opponent, hands instinctively reaching to his stinging eyes.

Mordraed laughed and struck out again, the top section of the bow cracking down on An'kelet's exposed right wrist; the Ar-moran was not wearing his archer's wristguard for he had only brought his daggers with him... This blow, however, was not as accurately aimed as Mordraed's first and failed to make An'kelet drop Fragarak. Vision slowly recovering, An'kelet lunged at his youthful enemy, sure that once he had his footing he could bring him down rapidly and finish this fight.

He was surprised when a dagger of bronze rose to meet his blade, not as long as the near-rapier he carried, but broad, with a deadly gleaming tip. Thrust into flesh and turned, it would wreak terrible damage. The hilt was of dappled horn and had several deep spirals grooved upon it, looking in some aspects like a spirit-face, the eyes of the Watcher. It slammed against Fragarak, and the bronze blades sparked as they sawed on each other. The hand behind the weapon was rock-hard, steady, immoveable...

An'kelet smiled grimly. Had he really expected any less? He had been training Mordraed himself these past months. But when had the youth become so strong of limb and fast? When had he, once the greatest warrior in the known world, begun to weaken and grow slow?

Still, he was not done yet. Suddenly pulling back from his opponent, he drew his other dagger, Arondyt, and made a sharp thrust at Mordraed's midriff. Fast as the serpent Mordraed recoiled, and then, as the blow went wide, he swung round in a semi-circle, kicking the weapon from An'kelet's hand with a blow so hard An'kelet felt the muscles tear from his forearm to the shoulder. He staggered and dropped Arondyt, his arm hanging numb and useless at his side.

Mordraed tossed back his raven-hued hair, laughing. He preened himself like the black bird of prey he resembled. "Surely you are not finished already? I am enjoying our little sparring match, Lord An'kelet! Our first real fight."

"You mock me but by the end of this day you will beg me for mercy..." gasped An'kelet, but even as he spoke the words a terrible sensation of doom and fear came over him, such as he had never experienced before. His words felt hollow, untrue. Pain lanced down his arm; his slashed eyes were still throbbing and blurring. He realised he did not have the heart for these battles any longer, nor the strength of a man less than twenty Sun-turnings.

He was done.

"An'kelet!" he heard Fynavir cry out. Having recovered from Mordraed's stranglehold, she rushed across the grass toward him, her unbound hair flying out in a white cloud. He grabbed her to him, uncaring now that any man should see them together.

And at the moment many did see... for the banks of the enclosure were full of young men, whooping and shouting, brandishing bronze and copper and stone axes, their faces flushed with misplaced pride and too much mead. He recognised them all, had given training to most, and with despair he realised that they were the displaced and dissatisfied, the youths he had told Ardhu would never be men of the warband—those who liked blood too much, or mistreated women and weaker men; those who imagined themselves stronger and greater than they were.

"You have done this, haven't you?" he gasped at Mordraed. "These creatures are your curs, eating the scraps of lies you throw them."

"Curs they may be," said Mordraed. "But I can assure you, Lord An'kelet, they have the bite of wolves."

He made a gesture with his hand to the young men on the enclosure bank, and with a frenzied roar they rushed in at their quarry, dragging along an axe-brandishing Agravaen in their mad headlong charge. Thrusting Fynavir behind him, An'kelet shouted a war cry of his own and hurled himself at the first line of youths, his unexpected burst of strength driving the first enemies back and bowling several of them over. He leapt upon the fallen, stabbing one man through the eye with Fragarak, and breaking the other's spine with a downward hard stamp of his foot. Screams rose to the heavens and blood fed the hungry grass.

Fynavir was screaming, hysterical, frozen to the spot by the horror and unreality of what was happening. Mordraed swung round and struck her across the face to silence her, his blow throwing her to the ground where she lay dazed, redness leaking from her cut lip.

An'kelet shouted in rage to see her struck in such a manner, and vented the full force of his fury on those before him, grabbing two of his assailants

106

and smashing their faces together, hitting them repeatedly as blood spurted and teeth cracked and fell from their red mouths to join the lost teeth of the long-dead in the grass. Casting their limp bodies to one side as a child would hurl a corn-dolly; he once more fought his way towards Mordraed at the edge of the earthwork. "I... will... have you..." he gasped. "You... are the rot in Kham-El-Ard..."

Mordraed cast him a pitying look, deliberately meant to infuriate. The look one might give a fool or simpleton. His eyes flicked across the circle.

In his rage and panic and eagerness to get to Mordraed, An'kelet had failed to notice that he was being stalked...

Agravaen son of Loth was thundering up behind him, wild and hostile, his archaic stone war-hammer upraised.

"Don't kill him, Agravaen!" Mordraed called out. "I want to see him confess to his crimes before Ardhu and be suitably punished!"

An'kelet whirled around, grappling for the haft of Agravaen's hammer... but he could not get a grip on the sweat-streaked wood with his damaged hand. If he dropped Fragarak, he might be able to over-power the stockier but less skilled man... but it would be a great risk to attack without any weapon save his own strength. Realising his opponent's disadvantage, Agravaen bore down on him like some rushing monster, a beast half-man, half-bull, and the youth's war-hammer smashed into his temple.

Lights exploded in An'kelet's head and he staggered and fell to his knees, blood running into his eyes. Seeing him fallen, his enemies howled and yelled and piled in on top of him, punching and kicking, tearing away his weapons and pinioning his arms behind his back.

Watching, Mordraed felt a sense of elation so great he thought his heart might burst. He threw back his head and screamed this first victory to the ever-changing skies.

CHAPTER ELEVEN
THE TRIAL OF FYNAVIR

The small party of horsemen cantered down the Harrow Way, the ancient track which crossed the summit of Harrow Hill, wound past the temple of Khor Ghor, and then fared on into the farthest West. Behind their shoulders the sky was the colour of an old bruise, filled with impending storm; a low rumble of thunder filled the charged air, and sullen flashes of lightning crowned the Eastern line of hills—Harrow, Beacon, and Magic Hill, where Bhel's face first rose at the beginning of the World of Men.

"Nearly home," said Gal'havad, leaning over his mount's neck and urging it to greater speed with the pressure of his heels. Despite the company's failure to heal the Maimed King, the young man's mood was lightening at the prospects of a homecoming—he wanted to see his mother again, to put things right with her after their last fraught parting, and to see his friend Mordraed, whom he had parted from without even a farewell, and tell him of his adventures as a Man of the Tribe.

Riding ahead of the others, Gal'havad soon reached the foot of Kham-El-Ard, raised like the prow of a sea-going ship that sailed into the Sunrise. He was surprised to see no workers in the surrounding field systems, and no one coming and going about their business on the hill. It was almost as if Kham-El-Ard had been abandoned. He bit his lip fearfully, and let his gaze travel up the earthen ramparts to the timber palisades rising above, but there was no sign of a battle or any destruction; all was as it should be, save for its eerie quietness. One thin streak of smoke came from one hut inside the Dun, to be dispersed in the storm-laden air.

Heart pounding, he slammed his heels into his mount's flank and drove it up the hill at great speed. Coming to the great gates, many times his height, he was stunned to see no guards on duty, as if they had all been called away elsewhere. He saw a few women in the distance, but they were scuttling between their huts like small beetles, faces downcast, moving rapidly as if terrified.

What was going on?

He glanced toward the Great Hall. He could hear voices now, a low ominous rumble just like the thunder in the distance. It was a different sound from what he remembered—no laughter, no song-singers, and no women chattering. It was a dark sound, an angry sound like disturbed bees buzzing in a hive.

"Ka'hai!" The name was torn from his mouth in almost a scream as he saw Ardhu's foster-brother suddenly appear in the door of the hall and glance out.

The older man's heavy brow furrowed and he strode forward, waving his arms, waving Gal'havad away. "No! Amhar... Prince Gal'havad... you mustn't come in here, you must not look! Where is your father? Where is Ardhu?"

Gal'havad flung himself from his steed and rushed toward Ka'hai and the gaping doorway behind him. "What is wrong, Ka'hai? Where are the people? Why do you bar me from my own home?"

Ka'hai caught the youth's shoulders, swinging him in a semi-circle, trying to turn him aside. "Gal'havad, a terrible thing has happened in your father's absence. You will be told all... but we must wait for the Stone Lord to arrive before more is said of this evil matter!"

"Tell me, Ka'hai!" Gal'havad wrenched himself free. His face was the colour of the chalk. "I am the Prince of Kham-El-Ard!"

Ka'hai began to weep, great unmanly sobs that made his broad shoulders heave and shake. It was like watching an oak tree fall, felled by an axe. "I cannot speak of it, Gal'havad. I cannot!"

Gal'havad raced past him, leaving Ka'hai bent with his grief. Running into the hall, he pushed through a sea of bodies toward the Eastern end where his father's high seat stood. As he drew near to the antlered chair, he could see his cousin Mordraed standing separate from the rest of the crowd. He was dressed in his finest warrior's garb, his hair braided with gold, and in his hand he held a black basalt stone axe of ancient type—a symbol of authority. Two white streaks were painted on each cheekbone—warrior's face-paint, worn in time of action—and he had darkened round the edges of his eyes with charcoal, making their blue colour stand out even more vividly. Behind him his lumpish brother Agravaen, also carrying a stone hammer and wearing his finest clothes and trinkets, stood like some shaggy and pugnacious hill-troll. Other youths that Gal'havad barely knew were clustered in the rear; they strutted about in unruly fashion, weapons clearly on display, full of pride and overconfidence.

"Mordraed!" Gal'havad thrust the crowds aside, struggling through the press of bodies towards his kinsman. "Tell me, I beg you... what has happened in my absence? Where is my mother, Fynavir?"

Mordraed jumped a little at the sight of the other youth but immediately regained his composure. "I am sorry to speak words that will grieve you," he said... loudly, so that all assembled could hear. "But the Lady Fynavir is being held a prisoner. And so is the Lord An'kelet!"

"A prisoner!" Gal'havad stopped in his tracks and stared at Mordraed as if he had gone insane. "But she is the Queen of Kham-El-Ard! And An'kelet is my father's closest friend! Mordraed, what madness do you speak?"

The insincere smile vanished from Mordraed's lips. "Your dam is a traitor and the Lord An'kelet, the foreigner, with her. There is no easy way to say it, my friend... but as you are now a Man of the Tribe I will speak to you as a Man and not a child. Fynavir of Ibherna has played the whore for

An'kelet of Ar-morah for many years and now she has been caught..."

Gal'havad stood as if he had been struck, blood draining from his face. Unable to speak, he mutely shook his head in denial.

At that moment, the crowds behind him parted. The angry buzz of voices within the hall fell still. Ardhu stood in the doorway, hard-faced as a sarsen stone, with Caladvolc a brand of fire in his hand. Hwalchmai and Per-Adur flanked him with weapons ready as he entered the Great Hall and strode purposefully toward Mordraed on the raised area near his seat of power. His gaze burned into the dark youth, taking in his stance and attire. Anger flared within him, and old mistrust.

"You!" he shouted. "Why do you stand there, as if you were lord of Kham-El-Ard? Where is my queen and my chief-warrior? What have you done with them, bastard?"

He raised his sword but at that moment Mordraed did something Ardhu had not expected. Casting down his weapons, the son of Morigau flung himself to the floor at his feet, falling face down in the rushes in a position of utter subjugation and humility, his back and neck exposed to potential blows from above. "Great Stone Lord," he said, "I beg that you do not bring the force of your wrath down on me, who only has the honour of your house foremost in my mind. I have done nothing to shame or betray you, you who are my close kinsman... unlike others who are dear to your heart."

Distrust still burned within Ardhu, and reaching down he grabbed Mordraed's tunic and hauled him roughly to his feet. "Do not seek to flatter me with words, son of a woman with a snake's tongue," he spat. "Speak now and speak clearly... and tell me what has happened here!"

Mordraed nodded toward Agravaen. "It is my brother who you must ask, lord. He is the one who first saw that a great wrong was being committed on you under your very roof."

Ardhu frowned, perplexed. Agravaen! He had watched the thick, rough boy blossom these past months, becoming dedicated to war-craft and eager to please him. Stupid he might be, but Ardhu had seen no malice or duplicity in him. He wanted to serve. He wanted to be in the war-band, away from the malign influence of the mother who thought of him as less than nothing, a child she would have exposed on a cliffside if she had had the choice.

"Agravaen..." Ardhu ordered, "Speak!"

The boy lumbered forward, licking his lips nervously. His eyes darted from Mordraed to Ardhu to the rush-strewn floor. "Terrible Head, please do not be wrathful, for I am loyal to you" he said, his voice cracking. "But I have ill news for you. When I was out... hunting... with my companions I saw An'kelet of Ar-morah and Lady Fynavir ride out into the Valley, their manner passing strange. Unbeknownst to them, I followed the trail of their horses to a hidden place and there I saw a sight that will burn in my mind forever—they lay together rutting like beasts upon the grass. My Lord..." his voice rose and his eyes rolled almost hysterically—he was obviously terrified, fearing that Ardhu's wrath at this evil news might be directed at him, "they must be put to death, given to the Stones! All will be made right then."

Ardhu went rigid. "Be silent!" His fist shot out, striking Agravaen full in the mouth. He fell backwards, lips swelling and bleeding.

Spinning around on his heel, Ardhu approached Mordraed, yanking him roughly towards him by the front of his tunic so that they were mere inches apart. "Take your brother and get out!" he shouted. "Remove yourself from my sight. If you have harmed them, my wife and chief warrior, I will have your innards ripped from your body as you watch…"

"They are both unharmed." Mordraed's voice was flat, cold. "My men have them bound in the cave below Kham-El-Ard, waiting for the Stone Lord's justice."

Ardhu stopped and suddenly stared straight into Mordraed's face, incredulous. "*Your* men? Mordraed son of Morigau… in this place *nothing's* yours!"

His arm shot out, striking the young man just as he had struck his younger brother. Mordraed staggered back but did not fall beneath the blow; he stood wiping blood from his lip where one of Ardhu's twisted bronze armlets had cut it, his deep blue eyes blackening with hatred.

Abruptly those fathomless eyes became shuttered, the face expressionless, revealing nothing more. He bowed curtly to Ardhu. "I will go as you decree, my uncle." Grabbing the arm of the still-reeling Agravaen, he propelled the younger man out of the hall and away amidst the huts clustered on the hilltop.

Ardhu turned, his visage grey, strained. "Ka'hai!" he called for his foster-brother, who knelt, still wracked with grief, by the doorway of the Hall. "You have been with me from the time I was a babe; brother of my heart, if not my blood. Come with me, and support me as you did when I was a child. I need you now as much as I need the arms of men like Bohrs and Hwalchmai."

Led by Ka'hai, Ardhu left Kham-El-Ard and took the long spiralling pathway down to the waters of the Sacred Pool that lay below the vast bulk of the Crooked Hill. There were signs of great trampling and tumult in the undergrowth, clods of earth torn up and smears of blood on foliage and ground.

"They are imprisoned in the cave, Ardhu," said Ka'hai tearfully. "Ba-lin and Bal-ahn are on guard, along with many others. An'kelet, as you might imagine, was not easy to subdue. He killed two of the yearling boys from the local settlements when Agravaen discovered his… treachery, and injured many more. He was only taken because Agravaen smote him unconscious with his hammer; but even that was only a small respite… once he woke the battle fury came on him and he slew again and again. Blood was spilled in Kham-El-Ard where blood has never been spilt before, and you can see by the gore around us that he was still fighting when we managed to drag him here."

111

Ardhu nodded stiffly. "Where are the dead?"

Ka'hai gestured to several biers lying beside the pond, covered with painted deerskins. Flies buzzed about them in clouds. "We have done no rites for them, Ardhu, to send them over the Great Plain to the Land of the Ancestors."

"And why has this not been done? Where is the Merlin?"

Ka'hai shrugged his shoulders. "That is the other evil news I must tell... we do not know what has happened to wise Merlin. He has not been seen for days, at Deroweth, Kham-El-Ard or Khor Ghor."

Ardhu ran his hand over his brown hair in an agitated motion. "Evil news indeed, Brother Ka'hai. All goes amiss for me in these dark times." He strode over to the biers and dragged back the deerskins one by one. Beneath the hides lay tangles of putrefying flesh, splintered femurs and ribs poking up from blackened stumps that seemed scarcely human, especially since beasts had been gnawing on them in the night. "Have them taken to the Old Henge and burn them on pyres," he ordered. "Have all the priests come from Deroweth to chant and sing and send their spirits on their long journey... then have them taken to Khor Ghor and interred with honour."

"But many of them were a bad lot," exclaimed Ka'hai. "Defiant and rebellious... they would have soon been sent home to their families."

"No matter," said Ardhu. "In rooting out the poison in the midst of Kham-El-Ard, they did me a great service and hence they shall have fitting burial in the Tomb of All Hope."

Leaving the reeking biers, he walked on toward the cave in the broad chalky hillside where An'kelet and Fynavir were imprisoned. As he neared it, he could see two dozen of his men surrounding its mouth; they had set up a great blockade in the entrance, an infill made of a stout tree trunk. They were clearly ill at ease, with drawn bows, daggers and clubs at the ready.

Ardhu approached Bal-ahn who stood nearest to the entrance, his bronze axe in his hand. "Unblock it," he said, nodding toward the makeshift barricade. "I will speak to them."

"Lord, no," said Bal-ahn uneasily. "An'kelet's strength in his anger is that of ten men... we could barely control him as it was. I would counsel you, as your companion of many years, to build a great fire here in the cave mouth, using the tree at kindling, and finish this vile matter in the only way it can end."

Ardhu's eyes glinted dangerously. "I do not ask for your counsel. Drag the tree away so that I may go inside. An'kelet of Ar-morah will not harm me."

Bal-ahn inclined his head and gestured to the other warriors to start removing the barrier. They chopped at the tree with their axes, hacking out a space where their chief could pass. "I will come with you, Ardhu," said Bal-ahn when the last cut was made.

Ardhu put his hand on his shoulder, more weary now than angry. "My thanks... but it is for me alone to do."

Taking a deep breath, Ardhu slid through the gap and entered the cave. The thin sunlight entered with him and lit up the mossy, stone-filled floor and the two figures crouched at the back amidst the rubble. He could see Fynavir's pale hair, unbound and tangled, and her tear-streaked face, marred by bruises, floating like a sad moon in the shadows.

Beside her An'kelet stirred. Abruptly he stood up, and Ardhu noticed that his tunic was stiff with gore. Blood also matted his hair and stained his arms and face. A wound on his temple leaked slowly, but most of the blood upon him was not his.

Slowly, he approached Ardhu. His eyes were wary.

Ardhu unbuckled his belt, with Caladvolc hanging from it, and cast it to one side. "I am not here to kill you," he said, his voice flat. "Not yet at any rate. I have come to hear, from your own mouth, what has happened. An'kelet of Ar-morah, my chief warrior, my *friend*... I want truth from you for once and for all. Have you lain with my woman?"

An'kelet took a deep, shuddering breath and suddenly fell to his knees before Ardhu. "Pick up your blade and smite me to the death!" he cried. "For I have betrayed you. I have lied to you long enough and would have an end. But do not harm Fynavir; I seduced her when she was lonely and weak."

"No, An'kelet, no!" Fynavir ran forward and threw her arms around her lover, almost as if Ardhu was not there at all. "If you die, then I will go with you to that Otherland!"

Ardhu stood unmoved, his cheeks grey. "She is as guilty as you. Her face tells me the truth about what has passed between you more than any words. You both deserve to die."

"Have mercy, Ardhu," An'kelet whispered hoarsely. "Not on me, for I know what I deserve. But on her. She is only a weak woman..."

Ardhu glared at Fynavir. "I did not say I would kill her, only that she deserves to die. No, she will stay here. She is the Land, or so the people think, and though she is barren soil, failing of even her beauty..." he spoke harshly, words deliberately cruel, "she is still considered the daughter of a Goddess on Earth. So she shall stay, by my side and in my bed, and she shall be punished besides in any way that I see as fitting."

"If she lives, I can ask for no more. Now take Caladvolc and drive it into my heart. We are undone, I have broken all my vows, and I cannot bear the shame."

Ardhu picked up the sword and drew it from its sheath. The blade gleamed red as blood as the faint beams of sunlight trailing into the cave struck it. Fynavir began to whimper, "No, no, no."

Ardhu approached An'kelet and placed the sharpened tip of the blade against his chest. Caladvolc shook in his hand. Tears streaked his cheeks as his arm muscles tensed, ready to thrust the sword into the heart of his long-time friend. An'kelet bowed his head, closing his eyes, lips moving in silent prayers to the gods of the Underworld, to Hwynn the White and his father Nud, asking that they might forgive him his crimes and still welcome him onto the Plain of Honey.

Suddenly Ardhu's arm dropped. He gave an awful, strangled cry of mingled grief, anger and despair and thrust Caladvolc, not into An'kelet's heart, but into his side above the hip.

An'kelet gasped and twisted in agony, grabbing at the blade that pierced him. The edges sheared into his fingers, drawing more blood.

Teeth gritted, Ardhu took a step back and yanked the blade from the wound. More blood flowed, pooling on the cave floor. Fynavir curled into a ball, sobbing. The redness from her lover's wound soaked into her hair, turning it bright crimson.

Ardhu slammed Caladvolc into its sheath, uncleaned, still dripping. "I will not take your life, in gratitude for the years you have served me. But now, wounded by my hand, I will send you forth to live or to die as the spirits see fit, but to receive no aid or succour from any man, woman or child in Kham-El-Ard, Deroweth, or the Place-of-Light. The Crossroads of the World and the entire West is barred to you also, and if you set foot in my territory, by Bhel's face and the Everlasting Sky, I will hunt you down and kill you like a wild beast."

He backed up to the barricade in the cave mouth and shouted for Bal-ahn and the others to come and widen the gap. The men of the war-band poured into the cavern, setting hands upon An'kelet and dragging him out into the open air. Curses they flung at him, for what he had done, and they spat at him and made signs against evil. Holding his injured side, blood welling through his bone-white fingers, he looked from face to face—the men he had fought beside and the lads he had trained as warriors. They had been his friends, his companions, his students... now they gazed at him with hatred, his sworn enemies unto death.

"What shall we do with him?" shouted one. "Let us take him to the river and drown him, and let her waters cleanse away his sin!"

"No!" Ardhu shoved the man out of the way. "Lay no hand upon him. He is a disease, a blight amongst us. Let him go and crawl into some hole and bleed to death, his blood feeding the land of our forebears, the land he has sullied!"

He turned to An'kelet himself, his eyes tormented. "Get you gone, before I change my mind!"

Gasping, hands pressed to his leaking wound, An'kelet limped down the steep, wooden slopes toward the riverbank, a red ragged figure of death and despair. "No, no, do not let him go to die in dishonour..." Fynavir ran from the cave and collapsed at her husband's feet, clinging in supplication to the fringe of his tunic.

Ardhu dragged her up roughly and grabbed her face in his hands, twisting her head so that she was forced to watch her lover stagger away into the trees.

114

"Look upon him well, woman," he said, voice heavy with weariness and grief. "It is the last you will ever see of him."

*****

That night at Kham-El-Ard there was a great storm. Thunder crashed overhead and shook the great posts holding up the hall to their very foundations. Men sat about silent and grim, holding their heads in their hands, while women squatted in the rain, wailing as if there had been a death.

Eyes red-rimmed, Gal'havad paced before his father's high seat, restive and anxious, angry and sorrowful in turn. Ardhu slumped on the chair of antlers, leaning his head on his hand, his visage ashen and his gaze unfocussed. "My father, listen to me," Gal'havad begged. "You must let me speak to my mother, to find out the real truth of what has happened!"

Ardhu's lip curled. "There is no need. All was confessed."

"You will not kill her." It was a statement, not a question, and edged slightly with danger.

Ardhu glanced up at his son; the youth's face wore a determined hardness he had not seen before... and yet it shone with almost an inner light, a pure flame that made him bow his head in shame and glance away again. "No, I will not have her put to death. She is the daughter of the Goddess on Earth. She is the Land. Whatever man takes the White Woman will be King."

Gal'havad sighed in relief, his shoulders slumping. He suddenly looked very young again, young and frail.

"But she will have to be punished."

Gal'havad raised his head, eyes starting to smoulder anew. "Punished? What punishment do you propose? Tell me!"

Ardhu raised his hand; his jaw was set. "It is not for you to question me. I am Stone Lord of Prydn, the Terrible Head, master of the Portal of Ghosts. Go from my sight until you are called for. I dismiss you from my Hall, Prince Gal'havad."

"Father, you cannot... !" Gal'havad's voice rose sharply and he took a long stride toward Ardhu's seat.

Bohrs blocked him, shaking his wild head. Gal'havad glanced down and saw that the burly warrior had his dagger drawn, gleaming in his clenched fist. "You have drawn blade on me," he said, incredulous.

"I wouldn't gladly use it, lad," the heavy-set warrior mumbled. "But you have to go as Ardhu commands. Just do as he says. He will come round... with time."

Gal'havad's mouth trembled. "Pray to the spirits it is so... and that this madness that is on him soon leaves!" Turning from Bohrs, he fled from the great Hall and out into the storm.

Ardhu stared after him, eyes dull and without emotion.

*****

Gal'havad staggered through the lashing rain, soaked to the skin, his hair plastered to his skull. He wandered aimlessly amidst the huts, not knowing where to go. His usual place was in a cordoned-off area at the back of the Hall, near the quarters of his parents, hidden behind a hedge of skins stretched over wooden frames to create a private space. He shivered, his teeth starting to chatter as water trickled down the back of his neck.

Suddenly he spotted a familiar figure limned against dull firelight in the low-hanging doorway of the hut where young warriors were quartered while they did their training in arms. "Mordraed!" he shouted, springing forward.

Mordraed stiffened as Gal'havad burst into the hut like some creature borne of the raging storm, his hair a slick stream the colour of old blood against his white forehead, frigid water showering from his short, ox-skin cloak. Gal'havad came to him and cast his arms around him in a deep embrace, seemingly unaware of the rigidity of the other youth's shoulders, the unfriendly set of his mouth.

"Mordraed, cousin, glad am I to see you." Gal'havad's voice was thick with emotion, bordering on tearfulness. "My world has grown dark and crazed, and I need to see one who is not part of that madness."

Mordraed forced a smile upon his face as Gal'havad glanced up; it would not do to let the boy see that he was annoyed by this unexpected intrusion. He put what he hoped seemed a comforting arm around his cousin's shoulders and drew him in toward the tiny fire that burned in the centre of the hut. The other lads who had fallen under Mordraed's sway stared at the newcomer, some with near-open hostility despite his rank. Gal'havad appeared not to notice their stares and scowls.

"Now, what is bothering you?" Mordraed poured a weak beer into a crude black pot and handed it to Gal'havad. "Has Ardhu chased you from the Hall too?"

Gal'havad nodded dismally. "He is maddened with grief. Somehow I must convince him that he must not hurt my mother. He intends to punish her, but will not say in what way. I fear he will harm her in his anger."

Mordraed rolled his eyes. "Gal'havad, consider it fortunate that she has not been put to death. She is, after all, a whore and a traitor."

"Do not speak of her so!" Gal'havad shot back. "It is not your place to judge!" His hand instinctively went to his dagger-hilt.

Mordraed's lips curled. So the boy had got some fire in his belly since going on his little quest into the East!

"Forgive me for my hard words, cousin. If it comforts you, my own mother is no better! Here, sit by our fire… we are all outcasts here, all those who do not quite fit into your father's plans. He blames me and Agravaen for his sorrow too, you know; for although it was through us the traitor An'kelet was apprehended, we still have been banished from the Great Hall." He sighed. "I just hope it is not a permanent ban. Otherwise, I will have to leave for distant lands to seek my fortune."

"No… you cannot do that, Mordraed!" cried Gal'havad. "You… you are my only friend here. I have no others my age, and now that my mother is in

116

disgrace and my father cold as ice to me and unwilling to listen, I would be greatly sore of heart if you left. You... you are like a brother to me."

Mordraed almost laughed at the irony of Gal'havad's words. "If you truly feel that I am your brother, then you must speak for me and for Agravaen... when the Stone Lord is calmer, that is."

"I will," said Gal'havad staunchly, "for all the good it will do."

They fell silent and Gal'havad squatted by the fire, drying himself, and downing the rancid beer Mordraed had given him. Eventually the flames in the fire-pit died to embers and youths began to sprawl out under their fur cloaks and sheepskins, coiling together on the rushes like a pack of weary hounds. Gal'havad glanced around unhappily, unused to sleeping in such cramped conditions; but eventually he lay down facing away from the others, turning his face into the darkness. Soon the sound of soft, rhythmic sleep-breathing reached Mordraed where he sat a few feet away, finishing the last of the sour drink in his beaker.

Mordraed put the mug aside and slowly eased himself down into the rushes, lying flat on his belly. If he stretched out, he could almost touch Gal'havad's back. One hand slid down to his hip, his finger hooking round the hilt of his dagger, drawing it an inch from its sheath. He had polished and sharpened it just the other day. One quick stab in the dark, and it would be all over... he would have done what he had intended to do in the Stones, had the malevolent Old Ones not prevented him. Eyes burning with a feral light, he reached out, his fingertips brushing his half-brother's shoulder blade. Here, right here... one swift deep thrust and the knife would pierce the heart from behind...

But no... what was he thinking! Suddenly he snatched his hand back as it had been burned. It would be foolish to act now. Yes, foolish. He would be the first suspect if the boy was found dead, he knew that. Already Ardhu had grave doubts about his loyalty. Possibly he might be able to pass the blame onto Agravaen—maybe claim that his younger brother had been jealous of his friendship with Ardhu's heir—but he doubted such a story would deceive the Stone Lord for long.

Vengeance must wait. But it would come.

Slowly his eyelids drifted shut over his death-blue eyes, and he sprawled next to the youth he had sworn to kill, throwing his arm over the sleeping youth's shoulders, seeing no incongruity in using his intended victim's body-heat to warm himself in the draughty hut. He slept deeply, his hand still curled round the hilt of his dagger—and did not dream.

*****

The priests came from Deroweth, highest priests and the Elders in flowing robes of bleached linen, with blue kirtles for the priestesses, green for the seers and speakers with the dead, and rust for the temple guardians and acolytes. They gathered in Kham-El-Ard before the doors of the Great Hall, and a huge beaker filled with mead flavoured by meadowsweet was passed

117

between priests and the highest ranked warriors of Ardhu's band. The pot was an enormous, ancient example, impressed with wheat grains and fingernail patterns; it was broken after the draught was drained and its shards buried in a pit near the threshold, alongside the offering of a newborn lamb. Then the priestesses poured fermented milk into coarse, rounded black pots and passed these to the women of the tribe, the ladies who accompanied the great warriors of Ardhu Pendraec, before depositing them at the fortress's entryway, symbolic of the fertility of man and beast and a tasty offering to passing ghosts borne on the bitter wind.

On his high seat, Ardhu sat decked out in his full regalia—the lozenge and belt buckle of gold, the shield that was the face of Evening, Little White hilt and Caladvolc the Hard-Cleft, sword from the Sacred Pool. Rhon-gom the Lightning Mace was in his right hand, wreathed in bright strips of rolled cloth decked with talismans. These adornments had been newly added to the mace, and men wondered to see them for they were tokens of coming change. Ardhu's gaze was still haunted, but the deadness of the weeks before had lifted from his eyes and a new purpose gleamed in them.

He gestured to the foremost of the priests to come before him. "Gluinval, is there still no word on the whereabouts of the Merlin?"

Gluinval shuffled forward in his pale and frothing robes, a spray of dog's teeth round his neck and a crow's skull plaited into his long sandy beard. "No word has come, Stone Lord of Khor Ghor. It is not unknown that wise ones of our order foresee their own deaths and go into the wilds to meet in their chosen way the shadow that stands at every man's shoulder. I fear this may be true with the Merlin, blessed be his name among us! None may ever know where the bones of wise Merlin lie."

Ardhu gripped the haft of Rhon-gom and a spasm of sorrow crossed his features. "I knew this day would come," he murmured, half to himself. "But why now? He is still needed… more than ever the good counsel of my friend Merlin is needed!"

Shaking his head to clear it, he focussed his attention back toward the priest Gluinval. "So, if Merlin does not return, who will take the place of High Priest of Khor Ghor?"

"It will be decided in a testing of wise men, as it has been done for centuries. But we must wait till at least three Moons have passed, and we are sure the Blessed Merlin has gone to the Realm of Ancestors."

"And for now? Who leads the priests; who guards the Doors between the worlds of the Living and the Dead?"

"The Merlin taught me, from my youth. I am senior among the wise of Deroweth."

Ardhu leaned forward, his eyes suddenly darkened, growing wolfish in his thin, sun-darkened face. "Then tell me, as a wise man of Deroweth, what do you deem the fitting punishment for a faithless wife? But not any faithless wife, who might easily be put away or given to a bog to appease gods and men. A wife who is also Queen, not just by virtue of marrying a man of status, but by her own lineage, which is bound to the spirits that rule the very soil we walk on."

Gluinval licked his lips, knowing full well that Ardhu spoke of Fynavir and her betrayal. "Lord, according to the legends of our People, passed down by many tongues since the days of Samothos and Bolgos, a capricious woman of great beauty called Tlatga once lived in Belerion. They said her father was Lord Bhel himself, that he came as lover to her dam while she made offerings inside a chamber of the Old Ones on Midsummer morn. Her hair was fire from Bhel, her body white as the chalk of our blessed Plain, but her heart was frivolous and her actions unwise. She played two brave chieftains false and set them snapping like dogs at each other's throats, driving their warriors to great battles not for cattle-wealth, lands or weapons... but to posses this faithless woman's body. The crops withered and failed, neglected in their fields, and common men starved, while noble warriors, cruelly slain, rotted in their barrows. When the foolish chiefs realised what they had destroyed for the desire of Tlatga the Fair, they put their enmity aside and turned on the one who had scorned them both. They decreed that Tlatga would atone by ploughing anew the earth ravaged by her folly. Alone, she would pull the plough through the ruined fields in the manner of oxen; a shameful task for the daughter of Bhel—but after the thing was done, the Land was at peace and returned to its health. Tlatga was given to both chiefs, one through the dark months and the other the light months, for the rest of her days."

Ardhu looked thoughtful for a moment, then he bowed his head. "To draw a plough like some humble beast, to grovel in the mud before the folk of Kham-El-Ard... I deem this a fit punishment for infidelity. No blood is spilt, no death will come, yet the affront to me and to the Land itself is made good. It will be done."

He rose from his seat and beckoned to Hwalchmai, standing on his right in the place that had been An'kelet's. "Cousin, with the departure of the traitor An'kelet of Ar-morah, I bestow on you the honour of being my right-hand warrior. Would that my eyes had not been blinded in the past and I had set you in that position from the start. Now I ask you to bring Fynavir of Ibherna to me, that her punishment is meted out without further delay."

Hwalchmai bowed. "It will be done, Stone Lord. I will fetch her myself."

He strode from the hall and returned shortly leading Fynavir, whose hands were bound with twine behind her back. She came without resistance, looking thin and frail, her uncombed hair matted over lifeless eyes circled with darkness. The same kirtle she had worn in the cave, streaked with An'kelet's blood, hung rank and stinking on her gaunt frame. She no longer looked beautiful, but as if she was half in the spirit-world and longing for death.

She stood before Ardhu's seat, unable to meet his eyes. "Kill me," she said dully, her voice a dry rasp. "It is what I deserve. It is what I want. It is what the Gods will ask of me as atonement."

"They would not desire the blood of one so faithless!" Ardhu's voice was the lash of a whip. "And so you shall not die as is your wish. But you *will* atone for what you have done; you have cursed the Land by your actions and brought it to barrenness... and so you will plough it by your own hands, white as the chalk, and perhaps make it whole again. And then you will lie in my bed and be as you should have been had you not shamed yourself with An'kelet... my right-hand man... my *friend* of long years! Maybe then the spirits will take away your barrenness and give us more sons, that my Lands may be guarded by strong hands and Gal'havad have many kinsmen to stand at his back when the time comes for him to assume my mantle."

Fynavir made a strangled sound in her throat and looked as if she might collapse at Ardhu's feet. Ardhu rose from his seat and steadied her, taking her arm with surprising gentleness, as if he was a doting husband and not a man betrayed, wrestling with his own anger and need for revenge, fearing also the darkness and desolation he had seen in the East, the creeping cold and the steady flood of the rain.

She did not resist him. Her eyes held nothing, no fear, not hatred. Nothing.

They left the Hall and processed down the hill, surrounded by Ardhu's chief warriors. The priests of Deroweth followed, chanting and making gestures against malevolent beings from the unseen world. Drums were beaten, and people from both the dun and Place-of-Light came running up from the river and the fields to see what was happening at Kham-El-Ard.

In the marshy lands near the Old Henge Ardhu stopped the procession. "Kneel, woman." He gestured to Fynavir and then to the ground. She slumped to her knees in the grass, obedient, her head hanging. Ardhu grasped her thick hair in one hand and lifted it, yanking her head up and back, while drawing Caladvolc with the other. The watching people gasped, imagining for a terrible instant that he intended to behead her on the spot. Instead he swung the sword is a sideways motion and the blade sheared through her snow-pale locks, leaving only a few inches curling around her head. "This is the first offering, the first penance of the faithless wife," he announced, holding up the hank of hair so that the gathered throng could witness its cutting. "Let the priests take it and give it to the Great Ones."

Acting as high priest in the Merlin's absence, Gluinval took the hank of shorn hair and, followed by his entourage of priests and seers, carried it through the entrance of the Old Henge. In the centre of the earthen ring, they built a cairn of small stones to which they added a magic brew—the bones of a frog, the skull of a bird, an eel and a dog's tooth, all mixed up with hazelnuts, yew-berries and toadstools. Fynavir's hair was spread over the top like a protective covering, and Gluinval used a flint strike-a-light to set the whole cairn on fire then danced wildly around it with his fellow priests, as the acrid smoke from the burning hair and magic stew coiled into the air.

When the pyre was reduced to ashes, the priests gathered up the remains and brought them in an urn to where Ardhu stood with Fynavir kneeling silently at his feet. The people from the local villages gathered round, wailing and crying out at this terrible sight they had never thought to see—their Queen shamed and their King seeking retribution for the wrong done to him. Fear gripped them, and horror; rumour had spread quickly of the Queen's infidelity, and all knew what that could mean for their continued existence. They knew the gods would be angry, and the Old Woman of Gloominess would walk long amongst them, bringing a long Winter. Already they had seen too many grey skies, too many tears from the sky that washed their livelihood away.

Ardhu gestured for Fynavir to get to her feet; she seemed unable to control her shaking limbs, so Hwalchmai lifted her up from the ground, his face grim, hating every moment, and forced her to face her husband. Ardhu stared at her, eyes unreadable, his mouth a tight, thin line, and then he raised Caladvolc to her neck and this time cut off her filthy rags, leaving her naked to the eyes of the assembly. Gluinval reached into the urn he carried and brought out a handful of still-warm ashes, blackening her face with them—a mark of shame—before tracing symbols on the rest of her body that told of her shame, her dishonour of her lord's bed. She recoiled as the priest touched her breasts and wept silently as two priestesses strode over, dragging a crude plough, and fastened the straps of its harness around her.

The crowd's hysteria was rising; people screamed out unintelligibly and fell writhing on the muddy ground as if possessed by spirits out of darkness. The throng pushed forward, toward Ardhu, toward Fynavir bound to the plough—to what purpose none knew, perhaps no real purpose, only to move and cry out and wave their fists in both protest and agreement at the punishment of the woman who had been their queen for so long. Ardhu's war band shouted at them and drew their axes, menacing the villagers as they drew too close, forcing them to take several paces backwards.

Ardhu turned angrily from them and grasped the handles of the plough, his knuckles bright white as he gripped the splintering wood. "Go, faithless bitch!" he snarled at Fynavir. "Let us finish this for once and for all!"

Fynavir lurched forward, struggling in the traces. Mud splashed up her ankles and she almost fell. The plough bit into the ground and partly sank, as the soil was so saturated from the unseasonable rains. "Go on, use some strength, woman!" Ardhu raged, all his anger and hurt and loss bursting forth in a frenzied tide. None in Kham-El-Ard had ever seen him so angry, he who was known for being measured and calm, who raised his hand in wrath only at utmost provocation. "You are the daughter of a goddess, aren't you? Special? An'kelet certainly thought you were special! He knew well the power in your thighs! Show me, your husband, what you are truly made of!"

Fynavir made a strangled sound and flung herself forward once more. Rain began to sluice down from the empurpled sky, making her shorn head frizz and curl like a lamb's fleece, streaking the ashes on her skin until she looked like some strange striped beast, a creature of light and shadow.

Someone laughed in the crowd of villagers and suddenly the mood became even uglier. A sod flew, striking the back of Fynavir's calf. "I curse you, White Phantom!" a woman shrilled, her voice so taut and high–pitched it sounded barely human. "Your lust has doomed us! My bairn has died, I have no milk… and the rains still come. This is your fault! You have cursed the Land. You are barren after one child due to your sin! You have brought evil on us!"

The crowd's wailing ceased and a dark murmur came from them, a sound like thunder over distant hills, a murmur low and ominous. Several people rushed forward, arms swinging wildly, to be forced back by the men of Ardhu's warband.

Ardhu ignored them, wrapped in his own private misery, intent on taking his own vengeance for the wrong that had been done him. "Pull harder, faster, woman!" he gasped to Fynavir, wiping the rain from his face with his arm. "Or do I have to smite you like a stubborn ox."

Fynavir yanked on the traces with all her remaining strength. Her eyes were screwed shut against the rain, against the sight of her vengeful, grief-maddened husband, and the people who, having been won to her cause over the long years, now cursed her name and called for her death. The priests and priestesses clustered together near the Old Henge, colourful damp blobs in the rainstorm, chanting and singing, swaying in a sickly rhythm that made her head spin and her stomach churn.

"I wish my heart would burst and this torment be over forever!" she suddenly screamed, and she threw herself forward, the hemp ropes of the simple harness biting into her bare flesh, burning like brands, cutting red channels. The world spun and she fell into the half-ploughed furrow, rain showering over her, churning the mud and the blood where the ropes had torn her flesh.

The crowd let out a terrible noise, a frenzied inhuman shriek, and they tried to surge forward once again. This time their intentions were clear; glassy-eyed, maddened by fear and superstition, they would tear her to pieces in the furrow and scatter parts of her body far and wide across the Great Plain in an attempt to restore the failing fertility of the soil of Prydn.

Hearing that awful, crazed cry, Ardhu suddenly seemed to come to himself, as if from a dream. He glanced at the roiling horde and a needle of fear pierced his heart. Not only Fynavir was in danger… they gazed on him with mad, accusing eyes too… the old king, the king whose power was waning, whose arm was growing weak. He abruptly dropped the handles of the plough and sprinted to Fynavir, drawing Carnwennan and slashing the ties that bound her.

The crowd broke free at the moment, one man rushing forward swinging a great club over his head. He shoved past Bal-ahn, who struck out at him with his axe, only to find his aim ruined as hysterical tribeswomen leapt up at him, biting and clawing, trying to pull him down, to rend him as they sought to rend Ardhu and Fynavir.

"Keep back... it is your King you threaten!" Ardhu warned in a great voice, reaching for Caladvolc's gold-pinned hilt.

The huge, wild-haired man staggered crazily on, showering mud, his eyes rolling and his club making whistling noises as it smote the storm-laden air. Per-Adur sprang into his path, thrusting at the man's throat with his dagger, seeking the great life-vein that stood out like a twisted pulsing rope. The attacker roared like a wild beast, and his club smashed into Per-Adur's arm and drove him backwards, his feet sliding in the churned-up mud. He tried to gain his footing, to reach his enemy's vital parts with his knife, but the wild man whirled the club again and with a crack it smashed into the side of his head. Silently he pitched face forward on the ground, his yellow hair reddened with blood, the left side of his face crumpled and ruined, the cheekbone and jaw shattered.

Ardhu reached for Fynavir, who lay floundering in the mud at his feet. Freezing brown ooze sucked at her smeared flesh, drawing her into its sombre heart, towards the Land of the Dead. Gasping, breath rattling, she lifted a pitiful, shaking hand to her husband. He hesitated for one moment, staring at her in her misery, then suddenly grasped her hand and pulled her free of the mud. Dragging her under his bearskin cloak, he held her tight against his left side so that his right arm was free to defend both her life and his own.

The berserker charged towards them, waving the club that was smeared with Per-Adur's blood. "Die... !" he cried. "I will loose your blood so that the Land will flourish once more and we will all live..."

"If you want blood to feed the earth, Man of the Tribe, let it be your own!"

A new voice rang out across the churned up field, making Ardhu whirl around in alarm. Squinting through the lash of the rain, he saw his son, Gal'havad, riding from the gates of Kham-El-Ard like the storm-wind, striking his steed with his heels to drive it on to greater speeds. He had the same strange, almost fearsome light in his face that Ardhu had seen in the East; the face of a man truly touched by the Ancestors, not quite in the world of mortal-kind. His red hair flamed upon the breeze; his eyes were the colour of the Otherworld and the grass that grows on dead men's barrows. Upon him he wore the true regalia of the princes of the West: golden tresses in his hair, beads of amber at his neck, sun-crosses on the buttons of his madder-red tunic. His Ar-moran dagger, Kos'garak, gift at his manhood ceremony, shone in his hand, hot and deadly, its blade thinner, longer and more piercingly sharp that those wrought in the Five Cantrevs.

Without a moment's hesitation he bore down on the berserker. The man raised his great club again, brandishing it in defiance, but Gal'havad behaved as though the weapon were a child's toy, a stick wielded by a petulant boy. Knocking the weapon aside, he forced his plunging mare straight at the man, his gaze riveted on the coarse red face, the mouth open like a dripping cavern. His arm shot out, his dagger shining, his blow straight and true, quicker than the lightning that came over the distant hills. Kos'garak bit the throat of his enemy and passed through flesh, sinew and bone in a crimson shower. The crazed man gurgled once and tumbled like a fallen stone into the furrow, lying amidst the mud, the worms and his own warm blood.

Gal'havad wheeled his horse around and faced his father. His breath came in ragged gasps, as if he was drawing in his slain foe's life force with every inhalation, and his dagger slewed off a shower of deep life's blood that struck Ardhu's lathered tunic.

"There has been enough bloodshed and unwholesome deeds for today," Gal'havad said chillily, and his voice held a certain authority that astonished and even frightened Ardhu. He knew he should have been angry—Gal'havad had been banished from the Hall after his first outbursts about Fynavir, and it was his intention that the boy not witness her ordeal, but he could not deny that Gal'havad's unexpected arrival may have saved both his life and hers.

The crowd was dispersing now, their wails and shouts becoming sobbing and low keening. Gal'havad edged his mount closer to his father and held out his arms. "Give her to me," he said.

It was not a request.

To his own surprise, Ardhu the Stone Lord complied, lifting the crumpled figure of Fynavir in his arms, mud and blood and streaking ash, and laid her over the front of Gal'havad's steed, across the young warrior's knees. Gal'havad steadied her limp body against his shoulder and covered her nakedness with his cloak, and then, without another glance at his father, he galloped back towards the black cone of Kham-El-Ard, the fortress of the Crooked Hill.

*****

Gal'havad came to his father's seat later than night. The warband had been sent from the Hall; outside, above the rumble of the storm, they could be heard drinking and carousing in the huts, while pipes skirled and drummers beat a strong tattoo that mingled with the thunder.

The Hall was dark, the fire nearly out. Ardhu sat in his chair, leaning back, feeling the ache in the leg that had been wounded so long ago, in the shadow of Mineth Beddun, the mountain of Graves. It was always so now, when the weather turned foul.

He peered through the smoky shadows at Gal'havad, still wearing his princely attire, although he had cleaned the blood from his arms and hands, even scrubbing his nails of any gore.

"You had been told to stay away until you were summoned," Ardhu said accusingly. "I swore I would not hurt her. You disobeyed me."

"I saved you," said Gal'havad softly, inclining his head.

124

Ardhu gave a deep sigh. "Aye, I cannot deny that. For that I am grateful." He stood, stepping up to the youth. "Sometimes I think you see things that I do not, Gal'havad, with your eyes that gaze into the spirit-world like a priest's. Even if you were disobedient I owe you for your actions this day... name what you desire of me, and it shall be given."

Gal'havad licked his lips and shifted uncomfortably. "My father, I ask that you admit my cousins Mordraed and Agravaen back into the Hall. They sought to help you when the Lord An'kelet's duplicity was exposed, and you have repaid their loyalty ill by driving them away. They should be rewarded, not punished! Both should be admitted to the warband as befits faithfulness and their rank as the sons of kings!"

Ardhu let out a long drawn breath. "Agravaen, he is stupid... but yes, I can see he would be loyal to me, and his arm is strong. But the other one, Mordraed... .you do not understand, Gal'havad."

"Do I not?" Gal'havad's fine brows rose. "Then maybe you should tell me, and not keep me in the dark! I know there is bad blood between you and his mother Morigau; maybe that should be put to rest at last."

Ardhu groaned and shook his head. "It can never be so."

Gal'havad folded his arms across his chest "You said you would grant me what I wish. That is what I wish—for Mordraed and Agravaen to join the war-band and have the rank in Kham-El-Ard that they deserve. If you do not trust Mordraed, you can trust me; I will keep watch over him and guide him if he goes astray. He will listen to me, I am sure of it... and I am sure he will serve you well; he is the best archer I have ever seen..." His voice rose and his eyes danced with delight; he sounded like a young child now, all enthusiasm for an older sibling or friend that he admired out of all proportion. "Together as kinsmen, I am sure we could accomplish so much, father! If we do quest to find the Maimed King's cup of gold, I am sure Mordraed will be a much-needed help on the long road."

Ardhu shook his head again, feeling suddenly old and drained. "You love this cousin from the North, don't you?"

"The spirits did not see fit to give me a brother to stand at my shoulder. They gave me Mordraed instead."

Ardhu went cold; he was glad the hall was dark so that Gal'havad could not see the sudden pallor of his cheeks. He longed to shout the truth, the terrible truth... but his tongue felt thick and heavy, and trembled like that of an old man shaken with palsy. There was nothing he could do or say that would not reveal the shamefulness of his past and condemn him. *He* should have been the one to pull the plough and heal the Land, not just Fynavir; he was as guilty as she.

"I will grant your wish," he said heavily. "Mordraed and Agravaen will be admitted back into the Hall and accepted into the warband. But if I get any scent of dissension or strife, they will both be cast out, not just from the Hall but from Kham-El-Ard itself."

Gal'havad bowed low; he was smiling, a happy youthful innocent smile that tore at Ardhu's very core. "Father, I swear you will have no cause to regret this day."

Gal'havad retreated from the Great Hall, feeling cheerful and light of heart. Almost immediately Mordraed appeared through the spray of the wind-driven rain and swooped on him like some dark bird of prey, drawing him into the lee of one of the round huts clustered around the dun. "What did he say?" he asked sharply, clutching Gal'havad's arm

"It is good news, cousin. His anger has abated. You—and Agravaen—are permitted to enter the Hall again... and he has said he will have you both amidst his chosen warriors. A time of great questing may be coming, you know, if the Stone Lord and the priests will it; what adventures we will have together, Mordraed!"

"What adventures indeed," Mordraed said dryly, his teeth a flash of white in the murk.

"And now we should go to our beds... it has been a hard and wearying day for all in Kham-El-Ard."

The red-haired youth looked suddenly drawn and he staggered slightly and leaned against the side of the hut; Mordraed wondered if he was about to have one of his fits and commune with the Otherworld. He hoped not; to witness such a vile event would be shameful and embarrassing. But luckily Gal'havad shook his head as if to clear it, then pulled himself upright and began to limp away. He paused after a few steps and glanced over his shoulder. "Are you not coming, Mordraed? Are you going to stand out in the rain all night?"

Mordraed drew up the hood of his sealskin cloak, which he had brought from Ynys Yrch and was sound protection from inclement weather. "I have an errand to run, dear cousin. Do not wait for me tonight, but look for me on the morrow."

He turned on his heel and stalked towards the gates. They were ready to be closed for the evening but the same simpleton he had spoken to weeks before was on guard, and he passed unchallenged. Like a shadow, he descended the ramparts and crossed the flooded field. Finding the riverbank, he followed the course of the Abona into the deep valley beyond, seeking out the hut of his mother Morigau.

CHAPTER TWELVE
THE LILY-MAID

An'kelet sprawled on his back amidst the growing greenery on the banks of Abona, staring with rapidly dimming eyes at the faded sky. The ground beneath him was soaked with river water and with his own blood. Around him river-reeds and lilies dipped and swayed in the breeze, as if bowing in honour of the passing of he who was once known as the greatest warrior in the West.

After Ardhu Pendraec had wounded him with Caladvolc, he had managed to stumble a few miles upstream from Kham-El-Ard and then bind his own wound, packing it with mosses and sap as he had been taught by his mother, the Priestess of the Lake in distant Ar-morah, Land of the Sea. However, as he tried to follow the river's course to safer lands where he could escape the Stone Lord's wrath, the wound started to go bad. Having lost his two famed daggers, Arondyt and Fragarak, when he had been taken prisoner by Mordraed and Agravaen, he had to quickly knap a blade of flint... with which he re-opened the wound to expel a stream of vile, reeking pus. Cleaning it till blood ran afresh, biting on a whittled tree branch against the excruciating pain, he began walking again, though fever burned in him, and the bleeding started once more, though at least the blood and the wound smelt clean.

Eventually, despite his great strength, blood loss and pain overcame him and he collapsed, expecting never to rise again. Gasping for breath, his lungs aching, he had turned his gaze on Bright Bhel, his face an umber ball trailing towards his rest below the Western horizon, and prayed for a quick death before the wolves and other scavenging animals smelt the scent of his blood and tore him to pieces.

But Bhel hid his bright Face behind a cloud, and An'kelet of Ar-morah did not die. He lay, staring up at the heavens as they changed from blue to gold to purple, his mind running over and over the folly of his life, the events that had led to this ignominious death on the riverbank. Fynavir... the White Phantom... he had known better than to touch her, to break oaths to both the spirits and to his King. A small bitter gasping laugh came from his peeling lips. But how could he have denied his own heart and not died anyway, just as bitter, just as destroyed in mind and body?

"Come, Hwynn, White One!" he groaned. "Take me away and be done with it! I wish no more to suffer the hurts of the world of mortal men!"

As he spoke he caught the sound of movement in the growing twilight, amidst the thick trees that grew along the riverbank. He tried to prop himself up on his elbow to see who was watching him. Maybe it was Hwynn himself, mounted on his horse of bones, his hair and his face and the blade he carried tongues of white heatless fire. If it was, he would welcome him in a strong embrace and draw in his cold breath that would still the heart forever...

Again, he heard a noise, the crack of a branch. Hwynn? No. Maybe a badger... maybe a brigand who was out to see if any rich pickings could be found on the fallen warrior in the forest. An'kelet flexed his fingers. Well, if any miscreant tried to rob him, he had just enough strength left to wring the bastard's neck and send his spirit shrieking into Ahn-un—the Not-World.

Ahead of him the bushes parted, showing dewdrops and sending up a flutter of moths. A figure stood in the shadows, bent forward, on tiptoes, almost like a frightened deer poised for flight. But it was no beast of the forest, nor was it skull-faced Hwynn.

It was a young girl.

She took another tentative step towards An'kelet and he could see her clearly now. She was tall for a woman and slim built, with long, straight, shining hair mixed between dark gold and leaf-brown. She wore a soft deerskin tunic belted with cord that was looped through a shale ring. The hem reached only just above the knee, leaving her long legs bare.

Slowly she approached and leaned over him, her hair falling forward like a stream of poured honey. Her face was a pure, sweet oval, her wide eyes a deep blue touched with violet... much like the twilight that even now cloaked the riverbank and all around it. She said nothing, and he wondered for a moment if he but dreamed; or if she was some sprite of the woodland or water, come to claim his life-essence for her own.

But then she spoke: "You are sore hurt! Can you hear me?"

He moved his mouth; suddenly his tongue felt tingly and he struggled to talk.

"Hush!" She knelt beside him. "You must not expend your strength. I will help you... if I can."

She reached to a bulging pouch fastened at her belt and opened it, revealing an array of herbs and seeds. "My mother was the village healer ere she died. She taught me her craft well... or so I am told."

An'kelet reached toward her, his shaking fingers, cold and numb, touching her arm, bronze from lots of sun and outdoor living. So different from Fynavir's snow-white flesh, the only other woman he had ever touched... Warm and alive... and he felt so cold, like the soil of the burial mound.

"Who... are... you?" he slurred.

"My name is Elian," she said. "I come here to pick the lilies every spring. The folk in the village where my father is chief call me the Lily Maid."

*****

Elian dragged An'kelet up river to a little grove of alder trees, where she had rigged a tent of hides for use as a shelter while she gathered her lilies and herbs from the forest. She had wanted to take him back to the small settlement where her father was chief, but he had begged her not to. He could not of course tell her why, but she had not questioned, just stoically grasped hold of his arms and pulled him along through the damp grasses. She was surprisingly strong for a woman, and he guessed she did much outdoors work and the tending of beasts, despite her father being a minor chief.

In the tent, she pulled away his sodden tunic, breath hissing through her teeth as she saw his wound.

"Is it bad?" he said.

"Bad enough, I will not lie. But I think, if the spirits will it, then you will live. I will clean the gash properly... but then I will have to sew it shut. Have you heard of that method of healing before?"

He nodded. "Yes, but I have never seen it done, and I have never taken such a deep wound before now. It sounds painful."

"It will be," she said with honesty. "But it is your best chance if you wish to recover."

He closed his eyes and lay back, face very drained and pale. "I am not certain that I do, lady."

"That is a wicked thought," she said, wiping at his wound with a large flat leaf. It brought immediate cooling to the tortured flesh. "You are not an old man yet. The gods would be angry if you willed yourself to an early death."

"You do not know what has befallen me, girl," he breathed, closing his eyes as she probed deeper into the gash and daubed unguents on the raw, torn flesh. "If you knew what an evil bastard I am, you would not lay your hand upon me."

Elian's lips pursed. "I do not know what has befallen you, but I can guess. I had a brother once, now dead. He fought with a local chieftain over some petty matter and died for his pigheadedness. If you are like other men, I imagine you too fought over some triviality."

An'kelet let out a bitter laugh, despite his pain. "It was hardly trivial, lady. But it was foolish, and the folly was mine. I betrayed my friend in the foulest manner... and left a helpless woman on her own, to face punishment and maybe worse."

Elian's eyes were fixed on An'kelet's injury. For some reason she did not want to hear of the stranger's 'folly'... or this woman he had left behind. "It is in the past now. The spirits have seen fit to let you live despite the ills you did. Now... I will give you something for the pain that you must face." Reaching to her bag, she drew out some willow bark. "Chew it," she ordered. "Suck the moisture from the bark. Old Saille the willow goddess sends a gift to soothe pain in her woody flesh."

An'kelet placed the shreds of bark into his mouth, then lay back as Elian took a long fine bone needle from her pack and threaded it with a thin strand of gut, the end of which she bit off with her teeth. "You must not move," she said. "You must stay completely still as I work."

"I will do my best." An'kelet closed his eyes.

Elian leaned over him and the needle entered his flesh. He bit his lips until they were ragged but made no outcry, no unnecessary movement as she darned his flesh, drawing the torn edges of his wound together. "You will have a scar," she said as she finished, "But I would not worry too much. You have a handsome enough face and every warrior has scars."

He was half-fainting with pain, but managed to utter a small, weak laugh. "I promise I will not worry about the scar, Elian."

She took her needle, cleaned it and wrapped it, then turned back to her patient. "I must go now. My father will be worried otherwise and I do not want him to come searching for me. He is very protective since my brother died. You do not want to be found, either... and..." her mouth quirked, "maybe I do not want them to find you. You are my secret, a gift brought to me by the Lady River. But tell me, what should I call you? There must be a name I can call you by, even if it is not your true one!"

He could barely think through the haze of pain and the weakness of his body. "Some have called me Longhand in the past. It was when I was a Spearman. But now..." He stared down at his hands, shaking faintly in the dimness. "You may as well call me Nohand, for I have not any weapons, not even one of my daggers."

"It will not always be so," Elian said firmly. "You shall be healed, Longhand, and will eventually take up arms and win back your honour."

He shook his head, his smile grim. She could not see it in the gloom. "No, my honour can never be regained. At least not in this land. But thank you for all your aid, Elian the Fair."

He heard the hiss of her breath between her teeth. "I will be back tomorrow, Longhand."

*****

Over the next few days An'kelet's condition worsened. Fever burned in him, and he knew not himself but raved and tossed on the ground. Elian knelt at his side in the little skin shelter, heating rocks on the fire to make the tent warmer. If he could sweat out the evil humours, there might be a chance for him. The girl scowled, shaking her head in despair. She did not understand why he sickened so. She had cleaned the wound well and treated it with the freshest plants; and even now, it did not stink of putrefaction, nor were its edges discoloured. It was as if bad spirits were at him, tormenting him, trying to drag him into the realm of Not-being. Well, by Bhel and the Everlasting Sky, those foul creatures would have a fight on their hands—if Elian daughter of Phelas of the tribe of Astolaht had anything to do with it!

Singing softly to herself to distract from the gravity of the situation, she went to the river and drew water into a big clay bowl. Taking it back into the shelter, she used a wad of dried moss to sponge down the feverish man, wiping beads of sweat from brow and body. It was frightening... not only was he hot, but his strength seemed to dwindle and his flesh with it, as if it was burning off in a fire that raged inside.

"You will not die, you will not die," Elian repeated over and over, as she held the moss sponge to his lips, squeezing it so that water dripped into his mouth. "But maybe..." She looked into his closed, pale face, the sweat standing out like jewels on his brow, "maybe the problem is that you do not wish to live. Well, if you stand on the dark edge, I will draw you back! Whatever you have done and to whom, one so fair of visage does not deserve an end such as this, surely!"

For several more days she tended him, staying awake all night least he should have need of her care. She had lied and told her father she would be gone for a few days to the distant home of the Ladies of the Lake, to worship at their women's hut and to learn more of herb craft and the like. It was her ambition to be the Holy Woman and healer of Astolaht, so Phelas thought nothing of her hasty departure—women's business was not for men to question—though he insisted she take a bow and quiver of arrows for protection. He had made certain that she knew how to protect herself since her eldest brother, Ro'chad, had died defending their livestock from cattle-raiders.

Elian had sworn not to sleep as long as she felt Longhand's life might be in danger. But on the fourth day weariness overcame her and she slumped on the floor next to the mound of skins where her patient lay, and she slept, curled into a tight ball beside him.

She awoke to the sound of the dawn chorus and, peering through the tent flap, saw the Moon was setting, a thin ghost sailing West through the trees. She cursed herself for her weakness; she should have stayed awake! Panicking, her eyes flicked to her patient, fearing the worst... she had been sound asleep for hours.

He was very still, very quiet. She could not hear the troubled breathing that had plagued him these past nights. *Oh no, what have I done!* she thought, reaching for his slack wrist... She found the beat of his life-force almost right away. His skin was cool, no more sweat washed over him; gazing at his face, she saw that, though pallid, he looked more relaxed. His breathing was slow, rhythmic.

A great joy welled up in her.

The stranger from the river would live.

*****

An'kelet recovered slowly. At first his legs would not hold him at all, and when he tried to rise he fell down again, almost taking the shelter of skins with him. Elian propped him up and helped him back onto the nest of skins she had made. "Too soon, friend Longhand," she said. "Recovery may take some time. I will bring you food and drink to cheer you and make you hale."

"I am shamed," he said, a shadow on his handsome though drained face. "You, a maid who is not my wife, must tend to my needs like a newborn babe. I cannot even piss by myself. That is shameful."

"It cannot be helped," she said. "And do not fear, Longhand, I live in a

131

house with no women, just my father and remaining brother, and I am not ignorant of what a man looks like."

He blushed furiously. Elian had to bite back a laugh; he was so much older than her, old enough to be her father, and yet he flushed like a young innocent lad at her joking words! She wondered where he had come from to have such strange manners and bearing; her father's age he might be but Phelas

was nothing like Longhand—he was a stout, balding man with wispy grey hair and a worried-looking face scored by years of wind and weather.

"I am sorry, Longhand," she said kindly. "I speak and do things plainly, which is how it has always been with women in my family. It is probably not the custom of your people for women to speak so freely of such things."

An'kelet dragged himself into a sitting position. "I feel filthy, having lain here for so long. Can you get me to the river?"

"Not yet... I fear its swell would be too strong and you would be dragged down to the bed of old River Mother! I would not let her have you after all my efforts to keep you in Tirr nambeo, the Land of the Living! A few more days... maybe a week... and hopefully you should be well enough to brave the cold waters. I will wash you as best I can in the meanwhile, if you do not mind."

He nodded, and she took out some soft wads of moss from her leather bag. Going outside she dipped them in the river then returned and began to slowly lave his skin, pushing aside the blood-stained and crusted tatters of his tunic. The palm of her hand came to rest on his chest, and she suddenly realised, as if for the first time, how strongly muscled he was despite the wasting of his illness. A warrior's physique... so different from the farmers and herdsmen of her small holding, short men who grew bow- legged and round-hipped from squatting round their fires. She also appreciated that, before his wounding, he had been well-fed... and she now suspected, of high status. She plucked a button from his ruined tunic and examined it in the dim light— although damaged and broken in two, it was a piece of jet with a rim of imported gold.. She had never seen the like; her mother had owned one bead covered in thin gold foil, but that was all. She stopped washing her patient, her hand still resting on his chest, and suddenly a shudder, half fear, half pleasure, shot through her and her face reddened to match his earlier. He noticed her hesitation and looked at her quizzically. She noted, as if for the first time, his eyes were almost an amber colour, warm and deep.

"I must do something about new clothing for you," She drew away. "This garb has grown rank and needs to be cast away—it will attract unwholesome spirits by its blood-smell. I will see what I can take from my village. I will need to be careful, though, lest I am questioned."

"Yes. No one must know. If you care for my life, my existence must remain secret."

"I do care for your life, Longhand." She gazed at him and suddenly her eyes were shadowed. She turned away abruptly, reaching for the flap of the tent. "I will return tomorrow. Rest well."

*****

She came back the next day, carrying a large spotted skin wrapped round her shoulders. She had taken it from Astolaht only after much harassment from her brother, who had stared suspiciously at her from over the rim of his beaker and asked why she was flitting back and forth from Astolaht like some piece of wind-blown marsh-gas. He wanted to know if she had a man, and was taking the skin so that she might lie with him on it. She had reddened to the roots of her hair, both angry and embarrassed, and smacked him in the face with her balled hand, making him bellow with anger, and then they had both railed at each other and tumbled in the grass outside their father's hut. It was only Phelas threatening to beat them both that made them spring apart and stand, breathing heavily, giving each other poisonous glares.

"And what *are* you doing with that skin, daughter?" Phelas had glowered at the dishevelled girl, her kirtle torn and hanging from one shoulder. "You have not been home much of late; you have been flying back and forth with scarce a word for your kin…"

"As I said!" snapped Tirre, his eyes flashing. "A lover!"

Chief Phelas swung his fist and struck Tirre, shocking him into silence.

"I told you," said Elian. "I have made a pilgrimage to the Ladies of the Lake. They have instructed me how to become one with the air we breathe, the earth we stand upon, the water of Mother Abona. And in order to accomplish that, I must have space to find peace, to enter the spirit world… and not be bothered by oafs such as Tirre!"

Phelas sighed, looking at his daughter with her gleaming oval face, honey hair and sun-bronzed skin. She was too old to be unwed, he knew that… but she was all he had left of her mother, whose marriage to him had been a love-match, and he did not want to part with her as yet. "I do not know if I believe you or not," he grumbled. "But whatever it is you do, daughter, take care. You are more precious to me than the sun-metal gold."

"You need have no fear," she had said, but she found her eyes darting away from his face, full of guilt. Throwing the deerskin over her shoulder, she had run into the dappled forest and not looked back.

But now she was here, back in her little shelter with Longhand, and was using her needles and gut strings to sew him a simple long tunic out of the deerhide. Carefully she scratched the hair away with her flint scraper, wanting to show him that she had some skill. She could have done better, making him both close-fitting trousers and a shorter, fitted shirt, but she did not dare be so familiar as to measure his frame with her hands. She hoped he would not mind her poor efforts.

He watched as she sewed, silent as he lay on his bed of furs. She noted his colour had all but returned and there was new life in his eyes and a renewed lustre to his hair. It fell in loose waves over his shoulders, rich amber to

133

match his eyes. She had not shaved him while he was ill, even though it had obviously been his custom, for she had feared she might cut him as he tossed in his sickness, and now there was red-gold upon his chin and round his lips. A lord of bronze and gold, born of the river and the sun.

Elian bit her lower lip and glanced down at the skin in her lap, sewing furiously. Why was she thinking such things? He was a stranger, she did not even know his true name, and he was old... for all that he still held the power of youth in his arms. He would get well, and then he would go...

Elian the Lily-Maid realised with sudden awful knowledge that she did not want the stranger to leave. She wanted him to stay, and be with her. She was not as the other girls in her village, already dandling babes round their fires; and he was not like the men of her clan. Whatever evil he claimed he had done mattered not one bit to Elian of Astolaht.

Longhand sat up, stretching out his legs in his old, cracking trews, stiff with dirt. "I thank you for your efforts, Elian. Do you think it possible I might enter the river today and wash the dirt from me, now that you have made new clothes? I feel stronger by the day. I do not think the river can take me."

"Yes... yes, I think so..." Her voice was scarcely more than a whisper. "But I must come with you, in case you fall."

They went down to the river and Elian sat upon the bank amidst the tufted grass. The wind was blowing and the lilies she loved to gather nodded their heads. Bits of blossom off the trees blew in white showers and curled on the river's swell.

Unselfconsciously, but with his back to her, An'kelet slipped into the cold Abona, releasing a little gasp as its coldness bit into him. Gingerly, he removed the torn and blood-smeared shirt and then the scored trousers, letting them drift away as an offering to the spirits who ruled the watery places, to Mother Abona, the Great Cleanser, and her consort, Borvoh the Boiler, churning and twisting in the weirs. He was reminded of his initiation at the temple of Khor Ghor so long ago, where the Merlin had dunked him in Abona's swell, purifying him before he took his oaths in the Throne of Kings before the Stone of Adoration and Ardhu Pendraec, the Stone Lord of Prydn. Oaths he had broken... His mind cast back to another river, dark under a midnight sky hard with stars like the inside of a broken bluestone pillar, where he had first betrayed his king and lay with the White Woman, Fynavir of Ibherna, Ardhu's chosen Queen.

The pain of the loss of both Fynavir and Ardhu, his friend since youth, was like a sharp twisting knife inside him, and he stumbled on stones in the riverbed. Buffeted by the waves, his knees gave way, threatening to throw him down to be swept to oblivion, to eternal forgetfulness. Elian gave a little cry and ran out into the water to steady him, and suddenly she found her arms around him, tall and golden bronze and naked, like some god of the Sun come to earth... even if that god was growing weary and faded, passing towards winter.

He stared down at her, her honey hair in damp coils against his chest, her tunic, wet from the river, clinging to her lithe young body. Suddenly he felt something he had not expected to ever feel again—the stirrings of desire. Until now, such sensations had been reserved for Fynavir, and guilt had accompanied them... guilt for the breaking of his oaths to both his priestess mother in Ar-morah and to Ardhu. Now those oaths were long gone, no longer binding him before man and spirits... he owed no loyalty to Priestess Ailin, on her Lake Isle where men died every nineteen turnings of the Sun, nor did he owe allegiance to the Stone Lord, who had cast him from Kham-El-Ard to die. He was going to live instead, though, by the art of this fair-faced girl who clung to him as if they were already lovers. She could heal him in more ways than she knew, freeing him from the ties that had bound him for so long... In the back of his mind he knew that this sudden rush of lust was not right, not in his state of mind and not as an outlawed man who must soon, now that his wound was healing, flee these lands before he was tracked down by Ardhu's men. To take her and then leave was against the honour he had always lived by, instilled in him by the virgin Lake Maidens in his mother's domain... but by the spirits, he wanted nothing more than to cast her on her back and quench the memories of all he had lost in soft yielding flesh.

Elian glanced up at him expectantly, her eyes wide and the pupils dilated, her mouth parted and breathing ragged, and he knew then that she felt what he felt too. She had not come there that day to nurse him; she wanted his body as much as he desired hers. Grabbing her shoulders he pushed her back towards the shore, ungentle in his urgency, rougher than he would normally have been with Fynavir. Reaching dry land, he swung her up into his arms and entered the shelter where she had tended him.

He dropped her onto the furs on the ground, hardly noticing how heavily she fell, and that her eyes had darkened, not with desire, but a hint of fear. Kneeling over her, he yanked the ties on her wet tunic, peeling it away from her body. He caressed and fondled her, none too gently, making Elian utter a small cry, though he did not know whether with pleasure or pain.

"Longhand," she managed to gasp, grasping at his bare shoulders, almost holding him off. "Please... I have not been with any man before."

He scarcely heard her but ran his hand up the inside of her soft thigh. She flinched. He could not wait, did not want to. Pushing her thighs farther apart, he lifted her slim hips and flung himself on top of her. She flinched again, more strongly and bit her lip, and suddenly he saw a tear of pain run down her cheek. A pang of guilt struck him and he wiped the tear with his hand, but then the need of his body overcame him, and he took his pleasure with little thought of hers. She cried out now, and he knew it was not with pleasure, and he pressed his hand over her lips so he would not hear. She writhed under him, suddenly frightened, as if fearing he would suffocate her.

Suddenly, it was all over, and with that rush of release, terrible shame flooded over him. "O gods, what have I done!" He dropped his hand from her mouth.

Hastily he rolled away from her. She lay on the furs like a frightened animal, breath coming in huge gasps, skin smeared with dirt and his sweat. Her knees were hugged to her chest, her eyes wide and fearful, and the whites too big.

"I told you I was tainted!" he shouted, loathing in his voice. "You should have kept well away and left me to die! I was meant to die... it was decreed so by Ardhu Pendraec!"

She struggled up, covering herself with her arms. "The Stone Lord? Why... what was he to you?"

"He is the one I betrayed! I took his woman to my bed, even as I took you. The Queen... the White Phantom. The one woman I should never have touched."

A look of horror crossed her smudged and tear-streaked face. Rumour had come down the Great River of the wrath of Ardhu at finding his wife unfaithful, and how he had punished her by sending her into the fields to pull the plough like a beast. "Who are you? What is your name?" She had half-guessed his identity already, but needed to hear the truth from his own lips.

He stood up, dirt-smeared, his hair a tangle of copper and leaves. "I am An'kelet, prince of Ar-morah, son of the priestess Ailin and King Bhan... once wielder of the spear called Balugaisa, once esteemed companion of the circle of Khor Ghor. Now I am an outlaw, bereft of all honour, a liar, a thief and a defiler of women."

She dragged one of the skins around her and rose to stand beside him. She was shaking, her teeth chattering. "This can be made well, just as your body was made well. You can come to my father's village with me... I will hide you. My father will be angered when he finds out we have been together, but when he knows it is my choice, he will come round and help you."

He glanced sideways at her and shook his head. "No. It cannot be. I will not hide away in any village till I am hunted down like a beast... and bring Ardhu's wrath down on your people. I will go this very day... back to Ar-morah, across the Narrow Sea." He strode from the tent, picking up the tunic she had made for him and yanking it on, before pulling on his worn calfskin boots with their felt inserts. "I thank you for the kind gift of this garment... and..." he stared down, fiddling with the belt, adjusting it to fit his dwindled waistline, "and for all else you have given me."

Elian scrambled from the tent, dropping the fur in her haste. "No... *no!*" her voice was a moan of torment. "Do not leave... not like this... not now, I beg you. I... I cannot face returning home full of shame. Oh, I have been such a fool... a fool! I beg you not to abandon me... I ... Over the days I tended you, I have come to love you, An'kelet of Ar-morah!"

"You will survive your wound of the heart, as I have survived wounds of both heart and flesh, lady," he said softly. Reaching forward he gently embraced her and kissed her bruised mouth—as a lover this time, rather than a ravisher. "You are fair to behold; any man would be glad to share your hut. But it cannot be me. I must go from Albu the White or spend all my life a fugitive."

"Then take me with you," she whispered.

"I cannot. I will not lie to you... my heart will always be with Fynavir, wife of Ardhu. That is the doom the Spirits have laid on me. You deserve more than to be second best."

He released her and began to stride purposefully down the riverbank, into the trees. "Don't leave me!" she shrieked at his back, falling to her knees. "I cannot bear it! I will not live with the shame you have brought to me! You have used me and now you abandon me... you may as well have put a dagger through my heart! You have killed me, An'kelet of Ar-morah!"

An'kelet broke into a run. He did not glance back. He vanished into the woodland as the rain began to fall, a thin, drizzly, drenching mist.

Elian the Lily-Maid of Astolaht tumbled to the ground like a sapling struck by lightning and lay unmoving, white and cold on the banks of Abona, with the rain washing her flesh as if seeking to rinse away the sorrow and the bitter truth.

CHAPTER THIRTEEN
OATH TAKING

Rain poured down out of a leaden sky, a solid sheet of water that slapped the stout timbers of Kham-El-Ard. Solstice was nearly upon the people of the Plain and the Place-of-Light but it was hard to believe it was summer. A chill hung in the air and the crops were dying where they grew, black rot speckling their roots. The fields were swamps, though the hills and hollows looked greener and more fecund than ever, but man could not live upon grass like a beast.

Ardhu Pendraec stood on the walls of his hilltop dun, staring at the winding, widened curve of the river, with the trees beyond sinking into mist-caps and the distant rises cloaked with helms of grey cloud. Despite the punishment of Fynavir and his own offerings to the spirits at Khor Ghor, nothing had improved in Prydn, neither with the weather nor with the actions of men. For the first time in many years a rumour came of a raiding party down on the south coast; dark-bearded men in sky-blue cloaks, seeking tin and copper and bronze, but with sword-blades rather than through legitimate trade. In the East, rumour had it, men raided cattle and women as they did in the days of their forebears, and rough brigands overthrew lawful chiefs and set themselves up as petty kings. And from the Middle-lands up as high as Peakland where the henge of Ar-bar stood on a limestone plateau, there were reports of a plague that killed men, women and children within a day. Pyres burned day and night on the Peaks and the air was black with the greasy smoke of the crematorium.

Ardhu frowned, his fingers twitching round the cold hilt of Caladvolc. Despite having broken An'kelet's influence and casting him forth to die, despite the atonements he had made to the spirits—sacrifices, prayers, fasts and dances, Fynavir had not quickened again. She was quiet in his presence and did not deny any demand he made upon her, and her shorn hair had grown swiftly and now lay on her shoulders like a boy's, but she had grown thin, the flesh burned from her with sorrow, and she did not ever laugh or smile, not even when Gal'havad came to visit her, holding her hands and speaking gently to her.

Ardhu knew there was only one thing left to do... follow what the Maimed King had suggested ere he gave himself up for the ruined Land. The Quest. The Quest for the Chalice of Gold, the beaker of Plenty, that had been taken by its makers and protectors back over the sea to the isle of Ibherna. He had lived long enough and seen enough to question in his heart whether the gods cared enough about men to place great powers in a thing wrought by mortal hands... but he knew others believed in its power, and, perhaps, that gave it the greatest magic of all. Its finding would be a token that he, as King, could still bring prosperity to Prydn, that age had not weakened his hand or his skill, and that the Cup of Gold could be the Cup of Plenty and the wheat sway in sun-burnished fields the next year.

And if it did not work, and the rains still came... he shivered and his blood felt as ice in his veins.

No, it *must* work, and he would announce the departure of the warband on an Imram, a Great Journey, as soon as possible. He would send messengers ahead to the ship wrights of Ynys Mhon, who would be well paid—with gold—to make two long, seaworthy boats in the style of continental craft that would hold twenty warriors and their weapons. From those rocky shores, dotted with the tombs of the Ancestors, his warband would fare to Ibherna where the Cup lay hidden in the Hollow Hills of the people who dwelt there.

But first the warband must be readied and new warriors sworn in at Khor Ghor. Replacements for An'kelet and for Per-Adur, whose head-wound caused him dizziness and ringing in the ears, and for Ka'hai who these days preferred to order the stores of Ardhu's household to fighting. Gal'havad would have his official Coming of Age ceremony before the Stone of Adoration, as befitted the Prince of the West... and also, as Ardhu had promised, Agravaen and Mordraed would take oaths as loyal warriors of the warband.

The Stone Lord's eyes narrowed slightly. Since the unhappy homecoming from the East and the banishment of An'kelet, Agravaen and Mordraed had worked hard to keep a place of respect in Kham-El-Ard. No ill word had come from any quarter regarding either of them... and yet Ardhu still felt uneasy. Not of Agravaen, guileless and eager to please, dreaming of glory. But Mordraed, always Mordraed, with his beautiful but closed face, and that slightly sardonic manner that none could fault yet none could trust. Yet he had done no wrong and Gal'havad was by his side most days, just like any adoring younger brother.

Of course, that is what he is, Ardhu thought, with a sudden stab of guilt. Does Mordraed know? Has Morigau told him the truth?

He prayed to Bhel and all the spirits of Earth and Sky that Gal'havad would never learn his father's darkest, most shameful secret.

*****

The Rites of the New Warriors began shortly before dusk on the Night of the New Moon. The rain had eased a bit, and clouds scudded across the vault of heaven, flickers of flame as the dying sun caught their underbellies. Up the Avenue came a stream of celebrants carrying burning brands, the men on the right side of the bank and the women dancing down the left. They lined up near Heulstone, the Stone of Summer, before turning to gaze down into the valley bottom, where the initiates were being brought up from the river Abona by the priests of Deroweth.

The three youths were guided past the Stone of Summer. They walked sun-wise around its grey bulk while the priests chanted and bowed and laid down offerings of dried wheat, little sheaves that tore apart on the rain-sweet wind.

They were then led into the heart of the circle past the Old Man and the Mother Stone, the two foremost bluestones, and the priests gave them beakers of mead to smash at the Stones' feet and burnt oat cakes to leave so that the spirits could sup as they pleased.

Upon reaching the Stone of Adoration, its greenish flanks glittering dully in the cooling light, the priest Gluinval, who performed the necessary rites for all religious matters in the Merlin's stead, squeezed through the narrow gap of the Great Trilithon, Portal of Ghosts, wearing a headdress with the bleached antlers and skull of a deer dead for nearly a millennium, and a robe painted with solar and lunar symbols of the Everlasting Sky. He raised a red-painted rattle and shook it, making a thunderous noise that bounced around the five inner Trilithons.

One of his acolytes lifted a perforated cow's horn and blew upon it, making a mournful noise that echoed alongside the din of the rattle. At that moment, Ardhu Pendraec stepped out from behind the mighty southern trilithon the Throne of Kings, with its inlaid carvings of daggers and axes. He wore a long woollen robe dyed with great art to match the colour of the sky, the colour of the holy ancestral bluestones, and on his breast gleamed the golden lozenge that proclaimed his kingship. He wore no helmet, for this was not a place of battle, but a thin band of bronze held the greying dark wings of hair away from his forehead. Blue beads dropped from the ends of his shoulder-length hair. In his hand he held the unsheathed Caladvolc, sword of bitter edge, undefeated in battle.

He gestured with his free hand for Agravaen to approach. The youth, his hair twisted into a knot on the side of his broad skull and blue paint running in zigzags across his eyes, lumbered toward his uncle, sweat beading on his brow in nervousness. "Agravaen son of Loth of Ynys Yrch, do you come here before the Ancestors to serve the Stone Lord of Prydn?" Ardhu asked, his voice sounding almost not his own in that sacred, enclosed space.

"I do, Stone Lord." Agravaen knelt on the packed chalk, and leaned forward to kiss the damp ground, the bones of the earth, as was customary. His flat, unappealing face came up white. "I will serve until my axe breaks and my dagger shatters and the breath goes forth from my body and my spirit flies over the Great Plain..." he mumbled the ritual words.

Mordraed watched him, lips compressed into thin lines. He knew his younger brother meant every word. It was embarrassing to watch him grovel and look up at Ardhu Pendraec with the eyes of a soft seal pup... but what else could one expect of a dolt such as Agravaen?

By the Throne of Kings, Ardhu touched the blade of Caladvolc to Agravaen's brow and then his heavily muscled shoulder. "You oath is accepted before your chief and your Gods. You, Agravaen son of Loth, shall join the warband of Ardhu Pendraec in this Round, this Dance of Great Ones."

Agravaen clumsily clambered to his feet and was escorted by priests to the Stones known as the Three Watchers, where he was given a ritual libation of fermented milk.

Ardhu and Mordraed stood looking at each other across the circle, silent, unsmiling. Gluinval made a hissing noise behind his antlered mask and suddenly downed his rattle. The air seemed to crackle between older man and youth; their gazes sparred, though neither spoke a word, and both wore expressions that were deceptively bland and calm. Ardhu was resplendent in his royal robes, the last beams of sunlight tracing the geometric patterns on the breastplate of Heaven... but Mordraed, standing before him, surely seemed his equal in that moment, almost a dark twin... but younger, the upcoming challenger, the future whether good or ill. Of similar height to Ardhu, his bare arms, wrapped in golden coils, were strong with the power of youth and his black hair fell in shining waves down his back, twined with feathers white and dark. His face was that of one of the Everliving Ones, too still, too perfect... almost pretty but yet with an edge hard as a sword blade.

"Come here, Mordraed." Ardhu's voice was a harsh rasp. He did not speak the usual formal words, but it made no difference.

Mordraed walked forward, gait stiff. He bowed before Ardhu and then, as Agravaen had done, knelt and kissed the earth. He made sure, though that his face remained clean; he would not root on the ground like a pig, as his brother had done. He spoke the ritual words, clearly; his voice as pleasing as his face and form.

Ardhu approached him with Caladvolc; the older man's hand shook slightly. Mordraed noticed it instantly and suppressed a mocking smile.

Ardhu touched the point to Mordraed's brow and then to his shoulder, as was customary... but suddenly he whipped it aside and pressed the blade's lethal tip against the base of Mordraed's throat. "You will be in my warband, and you will fight at the side of my son, Gal'havad." He emphasised the 'my son,' "And if you betray me—or—him... by the Ancestors I will take this blade and give you to the Stones. Do not suppose that... because we share... blood... ... I would not do it."

Mordraed's eyes blazed; people outside the circle and the priests were craning their heads, wondering why he had not been released from the Circle to join Agravaen at the Three Watchers. "I know exactly what you would do, lord," he said, rather impudently. "It is what any king would do if faced by betrayal." *As I would surely do to you, the biggest traitor of all—to the laws of our people and to your sister and your eldest-born son!*

"So, once again, we understand each other."

"I have always understood, my uncle."

"Good. Now stand beside me and await the coming of Gal'havad, your kinsman and my heir. I want you to swear not only to me, but to him."

Mordraed's expression became one of confusion; he had not anticipated being asked to perform such an act. "This is highly unorthodox," he spat, his eyes seeking Gluinval, as if hoping for intervention from the priest.

"Maybe it is," said Ardhu firmly, "but it is what I wish."

Gluinval began to move again, as if released of some spell. The rattle whirred, and Gal'havad came forward from his waiting place behind the outer ring of bluestones. On the journey up the Avenue from Kham-El-Ard he had worn a dark fur cloak and cloth hood which had stood in stark contrast to the high status warrior's garb of the other two youths, but now he had shed them and he stood forth clad as the Son of the Terrible Head, the Prince of Evening, Gal'havad the Hawk of Summer. He wore a long woven robe made by his aunt Mhor-gan of the Korrig-han; it was fringed with strands of glowing bronze and an inlaid chevron pattern ran around the hem. The colour of the robe was like nothing Mordraed or indeed Ardhu had ever seen on textiles before; a rich purple, the colour of the dying day, similar to the hue of the sacred cup Gal'havad carried as a talisman. Indeed, the dye used to get the colour had come from scraping the sides of similar stones within the Holy Pool below Kham-El-Ard—all carefully harvested by Mhor-gan and her mistress, Nin-Aeifa, Lady of the Lake. Besides the robe, he wore an archer's wristguard of greenstone studded with golden pins, and a vast crescentic necklace of amber beads. He also bore a new ornament, a gift from Ardhu upon this special day—a black jet lozenge, identical in design to the Breastplate of Heaven, a token of the symbols of kingship he would one day inherit.

He strode up to the Stone of Adoration and suddenly a shaft of light, the last of the day, streaked through the arch of the western trilithon, the Gate of the Guardian, and pierced the sanctity of the great circle. Stones turned green-gold then golden-pink; Gal'havad's auburn hair ignited, a stream of fire upon his shoulders; while his high pale forehead, struck by that glorious ray as it speared the gathered clouds of dusk, seemed to burn with an unearthly flame.

Ardhu stared in wonder, and Mordraed felt his belly give a queasy jolt. Gal'havad seemed more than just a youth of noble lineage come to take his vows within Khor Ghor. He looked like a priest-king, one who would mediate between the gods and men but who also had the authority to rule. Mordraed frowned, a twisting serpent of jealousy rising in him; he wondered if he, even with his years of practice, could keep the expression of hatred and envy from his face. But it was not just envy... a frisson of fear shot through him at the same time. What if Gal'havad prevailed against him, loved as he was by the spirits of this grim circle? He stared around at the Sun-touched Stones towering overhead ... by the Moon, he wanted to see those huge sarsens fall, shattered on the ground...

A moment later the clouds bunched and the light-beam failed. The Stones descended into darkness, turning slatey then a sullen blue. Cold shadows fell over Gal'havad, extinguishing the light in his face and the fire of his hair. Mordraed smiled to himself, coldly; yes, that is how it should be and would be... the light of this touched and tainted youth diminished, cut off. Forever, when Mordraed found the right moment to remove his rival and claim the inheritance that was rightfully his.

Ardhu gestured to Gal'havad and his son went to him, walking three times around the Stone of Adoration and then laying his hand upon the inlaid golden dagger on Throne of Kings. The Terrible Head spoke to the youth of the Land and of duty, and the sacred responsibilities that came with being the Stone Lord of Prydn. Watching, Mordraed stifled a yawn; these pretty speeches seemed nothing but meaningless babble to him. A waste of time. For Gal'havad would never rule after Ardhu. Never.

Suddenly he felt Ardhu's sharp hazel eyes upon him. He jerked back into total alertness, schooling his face to look serious and sincere. Ardhu held out a hand toward him. "Remember what we spoke of, Mordraed Sister's Son," he said softly. "It is time for you to swear to the Prince Gal'havad, that he may have a faithful and loyal protector and servant."

Gal'havad's expression was one of surprise, but also of warm gladness. Mordraed came before him and knelt in a way he hoped would seem humble, and took his hands in his own. "I swear," he said, his voice barely above a whisper, "to serve you and be at your side, as if you were my brother..." His lips curled slightly, hidden by the raven-wing fall of his hair.

"Swear..." Ardhu loomed over Mordraed, vaguely threatening, his fingers playing with the hilt of Carnwennan, his dagger. "Swear that you will bring him no harm. Swear by the Everlasting Sky."

Mordraed writhed in irritation. "I swear..." he suddenly raised his voice, glad to see the black birds that nested in the Stones fly in fright at the unexpected sound, "that I will never raise blade in anger against my kinsman and my prince, the Lord Gal'havad of Kham-El-Ard. And if I should in madness and folly commit such a base act, may the Everlasting Sky fall upon my head and my bones remain unbarrowed for eternity." *I may speak the words you crave, father, but how can such an oath be binding when you have forced it upon me? And my mind is quicker than yours... there are many other ways to rid oneself of troublesome kin besides daggers and axes...*

Ardhu grunted and gestured that he might rise. Mordraed got up, and Gal'havad embraced him, giving him the kiss of peace on either cheek. "I am so glad you have sworn your loyalty to me, Mordraed, my dearest cousin. You will be as high in my esteem as An'kelet was to my father... before... before..." He abruptly bit his lips and glanced down, realising that he had spoken rashly.

Ardhu appeared not to have noticed. "Let us go forth and let the people of Kham-El-Ard and the Place-of-Light see their Prince. Then we must make ready for a great *Imram,* a great journey...to find the Golden Cup that lies across the sea in Ibherna."

143

CHAPTER FOURTEEN
TRIPLE DEATH

Ardhu sent messengers to the far west the next day. Boats would be built, sturdy enough to carry his war-party to Ibherna's shores. Gold he sent with the horsemen, as payment to the shipwrights, who lived on the headland on the tip of Mhon, and also to the priests of the Shrine of the Dark Grove, for their prayers in seeing Ardhu's men across the treacherous waters that separated the sister isles.

Then he called his men to his Hall and chose those who would be his companions—chief amongst them being Bohrs, Hwalchmai, Betu'or, Ba-lin, Bal-ahn, Mordraed and Gal'havad. "Go to your women and your families and make your farewells," he said sternly. "We will not linger long, but will leave at first light tomorrow. We will go for blessings at the Crossroads of the World, then hasten to the shores of Mhon, where we may depart Prydn if the seas are calm enough. If they are not, we will wait and sacrifice a horse to the waves. Bring your talismans, and bring your sharpest blades, your most doughty axes. We dwell in dark times, when even the Sun is not so mighty as he used to be... Let us show the people of this land, this holy isle of Prydn, that still their King fights for them, that he is still strong and one with the Land itself and will bring its flourishment once more!"

He finished his speech to great cheers, and men began to beat drums and dance, while others ran about packing provisions and attending to the horses of the warband.

Mordraed walked with Gal'havad through the heaving throng. "Are you excited, cousin?" asked Gal'havad. Little children were clustered around him, trying to touch his purple robe for luck. "To go out into the world and see the great and magical things that lie beyond?"

"Very excited," said Mordraed dryly, not meeting his eyes.

"I must say farewell to my mother." Gal'havad sighed. "She seldom smiles or even weeps these days... but I know, beneath her ice, the pain is raw, and that she would not have me leave."

"I have a woman to see as well," said Mordraed. "Do not expect me back in Kham-El-Ard before our leave-taking at dawn."

Gal'havad glanced at him, brows lifting in surprise. "What is this, Mordraed? You have not told me of any woman!"

"I do not tell you everything, little cousin," said Mordraed mockingly. "And do not ask me... I will not share her with you!"

He turned and left before Gal'havad could ask any more questions, striding through the open gates, and down the hillside towards the shining band of Abona without a backwards glance. Pressing forward without delay, he soon reached Morigau's hovel, its roof even more unkempt than he remembered and its door-frame leaning at an awkward angle. The oracular pig in its pen lifted its ugly porcine head and grunted at the sight of him.

Hearing the snorts and squeals of the pig, Morigau stuck her head out of the doorway. When she saw the arrival was her son, she ran forward with a glad cry. "Again... it has been too long, Mordraed. How fares my boy?"

"Well enough," he answered. "Tomorrow Ardhu's warband, of which I am now a sworn member, sets out for Ibherna, on some fool's chase to find a Golden Cup."

"A cup?"

"Yes. Ardhu believes it will bring hope and goodness back to the Land. The fool."

Morigau's thin but strong arms wrapped round Mordraed, drawing him against her lean, wiry body. He tried not to flinch in revulsion as she stroked his back with her long-nailed hands. "There is only one way to restore the failing of Prydn," she whispered her breath hot against his ear. "A new king, young and virile and beautiful. You, my Mordraed."

"I will be ready for it when that time comes," he said.

"It will be soon." Her deep eyes misted, seeing into Otherness. "There is change... in the air about us, in the water that flows, in the earth in which we barrow our dead. An old king will die, another one will come to replace him."

"I will need your help," he said. "I have sworn an oath to raise no hand against Ardhu's heir, Gal'havad. And yet I must. I know it is weak of me to even question what I must do, but an oath is powerful..."

"Any oath sworn to Ardhu is not valid... he who is no rightful king, who broke the greatest of taboos..."

Mordraed glanced at her, amused since she also had committed the sin of which she accused her brother... and he was the fruit of that folly. She appeared not to notice.

"But if it troubles you, there are other ways. I can make poisons that could fell a hundred strong men! Use such a draught to kill the boy and you would not be forsworn; you would have raised no hand against Ardhu's heir."

Mordraed rubbed his chin thoughtfully. "It could work. No marks and no trace. What brew can you give me that will do the deed but with little outward sign?"

"Come with me, Mordraed."

She took him into her hut. It was a little less rank than he remembered but still close and smelly; Ack-olon was cleaning a skin by the sputtering hearth while La'morak chewed on a piece of meat in the corner. Khyloq was stirring a pot full of some revolting gruel, her face smeared with ash and grease and her expression one of bored annoyance. As she saw him, her green eyes flickered in the thin oval of her face. After the initial awkwardness of their forced marriage, she had swiftly warmed to him, perhaps seeing him as her

145

protector from the excesses of Morigau and her two warriors. Any shyness gone after the first clumsy night, she was eager to please him every time he visited, dragging him out behind the hut and down to a secluded spot down by the river, where she would lift her ragged skirts for him.

"Mordraed, you have come…" She dropped her ladle and stroked his arm with her grubby work-worn fingers.

He shook her off. "A moment, woman," he ordered, his gaze fixed on Morigau. "I must attend to more important things than you."

Morigau was prying amidst clay vials and pots lined against the wall. She sniffed at some and eventually brought up a little urn stoppered with blue clay. "This one," she said with satisfaction. "Mixed in a drink it will not smell and will have little taste. It is fast and it is deadly."

Mordraed took the urn and carefully tucked it into his belt pouch. "That is what I need. May it work as well as you claim."

"I am mistress of the art of creating poisons," she said. "What do think happened to Loth of Ynys Yrch? Do not doubt me… I, who, through my gods-given craft, shall be mother and priestess to the new King of Prydn before this year is gone!"

"I do not doubt you—I would be afraid to, mother! Now, I will say you farewell—until this quest of Ardhu's is over. Listen to word brought down the great Ridgeways, that you will know when to expect me home."

She clutched him to her, kissing his mouth in a way that was not altogether seemly, as Ack-olon and La'morak sneered in frustration. Pulling away from her, he grasped Khyloq's grimy wrist and led her from the hovel and away down the hillside to their usual spot. She undid the ties on her scruffy brown kirtle but he seemed distracted and did not look at her. "Go take a bath, girl," he said. "You smell of the pig."

She quickly ran down to the river, then returned dripping wet and wrapped herself around him, shivering in the cold. He still seemed barely interested; he kept reaching to the pouch at his waist, fingering the small urn tucked inside that carried death. "Mordraed, won't you touch me?" she breathed in his ear. "I have missed you, though I know you have many things to think of. Killing people… becoming King… doing what your mother says…" She spoke the last words with a hint of jealousy and spite.

Mordraed swung round on her, grabbing her long water-darkened red hair. "Do not speak of Morigau like that! Who do you think you are?"

She tried to tear herself away but he dragged her closer. Rather than looking fearful, however, she looked rebellious. He liked this expression far better than when she appeared meek and cowed. He felt the stirring of desire.

"I know who I am," she panted, standing with her hands on his shoulders, almost as if pushing him away—except that she was in fact leaning towards him, her white skin dappled with shadows, smelling of river water and the woodlands. "I am Khyloq, daughter of a noble chieftain and of good blood… and I am wife to Mordraed son of Ardhu son of U'thyr Pendraec the Terrible

Head. When he is King of Kham-El-Ard and all of Prydn, I shall sit beside him as his best woman, for even if he must wed the White Woman as Morigau claims, I will be the one to bear him sons. Sons that will rule Prydn after him"

She suddenly snatched his hand and pressed it to her bare stomach. "Stupid man! Do you not notice that my belly has grown? Already you have put a bairn inside me. The Ancestors have smiled on our union"

His jaw dropped. "Why did you not say something sooner?"

She flicked back her fiery mane. "I would not tell of it before a few moons had gone by, lest evil spirits snatch the baby from the womb. Stupid man... why do you look so surprised by my news? A baby is what comes when you plough the furrow. Surely Morigau taught you that!"

"You are a sharp-tongued little shrew, aren't you?" he said, half-laughing, drawing her close against him and running his hand over the slight swell of her stomach, wondering at the strange, old magic that had seen fit to make his seed quicken to life.

"I am," she said. "And one day I will be lady of Kham-El-Ard, and my son and yours will be prince of all Prydn!!"

*****

Shortly after sunrise the next morning Ardhu's war party set off toward Suilven, the Crossroads of the World, as he had decreed. It rained and the wind blew, howling across the sky as though winter still held sway in Prydn, although it was actually nigh on the Summer Solstice. Several men had whispered that it was ill-luck to leave at such a time, before Bhel Sunface had sent his shaft of light into the holy circle in the red sunrise of the longest day, but Ardhu paid these whispers no heed. He knew it would be deemed equally unlucky if he stayed to lead the ceremony, and no Sun and no warmth came. Instead he gave the honour of his place to the newly appointed high priest, Gluinval, and Fynavir, an unusual move, for such acts were not often the province of women, but he was eager to show the people that he had accepted her back and she him... though he knew the truth of her silence, and to even look on her half-grown hair and thin, wan face felt like a dagger was being turned in his gut.

A few paces behind Ardhu and his chief warriors, Bohrs and Hwalchmai, Gal'havad rode beside Mordraed, happily surveying the rain-washed countryside. "I look forward to seeing Suilven," he said. "I have heard it is much different from Khor Ghor... much bigger... and there is a mighty hill where some say Bhel sleeps and is reborn... and a tomb of the Old Ones where the spirits fly after dusk..."

"Aye, and it's such a magic place, all the priestesses have three tits and an extra eye in their forehead," said Mordraed dryly.

"Do they?" gawped Agravaen, who was riding just to the rear of his older brother.

"Of course not, you dolt," laughed Mordraed, and Gal'havad laughed

147

too, while Agravaen flushed red and murmured, "I knew that!"

Other than Mordraed occasionally tormenting Agravaen, the ride across the Plain and beyond, following the great Ridgeway track, was uneventful. Mud sloshed underfoot and hail beat into the company's faces as they crested Red Horn hill, but it did not slow their progress, and soon the wooden posts of the Sanctuary became visible on the horizon, dim under a soggy cloud cap. The door was barred and no fires burned.

As they drew near, Ardhu reined in his stallion and paused for a moment, remembering a time he had been here as a young man no older than Gal'havad, and how his actions could have ruined all he had worked to obtain. But it had all turned out for the best. None save Merlin knew of his dark secret... unless Mordraed himself knew.

Ardhu glanced furtively over his shoulder at the dark-haired youth riding behind him, the wind blowing his black mane straight back from his high forehead. He still didn't trust him, but looking at the boy, relaxed and even smiling as he talked with Gal'havad and Agravaen, he found himself wishing the path of fate had been different. Maybe he should have killed Morigau and taken the child, raising him as his own... well, he *was* his own. Then, perhaps, there would be no fear of what darkness might be lurking in Mordraed's head. Certainly he was a warrior one could be proud of, bold, fearless, a lethal archer... with a face and form that spoke of the ancient lineages of the West. It was cruel fate that Mordraed resembled Ardhu's family so much, when Gal'havad resembled no one...

He scowled, not allowing his thoughts to travel any further on *that* road, and slammed his heels into his steed's flanks, driving the beast away from the shuttered Sanctuary towards the twin lines of menhirs, diamonds and longstones, which wound down from the Ridgeway toward the heart of Crossroads of the World. The rest of the warband followed him, unaware of the doubts and fears that roiled within their leader's mind.

They did not enter the great circles of Suilven, protected by their monumental chalk-cut ditches, but instead turned toward the Hill of King Zhel, rising like a snowy cone with a pool of wind-rippled water hugging its feet. Passing by, with an offering of gold and bluestone chips given to the waters, they came at last to the tall rows of wooden buildings that formed the Palisades. There they were greeted by the folk of Suilven, who took their steeds to pens and fed and watered them, and brought forth champions' portions of meat and huge ceremonial beakers slopping thick, honey-rich mead.

Once this greeting was over, Ardhu travelled on foot back into the Great Circles to meet with the priestess who presided over Suilven. In his youth, the Holy One had been a great, fat old woman called Odharna, but she was long barrowed, her spirit now dwelling among the Ancestors, and her place had been taken by the Esteemed High Lady Mako'sa, She-who-dispenses-Food.

Mako'sa was unusually tall, with a thin brown face and grey-black hair threaded with blue faïence and wrapped into coils on either side of her head; an added pad of horsehair gave her tresses towering height. Madder dye had given her robes a blood-red hue, and her cloak was wrought from the skins of hares—her totem animal. The hares' heads had been left on and were bound with fine bronze thread.

"Welcome, Stone Lord," she said, as she sat cross-legged outside of her cult-house within the great earth-ring of Suilven. "It has been long since you came to visit us at the Crossroads of the World."

He nodded. "My business has always been at Khor Ghor. I do not think the great priestesses of this place need the help of any mortal man to run their temple."

"No, that we do not," said Mako'sa. "But we are surprised to see you now, unbidden and carrying your axes and daggers of war. "

"The world is changing, priestess. You will have seen how Bhel fails and the rain comes." He held up his hand to the sky; it was raining again now, a thin drizzle. Water beaded on his greenstone wrist guard.

"Yes, we have seen it." Mako'sa's eyes turned grey as the soggy sky. "There is little that the Eye of Suilven does not see, Ardhu Pendraec. So a quest it is, for you and for your men. A quest to save the Land? Or to save your life?"

He went ashen. "What have you seen, Lady?"

Rain trickled between her dark brows, furrowed from age and weather. She must have been over fifty, a great age for a woman; though such advanced age was not infrequent among the priestesses of Suilven. "I have seen the fate of kings, Pendraec. As it always must be."

"We all die and go to the Ancestors, that is true," he said gruffly. "But I have no intention of going anytime soon, and it is my Land that worries me more than the fate of my body. Crops are failing, Lady Mako'sa; children with bellies swollen from hunger die in ditches."

"And so you will fare over the Sea to seek the Cup of Gold, the Cup of Plenty, that stands within Spiralfort, where the lamps of Uffern burn. Hoping its powers will restore what has been lost."

"Yes... the tale of the Cup was told to me by the Maimed King of the Wasteland ere he died."

"Perhaps hope in the quest is the thing... rather than the finding," Mako'sa said quietly.

He ignored her; perhaps not understanding her words or choosing not to understand them. "I have brought my men here not just for rest and food but for your blessing."

"And they shall have it, for what it is worth," said Mako'sa, bowing her head. "Bring them to me."

*****

The warriors of Ardhu's band came one by one to the cult-house of the

149

Esteemed Lady Mako'sa, each one bowing before her door with its carven poles that showed the faces of many beings both foul and fair, their eyes made out of pebbles polished from years of supplicants touching them for luck. Whatever she said or did with each man of the tribe within the stout walls of the house was never spoken of, either by the priestess or the warrior, who, his brow marked with a sign made of animal fat, marched back to the encampment at the Palisades. It was secret and made sacred before the spirits.

Gal'havad, looking a bit pale and queasy, went into the cult house before Mordraed, who waited impatiently outside the skin-hung door, striding back and forth with a petulant expression. Gal'havad wasn't long and came out bone-white and quite unsteady on his feet. Mordraed saw him stagger and lean against one of the totem poles, hand pressed to his midriff as if he was about to be sick.

"What is wrong with you?" Mordraed caught him, as his knees buckled.

"It is nothing. Go and have your blessing from the Great Lady."

Mordraed cast a distasteful glance toward the hut door. Scents of burning herbs, unwholesome and possibly hallucinogenic, drifted out towards him. "I think not, cousin. My fate was already mapped out by the spirits at the hour of my birth... that is my belief; I do not think a blessing, even from a powerful priestess, can change what is destiny."

He helped Gal'havad from the henge and out into the now-darkened fields. The Moon came out above, slicing through the sky; the stars were hard eyes, watchful and unfriendly. Mordraed breathed a little sigh... he was well aware that out here, beyond men's comforting fires, there was no one around. No one but him and Gal'havad, cousin, half-brother... and rival. It seemed the perfect place to finish his unsuspecting kinsman. Yet somehow he could not bring himself to find his dagger hilt. Not here. Not yet. Striking down a man who looked as weak as a babe was not honourable. And of course there was the forced oath, sworn before the Stone of Adoration, that he would raise no hand to Gal'havad.

Inside, he felt something he had not expected.

Pity.

It was as if he gazed at one of his two youngest brothers when he saw the ailing Gal'havad. He shook his head, wondering at his own feelings, despising himself for this unbidden weakness. He cursed silently and dropped his arm from his companion's shoulder ... and at that moment Gal'havad toppled over into the growing corn and was noisily sick. His limbs jerked and Mordraed realised he was having one of his fits where he entered the Otherworld.

The sight of Gal'havad helpless and unmanned, lying twitching in the corn, filled him with revulsion, but again... that sense of pity rose up in him, snaring him, twisting his gut. Gal'havad could not stop his spells, could not control the forces that tormented him... Mordraed would hate to be so out of control, used by spirits for reasons unknown...

"Gal'havad." He crouched down beside his half-brother. Mercifully he had ceased shaking and lay crouched on his side like a corpse in a barrow, pale-faced and with closed eyes, his breathing rapid and shallow. "Gal'havad, can you hear me?"

Slowly Gal'havad's eyelids flickered. His expression was one of disorientation. "I am sorry, Mordraed," he whispered, "that you have seen me so."

"I know of your strange spells," said Mordraed bluntly.

"Will you help me back to the encampment, cousin?"

Mordraed put his arm around Gal'havad's narrow waist and assisted him to his feet. He staggered slightly and put a hand to his face. "They are getting worse, Mordraed," he whispered. "The fits. There is great pain in my head too, and a blinding light. In the morn I ofttimes void my stomach; the other youths think it is because of too much mead but it is not."

"You bear a burden, Gal'havad." *And so you should have been a priest and not a king's heir... and then I would not have to kill you!* "Come; let us get you back to the Palisades."

*****

Reaching the encampment, they entered the hut that had been set aside for the younger members of Ardhu's warband. As Ardhu's heir, Gal'havad had a section separate from the others, with fur-draped screens separating his bed-space from that of the others. Mordraed shoved the hangings aside and ushered Gal'havad through, and the red-haired youth collapsed in a weary heap on the bare chalk floor, still looking wan and weak and drained. "Mordraed, will you stay with me?" he asked, almost plaintively, as if he were still a little boy, and not a warrior who had already proven himself at Pendraec's Mount and who had ritually taken the life of the Maimed King.

Mordraed shifted uneasily; he did not wish this, but what could he say? "Yes, if that is your will."

He sat down uncomfortably on the ground near to his half-brother, stretching out his legs before him. Gal'havad shifted and laid his head on Mordraed's knee. He turned his head to gaze up at Mordraed, "I am afraid," he said quietly.

A cold sensation passed through Mordraed. *Do not look at me... Do not look at me...* He tried to ignore the intense, unwavering stare of his young half-brother. "There is no need to fear." His voice sounded harsh, the caw of the gorecrow.

"I dream of the barrow, Mordraed... Sometimes I cannot see myself upon my father's high seat or ... growing old."

"All who live dream of the barrow now and then," Mordraed said shortly. "Do not think of it more; it can make a man mad. Rest or you will not be able to continue with the Pendraec's quest. I will watch over you; if you sicken again I will call the priestesses."

"My thanks, Mordraed." Gal'havad closed his eyes. "You are good to me.

151

I often feel bad that you have no inheritance like I do, that your lands were lost when your father Loth died. I swear that one day I will see that you have lands aplenty and many head of cattle."

Mordraed was taken aback. "You… you would? You would give me those things, which would make me nigh as powerful a chief as yourself?"

"Of course I would. I swear it by our shared blood."

His voice was growing faint, heavy with need for slumber. Cushioning his face with his hand Gal'havad was soon asleep, head resting on Mordraed's knee. The older youth sat as if frozen, horrified by the intimacy of Gal'havad's touch, his face nearly as white as his half-brother's. Oath or no, he should end this now, snap this sickly boy's neck like a wounded animal's, free the wretched spirit-touched youth from his blighted life… He could claim he had another fit, that he fell at an awkward angle and his neck snapped…

But he could not bring himself to touch him… Anger and emotions he could put no name to welled up, a coil of conflict. Moving Gal'havad's head onto the ground with a gentleness incongruous with his inner turmoil, he covered his half-brother with his own cloak, then raced from the hut out into the darkness.

*****

Merlin paced around the bottom of the sacred shaft, a caged beast trammelled by walls of chalk. He touched the place on the wall where he had tried to mark off the days and nights of his imprisonment… how many had it been? He was losing track of time now, as he grew weaker and more despondent.

"I must get away!" he muttered to himself, staring up at the tiny circle far above that allowed a glimpse of the darkling sky. He knew, felt it in his bones, that there was much amiss in the outside world. Ardhu… he must go to Ardhu, warn him, help him before it was too late.

He sighed and sagged against the chilly chalk wall. Yes, he was wrong to try and stave off what the Ladies of the Lake termed as 'Fate'… but how could he not? He had made Ardhu, engineering even the union that brought about his birth… how could he abandon him to wanton destiny now?

Suddenly he heard a noise from above, the sound of feet skimming grass. He stared up, rheumy eyes straining in the gloom. Moments later, Mhorgan's face appeared at the lip of the shaft, gazing down. "Merlin?" she asked. "Are you hale? I have brought more food and a warmer garment."

Merlin made no answer. It was doubtful Mhor-gan would fall for his wiles, but he must try. She would be the one to appeal to if all else failed; Nin-Aeifa's heart was long ice towards him, and Mhor-gan had always been the softer of the two priestesses, her heart fair and true, like her brother's.

He crouched down, curling into a ball and putting his arms over his head. Opening his mouth, he let out what he hoped sounded like a pain-wracked moan.

High above him, Mhor-gan looked alarmed. "Merlin, what ails you?"

"The elf-stroke..." He touched his cheek. "It has happened again. You must help me lest I die here like a trapped animal."

"I will come down at once." She dropped the rope ladder down the side of the pit and began to descend.

Reaching the bottom, she knelt beside Merlin as he crouched on the floor. His heart was pounding and he resisted the urge to lunge at her and battle with her for the ladder and freedom. Instead he held out what appeared to be a weak, quavering hand. "Help me, Mhor-gan," he implored. "I wish to smell the pure night air one more time if I am to die."

"You will not die," she said fiercely. "Here, put your arms around my neck and I will bear you to the surface. I will take you to Nin-Aeifa's abode for warmth and healing."

Merlin staggered to his feet and climbed upon her back. He trembled as he wrapped his bony arms around her neck. She did not know the trembling was from excitement, from anticipation of freedom.

"How is your grip, Merlin?" she asked, concerned. "Can you hang on?"

"My fingers will hold... I think..." he said in the weakest whisper he could muster.

Mhor-gan began to climb the ladder, clinging to the ropes till her fingertips turned white. Like her brother she was not overly tall, with Merlin being slightly the taller, and he could tell that it was a strain on her to carry him in such a manner, tiring her, sapping her of strength.

He smiled, there in the dark, out of sight.

After what seemed an eternity, they reached the top of the ritual shaft. Gasping, Mhor-gan crawled on all fours upon the grass, Merlin still with his arms looped around her neck, dragging on her like a dead weight.

"Are you well, Merlin?" she panted.

"I am..." he said, and suddenly his voice was deeper, stronger... and the quivering hands that flapped so feebly at her throat were now tightening on it with intent.

She tried to cry out, but Merlin pressed her face down into the grass. "I will not harm you, for you are a priestess and the spirits would not be pleased," he said, drawing off his belt and binding her arms together. Then, still pushing her into the ground, he tore strips from the hem of his robes and threaded them through the belt, tying her arms to her ankles so that she could not rise and pursue him.

"Merlin..." Gasping, Mhor-gan rolled onto her side, red marks from his fingertips glowing on her neck. "I meant you no harm; you know that; we only wanted to keep you from rash actions ..."

"Rash actions—what? Saving Ardhu? Killing myself? No matter what you think is the right course for Prydn, woman, I will tell you one truth... you and your sisterhood will have no say in the fate of Merlin."

Leaving her struggling against her makeshift bonds, he began to run jerkily uphill. Adrenaline pumped through him, giving him a strength of body he had thought long gone. He knew he teetered on a dagger's edge, pushing himself beyond the limits of his failing flesh, but he no longer cared. This would be the last quest of the Merlin, and he would gladly look good to those Ancestors who awaited him in the spirit-world upon the Plain of Honey.

Following the top of the ridge he set his course toward the East and the hill of Kham-El-Ard. His heart leapt in his bony chest as he saw its dark hump rising like a land-locked ship against the star-strewn sky. He could see torches flickering on the ramparts; smell the comforting scent of fires and animals, of human life.

Ardhu, Ardhu, my son... I pray you are still there, and that you are safe...

He puffed up the hill, staggering over to the gate guards who stood on duty all night. They gawped at him like simpletons but opened the stout oak gates at once to allow his passage. Hair wild, robe flapping around his knees, he stumbled across the inner yard and burst into Ardhu's Great Hall...

And found it almost empty. Neither the Stone Lord nor his prime warriors were to be seen—no Ardhu, no An'kelet, no Hwalchmai, no Bohrs. A few idle-looking louts lounged around the fire-pit, frowning in Merlin's direction as the freezing night air washed in over them.

The old shaman felt fear grip beneath his breastbone. "Where is Ardhu Pendraec?" he rasped. "Where are Prince Gal'havad and Lord An'kelet?"

One of the youths sitting at the fire snickered. "An'kelet? You are out of touch, old man! He is gone from here, by Ardhu's will. By now, he is probably dead in the forest and being eaten by beasts. Where in Prydn have you been? He was fucking the bloody Queen!"

Merlin's face went bone-white and dizziness washed over him. "And Ardhu?"

"Gone to find the Cup of Plenty over in Ibherna." The youth, Mordraed's friend Wyzelo the Weasel, belched and flicked a greasy pig-bone into the fire. "Waste of time, if you ask me. We should be fighting the tribes who have become unruly, not chasing such womanish dreams!"

"And Gal'havad is with him?"

"Yes, pretty boy has gone."

Merlin felt his dismay turn to sudden anger. Striding to Wyzelo's bench, he caught the youth's throat in a clawed hand, almost knocking him from his perch. Wyzelo's beaker went flying and rolled in the dirt. "Who are you to speak so of the prince who will one day rule you? And who do you think it is that you speak to now, boy?"

Wyzelo made a squeaking noise, so high-pitched and effeminate that his half-sotted companions fell about the place laughing.

"I am the Merlin," snarled the old man, his eyes burning into Wyzelo's. "Have I been gone so long you do not recognise me? Or has this place gone to ruin so swiftly that men no longer honour those whose hard work brought them here?"

154

"Merlin!" He released Wyzelo as he heard a familiar voice behind him. Turning, he saw Ka'hai striding towards him from the outside ward, pinch-faced and worried. "Glad am I to see you... but so surprised that I shake like a leaf in the wind! It was rumoured you were dead!"

"It seems reports of my death were highly exaggerated," said Merlin dryly. "Do I look like a dead man to you? Now tell me, for you I know I can trust... has Ardhu indeed gone to Ibherna for this Cup of Gold?"

Ka'hai nodded. "Yes, he left a few days ago, travelling first to Suilven for blessings on his quest, and then intending to ride for Mhon, where he has paid for ships to be built on the strand. He has taken twenty of his best men, including Gal'havad. Mordraed his sister's son also rides with the company."

Merlin's face whitened. "Mordraed! I can hear by your voice, friend Ka'hai, that you feel about this news as I do. Why should he take on the whelp of the bitch who tried to bite him?"

Ka'hai sighed. "Gal'havad wishes it... he seems besotted with the man, as if he has been bewitched! Mordraed also exposed the treachery of An'kelet and Fynavir—maybe Ardhu feels he owes him something for that deed."

"He owes that one nothing! This is evil news indeed." Merlin shook his head, chewing his chapped lips as he thought about what he should do. "Ka'hai, I cannot linger here... I must ride and catch up with Ardhu if I can. Have a horse brought for me. Quick, man... all we hold dear may depend on it! Ardhu is as your brother, and if you love him, you will do as I say!"

Ka'hai opened his mouth as if to protest, but Merlin's eyes glowed like brands, feral and bright, and the warrior dashed off into the gloom, returning shortly with a fine, grey-maned horse. "This is Per-Adur's steed. He is injured and will not ride again for a long time, maybe never again. Take it, with his blessings, and may the spirits smile on you and on my chief—and foster-brother—Ardhu Pendraec."

Merlin clumsily pulled himself up onto the horse's back; he was never much of a rider, less so with his weak elf-shotten side. But he would do what he had to. "Watch these dogs well," he said, pointing with a sideways motion of his chin toward Wyzelo and his loutish fellows as they lounged about inside the Hall. "I think they have been fed scraps that tempt them, and would soon gladly bite the hand that feeds."

Clapping heels to the grey mare's flanks, he shot out of the wooden gates of Kham-El-Ard and into the night, heading toward the circles, avenues and ditches of Suilven, and the great Hill of the Eye in its pool of moon-silvered water.

*****

The second night at Suilven rolled round. Ardhu himself had gone for purification and blessing at the springhead near the Hill of Zhel, and none were allowed to witness this ritual cleansing of a King save Priestess Mako'sa and her acolytes. Even the lesser holy men and women were forced to wear blindfolds and masks to hide their eyes from what it was forbidden to see.

Sitting alone on the towering bank of the henge, watching the sharp sickle of the moon rise in the east, Mordraed felt uneasy and restive, eager to be off. Too many women here, intelligent fierce women whose sharp gazes could scry a man's soul. Too much like his mother, only worse, for they did not hold him dear. He feared to look them in the eye, lest the truth of his heart be read and they should fall upon him, rending him limb from limb in fury and feeding his blood to the earth.

His blood instead of Ardhu's; he—Mordraed—the tanist sent to try and appease the Spirits so that the old king could live to fight another day...

He shook his head angrily. Such an end would be unnatural and wrong... the young should not die before the old; the weak should not hope that the young offer themselves up to the gods in their place.

Suddenly he heard a noise, the faint thud of hooves on chalk. Turning, he peered into the gloom, his keen eyes catching sight of a figure at the end of the avenue of stones that ran from the portals of Suilven to the Sanctuary on its plateau overlooking the shallow vale.

A man on a horse, riding at great speed toward the sacred Circles. Riding as if he fled from, or to, the world's ending.

A sense of alarm filled him, though he did not know why, and slinging his bow across his shoulders, he leapt from the bank and jogged down the Avenue, keeping close to the flanks of the giant pillars that marched away into the gloom, an army of stalwart stone.

The thundering hooves drew closer, and he could hear the heavy laboured breathing of a horse pushed almost beyond its endurance. Hastily he slunk into the lee of an enormous diamond-shaped menhir, leaning against its craggy face, willing himself to appear invisible, to become part of the stone itself. He could feel its cold surface burning into his back through his thin summer tunic, and see the rough lichens that made patterns like gurning faces on its broad spine.

Out of the gloom the rider came flying... grey-white steed, grey-white man with long hair and beard a ghost-like misty trail on the wind. He caught a brief glimpse of an intense hawk-like face, withered as an old apple, but with eyes burning like fire, like fallen suns.

A face he knew and had hoped never to see again.

The face of Ardhu's counsellor, the shaman Merlin.

Merlin, who had used his unclean magics so that U'thyr could bed Y'gerna of Belerion and beget Ardhu, throwing Mordraed's mother aside as if she were an unclean rag, taking her inheritance and birthright from her. His mother, who was a powerful magic-woman in her own right, who could have been as great as the Merlin himself if given a chance. Or so she had always told him...

Like most of the others in Kham-El-Ard and Deroweth, Mordraed had thought Merlin was dead when he vanished without a word... or that he had become crazed and run amok in the woods as his kind were wont to do,

156

struck moon-mad by their constant communication with the spirit-world and by the potions they consumed all their adult lives.

"You may wish you were dead, old man," he muttered between clenched teeth, sliding out from behind the great stone, a darker shadow blending with other shadows. "And then you may well find yourself in the spirit-world in truth!"

Bow in hand, he began to track the trail of the Merlin across the circles of Suilven. His face became very still and white, intense, between the midnight wings of his hair. All his senses felt heightened; he knew he was on the edge of something great, something terrible, something that would change the course of his life forever.

Tonight Mordraed was what his mother had taught him to be.

Tonight he was the Hunter and the Merlin was his prey.

*****

Merlin rode his lathered horse over the fields and into the sacred hollow near the springhead of Suilven. Ardhu's ceremony was over and the King was gone, returned with his retinue to the Palisades, but Mako'sa remained at the spring, reading things from past and future in the deep, clean water that flowed from the body of the Earth in that hallowed space. The masks of her followers, removed once Ardhu's cleansing was over, had been thrown into the bubbling waters where they hovered and eddied a few inches below the surface, like the images of strange otherworldly creatures, unravelling and unbinding as the gentle current buffeted them to and fro. Torches set along the banks sent fiery ripples across the swell and made strange shadows dance.

Mako'sa watched, visage solemn, painted with white chalk so that her long thin face almost appeared a skull. A time of unravelling and unbinding... a time for new beginnings. Kneeling on the flat sarsen stones that spanned the spring, she drank of the holy water, hoping to receive blessing and wisdom.

And saw, to her surprise, a reflection appear in the water behind her left shoulder, grey and ghostly, as if an Ancestor had wandered from the old chambered barrow on the hill and come to gaze upon her rites. She sat up immediately and turned, the decorative bronze wires and faience beads on her elaborate hairpiece clattering and clacking with the speed of her motion. Her hand went to the little flint dagger, sharp as a razor, that hung at her belt, its blade painted with protective symbols. It was the life-seeker for taking sacrifice, but it could also command the dead should they rise from their sleep as fractious ghosts.

But it was no ghost that stood before her, silvered in the starshine, hair and beard wildly tangled and his robes drenched with sweat. She knew that face, lean as her own, a bird's face within a man's. It was the Merlin, chief priest of Khor Ghor.

Merlin, who Ardhu had told her was reckoned amongst the dead. But who was clearly not, his breath steaming hot with life before his cracked lips.

"High one," she said "why do you come to me like this, weary and wind blown? Where have you been for so long, O wise one, making the song-singers and the priests and priestesses mourn you as one who has gone over the Plain in the Snare of Nud the Catcher?"

"A prisoner have I been," he answered, "held by ones who I never thought would mean me ill." He was at the top of the little dell that encircled the spring, still mounted on his froth-mouthed steed. Carefully he slid from its back, letting the reins dangle, and walked stiffly towards Mako'sa. "But no more. I seek Ardhu Pendraec, to advise him as I have always done. To keep him safe."

Her brows rose slightly. "He is not some youth to keep safe anymore, Merlin. He will be what he will be. He has proposed a quest of great holiness and he has had blessing from the Eye of Suilven, and bathed in the blood of the Great One who birthed the Sun Himself, whose body is represented in the Holy Hill. He will fare forth to Ibherna with his band of chosen men to find the Cup of Plenty, which lies in the valley of the River of the Great White Cow—locked within Spiralfort, fortress of the Flaming Door, where the lamps of Uffern burn both night and day."

Merlin seemed to sag, his shoulders slumping. "I can see no good in this quest. Only death. A symbol of Hope he seeks and maybe he will find it… but I feel it will be bought at a terrible price."

"What would you have me say, Merlin?" said Mako'sa quietly. "Should I have denied my blessing? He would have gone anyway, without even asking the spirits to strengthen his hand."

Merlin knelt by the water, staring at his own ragged reflection. The ends of his beard and his snarled hair fanned out on the swell. "Does the Land need blood so much?" he said hoarsely.

"The Land fails… the Moon is red, Bhel himself bleeds and turns his Eye from us. Ash of the pyre has fallen in the North."

"Could I not stand for him? It was done so in older times, Mako'sa."

She pulled her cloak around her, as if suddenly chilled by the wind. "No. I think you know that you have grown too old to take his place."

"So others have said… but I am still the Merlin!"

"And may you be long among us, with your wisdom. But making of yourself a sacrifice will not avert Ardhu's doom. I certainly will not be the one to lay hand upon you, nor would any of the wise."

Merlin's shoulders slumped. "I would speak to him at least."

She touched his arm lightly, an expression of pity on her face. "There will be no harm in that. You were as a father to him as well as mentor."

Suddenly the Merlin raised his head. His eyes narrowed, became secretive, and his nostrils flared as if he was scenting the breeze like a beast. A strange expression crossed his thin features and he licked his lips in nervous agitation. He was gazing intently over Mako'sa's shoulder and the priestess felt a shudder of fear ripple up her spine.

She wondered if her initial thought had been correct... that an old spirit was indeed wandering about out of its bone-chamber, creeping closer to the place of power where the water flowed from the womb of the earth, feeding the Khen and the great pool at the foot of Zhel's hill. "What do you see, O Merlin?" she asked.

He shook his head. "N... nothing... just an old man's fancy." He knelt on the sarsen stepping-stone bridge again. "Lady, would it be possible for me to stay here awhile on my own? To pray to all the Mighty Ones that these troubles will pass?"

Mako'sa hesitated then nodded. "To any other I would give only refusal. But you are the Merlin, and the events of these grim times are bound to you, heart and soul and body. Stay here awhile, as you wish. I will not stop you. I will go to the Palisades where the feasting has begun."

She bowed to him and then, drawing her cape around her, walked away beyond the ring of flickering torchlight and out across the fields of blowing grass. She did not gaze back... perhaps was afraid to, fearful of what she might witness.

Merlin wiped a hand across his sweat-stained face and clumsily rose to his feet, stepping off the bridge and raking the nearby shrubbery and trees with a burning gaze. His stance was not one of a man about to pray to his gods but one who expected to face an enemy "Come out, son of pestilence," he snapped. "I know you are out there. Let us not play these games but put an end to this foolery for once and for all."

The bushes rustled, and it was not the wind.

Out of a haze of green boughs stepped Mordraed, the Moon shining behind his dark head, the light of the guttering torches around the spring giving a bloody hue to his features. He looked so like Ardhu at the same age that a terrible pang of sadness ripped through the Merlin—sorrow for what was gone, for what was fading from Prydn, for all the bright summers of the past years that were now blurred into a rosy memory. He even sorrowed for Mordraed, beautiful but twisted, child of a broken taboo, pawn of a malevolent mother who had groomed him to the darkness for so long he could never see the light.

"What do you stare at, old man?" Mordraed's voice was cool, silken, deadly.

"A traitor. A would be kin-slayer." Merlin spoke softly.

"You presume."

"I know."

"And why are *you* here, after going missing for many months? Your own loyalty is in question, vanishing when Ardhu Pendraec needed your counsel most!"

"I do not tell serpents such as you my business. Step aside, Mordraed. I will go now to Ardhu's side and speak to him." He took a long, determined stride in Mordraed's direction.

The young man blocked him, sneering down into his face. "What lies will you whisper to him, old man? He doesn't need to hear the prattling of one nearly in his dotage!"

"I'll tell him the truth and he will believe me. The truth that you seek his chieftaincy, to cast him down. You have already cut him like a dagger when you disgraced his queen…"

"The whore disgraced herself…" retorted Mordraed.

"And caused him to drive away his strongest warrior…"

"A traitor of the greatest kind… I would have killed An'kelet for his actions had it been up to me!" Mordraed tossed back his hair, his eyes on fire. "Besides, you can say what you will… he has heard all these things about me and more and still has allowed me into his band. You tell him nothing new."

"But there is more, and this will interest him—your trips to the hut of your mother, Morigau, who was forbidden to meet with you. What does she tell you, what has she given you for your journey to the West? Come, Mordraed, we both know she is a master poisoner! And the red-haired girl that you rut with down by the river; who is she? Not a local woman, that is for sure. My watchers have said you call her wife and that her belly is full. And even if your sly secret doings do not move Ardhu to anger, I will lie to him of more dark deeds… not because untruths fall easy from my tongue, but because I know what you are and what you will do. He will believe any tale I tell him of you, for he trusts me… and not you."

Mordraed blanched. He had not thought the old man might have been having him watched. Nor that a holy priest of Khor Ghor would admit to telling blatant falsehoods to get what he wanted.

Merlin reached out, shoving Mordraed backwards with a sharp motion of his hand. A strange expression was in his eyes; desperate and feverish. Sweat sprang out on his forehead. "So out of my way, Mordraed son of Morigau."

"You will tell my father nothing!" Mordraed flung down his bow onto the grass and caught the old man by the shoulders, whipping him around.

"You will have to kill me then." Merlin's eyes, struck by the moonlight, were two eerie silvered pools.

"I should have done so long before now!" cried Mordraed, and he lunged at Merlin catching him around the throat and hurling him down on the sarsen stone bridge that spanned the bubbling waters of the sacred spring.

Merlin's head hit the ground with a crack and he lay there gasping. Mordraed was kneeling over him, hands clawing at his neck, seeking a stranglehold. Merlin choked and spluttered, writhing, but he managed to tear the clutching fingers away from his windpipe and throw the youth back, half into the water. "Come on…" the old man sneered, between gasps for breath, livid marks already glowing on his throat. "I am but a dry stalk, and you young and fresh… is that the best you can do? I had imagined your dam raised you as a killer…"

Mordraed flung himself forward, grabbing a handful of Merlin's robes, pulling him off the bridge into the water. They stood together in the swell, facing each other, the old man all grey and white, a spectre seeming half of the spirit-world, and the youth all darkness and fire, with eyes like the night sky, sucking in the torchlight.

Mordraed lunged, throwing his adversary backwards in a violent motion. Merlin stumbled and his head struck the bridge with a crack. Blood suddenly poured into the swirling waters, curls of it flooding outwards to stain both opponents with red. Merlin raised a hand to the stream, his palm coming back crimson. Lights fragmented in his brain. "And so the first blow is struck..." his voice was tremulous and yet full of rapture at the same time.

Mordraed stared at him; he could almost fancy the old fool was laughing through his pain, while staring at the blood coming from his head as if it was a marvellous, wonderful thing. The most wonderful thing he had ever seen.

Mordraed snarled in perplexed frustration and laid hold of his adversary again, hurling him bodily into the shallows. He collapsed, face down, in mud and water and blood, his arms flung out, his fingers digging into the streambed. Panting, eager to end this madness for once and for all, Mordraed flung himself on the aged shaman and thrust his head under the water. Merlin jerked and writhed and blood-tinged bubbles rose to the surface, bursting horribly like boils on the swell.

Merlin went limp and Mordraed backed away, panting, but then he heard a tormented groan... he was still not dead, and there was a disturbing hint of mocking laughter even amidst his agony. He lifted his head and craned around, his bloody, muddied face staring up like some horror from the Un-world realms. "I thank you, Mordraed," he croaked. "You have killed me by the sacred way, as no other dared to do—the threefold death of strangling, wounding, and drowning. My sacrifice may not save Ardhu, but maybe if the Ancestors are pleased it will give him more time, more strength. Strength to defeat the likes of you. And as a dying man, and high priest of the Door into Winter, I will speak one last prophecy meant just for you—you will never be king in Ardhu's stead. By the Everlasting Sky, if I have to fight Hwynn and Nud themselves, I will return from the Otherworld to stop you!"

"Be silent!" Mordraed grabbed a heavy chunk of sarsen from the stream-bed and slammed it into his victim's head.

Merlin ceased to move. Shaking, Mordraed pulled him into the centre of the spring and weighted his body down with stones. He yanked off Merlin's talismanic pendant, the bronze-wrapped skull of his totem hawk, and tossed it far out into the water, in case the shaman's spirit-beast might rise and attack him. Swiftly Merlin sank, bubbles rising and breaking around his body. The blood trails slowed to trickles and dispersed on the swell.

Mordraed crawled onto the bank, shivering, staring at the spot where the corpse had vanished. The unfurling masks from the earlier rites bobbed around it like sinister guardians. Hot and cold shudders ran through him. He had done what he intended, what he knew he had to do. The old man would

161

have destroyed him otherwise; he had always been an enemy. But his last words… a curse and a powerful one, born in blood.

"But it will not come true!" Mordraed made the symbol to avert evil with his hand, though he knew it was too late for the words had been spoken. "By Bhel and the Everlasting Sky, I will be King!"

CHAPTER FIFTEEN
THE SPOILS OF AHN-UN

Ardhu's warband left the Crossroads of the World at the rising of the Sun. Horns blew mournfully and drums beaten, dull rumblings bouncing from the enclosures of the Palisades to Zhel's hill and back. The Sun, to everyone's surprise, showed its face after days of gloom, the rain-clouds rolling back from the East like great moving bruises staining the arch of the sky.

It was a good omen. Ardhu sat astride his horse staring up at the brightness, letting the meagre warmth caress his face. The Sun-rays caught on the Breastplate of Heaven and Caladvolc's gold decorated hilt and turned them to flame. He raised the Lightning Mace in salute to the glowing Face of Bhel and the company began to move, leaving the Palisades and heading uphill in a westerly direction.

Mordraed stared over his shoulder as the warband moved off. He was white-visaged and twitchy, expecting at any moment to hear screams from the direction of the sacred spring. Perhaps he had not pinned the body down well enough or deep enough... maybe there was bloody residue along the waterline that the priestesses would notice.

But no sound of discovery came, only the shrill shrieking of the wind as it whipped over the crest of the hill, past the hump of the chambered long barrow on its summit. Mordraed forced himself to look ahead and suddenly smiled grimly, realising the significance of this place. The tomb of the Ancestors... where Ardhu had broken the great taboo and mated with his own sister. Mordraed raised his hand to his forehead and saluted the Old Ones who had gathered around the illicit lovers that night and breathed upon them, ensuring that a spirit would enter Morigau's womb to be reborn in flesh. Ensuring that he would be—a new powerful life come out of the Un-world of the ancient Dead.

The huge blocking stone of the mound flashed by, stern and forbidding, and then the company was beyond the boundaries of Suilven and out into fields full of blowing grass and fleeting cloud-shadow. Mordraed clapped his heels into his horse's flanks and galloped on ahead of the others, even outstripping Ardhu, although it was insulting and inappropriate for him to outride his chief.

Ardhu frowned as he saw Mordraed race past, a blur of darkness, but decided to hold his peace. Why make trouble, just for the sake of reeling in one invigorated by the high spirits of youth? He had more on his mind that making unfriends with his wayward and trying bastard.

He had the Imram to think of, his Quest. The journey to the West that would either save his kingdom ... or destroy it.

The two ships glided across a smooth and silvered sea, under a pale sun enfolded in thin cloud like wisps of a sky-goddess's hair. Ardhu knelt in the prow of the foremost, that he had named Pridwen, pleased that the weather had been fair and the crossing easy—the sea between Ibherna and Prydn was often treacherous and cruel, swallowing the craft of even the most experienced sailors. He glanced over his shoulder, noting the sea-sick greenness of Gal'havad's face and the almost rapt, excited expression on Mordraed's. He felt uneasy and turned back into the spray.

The lead ship ground ashore in a narrow estuary, its banks lined with drifts of wind-carved pale sand. Ardhu and his men leapt ashore and dragged the boat up onto dry land, then stood knee deep in the tide to take hold of the second boat and haul it in beside the first. When both boats were secured, the companions scanned their surroundings. They were at the mouth of an estuary filled with islets and sandy banks; a river as wide and bright as Abona coiled away into a smoky green distance. There were no signs of any habitation, just a few stark cairns on the nearby hills, their ruined portals gaping at the sky. Seabirds wheeled overhead, wings flashing in the pallid sunlight, their cries mournful as those of barrow-ghosts.

Ardhu put his hand on the shoulder of Betu'or, one of his oldest companions, whose life he had spared in his manhood rites at Marthodunu. "Will you stay with the boats, my old friend?" and when he saw the warrior look downcast "someone must, Betu'or. We cannot risk that they are stolen or destroyed; if anything should happen to them, it is likely that we will never escape this island."

"I will stay," said Betu'or, "although I would rather be at your side. I want to do more for your cause, Lord Ardhu, than sit on a beach with my feet in the sand."

"You will one day, Betu'or, the Knower of Graves," said Ardhu softly, clasping the warrior's arm fondly. "Your day will come when you can do more for me."

Leaving Betu'or to make camp on the strand, Ardhu led his small warband away from the water and into the hilly lands beyond. Hwalchmai trudged next to his kinsman, loosening the peace- bindings on his axe in case he should need to use it. "Do you have knowledge of where we must go? Although Ibherna is small compared to Prydn, yet I think we should be weary treading all of it!"

Ardhu nodded. "I spoke for many days with the wise of Deroweth about this very matter. If our calculations are correct, we have come aground at In'var Kolptha, named for a great warrior who drowned here in the tides at the dawn of time. If we proceed inland, following the River of the White Cow past the Stones of Balytra, we should come to the place we seek, that our people name Spiralfort and the God's Peak, and the men of Ibherna the House of the Good God and Young Sun. What reception we will have there, I cannot say... so we must be careful in all we do and say. The men of Ibherna, it is rumoured, are even fiercer than our own warriors and follow ancient ways that we now shun."

"Well, if they start aught with no good reason, they will have a taste of my axe," grumbled Bohrs, stomping up beside Ardhu and smacking his unsheathed weapon against the palm of his hand.

"I would have no fighting, unless it is absolutely necessary," said Ardhu. "We do not come to fight."

Bohrs looked disappointed. "Just a few heads to crack, Ardhu... just to show them who is mightiest."

"No! Not unless there is no other choice!"

"Well..." Bohrs scratched his beard," I cannot see them giving up this Cup of Plenty or whatever it is, just like that. So I am sure there will be head-cracking to be done. And lots of fighting."

Walking at Ardhu's side, Hwalchmai shaded his eyes with a hand. "Maybe you will get your chance soon, Bohrs. I see armed men on the rise up ahead."

The warband moved on, grouping together to create the impression of solidarity. On higher ground in the distance stood three standing stones, weirdly whittled by the wind, the tallest aligned with a rocky island out at sea which faced the rising Solstice Sun in Winter. Between these gnarled pillars, dwarfed by their lofty height, stood a group of warriors, not as many as Ardhu's band, but fierce of visage and strange and magnificent in manner of dress.

Ardhu was the richest chief in all Prydn, but these men dripped gold as if it were no more precious than clay beads. Huge crescent collars gleamed like Moons around their necks, and twisted, spiralling armbands shone on tattooed arms. Cloak fasteners with terminals the size of a man's fist glowed in the sunlight. Gold coils hung from earlobes, and dark and fire-hued tresses were bound with scores of golden rings. It was no surprise that they were wealthy though, even those who were not chiefs—Ibherna's mines exported massive amounts of copper to the mainland coasts all the way to sun-soaked Ibher, and gold was traded as far away as the Middle-lands between the Rivers Rhin and Rhon, and even to the farthest North near the Bheltis Sea.

Ardhu approached the warriors cautiously, holding out his empty hands to show that he brought no threat. He knew a little of the tongue of Ibherna, from Fynavir who was daughter of the red Queen Mevva, who still lived, although now a very great age, in vast holdings further North. Not that the language was too difficult to comprehend if spoken slowly; the Tin-men had colonised Ibherna as well as Prydn and brought with them what became the language of trade. Once established, this tongue swiftly became the common speech, with older tongues falling aside and vanishing in its wake.

One of the men stepped forward; obviously a leader or shaman. He had a face much beaten by the sun, with rheumy blue eyes bright against the leather of his wrinkled skin. A huge red eye was drawn in ochre on his forehead, and on the end of his staff perched a skull that was also daubed with the same eye. He wore a bell-shaped tunic, with zigzag patterns threaded with fine hairs of bronze crossing it many times.

"I am Kichol, priest of Bal'ahr, he who is the Eye of the Dying Winter Sun," he announced. "Who are you who come unbidden to Ibherna, bearing weapons of war?"

"We carry our weapons because we are men and warriors," replied Ardhu. "Not because we choose to offer battle to the brave and noble folk of our kindred-isle. We come to visit the sacred sanctuary on the River of the White Cow, where it is said the God sleeps in his mound with white swans circling."

"The road to that place lies hither." The shaman of the Red Eye of Bal'ahr pointed with his staff toward the river. "Not just to the Home of the Good God, House of the Sun, but also to Dubad, The Hill of Darkness and Cnobga, mound of Bui the Hag. But there is a toll for foreigners who use the old way to the Palaces of the Ancestors."

"And what is this toll?" said Ardhu uneasily. He mistrusted this man, with his silent comrades who had neither smiled nor spoken, but stood still as the stones behind them, glittering in their masses of gold.

"You must leave one of your companions to be given to Bal'ahr with the turning of the tide," Kichol replied, almost hungrily. "When the sun rises he will be bled into the waters. It will be an honourable death."

Ardhu's face darkened with anger. "What you ask can never be, old man. I do not give up my sworn warriors lightly, and never to strange gods!"

"Then you shall not pass my lands!" Kichol struck the butt of his staff against the ground and the warriors beside him drew copper blades from their belts. At the same time a dozen other men sprang up from behind rises and bushes. Men with bows, men with blow-pipes, men with spears and gleaming daggers.

"I knew they would prove false! They wanted this from the beginning, I could see it in their eyes!" roared Bohrs and he flung himself toward the Shaman of the Red Eye with all the fury of a charging boar, his axe swinging in his hand.

Kichol's warriors loosed blood curdling war-cries and circled around Ardhu's band, spitting and cursing at them, making magical signs against them as if they were demons. But it was these servants of Bal'ahr who resembled demons; these warriors with the lurid red eye of their fierce and ancient solar god daubed upon their foreheads and the skulls of small birds and animals plaited into lime-caked hair—crows, eagles, voles and mice—all making a macabre tinkling as they moved.

One leapt directly in front of the warband, defiant, hungry for engagement, a red whorl of paint bleeding on his bare chest, a dagger in one upraised hand and a blow-pipe in the other.

"Take him down!" yelled Ardhu as the man put the reed pipe to his lips and glanced about him seeking a victim. Bohrs was standing on the warrior's right; the man shifted in his direction and filled his lungs with air.

Hwalchmai shouted out and hurled himself at the warrior with the blow-pipe, stabbing his flank with his rapier and ripping upwards toward the ribcage. The man staggered and dropped his own knife under the onslaught, but kept a tight grip on his blow-pipe. Shoving Hwalchmai away from him, he blew hard upon the carved tube, showering the men of Ardhu's warband with deadly spikes like so many thorns...

Mordraed spat a curse and dived into a nearby bush, dragging Gal'havad with him; he had used the blow-pipe to hunt birds for sport as a boy and guessed the tips were poisoned. Ardhu flung up Wyngurthachar and the spikes struck harmlessly against the bronze surface of Face of Evening.

Not all were so lucky. Agravaen was struck, a dart protruding from his cheek. He roared in fear and anger, swatting at his face. Staggering, he thudded toward his assailant and smote his head with a dozen frenzied blows of his war-hammer, spilling the man's brains on the ground before collapsing, hands pressed over his swelling flesh.

Several other members of the warband likewise fell, rolling in spasms on the ground, froth bubbling on their lips as poison seeped into their blood. Next to Ardhu, Glu Mightygrasp went down with a thud, gurgling as his throat constricted, and a flying spear went into him, pinning him to the earth and finishing him. Arrows whined, killing Anwas and Ellidur outright, going right through their shields of oak and leather, and giving Bal-ahn a scraping wound to the shoulder. The arrow-fire was returned by Mordraed and Gal'havad from their position in the bushes. Their lower angle helped them as they fired upwards with lightning speed, their hands a sweaty blur, their white fletched arrows arcing toward the enemy on the rise. Screams rent the air and several of Kichol's warriors tumbled down the rise—eyes and throats and hearts pierced by the deadly barbs of the arrows of Ardhu's two sons.

More warriors arrived, though, running pell-mell from the tangle of birch, elm and alder that grew along the waterway, and they charged toward the Stone Lord's warband with almost crazed abandon. Ardhu had Caladvolc out and slashed around him, fighting his way toward the Shaman of the Red Eye, who was screaming and dancing and chanting in frenzy, inciting his men to slaughter, calling down the wrath of spirits and gods on the strangers who had set foot upon the blessed island without leave. A warrior leapt out at Ardhu, wielding two long knives of Ibero bronze; Ardhu flung up Wyngurthachar on his left arm and smashed it into the man's jaw, shattering it until it hung at a strange disjointed angle before cleaving his skull with Caladvolc and kicking the body away.

"I will kill them all!" Ardhu shouted at Kichol, holding up his dripping blade as proof. "Call them off or they all die this day and your bloody god will have his red tribute!"

Kichol halted for a moment, and Ardhu, drawing ever nearer, could now see his eyes, blood shot and wild. There was fear in them. Adrenaline shot through Ardhu, the excitement of the hunt, the kill, the anger of being attacked so needlessly. Casting aside Wyngurthachar with reckless abandon so that he could use weapons in both hands, he raced towards his opponent. The shaman's remaining men saw the shield fall, and rushed in toward Ardhu's unprotected left side, but Mordraed rose to his knees, all darkness and serpent-grace, and fired a stream of arrows that felled many. Sprawled in the grass at his side, Gal'havad had run out of arrows but grabbed a miscast spear and flung it with all his strength at the bare legs of the opposing warriors, impaling one and tripping others, who went down shrieking like demons from the deepest pits of Ahn-un.

Ardhu had almost reached Kichol. He still held Caladvolc in his right hand, but now in his left he held the Lightning Mace, symbol of his authority as Lord of the Great Trilithon. With a cry he brought the mace down on his opponent's skull staff, splitting the pate of the death's head in twain in one motion, breaking the other man's symbol of power with his own.

Kichol fell back, recoiling in terror, but Ardhu launched into him, battering him with many blows from the huge polished fossil head of the mace. One blow struck the man's brow where the bloody Eye of Bal'ahr was painted and blood spurted out, streaking Ardhu's tunic and face like war-paint. The priest of the God of the Winter Sun crashed to his knees, and as his head lolled forward, Ardhu brought down Caladvolc with as great a force as he could muster, shearing the head of his enemy from his shoulders. The body fell back, headless, against one of the three tall pillars crowning the slope. Rooks and ravens began to wheel overhead, cawing and cackling as they awaited their meal.

In the distance there came the yammer of hounds, eerie howls that grew in intensity. Someone else was coming.

Ardhu whirled away from Kichol's corpse and snatched Wyngurthachar from the ground. "Run!" he shouted to his men. "More of our foes are on the way… and they have brought beasts to track us. Leave the dead; we can do no more for them!"

"And the wounded?" Ba-lin shouted, staunching the bleeding flesh-wound that scored his twin brother's shoulder.

"If they can run with us, bring them… if not, drag them if you have the strength. But if their injuries are too great…" Ardhu closed his mouth with a snap, his eyes grown hard and steely. All knew what he meant.

Bohrs's big, rough face creased up and he began to weep—he who was as hard as the sarsens of Khor Ghor. "I will do the deed, Stone Lord."

"No, I will," said Ardhu grimly, drawing Carnwennan, his white-hilted dagger, from its sheath against his lower leg. "Turn away, all of you."

Mordraed and Gal'havad scrambled over to Agravaen who lay thrashing on the bloodied ground. A purple stain smeared his cheek; his eyes were glazed, unseeing. With a grunt of exertion, Mordraed yanked him up and slung him over his shoulders. He staggered under the dead weight; Agravaen was a good hand taller than him and heavily built.

"I will help you!" cried Gal'havad, rushing to his side.

Mordraed scowled at him. "Help me? Why should you help me! Don't get in my way, boy!"

"I want to help! He is my kinsman too!" Gal'havad grasped Agravaen's dangling legs, taking some of his weight. "Let's run. I can hear the dogs getting closer."

The two youths staggered down to the riverside, plunging through the marshy pools that rimed the overgrown banks. The remaining warriors of the warband raced at their heels, followed in the distance by Ardhu, ashen-faced, his hands crimson from his last, lethal gift to those who had served him.

On the distant horizon another warband appeared, wearing the same mark of Bal'ahr the Winter Sun on their foreheads. Before them loped great grey-coated hounds the likes of which the men of Prydn had never seen, shaggy and near as tall as a man. They raced before their masters like dogs of the Un-world, howling and baying, their tongues lolling horribly.

Catching up with the main body of the survivors, Ardhu gestured ahead to a curve in the river, where a thick patch of elm, ash and alder grew on the far bank. "Get into the water at that spot!" he shouted. "Cross to the trees. Maybe the dogs will lose the scent." He sounded doubtful. Desperate.

The band plunged into the river, splashing and going under as the muddy river bottom gave way beneath their feet. Mordraed slipped and was momentarily pulled under by the slow, strong current; he resurfaced cursing and blinking water from his eyes; not only briefly blinded, but with a wet bowstring that would render his weapon unusable. And Agravaen... where was he? He had lost hold of him... He glanced about wildly. He had no great feeling for his younger brother but he could not let him drown or fall to a bunch of savages.

A few feet away he saw Gal'havad struggling in the swell, bracing the supine body of Agravaen against his shoulder and fighting to keep his head above the water. "Over here, Mordraed!" he gasped. "Hurry, I cannot hold him much longer."

Mordraed struck out swimming and managed to get hold of Agravaen again. Between him and Gal'havad they hauled his limp form to the shore and then into the relative safety of the trees. Once hidden in the tangle of foliage they halted, staring back at the progress of the other men. Most were nearly across the river, showering mud and water as they slogged through the shallows. Only Ardhu and Bal-ahn hung back, standing on the far bank amid the swaying reeds. Bal-ahn with his shoulder streaming dark blood and a face as deathly as that of Hwynn, god of the Mortuary.

"With this wound bleeding freely, the hounds will sniff me out for sure." Brought on the wind, Bal-ahn's words were carried across the holy river of the Great White Cow. "And I am too weakened to swim such a current. I will stay and hold them off as best I can. It may give you more time, Lord."

"Bal-ahn... you cannot." Ardhu's voice was weary, heavy. "You know what that will mean. You know there can only be one ending if you remain here."

Bal-ahn drew his dagger, an imported blade from Ar-morah, long and deadly. "I do."

"I cannot ask you to do this."

"You have not asked me, Lord. I choose to do it."

Standing ankle-deep in the mud on the opposite bank, Ba-lin listened to his brother's words and his cheeks drained of colour. Splashing back across the river, he reached Bal-ahn's side and grabbed his uninjured arm. "We were born of one womb; it is said we share one soul between us," he said fiercely, though his voice trembled. "If you make a stand here, my brother... you will not stand alone!" He drew his own dagger and stood at Bal-ahn's side, ready to share his twin's death as he had shared his birth.

"Go, Stone Lord." Bal-ahn glanced desperately at Ardhu. "I can hear the enemy drawing close; they have not given up the chase!"

Ardhu embraced each of the brothers quickly. He was as white as they, his eyes dark hollows, his hands trembling with emotion. "Farewell, my greatest friends of these many years. May we meet one day in the banquet halls of the Ancestors on the Plain of Honey!" Whirling on his heel, he dived headlong into the river and swam with the agility of a salmon to the far shore. He had just reached the bank and scrambled into the shadows of the trees when the first of the great hounds padded into view, a great creature near as tall as a pony, with a dun coat and swinging tail like a club. Its lips peeled over its fangs as it saw the twins waiting with drawn daggers on the riverside.

And then, with a blood-curdling howl, it bounded towards them.

*****

In the little wood, Ardhu gathered his band together. Nine... that was all that were left. Nine, including an injured Agravaen. All had come to ruin... why had the Ancestors turned against him in such a manner?

"We must keep going," he barked gruffly. "Ba-lin and Bal-ahn will hold them as long as they can but they are far outnumbered, and our foes know this area while we do not."

"Which way?" gasped Hwalchmai, slapping his sodden hair out of his eyes.

"Down the river. Keep following the water but do not go too close to the edge lest you are spotted by enemies on the other shore."

Mordraed fumbled in the calfskin pouch hanging at his belt. He felt the vial of poison there; undamaged, its stopper still sealing its contents, praise the spirits. "My bowstring is wet; I cannot shoot at our foes. But I also have a slingshot. I will take any down with that, if I can."

They began to run again, Mordraed and Gal'havad pulling Agravaen's supine form along the ground, one arm each; he was proving too weighty to carry between them. Woodcraft was forgotten as they crashed through vines and growing shrubs, desperate to put as much space between them and their pursuers as possible. In the distance they could hear the great dogs barking and howling in canine fury; then men were screaming, shouting, their voices eerie and hideous and distorted on the rising wind.

They forced their way through the greenery for what seemed an eternity. Eventually Ardhu held up a hand for a halt. "I hear nothing now. We will find a place where we may rest and tend the wounded. Leave the river and head for that rising ground…" he pointed through the tangle of trees to a grey outcrop of stone furred with mountain-ash and ferns. "There's an open spot above the treeline where we can watch for the approach of any enemy."

The companions veered away from the River Boann and began to climb the escarpment. A few hundred yards below the top, in a bald space denuded of greenery, stood the retaining circle of a ruined round-house. The band climbed into the safety of its sheltering walls and then collapsed, some leaning against the tumbled stones, panting, others falling full out on the ground, their strength almost completely sapped.

Mordraed and Gal'havad placed Agravaen on Mordraed's skin cloak and Mordraed tried to give him some water. He could not swallow. "Let me try," said Gal'havad and he took his little violet-coloured cup from the safety of his tunic, filled it with a bit of weak ale from his flask, and pressed it to Agravaen's dry and peeling lips.

Mordraed scowled, sitting back on his haunches. Gal'havad was like a child, playing with his silly talisman, a stone scraped out of the bottom of a pool. And yet… he saw Agravaen's eyelids flicker. The big lad glanced around dazedly. "I… I have done well this day, haven't I?" he asked. His voice was strange, lost; his eyes glazed and unfocussed.

"You killed your enemy, so yes," replied Mordraed.

"I have done well for the Stone Lord, then?" Agravaen asked, letting his head fall back on the earth with a thud. His mouth trembled slightly; a purplish stain deepened his lips.

"Aye." Mordraed's voice was sharp. "What a good warrior should do for his chieftain."

Agravaen's hand shot out, catching Mordraed's wrist and drawing him down until their heads were close together. His fingers were icy. "I know… what is in your heart… brother…" he whispered, and suddenly there was bloody foam leaking from his mouth. "Don't do it. Our mother is not right. Turn from your path, Mordraed, or you will die…"

Mordraed listened in horror. What if Gal'havad or any of the others heard? Leaning down, he pressed his hand over Agravaen's mouth, trying not to recoil at the feel of his hot spittle against his palm. "Be silent… the poison makes you rave. Be still, we will do what we can for you, perhaps the dart did not go too deep."

Agravaen stared up at his older brother, unable to speak due to the pressure of his hand. His eyes suddenly darkened with a look akin to hatred, and then he made a gasping, wheezing noise and began to jerk and spasm.

Gal'havad heard the sound of his heels drumming the loose stones. "Mordraed... what is happening?"

"Get back!" Mordraed swung out at him with his arm, gesturing him away. "This is not for you to see, Prince of Kham-El-Ard!" Bitterness and rage dripped from his words and Gal'havad stood as one stunned, too fearful to move.

Agravaen lay still. His eyes were wide open, sightless, and a trickle of yellow foam ran from his mouth. Mordraed wiped his hand on the grass, face contorted. "He is gone to the Ancestors... Leave me, Gal'havad. I will make a burial pyre for him."

Having heard the commotion, Ardhu strode over and looked at the inert body. "I feel grief that Agravaen has gone to the long-house of his fathers," he said formally, "but there can be no pyre. The smoke would be a clear sign to our foes."

Mordraed's eyes crackled. "So you think it acceptable that a man of your own royal house, your sister's son, lays unbarrowed as food for wild dogs and wolves..."

"I do not," said Ardhu wearily. "But we are in danger and the needs of the living must outweigh those of the dead. Remember, Mordraed, in the days of our forebears, the bodies of the dead were laid open to the sky for many Moons before they were burned or placed within their mounds."

"I will build him a small cairn at least," snarled Mordraed. "High on the hill above, where the Sun will touch. No thanks to you, Stone Lord, and no honour to your kin."

Ardhu turned his back to his bastard son. No use in argument that would solve nothing... especially with Mordraed who seemed to crave argument at every turn. He was sorry to see Agravaen dead, he had been loyal despite his upbringing in Morigau's household, but he could not make exception for him.

Mordraed angrily grabbed Agravaen's body beneath the arms and started to drag him out of the hut circle and further up the slope, while the other members of the warband stared, motionless. They knew him little, as he was one of the younger members, and had rarely mingled outside of his group of fractious youths who had few prospects.

Gal'havad, who had watched the exchange between his father and friend, suddenly leapt forward as if released from a spell. "I will help him!" he cried, and raced after Mordraed.

He soon caught up with the dark-haired youth and in silence grasped hold of Agravaen's legs. Mordraed stared at him, surprised, then nodded curtly in acceptance of his help. Between them they wrestled the young warrior's body to the crest of the hill, where they found the shattered cairn of an earlier people, its inner stones, covered with Suns and spirals, now open to the frowning sky. They placed him in the unroofed entrance passage and tucked his knees up to his chest, laying his head to the North so that his unseeing eyes faced East toward Bhel's glory. Mordraed began to hunt out rocks from the fallen dome of the mound and placed them over him, one by one, heaping them up into a pointed cairn. Unspeaking, Gal'havad worked steadily beside him, until, by the time the sky had darkened to purple and the light of a big Moon turned the hilltop to white-silver, the body of the dead youth was completely covered, safe from the predators that roamed the wild places beyond the firelight.

Upon finishing, Mordraed fell back against the retaining circle, breathing heavily, rubbing his blood and earth-stained hands over his hot, sweating face. He felt wearier than he had ever felt... he who was graced by the spirits with good health and strong limbs... and his mind was in turmoil. Agravaen dead... his ally, even if only to use as a shield against the hostility of others. And if that was not bad enough... there, across the river when they were attacked, he had lost yet another chance to claim his birthright. He could have finished it off then, quickly and easily. Two arrows gone astray in the heat of battle... Ardhu Pendraec and his son Gal'havad dead in one tragic accident. None would have dared blamed him, and he would have made the suitable show of grief.

He moved his knuckles across sore, burning eyes. What was wrong with him? Why had his arm turned soft? No... no, *nothing* was wrong! It had just not been the right time to make such a decisive move, that was all... if he had killed them, the remaining warriors of Prydn might have lost heart and been overwhelmed by their enemies, and he would have swiftly met the same fate he had dealt out.

"Mordraed... are you all right?" he heard Gal'havad's voice through what seemed a heavy mist. He managed to force his eyes open and glare blearily at his half-brother, who knelt on the lichenous stones, hand on his shoulder.

Mordraed shrugged him off. "Why?" His voice was dry, cracked. "Why did you come up here to bury Agravaen with me?"

"It was right. Agravaen deserves to lie in honour. My father was wrong not to help you himself." Gal'havad hung his head. "I would aid you in whatever you asked, Mordraed. You are my brother."

A cold chill swept through Mordraed, piercing him to the heart. It was as if a barrow ghost had prodded him with an icy skeletal finger. The heavy mist of exhaustion fell from him, and his dark eyes narrowed. "Brother... what do you mean?" Could the boy know? Had he known all along?

Gal'havad's face was open and guileless. "I know we are really but cousins, yet I have no brother of my blood and I have always looked to you as I might a brother."

"You are a fool, then..." Mordraed scrambled up.

Gal'havad stared at him. "You are not yourself... but I understand."

Mordraed stormed down the hill, slipping on the shale, eyes burning, tearing with an emotion he could not fathom. *Oh my little brother... it is you who does not understand. I AM myself. Completely myself. And that shall be your undoing...*

*****

Ardhu led his remaining men down the river in the dark. Fish flopped in the swell, the wind sobbed in reeds and withies. Animal eyes, luminous as floating moons, shone out of bushes, then vanished into the tangle of foliage on the banks.

"I can smell a tang in the air," hissed Hwalchmai. "Can you smell it too, Ardhu? Wood smoke."

Ardhu lifted his head, scenting the air like an animal. "Yes, I smell it too. But not just wood smoke. Flesh cooking. Let us hope..." his smile was grim, a shadow deepening his eye sockets till his visage looked a skull, "it is animal flesh. Although men say the folk who dwell at Spiralfort are wise and peaceful. If what I have deduced by the stars is correct, we should be drawing near the bend of the River of the White Cow, and will soon see the great sanctuary of God's Peak."

"Let us pray to the Ancestors that you are right about the peacefulness of the folk who dwell there," murmured Hwalchmai.

"They wrought the Cup of Gold for the Maimed King," said Ardhu.

"Aye... but they took it away again," said Hwalchmai darkly. "A capricious folk, whose motives we do not know."

Ardhu glanced over his shoulder at his dwindled warband. Their faces glowed pale in the starshine. Mordraed and Gal'havad were at the rear of the party, walking side by side... Mordraed's visage was dark, shuttered, his lips drawn into thin lines, his hair whipping his cheeks like the wings of the flesh-hungry raven. Ardhu felt a sudden, irrational surge of fear; the like of which he had never felt before, even in his first battle by the Glein, when he was scarcely more than a boy. He gripped the hilt of Caladvolc, tempted to draw it, although he knew he would appear mad to his men.

Trying to get hold of his emotions, he turned in his saddle and gestured to the two youths. "Come to me, both of you. Gal'havad, you must stand with me as Prince of the West. Mordraed, I take it you have restrung your bow? We may have need of it."

"It is done," said Mordraed flatly. "My weapons are always close to hand, Lord Ardhu."

I would wager that they are indeed, my serpent son born in shame and shadow! But oh gods, I must trust you now because I have no choice and almost no men left...

The course of the River Boann turned abruptly, and in an instant the trees vanished, leaving a wide open vista. The companions stopped and stared, for before them, on the northern side of the Holy River of the White Cow, was a marvellous complex, with features both familiar and alien to them.

On the top of a slight slope stood a huge mound, not as large or as conical as the Hill of Zhel, but wide and drum-shaped, a sun-disc with a mighty white quartz revetment and decorated kerbstones that gleamed blue in the moonlight. A circle of about thirty massive stone blocks surrounded it, shutting out the profane world and holding the powers-that-be in. Two timber structures stood close at its side—a smaller, linear one in the West, facing the Land of the Ancestors, and an enormous circular one in the South-East, filled with many rows of pits and posts and fronted by a pair of gigantic stones similar in function and appearance to the Three Watchers of Khor Ghor. Torches and fires flickered by stones and wooden posts, making shadows dance, and the smell of roasting flesh permeated the night air. By the entrance passage of the great mound a pair of stone lanterns could be seen burning—the famed eternal night-lamps of Uffern, the Very Deep.

"So this is it!" Bohrs stood staring, arms folded over his barrel chest. "The place they call Spiralfort, the God's Peak."

"And also Kar Pebir, the Flaming Door, and Fortress in the Middle-of-the-Earth," said Hwalchmai. "or so the song-singers tell, when they fare across Severna's sea."

Gal'havad looked across the rippling waters of the river at the mound and its satellite structures. A strange sensation gripped him; fear and yet elation, a sense that here destinies converged... it was just as he had felt when he first set eyes upon his cousin Mordraed walking through the snow across the barrow-grounds of the kings.

"Father..." he swivelled round in his saddle to face Ardhu. "Let us cross the river and come to this place. I can sense the Cup we seek is here, waiting for us to claim it."

"We will not be hasty," said Ardhu. "We must be cautious, though I have heard the folk of the God's Peak are hospitable, enemies of those who attacked us on this bitter day. The headman is said to be a wise man called Maheloas."

The companions walked a little further, crossing the Boann at a place where there was a natural ford with signs of passage. White cattle sacred to the spirit of the river moved through the waters with them, passing to and fro under the vast haze of the Milky Way, the cloak of Nud and skyward path of the Dead.

Trudging across the grass towards the great mound on the height, darkness suddenly swirled and shattered and the band were confronted by an unbroken line of men and women. Torches flared and they gazed at rows of faces, young and old, some masked, others bare. The strangers were impassive, neither friendly nor fierce, and it seemed their eyes, glimmering in the red torchlight, scryed the truth of their souls.

Ardhu stepped forward, hands held apart, far from the hilt of Caladvolc. "We come in peace. Is there one here who goes by the name of Maheloas?"

An old man left the throng and walked in stately manner towards Ardhu.

175

He reminded him of the Merlin, a lean wiry figure with sweeping grey-black hair and a long beard plaited with beads wrapped in golden foil. Beneath bushy brows that rose like wings, his eyes were a pale, striking blue, the colour of thick winter's ice upon the tarn. He wore a shaman's robe with a great wheel painted upon it in ochre; the wheel was crisscrossed with lines that showed the movements of the Moon. "I am Maheloas," he said. "High Priest of the Houses of the Holy—of the Cave of the Sun, and of Cnobga the Hill of the Hag Bui, and Dubad the Hill of Darkness where the Winter Sun is swallowed. And you I know, though we have never met. You are Ardhu Pendraec, King of Prydn, and husband to Fynavir, daughter of Mevva the Intoxicator."

Ardhu's eyes widened in surprised. "How do you know who I am?"

Maheloas smiled, his face creasing into a thousand lines. "Wanderers come bringing tales of strife and sadness in Prydn. They say the King, the greatest lord since the days of Samothos the Tin-Lord, seeks to find the Cup of Plenty that will bring new life to a barren old world."

"That is what I would do." Ardhu inclined his head.

Maheloas scanned Ardhu's face with his ice-cool eyes. "And yet... I do not feel belief coming from you, Lord of Prydn. You do not believe any Cup of enchantment can save your land."

Ardhu glanced up again, suddenly fierce, his gaze green-dark fire. "What I believe or do not believe is of importance to no one but me. I do what I must and have the blessings of Deroweth and Suilven for this quest."

"You will be welcome here." Maheloas smiled benevolently and held out his hand. "But if you do not believe, the Cup will never go with you. And if you try to take it by force, not one of your men will leave this place alive. I do not threaten this in anger, King of Prydn, I tell you only what must be. We took the Cup back from the Maimed King long ago, when he fell into folly and ruin; it is precious to our people because the gold from which it is beaten was bathed in the blood of our Good God Dag who, with his consort Ahn-u makes all the land fruitful."

Ardhu bowed, and then ran his hand across his tired eyes. "I speak from weariness... half my men are dead, including kin and friends of many years, and we have been running from foes for hours. I beg you, Maheloas, to let us rest awhile and then we may talk of the Cup."

Maheloas nodded. "I will agree to that, Stone Lord of Prydn. Follow me."

*****

The priest led the band to the Eastern enclosure beside the great Mound of Spiralfort. An outer ring of mighty totem poles surrounded an inner ring of cremation pits lined with clay, where animal carcasses burned, tended by veiled women in strange broad hats of woven river rushes. The ground was thick with ash; the air greasy and rank with smoke. Beyond the crematory hearths were three inner rows of pits in which the charred remains were strewn—burnt, blackened ribs and cow's heads with horns, parts of goats and sheep and deer, even a wild horse. A large clay mound, pale and tumescent, stood at the end of the vast enclosure, reminding the warriors of Prydn of their own sacred space at Marthodunu, lying in its valley midway between Suilven and Khor Ghor.

"This is Wheel-of-Offering," said Maheloas. "Where we give to the spirits the bounty of our land both night and day."

"You do not feast here yourselves?"

"At the times of darkness and light—yes. Now and for the next few months only the spirits will sup. We have enough for ourselves in our settlement on the hither side of blessed Boann. That we have so much to spare should show you, who has ceased to believe, how we are blessed by the Ancestors and Great Ones."

"But have you not noticed the change in the weather, the gods turning their faces away? Surely it has come to you too."

Maheloas did not meet Ardhu's probing gaze, but continued to walk amidst the smouldering and bone-filled pits. "If the rains come, we pray harder and make more and greater sacrifices... The Old ones will listen."

More sacrifices... Ardhu's stomach lurched; he had had enough of sacrifice. The loss of Ba-lin and Bal-ahn burnt his memory like the fires around him, while the smell of hundreds of lumps of burning meat made hot acid leap into his throat.

Maheloas took the men of Ardhu from the great Eastern circle to a more intimate structure in the West, where twin rows of massive parallel posts stood like sentinels, the early morning mist swirling around their bases. One of the standing stones of the circle surrounding the passage tomb was trapped within this artificial forest, a lumpen grey ghost glimmering in the torch light. A low roof made of plaited river-reeds lay over the top of the posts, casting deep shadows that hid whatever lay in the sacred space at the back of the structure.

Out from the entranceway of this mysterious cult-house stepped a girl who greeted Maheloas in a soft, musical voice. Next to Mordraed, Gal'havad made a small noise in his throat. Mordraed was about to cast him a scathing glance... but then he saw the torchlight illuminate the maiden who walked gracefully towards them.

She was slight and her hair was as black as his, curling to her waist, twined with blue beads and roundels of carved bone. Crescent earrings imported from the realm of Ibher hung from her lobes, and an intricate gorget ribbed with golden beads clasped her neck. In contrast to the darkness of her hair, her skin was white as if she seldom walked under sun, flawless and unmarked—this proclaimed her status, that she need not work tending the crops or herding the cattle. In the small, perfect oval of her face, her eyes were a clear, deep blue, the colour of Mordraed's own eyes, but lacking their coldness—instead they were filled with a calm clarity. In one hand she held a bowl bound with bronze, in the other a sceptre similar to Ardhu's Lightning

Mace, its shaft cut with deep spiralling grooves and its polished stone head pinned on by golden studs.

"I am Ivormyth daughter of Maheloas," she said simply. "I am the Maiden of the Holy Cup, its servant and its Guardian. Be welcome here, to the House of the West."

She gestured with her hand and the companions entered the cult-house, bowing to the great standing stone confined within its walls. Inside were two other young women, near as beautiful as Ivormyth, who brought out bowls of ancient design, wreathed in spirals and brimming with pork, and tall fine beakers impressed with wheat and nail-marks like little crescent Moons.

"This is the House of Vedu," said Ivormyth, placing the symbols of her rank on a dresser of stout withies at the back of the hut. "House of Intoxication." She handed Ardhu the largest of the beakers, a huge drinking vessel as red as fire. Honey-mead swirled in it, with tiny flowers added for sweet flavour dancing on the swell.

Ardhu clasped the beaker and raised it above his head as expected, then drank it to the dregs in one. Ivormyth took the empty pot from him and smashed it against the single standing stone, the pieces spinning out across the room. "The spirits welcome you," she said. "Sit and rest and my sisters will tend your wounds."

The warband sat down on the floor, humble and quiet in the presence of these sacred maidens. Ivormyth and her two companions went amongst them, bringing food and drink and bowls of clean water and moss to tend their scrapes and gouges.

Mordraed was unable to keep his eyes from Ivormyth as she bent and knelt beside the warriors, graceful as a willow wand. Khyloq and the child in her belly were forgotten; they fled from his mind like mist. House of Intoxication indeed! He had not expected this... suddenly he felt a little less angry and confused. If he could take this girl back to Prydn it would please him; there was no law that said a man could not have many wives, it all depended on wealth... and stamina. He grinned. Once Ardhu was out of the way and Mordraed claimed his rightful place, he was sure he would soon be richer than Samothos and Bolgos in their golden barrows!

And then Ivormyth was there, standing demurely in front of Mordraed, offering him a beaker. He leaned forward, taking the drinking cup slowly, letting his long, slim fingers slide against hers. He smiled, tossing back his hair, confident that she would look upon him with favour; he had long known how the women of the tribes desired him. Why should she be any different? They were alike; both beautiful, both high status; it would be an excellent match.

To his surprise she did not return his smile. Her lips were pale straight lines and her eyes cool. Without a word or gesture she turned away... and faced Gal'havad, who sat beside him. "You are the son of Ardhu Pendraec?"

she said. Her voice was lilting music; it infuriated Mordraed to hear it wasted on his younger brother.

"I am. I am called Gal'havad, the Hawk of Summer, Prince of Evening. My mother, Queen Fynavir, is from your fair country." Gal'havad got to his feet and made a small, courteous bow. "The Ancestors bless the day of our meeting, Lady Ivormyth of Spiralfort."

Mordraed's eyes widened in fury. The little bastard was trying his wiles with the girl! Gal'havad, the pure one, the different one who was more apt to speak with ghosts on the Plains than women!

New hatred coiled in Mordraed's heart; how did Gal'havad dare, when Mordraed had made it obvious where his interests lay! He let his thumb touch the hilt of his dagger. He should have finished it before; well, the time was coming. None would gainsay Mordraed son of Morigau and the Pendraec.

Ivormyth gave a hand-signal to the other maidens and together they left the cult-house. Dawn was coming; light seeped through cracks in the roof and the torches were guttering, but the companions were all weary, and lying down they slept like dogs round the hearth, sated with meat and drink.

Gal'havad and Mordraed alone remained awake. Mordraed would not look at his brother, but stared moodily into space. Gal'havad seemed not to notice. "Cousin, I am filled with a great joy," he said impetuously. "This is a great and holy place; I can feel the spirits of the Old Ones all around me. And the Lady Ivormyth... it is as if she holds my destiny in her hands, I can feel it."

"I would imagine that is not all you would like to feel," said Mordraed with heavy sarcasm.

Gal'havad frowned, his brows drawing together. "Mordraed, what do you mean?" And then, as the words registered, "Mordraed, that is an unjust thing to say. I would not dishonour a lady of such high rank and beauty. Or any other, for that matter."

"Oh noble Gal'havad," mocked Mordraed. "Spare me your words of honour and let me sleep."

He flung himself on the ground, back to Gal'havad. The red-haired youth stared at him for a while, noting the tenseness of his back and shoulders. His eyes were closed but Gal'havad knew he did not sleep. For the first time a little cold finger of doubt touched Gal'havad. Mordraed had always been quick to anger and sharp-tongued... but in the last few days there had been strangeness in him. Reaching into his tunic, he pulled out the violet cup from the sacred pool at Kham-El-Ard, given him by his aunt Mhor-gan. He held it to his face, feeling the stone, washed smooth by five thousand years of gentle waves, against his cheek, reminding him of home, of the forests and the Plain, of the Stones of Khor Ghor in the morning mist, and the great hump of the Spirit-Path streaking toward the rising Sun.

He wished he was home now, and that this quest was over.

But that was not to be. He was in the Land of the Setting Sun, at the

Temple of Spiralfort, for good or for ill. Stretching out on the ground, he fell into an exhausted sleep alongside the rest of the companions, the little violet cup clasped like an offering between his fingers.

*****

Gal'havad woke later in the day. He could hear people moving around him, and the sounds of dogs, animals and people outside the cult-house. He sat up, scrambling to his feet, and suddenly he realised something was wrong. Something terrible.

His talisman was gone.

Cursing, he searched through the rushes on the floor, searched through the calfskin bag at his waist and in the folds of his clothes.

It was gone. The violet cup of twilight, his talisman of protection, his gift from Mhor-gan.

Angry and desperate, he whirled around to see who else was in the hut. His father was standing by the doorway, with Bohrs, and Hwalchmai... all trustworthy, kin or as close as kin. The other men too, he trusted; they had not even been lying near him. Mordraed had slept at his back, of course; he was still nearby, sitting cross-legged in the rushes, honing his dagger blade and seemingly unaware of Gal'havad's distress.

"Mordraed!" he called out. "Have you seen my cup?"

Mordraed craned his head around, continuing to work his blade with the flint sharpening-stone. "No. Should I have?"

"It is missing. I had it in my hands last night!"

"And you went to sleep with it on show?" Mordraed rolled his eyes. "Not wise, little cousin. No doubt one of these foreign savages has made away with it. Don't worry yourself... it was just a trinket. I am sure Mhor-gan will dig up another one for you when we return home."

Gal'havad's shoulders slumped. Maybe Mordraed was right; he attached too much importance to his aunt's gift. No matter the truth, he could do no more to find the talisman; he could not accuse Maheloas and his people of theft for fear of causing an affront that might lead to all their deaths...

Sighing, he gathered his cloak up and walked toward Ardhu, trying not to think of his missing gift. Mordraed rose and followed him, hiding a slight smile behind the fall of his hair. The little fool wasn't looking so sure of himself today...

Ardhu peered out of the cult-house into the bright sky. "Maheloas is coming for us. I believe we are to have a testing of sorts."

"I would test my axe on some heads," murmured Bohrs.

"Again..." Ardhu cast him a warning look, "no fighting unless we have no choice."

A shadow fell over the threshold, stretching inward over the great stone that was the heart of the house. Maheloas was there, a fox skull bound in the upper section of his hair and its bright pelt falling across his shoulders. Skulls of cranes and swans dangled from his cloak, making an ominous clack and

180

clatter. In his hand he carried a great, antiquated crook made of stone, its front wreathed in jagged patterns. "Come, my guests." He gestured with his thin, knotted hand. "You will eat with us and we will speak of the quest you have come upon and what you desire."

He led Ardhu and his warriors across the green vista outside the great Ancestor tomb. Even in broad daylight it was a magical place, all its features now clearly revealed. The grassland swept away toward the river, dropping in stepped terraces toward the foaming, frothing cauldron that was the heart of Boann, River of the White Cow. Birch trees tossed their branches on the far riverbank, silver dancers amidst more solemn alder and magic hazel, so beloved of shamans for their wands. Deer flitted amidst the trees, passing like shadows as they migrated towards the distant peak of Redmountain, the source of many streams and tributaries that merged their strength with the holy river.

The group passed East toward the rising Sun, back toward the crematorial pit circle with its still-burning offerings. The vast entrance of the passage tomb came into view, clear now in the light of day, a place of power, of the spirits, of life and death. White quartz fronted the mound here, a wall that had buckled and slumped, fallen after uncounted nights of rain and wind and erosion. A huge stone blocked the way to the passage, an enormous prone block carved with art such as the men of Prydn had never seen—huge swirling spirals, locked together, looking to some like the orbs of the Watcher who protected the souls of Men, to others like a vast proud bull ready to charge, to yet others a vast sea with the waves curling and the bright stars that were the watching Ancestors above.

Behind the portal-stone, above the dark womb-passage, was a stone box... the place where the beams of the Midwinter Sun would pierce the mound, lighting the holy of holies, drawing the spirits from the cremated ashes that lay in huge carved bowls in niches inside. Ardhu recognized the significance, even as he observed the box, for its purpose was similar to that of the Great Trilithon, which on the same day also framed the Sun, drawing its rays into the circle and bringing life to the spirits.

Leaving the entrance of Spiralfort behind, the company circled the mound alongside its vast decorated kerbstones, partly hidden by the collapse of the heavy cairn material, which was already over a thousand years old. In the East loomed the pit-circle with its many rings of posts, and by its entrance, guarded by the two flanking stones like grey needles, a small domed hut that they had not noticed last night amidst the flickering fires and the smoke of the cremated offerings.

Maheloas guided them to the hut door. Inside, the beehive hut was dark and dank, the clay walls oozing moisture. Incense cups burned, the fragrance of herbs mixed with the ever present aroma of charred meat. Ivormyth knelt on the floor, her two attendants beside her. Her bowl stood before her knees, while the sceptre lay near her right hand. She had assumed a new robe, thin as mist, her flesh, painted with ochre, gleaming tantalisingly through the folds.

Maheloas gestured for Ardhu and his band to be seated and they settled themselves on the floor. Ivormyth's women rose and, as before, brought mead and bread and meat, which were consumed in silence. When the remnants of the meal were cleared away, Maheloas rose to his feet and gazed first at Ardhu then at each of his men in turn.

"You have come many miles from Prydn to Ibherna to see the Golden Cup of Plenty, Blessed by the Good God, old master of all," he said. "The Maimed King held it once but it passed from him when he became unclean and doomed. You wish to take it again, to bring hope and maybe more, for it is said all things of goodness flow from its depths. But not all may touch the Cup, and already once have hands not worthy enough held it, diminishing its power. Ardhu Pendraec, Stone Lord, you have already admitted the belief is not in you—you will not touch or bear the Cup of Gold. But of those who travel with you, your loyal companions, I cannot say."

The old man gestured to the warband. "Look upon what you see here before you... the Cauldron that is always Full, the Sceptre that a king bears, the Maiden that is the Land. Choose between them, warriors, and choose wisely. One may be He Who Sees Beyond to the true Nature of the Cup."

Bohrs pushed forward, ever eager, and grasped the bowl in his thick hands, lifting it above his head. "A full bowl of food and the full bellies of the people is always a good thing! Without food, where would we be? Dead!"

The companions laughed, though Ardhu with unease. What if this game was played to deceive and the prize would be snatched away, with no real chance of winning it?

Hwalchmai stepped forth next, reverently lifting the sceptre with its flashing pins of gold. "A peaceful land with a strong lord to rule over it is good land. When chiefs fall to warring, the land and its bounty is diminished."

Hwalchmai placed the sceptre back into its place and was about to sit back down at Ardhu's side, when Mordraed shoved him aside, almost making him drop the holy relic in his hands. Mordraed's eyes were hot as brands as he stared at Ivormyth, who sat head bowed, her hair pooling around her like black water. "It's the girl, isn't it?" he cried. "The other objects merely fool the greedy and the power-starved... the food bowl for Bohrs who dreams of naught but haunches of roast pig and beakers of beer, and the sceptre for Hwalchmai, a landless kinsman eternally basking in the glory of his betters! The girl is the key... She is Sovereignty, the Cup is her, and I will claim her here and now!"

Reaching down, he grasped Ivormyth's slender wrist and yanked her to her feet, his expression one of triumph.

Ivormyth glanced up, eyes flashing, and slapped him with full force across the face.

"Bitch!" He dropped her arm and drew his dagger as Maheloas leapt up to pull Ivormyth away. Ardhu and Hwalchmai swung into action, grabbing Mordraed's arms and pinioning them behind his back, while Bohrs ripped the knife from his hand and flung it upon the ground.

"You dishonour me!" Mordraed screamed, incandescent with rage. "It was the true answer, the meaning of the Cup... but you have no intent of giving us the treasure, do you, Maheloas? Your savages probably want to cut out our hearts and give them to your god, Bloody Crescent!"

"Enough!" Ardhu's fist shot out, striking Mordraed in the mouth and drawing blood. The blow was strong enough to drive Mordraed to his knees, head reeling. "You will not insult our hosts. If you do not hold your tongue, I will give you to the spirits myself!"

Maheloas walked across the hut and stared down at Mordraed. "You were wrong, boy. Wrong. As were the others. The Cup is bound with all you have seen, and yet none. Its true meaning remains locked from you, and none here is noble or pure enough to witness its brightness, the Sun bound in a Cup of Gold. I would ask you now to leave the Mansion of the Good God and his Son. Follow the river back to the shore, take ship and do not look back. We will not harm you if you agree to this, but if you do not go in peace, I cannot guarantee your safety."

"Wait!" It was Gal'havad who spoke now. Clambering to his feet, he faced the shaman. The light shining through the door at his back turned his hair into a halo of fiercest flame. His face was translucent pale, the face of one of the Everliving Ones who guarded the islands of the West. "I have not spoken yet. I beg you listen to me. I know the secret of the Cup of Gold."

Maheloas's brows rose; his shrew gaze scanned the young, ardent face before him, lit by an inner light that was almost not of the world. "Speak."

"The mystery of the Cup is not in plenty, power or sovereignty. The secret is in here." He laid his hand on his chest. "Its power is what is means to the man who holds it, who believes in its worth. It is nothing and everything."

Maheloas's lips drew to narrow lines. "Who are you, boy, who speaks words of a priest but wears a warrior's garb?"

"I am Gal'havad, Hawk of Summer, prince of the Twilight."

A sigh slipped from Maheloas's lips. Unexpectedly, he sank down on one knee and clasped Gal'havad's hand in his own. "You are the one. Dark and light, youth and death, warrior and mystic. You have won the right to the Cup of Gold for your people."

Ardhu and his men stared, overjoyed at this sudden change in fortune, victory snatched from the jaws of defeat. Mordraed half-scrambled to his feet, snarling, and was slapped down to the ground again by Ardhu, who planted his heel upon his son's wrist, pinning him to the spot.

Ivormyth, with great dignity, collected the bowl and the sceptre. Gravely she bowed to Gal'havad and placed them into his hands. "These will you

183

have, lord of the Golden Cup: the Bowl of Plenty, the Sceptre of Power... and I will also be yours if that is your wish."

"I wish it, lady," he replied, blushing.

Maheloas came between them and took their hands and clasped them together. "An alliance between our people. This is good. On the night of the third day the Moon is reborn and then will the Lord Gal'havad claim the Cup and all the other treasures he has won."

*****

The warriors of Ardhu Pendraec rejoiced, and so did the people of God's Peak, the Spiralfort of the Good Dag and his Son. People danced around the stone circle throughout the day and night, and beakers were filled, and drunk and smashed. Offerings were given in the pit circle and to the maiden of the Holy Chalice and her chosen one, Gal'havad, winner of the Cup of Gold. The folk of Ibherna came from all around, climbing up the terraced hillside from the river to gift them with fruit and wheat sheaves and to give Ivormyth ancestral gifts to take to her new home in Prydn, the Isle of the Mighty—barrel-shaped beads and schist plaques of jadeite, a miniature axehead pendant and two polished balls for fertility.

Ardhu relaxed for the first time in many days. He drank from the same beaker as Maheloas, as they would soon be kin with the joining of his son and Maheloas's daughter. He vaguely wondered how Fynavir would react when Gal'havad returned from his travels with a bride as well as the holy vessel; shocked no doubt, but perhaps since Ivormyth was of her own folk she would come to be glad.

As Ardhu drank to the health of the couple and the renewing of Prydn, Mordraed sulked, sitting in the blue shadows of the mighty God's Peak, his back against a slab of intricately carved stone. He had been made a fool by the riddles and games of Maheloas and his haughty daughter, and by his own father, who should have stood up for him and not treated him like some miscreant. As for Gal'havad... envy gnawed at Mordraed. He could scarcely believe it. A mere few months ago, his half-brother had been just a boy, not even accepted as a Man of the Tribe, and now he was some kind of hero and about to wed the woman Mordraed desired for himself...

Cold snakes of fear writhed in his belly and suddenly he felt deathly ill. Gal'havad was becoming too powerful, too popular, despite his physical frailties, his shaking illness. It was time to act, time to make an end as he had sworn to do. He had been weak, and too merciful, sparing his half-brother too many times. It was time to do the will of Morigau, and to take the destiny he was owed.

He rose, heart hammering, gazing toward the cult-house where Gal'havad was ensconced with the girl, receiving gifts from the tribesmen of Ibherna. This deed had to be done; it was what he had been trained for, what he was sworn to do. So why did he feel so sick and shaken and sad... somehow so *appalled* and yet so intent on Gal'havad's death?

"Am I falling ill?" He brushed his arm across his forehead. He did feel slightly hot. A fine sheen of sweat glistened on his brow. He did not understand this; he was never sick. But it would make no difference.

The deed had to be done.

When the Moon was reborn, Gal'havad would claim the Cup of Gold as Maheloas had decreed.

When the Moon was reborn, Mordraed would be waiting.

For he was the Dark Moon, eclipsing the light, son of a broken taboo. Fingers trembling, he touched the scar on his face where Morigau had marred him, marking him as the chosen one of her malevolent lunar spirits.

In the time of the Dark Moon, death walked.

*****

Ivormyth moved like mist across the trampled earth before the portal stone of God's Peak. Twilight had fallen and a purple haze hung over the land, giving it a surreal glamour, where trees and rocks and river seemed strange and distorted, half in the world of reality and half fading into an Otherness. Reverently she knelt in a dip in the ground before the tomb's entrance and left an offering, a rounded ball of quartz, amidst a pile of older gifts peeping through the soil—pebbles from distant seashores, a stone phallus, tools that had been used to prepare the dead before they were cremated and their ashes placed inside the passage-grave. Then, rising, she stoked the eternal flames–the Fires of Uffern—that burned in stone lanterns on either side of the portal of God's Peak. Imported oil spat and flames curled into the dusk, spitting and sizzling. The vast carved stone of the many spirals lit up, its tangle of lines seeming to curl and coil as shadows raced over its surface. The white quartz revetment behind gleamed with a spectral bone-light as the Moon, reborn, rose in the East and soared toward that ancient place of Ancestors.

Ivormyth bowed to the entrance-stone and then sprang lightly up and over it, vanishing into the blackness of the great cairn.

As she vanished from sight, Mordraed slid out from behind one of the boulders of the surrounding stone circle. He was not quite sure what he intended to do—only that something this night would change... change forever.

Carefully, quietly, he slithered on his belly over the spiral stone, and crawled on hands and knees into the passage, keeping low in the darkness to avoid detection. Gravel and bits of charred matter ground into his palms but he made no outcry. Glancing up, he could see spurs of stone jutting into the long, narrow tunnel; this ancient grave was almost barricaded across its width, as if to dissuade from entering all but the most reverent or determined.

Continuing on, he eventually spied Ivormyth in the furthest chamber. She had lit another stone lantern and was on her knees making obeisance to whatever spirits her tribe worshipped. Her back was to him, and she faced a niche carved with a triple spiral; it was here the Winter sun fell at dawn, the shaft of the sun piercing the dark womb of the holy hill. Other recesses also became visible, dark mouths in the tentative light; in them stood vast stone basins, decorated, filled with a jumble of cremated human bones. An astounding cantilevered dome covered the final chamber—the true turret of Spiralfort, the God's Peak.

Mordraed gazed on this holy of holies with awe and for a moment his resolve wavered. The spirits here were strange to him; they almost seemed to sap his power, making his hand tremble and his heart heavy. But despite his sudden unease, he crawled over the shallow sill-stone into one of the niches and wedged himself in behind one of the cinerary basins.

He was quiet, using all the arts of moving silently that he had learned from the hunt... but Ivormyth heard something nonetheless, a shuffle, a breath in the shadows, and she turned her head swiftly and for a second he thought he was undone.

But she made no move, perhaps thinking it was a friendly spirit, some old mother from times past, or even just a small animal rummaging in the tomb, or leaves blown in on the wind. Turning back to the holy of holies, she reached into the fire-lit niche and drew out a beautiful cup.

Mordraed had never seen its like before. Fashioned like a drinking beaker, it was wrought from a single lump of pure gold, with descending rows of corrugated rills whose edges caught the flickering light. Unusually it had a grooved handle, also of gold, riveted on by tiny lozenges that resembled Ardhu's breastplate. Reverently she lifted the Cup, touching the cold metal to her lips. "Blessed Cup of Plenty, one of the Hallows of these isles," she breathed. "Wrought by the bright lords from Murias, across the sundering sea, fashioned in the breath of Dag the Good God whose Cauldron is never empty. Now to pass to the Prince of Evening, to restore the fortunes of his land and augment those of mine."

So saying, she reached to a woven basket she had brought with her and removed a wooden keg and poured a draught from it into the Cup. She tasted it herself; allowed to touch this man's drink because of her priestly status. Satisfied the drink was properly brewed, she set the Cup carefully on a jutting ledge of stone, where it gleamed like a fallen sun. The drink within it, whatever it was brewed from, shone the colour of dark, arterial blood.

Rising, Ivormyth bowed to the Cup, to the Ancestors that surely swirled, bone-dust and ether, in such a holy, ancient space. "I will return, O Mighty Ones," she murmured, "with he who will become one with me, who will drink the Breath of Life from this Cup of Plenty and unite our isles forever."

Turning, she swept down the passage, her robes trailing behind her like mist.

Mordraed's heart almost leaped from his chest it beat so hard. This was the moment... the moment of his destiny, his triumph. Surely it was meant to be, all his mother had worked for. The spirits had guided the arrogant bitch

Ivormyth away, and left the Cup unguarded. The Cup that Gal'havad would drink from.

The Cup he would poison.

Laughing under his breath, he reached inside his jerkin and drew out the tiny clay vial Morigau had given him. At the same time he drew forth Gal'havad's tawdry purple cup, which he had stolen in the night. Hurling it to the floor, he smashed it in two and ground the bits into the dust. If it did protect from poison—and of that he was doubtful—its power was truly shattered now.

Slinking forward, he approached the shimmering Cup of Plenty. It beckoned to him, almost daring him to take it for his own, but he resisted. It would be more useful as it was... the Cup of Life... but by his design an instrument of death. Unstopping Morigau's flask, he poured its contents into the Cup. Acrid fumes rose then dispersed throughout the chamber.

The sound of approaching voices at the passage of God's Peak made him whirl around in alarm. Ivormyth and Gal'havad were entering the tomb. Quickly he shoved the empty poison vial in his tunic and scuttled away to hide behind the huge funerary basin in its niche. Hot-eyed, he watched as his half- brother and the girl Ivormyth came into the terminal chamber of Spiralfort.

Ivormyth gestured for Gal'havad to kneel and he did so at once, bowing his bright head. With her thumb she traced patterns in ochre on his brow and cheeks. "Tonight you take the Holy Cup as your own; you are chosen, you will unite two lands. A new Sun will come, dawn will be bright. I will leave you here a while to ask the spirits about your path; what they will desire of you when you are a king of men. Drink freely of the elixir whose secret was passed down to us, time out of mind, from Ancestors long dust upon the Fields of Gold. It will help you see the Otherworld and know the Truth and your ultimate Destiny."

"Will you stay with me?" he asked.

She shook her head but reached out and squeezed his hand. "No, it is for you alone as the one who is pure and holy enough to claim the Cup of Dag. But when it is over, my father Maheloas will join us and we will lie together this night and every night until forever."

He grabbed her then, rough in his haste, and kissed her lips, her cheeks, her hair, and Mordraed, in the niche with the old bones scattered around him, grimaced in revulsion and envy. But then he stifled a laugh upon his sleeve. Envy? No need. Ivormyth would have a cold bedmate before the light of dawn...

Ivormyth pulled gently away from Gal'havad and, casting him one last smile, retreated down the corridor. Gal'havad knelt on the floor, hands spread out as though in supplication, staring at the Cup on the ledge before him. It seemed a long time before he moved; Mordraed chafed impatiently in his cramped hiding spot, willing him to drink.

Finally he climbed to his feet and took hold of the Cup. Light from its pure gold surface cast a warm glow on the cold grey stones of the burial chamber. "Spirits, I know not what your plan is for me. Whatever it is, know that I have always served you well. Maybe, within the draught from this blessed Cup, all the mysteries of the heavens and earth shall be revealed to me."

Mordraed shuddered as the younger man spoke; it was almost as if he knew, suspected. And yet... he raised the Cup, first holding it above his head as if to show the Spirits that he was ready to accept what Fate they brought him, then bringing its shining rim to his lips.

He drank deep, finishing the Cup in a single draught.

He stood for a few minutes, eyes closed, arms outstretched, almost god-like in the flickering of the stone lamp. Then, he began to choke. His eyes shot open and he fell to his knees, hand clutching at his throat.

Mordraed did not know why, but he could not watch in secret any longer. He burst from his hiding place and skidded across the cairn floor to tumble down a few feet from Gal'havad. His heart was racing, its furious beat making him nauseous, and sweat sprang on his brow, but it was cold as ice-water. *What have I done? What have I done?* his mind screeched, unbidden.

"Mordraed..." Gal'havad's voice was a croak; he dragged himself towards his half-brother with an effort, his arms trembling like leaves in a high wind. "The gods, the Eternal Ones on the Plain of Honey... they have called to me... I must go to them... For me, the Cup has come with a great price, but I am sure this is indeed a gift and not punishment by the Great Ones... I will never again shake with the illness-inside-my-head when I am gone across the Plain..."

His face was white and earnest, his eyes unfocussed and dazed. "Mordraed," he suddenly said, his voice small, like a child's. "Take my hand. It is growing dark... so dark..."

Mordraed hesitated, waves of sickness rushing over him. *To take the hand of the man he had slain...* Slowly, reluctantly, he took the other's hand, not quite knowing why he did so, when it would be so easy now to turn away. This ending was not as he expected; in his mind's eye he had seen himself standing over Gal'havad's inert form, the proud conqueror, shouting his triumph to the world. Instead he felt sick, as if heart and guts were being wrung from within, and all he had striven for and desired so much seemed bleak and pointless as an old worm-eaten skull. Gal'havad had stood in his way, but he had helped him too, had sworn to give him lands and riches had he lived to be king. And surely he would have kept his word, for Gal'havad was a man of honour... unlike Mordraed, son of the serpent-woman, with her cold blood running in his veins.

Unexpectedly Mordraed began to cry. It burst from him like a wave from the sea, unwanted and unstoppable.

"Don't grieve for me," Gal'havad whispered, squeezing his fingers with rapidly dwindling strength. "It is the will of the Ancestors. That must be why my own cup went missing, it was taken from me by the spirits so that I could enter the doors of their domain."

Mordraed wept even harder, guilt and remorse and anger and other feelings long suppressed rose in him like a furious storm. The remains of Gal'havad's talisman lay a mere foot or two away, crushed by his feet. *His!* Not the spirits'... Even in dying, Gal'havad was deluded; there was none whom the Gods loved, only those whom base men hated... Men like Mordraed, lusting for power at any price...

Was the price too high to pay?

Gal'havad slumped back onto the cold flagstones, the Cup lying fallen beside him, his hair a radiant sun wheel around his drained face. "Farewell, my friend," he muttered. "I can see the steeds of the sea with white warriors riding on them wielding long spears of light. They come for me, to bear me to the lands where falls not the rain, nor snow, nor any tears, where Sun and Moon are never dim, and there is no sorrow. I... I..." His voice was barely above a whisper; a haze of bloody mucus marred his pale mouth. "I... will miss you... you were like my brother..."

"I... I am your brother." Mordraed leaned over him, his tears falling freely onto his pallid face, and kissed him on the mouth, as if hoping his pain and the poison that destroyed his innards would pass to him too.

Gal'havad gazed up at him and smiled through his pain. Then suddenly he took one great gasping breath and no more.

A dark madness grasped hold of Mordraed, a monster lurking in his head that sank claws and teeth into his brain, into his very spirit. He flung himself down across the inert body of Gal'havad and screamed his rage and fear and grief and confusion into the echoing chambers of God's Peak.

*****

Ardhu's men heard the first cry, a haunting howl so agonised it sounded scarcely human. Standing beside her father Maheloas, Ivormyth gave a terrified gasp and dropped the beaker she had been holding for a celebratory draught when Gal'havad emerged from Spiralfort. It smashed on the cobbles, dark contents staining white quartz like blood.

Ardhu sprang forward, throwing himself with abandon into the mouth of the tomb, Hwalchmai and Bohrs hot on his heels, and the other three men behind them with drawn axes. They skidded and slid in the darkness, shouting in anger and pain as they crashed into the jagged juts of stone that thrust out into the narrow passage.

At last Ardhu stumbled out into the awful, flickering light in the terminal chamber. He saw the corbelled dome, stained with soot; he saw the side transepts with their beautiful yet sinister basins filled with pale ash and clinkers of welded human fat and hair.

He saw Mordraed crouched down on the floor, a hunched shadow on the dusty flagstones. He saw the Golden Cup, the prize he had sought for his

Land, fallen, dented, rolling in the wind that blew up the central passage.

And he saw Gal'havad lying as if asleep, his hair the setting sun around him, his face as white as the chalk of the Great Plain, or the Mother Moon, or the bones of the dead. His lips curved in a faint, unfathomable smile, as if he knew some eldritch secret, some special mystery reserved for him alone... but they were blue, with no breath passing between them. The Prince of Twilight had passed into the twilight of Ahn-un... and his passing brought darkness and night to the heart of Ardhu Pendraec.

"What have you done?" Ardhu screamed at Mordraed. Grabbing his shoulder, he wrenched him up and flung him away from the body of Gal'havad.

Mordraed hit the wall and slumped back to the ground, throwing his arms up over his head. "I did not touch him!" he gasped. "I swear it. The spirits have taken him; he was always close to their world!"

Ardhu drew Caladvolc, its long blade a tongue of blood in the fluttering lantern-light. His eyes were stony, maddened. Hwalchmai clutched his chief's sword arm, trying to wrest the weapon from him. "No, Ardhu... do not do this, you cannot shed blood here... You have no proof, it may not be a lie... the boy is clearly grieved!"

They strove together for a moment or two, then suddenly Ardhu let go of the sword hilt. Caladvolc clattered to the ground. Ardhu stared at his fallen weapon, and then at Gal'havad's body. Mordraed was forgotten. Ardhu's visage drained, becoming nearly as pale as that of the dead youth, and he crashed down on his knees.

At the entrance of Spiralfort, the warriors of Ardhu could hear Maheloas and others moving, calling out and asking what was wrong. The men drew their axes and daggers, ready to defend their mourning chief and the body of his son, though there were only four of them. Mordraed, slouched against the wall, choking with the madness of his unforeseen grief and guilt, was forgotten.

"Do you think they have murdered him?" Bohrs glanced at Hwalchmai. "Was this their plan, to poison Gal'havad? But why? They seemed peaceable and kindly hosts!"

"I do not know." said Hwalchmai shook his head grimly. "But in my heart I do not think they are to blame. Maybe the gods did but act... Gal'havad, may his spirit travel light to the Uttermost West, was purer of mind and body than the rest of us... but he was unwell and becoming more so. Whatever the truth, Maheloas's folk must not come in here and see Ardhu in his grief... We will come out when we are ready. Block the entrance if you must, till Ardhu is himself again."

Bohrs thrust his corpulent frame into the narrow passageway. "Hold, friends!" he shouted down the shadowy corridor. "A great evil has fallen upon us. Let us deal with this as best we can, in the way of our people, and when we are ready we will come out to you."

Hwalchmai went to Ardhu and laid a steadying hand on his shoulder. "Kinsman," he said gently. "We need to take him from here. The people of Maheloas are wondering what has happened. This is their tomb of Ancestors; we cannot keep them from it for long."

Ardhu lifted his head; Hwalchmai gaped for it was as if the hand of time had struck his cousin a resounding blow. He looked as deathly as Gal'havad, waxen, suddenly aged. Slowly, like a very old man, he clambered to his feet. "Lift him," he murmured his voice grating in his throat. "Bear him from this place as one would a returning warrior."

Hwalchmai and Bohrs went to Gal'havad and gently lifted him, wrapping him in his cloak. They supported his head, while the other men lifted his legs, and they raised him to their shoulders. Ardhu picked up Caladvolc from where it had fallen, and holding it aloft like a brand began a slow march from the heart of God's Peak, leading the makeshift funeral cortege. Mordraed scrambled up and staggered behind the others, ignored as if he did not exist.

The warband exited the tomb with grave dignity, watching the faces of the tribesmen gathered in the forecourt. The horrified expressions of Maheloas and Ivormyth immediately told them that their hosts had not played them false; that they had nothing to do with the death of Gal'havad.

Ivormyth began to wail and keen, tearing her hair; Maheloas tried to draw her to him but she pulled away and ran toward Ardhu and his men. "What evil had befallen? What evil?" she cried. "Oh, let me see him, who was the Prince of Twilight, who was to be my husband!"

In silence Ardhu gestured to his men and they laid their burden on the earth before the spiral stone that was the Watcher's eyes, a Bull, a Wave of the Sea. Ivormyth knelt beside Gal'havad, leaning over his body and rocking with grief. Briefly she kissed his pale lips, and her face twisted. "There is death in his mouth! I can taste it. Such bitterness was not in the draught I gave to him!"

Immediately Bohrs's gaze swivelled to Mordraed, crouching by a kerbstone like some crushed spider, his hair a tangled web over his white, red-eyed face. "You! What were you doing in there? You had no right to be within the sacred space!"

Mordraed raised his head; he looked haunted... and hunted; he knew his position was a precarious one. "You cannot blame me!" he gasped. "He was my... cousin, I loved him, we fought side by side! I went in there to... to protect him! I suspected from the start that all was not as it should be. The girl... she attached to him as a burr sticks to a horse's mane! She hardly knew him, it was not natural! I hid to make sure he would not be harmed... but I failed him; he drank that cup of poison before I could make myself known and strike it from his hands."

Hwalchmai frowned. "Inside God's Peak you said that you thought the spirits had taken him. You mentioned naught of poison."

Mordraed licked his lips; he pointed a shaking hand of Ivormyth.

"She mentioned the poison; she damned herself out of her own mouth."

Ivormyth cried out, angry and grief-stricken at once. "I noted the taste of it upon his lips; I would hardly have done the act then announced it to you and my folk!"

The tribesmen behind Maheloas began to murmur, angered by Mordraed's accusations. The flames of the eternal lamps of Uffern gleamed on newly-drawn daggers.

Maheloas held up his arms, shaking his head is dismay. "Enough, all of you! Put up your blades! Evil has marred this night already. Ardhu Pendraec..." he took a stride toward Ardhu and clasped his arms at the elbow; Ardhu barely moved, hardly reacted; his face was near as lifeless as that of Gal'havad, "I swear by the Almighty Sun, by the Good God, by Ahn-an whose breasts are the Mountains, and by Crooked Krom who carries the Grain-of-the-World upon his back, that my people and I are blameless of any wrong doing in this matter. I can only guess what happened to your son. Maybe the spirits did reach out to take him; it is not for me to say. Or maybe you can think of other possibilities..." His pale blue gaze, glistening, slid toward Mordraed. "But be that as it may, do not bring your anger and your bloodshed to this place. I would counsel that you go back to Prydn as soon as your grief is no longer raw. You may take the Cup with you; for it was won by the Prince of Twilight."

Ardhu jerked into life, shaking his head as if to clear it from evil dreams; perhaps he hoped he truly did but dream and he would awake and the world would be in its normal balance once more, and Gal'havad would rise from the ground, with laughter on his lips and the sunset trapped in his locks. "There is no point in taking it, this Cup of Life that brought his death! If the world was barren and failing before; it is truly the Wasteland now, at least for me. And so it shall ever be."

Stooped like some hoary elder, he turned to his warband... what remained of them. Only five still lived, including Mordraed. All in all, including himself and Betu'or, if his loyal friend had survived the wait upon the sea-strand, only seven of his once mighty warband would return to Prydn from Spiralfort. He had failed utterly; once he had been as the rising Sun, growing brighter and more powerful in strength... now it was as if his Sun had tumbled from the sky, leaving a bleak world of Winter and despair in its wake.

Hwalchmai made a coughing noise. "Ardhu, I know this is a time of great sorrow but we must decide and decide quickly... what are we to do with Gal'havad's body?"

Startled, Ardhu glared at him. "We take him home, to the sacred cemeteries of Khor Ghor."

Bohrs nervously shifted from one foot to the other. "Ardhu... my friend, my lord of these long years, it is not possible. You know that. We cannot carry a body with us while travelling many days, nor can we afford to tarry here while he lays open to the sky. We must bury him in Ibherna, wherever we are permitted…"

"No!" A muscle jumped in Ardhu's jaw. "He will not stay in the land where he died! I forbid it!"

Maheloas stepped forward, his hands clasped, his fingers knotted together, working nervously. "He died while in our territory; we will help you," he said gravely. "Our great Ancestor-tomb has been made unclean by the evil that has happened today. We must sanctify and purify… with fire."

"You would cremate him. Burn him on the pyre."

Maheloas bowed his head. "If it is your will."

Ardhu passed his hand over his brow, lines of strain clear on his face. "So be it… I can see no other way. Once the deed is done, I can take his bones back to Prydn to be buried in earth-houses of his own Ancestors."

Maheloas gestured towards his waiting people, the grim-featured warriors, the weeping women. "We must make ready a pyre for the Prince of Twilight, the holy one, the Cup-winner… he whom the gods loved so much they have taken him to the Plain of Honey this very day. Go to the House of the West and prepare it to receive Gal'havad, son of Ardhu Pendraec."

*****

The pyre was ready by Sunrise. Gal'havad had been laid on an oak plank in the centre of the timber cult-house, knees curled up as if asleep, his face turned toward the East as was the custom of his people. Burnished copper, his long hair lay spread out over his shoulders and around his face, and his woven cloak, coloured violet with the dye from the magic stones in the Sacred Pool behind Kham-El-Ard, covered him from mid-chest to feet. His amber necklace hung about his neck, glowing, its strange insects frozen in time; and he too, given false semblance of life by the dawn, seemed to be caught in time, a vision to be remembered for eternity by all who gathered there.

The men of Spiralfort gathered around him, placing brush and dried reeds around his bier to help fuel the fire. Heaps of skins lay round as offerings, and women brought meadowsweet and wild flowers in great bunches and beakers of drink so that he would not thirst upon his Great Journey. Maheloas danced and invoked the Sky, the Ancestors, the Earth itself, and with Ivormyth laid protective lumps of quartz, the stone of the Moon, the stone of the Sun, around Gal'havad, placing one clear fine rock before his face so that his spirit, if still travelling to the West, could clearly see the way within its depth.

Ardhu took up Gal'havad's dagger, the gift from An'kelet for his manhood rites. He broke the tip, drawing blood from his own hands as he killed the spirit of the weapon, sending it to the Deadlands alongside his son. Likewise he took Gal'havad's bow and with a great cry snapped it in two across his knee before placing the fragments across Gal'havad's legs and tipping the contents of his quiver of arrows after it.

Lastly Ivormyth brought the Cup of Gold, the fatal Cup that had brought death and not the renewed life Ardhu had hoped. Hands trembling, she set it down on the bier close to Gal'havad's hand. It had been a relic, sacred to the God Dag, but her people wanted nothing to do with it now; its magic had turned bad, feast falling to famine.

This last act done, Ardhu and his men and the folk of Spiralfort departed the House of the West, Maheloas cutting the throat of a black-faced lamb against the blocky standing stone in the doorway to sanctify and seal the funeral chamber with blood. Once outside, he gestured to his followers and they set many brands alight with their flint strike-a-lights. Solemnly, he handed one to Ardhu. "It is your right, Ardhu Pendraec, to start the flames that will light his way to the land of the Ancestors."

Ardhu walked toward the cult-house, grey as a winter's night, no life in his eyes, like a dead man who yet walked. He paused for an instant, gazing into the gloom of the chamber, taking in one last glimpse of Gal'havad that must last him to the end of his days... and then, with a violent motion, he thrust the burning torch into the reed thatching.

A whooshing noise filled the air and the thatch caught alight. Flames raced up the roof and over it in a searing sheet. Ardhu's warband and the people of Spiralfort hurled their torches after it, adding to the conflagration. A wind, blowing from the East, fuelled the fire and it sprang ever higher, roaring and crackling. The chamber was consumed, as twisted orange flames spiralled into the air and oily smoke belched above the quartz-faced mound of God's Peak.

Maheloas began to chant before the burning house, and his men followed suit, rubbing ash and dirt on their cheeks to emulate the dead man within the tomb of fire. The women hewed off hanks of their own hair and flung it into the inferno as an offering to any passing spirits; it sizzled and sparked, sending up a horrible, acrid scent that mingled with that of the pyre.

Then Ivormyth walked toward the pyre, slowly, stately, a strange twisted expression on her face—suffering mixed with determination. She dropped her spotted cowskin cloak to the ground and the watchers gasped as they saw that she was arrayed with gold from head to toe—a gorget with flower-faced terminals, buttons like rayed suns with jet surrounds, a belt of woven strands closed with a massive polished buckle. She drifted towards the burning hut, her hair streaming out behind her like a tendril of escaped smoke.

She halted near the entrance, blinking as smoke and glowing embers billowed around her. Nothing could be seen of Gal'havad amidst the smoke and fire. The stone in the mouth of the hut seemed to glow with a sullen reddish light as flames licked greedily around it.

Ivormyth looked from her sire, Maheloas, to Ardhu and then to Mordraed, who stood behind the rest of Ardhu's warband, pushed to the back, forgotten in their grief for their lost prince. White as bone, his countenance was wracked by sorrow… and guilt. He held his arms protectively across his body, as if expecting blows from some otherworldly agent.

"I was named as the killer of Gal'havad son of Ardhu by one of this company," Ivormyth said in a clear, ringing voice, her gaze still locked on Mordraed. "That was the cruellest lie ever spoken by man's lips on this Isle of the Blessed. I have harmed none in my short life; I served my father and the Ancestors well. I was to wed the Prince of the Twilight, and was glad to do so. I was happy to lie at his side in life… and to prove that I am no murderer, I will show all how true I am to him and to his blessed memory. Today I will join the Prince of Twilight as his bride in the realm of the Not-world."

Maheloas gave a terrible scream and lunged for his daughter, suddenly realising her intent, but Ivormyth was too swift for her elderly father. Swift as a deer, she hoisted her robes round her calves and sprang forward, hurling herself into the flames of Gal'havad's funeral pyre. She began to scream as the hungry flames roared up to meet her, but as if by the hand of a merciful god, the roof-beam of the house cracked and collapsed inwards with a resounding roar, bringing the walls down with it, and scattering red-hot embers everywhere. Ash and hot sparks fountained up then showered over the horrified onlookers. The standing stone inside the hut seemed to wobble in its pit, and suddenly it cracked at the base and shattered, spewing steaming fragments all over the scorched ground.

Maheloas was on his knees, rocking with agony. His hair smouldered; his mouth hung open in a soundless scream. He ripped off the ceremonial mask he wore and hurled it into the fire. "Get your son's bones and go from here," he said to Ardhu Pendraec, when words would come. "It was a black day for both of us when you set foot upon this isle!"

CHAPTER SIXTEEN
THE LADY IN THE RIVER

The remnants of Ardhu's warband trudged back to the sea-strand where they had first set foot ashore. For the first time since they had entered Ibherna luck was with them, and they were neither attacked by the tribe of Bal'ahr nor any other man or beast upon the road. Ardhu walked ahead of the others, face sarsen-hard and unnaturally aged, holding in his arms a coarse cinerary urn that contained the charred bones of Gal'havad. Bohrs and Hwalchmai flanked him, axes upheld in a symbol of respect to the remains of the young lord of Kham-El-Ard—while Mordraed, shunned by the others, staggered in the rear of the party, haggard as a wraith, a figure almost to be pitied in his abject misery.

Betu'or was sitting down by the boats, still faithfully on guard, a spear across his knees. He leapt up, kicking sand over his small fire, when he saw familiar figures crest the rise... then stopped in horror as he counted the men before him and realised what his chieftain bore in his arms.

"No, it cannot be so!" he cried, falling to one knee as the sand eddied around him, as golden as the Cup they had sought... and left behind, charred in the ruins of the cult-house at God's Peak.

"Sadly, it is indeed so. Gal'havad son of Ardhu has gone to the Ancestors." Hwalchmai came down beside Betu'or and raised him with a hand. Ardhu said nothing; he merely clutched the urn and stared out, stone-eyed, to sea. "And only seven of us will return to Kham-El-Ard... and that is if the tides are with us and we do not founder." Hwalchmai followed Ardhu's gaze out to the choppy grey water; bunched clouds loomed like giant's heads on the horizon and the wind was singing.

"The wind is not right." Betu'or held up a string of lank seaweed, watching the direction in which it swung. "The Moon had a sick hue last night, and the dawn was the colour of blood... both ill omens for sailing."

"I will stay no longer, not even if Ga'o the Wind Spirit blows his fiercest blasts and Mahn-ann brings down the roiling mists of Symmerdim." Ardhu's face was impassive, like granite. "The very soil of this place screams out against us, and if we linger too long I am certain not one of us shall return to Kham-El-Ard. Betu'or, we will only need Pridwen for the journey home, for there are but seven of us left; destroy the other boat, so that none can follow us. We have met many here who have no love for the men of Prydn."

Betu'or drew his axe and started to hack at the lesser of their two sturdy boats. Wood cracked and splinters flew. Hwalchmai and Bohrs joined him, smashing the carefully-wrought timbers with great force until the craft lay in shattered pieces upon the strand.

Then the warriors gathered together and pushed Pridwen out into the swell, with Ardhu seated in the prow, facing his homeland, the urn and its precious contents held fast between his knees. Once Pridwen was afloat in waist-high water, they hauled themselves over the side and took up their flat paddles—all except Mordraed, who crouched at the far end away from his fellows. He looked ghastly and began to heave over the side, his hair hanging in the salty water. The others ignored him, disgusted.

The crossing was bad, with a high wind taking them farther down the coast, but not as bad as it could have been; at least no storm-god had swept in to try and capsize them, and no Maidens of the Waves tried to draw them onto hidden rocks. Before long the shores of Prydn became visible under a helm of grey drizzle. Pridwen had been driven off course by the capricious winds, but it had turned out to be no bad thing... the cliffs on the horizons were not unknown to the warriors; the red and pale cliffs and sea stacks were the bastions of the Land of the Dwri, the People of the Water, one of Ardhu's own holdings through his father, U'thyr Pendraec.

Sailing into a sheltered cove with a huge, storm-carved arch that opened to the wild seas, Hwalchmai, Bohrs and Betu'or leapt into the shallows, dragging Pridwen up across the loose shingle on the beach until its prow came to rest against a vast weedy rock. As the company disembarked, climbing stiffly out onto solid land, the towering cliffs above became filled with spear-carrying men who waved their weapons with menace.

Ardhu set down the precious urn that contained Gal'havad's remains and took Rhon-gom from his belt and held it aloft so that all could see the symbol of his sovereignty. Immediately the tribesmen on the heights cast down their spears and began running down paths on the cliffside to greet the King of the West upon the cold sea-strand.

Their leader was a man known to Ardhu; a youth of twenty summers called Ithel who had been at Winter Solstice celebrations at Deroweth for the last two years. He was distant kin, a grandson of one of U'thyr's sisters.

As Ithel jogged down the beach, shouting out a greeting to his kinsman, Ardhu held up his hand for him to halt. "Ithel, we come to the lands of the Dwri with no tales of glorious questing and its rewards. We went over the waves with death at our shoulders, and death is all we have brought back to Prydn." He nodded grimly towards the rough black urn at his feet.

Ithel stared at the coarse pot, not understanding its significance.

Ardhu bowed his head. "That urn contains the bones of Gal'havad, prince of Kham-El-Ard, my only son and heir. He died upon the Imram, the... gods..." he swallowed, fighting for control, '... took him at the moment of our victory... for he was too good to walk longer amidst mortal men."

Ithel looked thunderstruck, his cheeks draining at the gravity of this news; he made the sign against evil with his hand. "My ... my lord... these are unwelcome tidings indeed! Sorrow is in my heart and will be in the hearts of all true men of Prydn, Great Stone Lord. May the spirits give you ease."

197

"I will have no ease for the rest of my days, be they long or short," said Ardhu bitterly. "And the spirits? They have turned their faces from me. But if you would aid me, there is something I would have you do... to honour Gal'havad. Send your most reliable men across Prydn, to every camp and settlement you know. Let them spread the news of the death of my son, the Hawk of Summer, who has now passed from us as summer passes to winter. Let all of Albu the White and even beyond weep for the Prince of the Twilight."

Ithel bowed. "It will be done, Ardhu Terrible Head. I will see that all men know and honour the memory of Gal'havad. Fires will burn to light his bones home to the houses of his forebears." He turned, shoulders slouched with the heaviness of his assignment, and scrambled back up the cliff, gesturing to his men to follow. Once they reached the cliff-top there was scuffling and commotion on the height, and then, against the faded, dismal sky, a tongue of flame blossomed. It spiralled upwards, smoke trails billowing above its burning heart like the hands of departing spirits. It was joined within a short while by a blaze upon the summit of the opposing sea-cliff, matching the first in ferocity and intensity.

Ardhu picked up the heavy urn, cradling it in his arms, and began to climb the steep slope from the cove, his steps slow and lacklustre, the steps of a mourner.

And so the bones of Gal'havad the Son of Ardhu, the Prince of Twilight, began their long journey back to Kham-El-Ard.

*****

The Land was in mourning. Ithel's messengers had spread the unhappy news, carrying it through all of Dwranon and as far afield as Khor Ghor and Suilven, while other men continued to pass the tale of woe on through all the villages of the West right down through Duvnon with its twisted tors to the craggy tip of Belerion where the land meets the sea. Mounted on a steed borrowed from Ithel's holdings, Ardhu rode slowly through Dwranon with the cinerary urn in its place of honour before him on the horse, and his men gathered around him like a guard, marching sombrely on the long road home. Mordraed, though still pale and wretched, had regained some of his equilibrium and even marched at their side, though the others still ignored him. They could accuse him of nothing, and his grief seemed real enough, but his behaviour in Ibherna and its consequences had estranged them even more from him. But he was Gal'havad's kinsman, and had been his friend, so they had no right to bar him from the funeral procession.

They passed the great Mai Dun Fort of the Plain, where a causewayed camp had crowned the hilltop in the days of the Ancestors, a place where feasts had taken place and marriages were contracted and the silent dead had watched over all from platforms raised to the Everlasting Sky. A great long barrow, so large it seemed more a bank than a mound, stretched along the brow of the hill like a dark, undulating worm. As the warband passed on the

198

track that skirted the foot of the hill, small figures scurried along the barrow's length and suddenly its humped back burst into flame—beacons lit to honour the dead youth whose charred bones were carried ever onwards towards Kham-El-Ard.

It was the same at the Great Dragon Path of Dwr, white-banked and massive under a stark crescent Moon, trailing away into the distance as far as the eye could see. As Ardhu and his companions processed along its length, the night air was suddenly filled by smoke and ash, and the Spirit-Path and all its satellite barrows were lit by flames from hastily ignited brushwood pyres. And the people of the Dwr came from hut and farm and settlement, some travelling many miles, whitening their faces with chalk and smearing their bodies with charcoal, and they wailed and keened and cried, dancing and drinking themselves into a frenzy in honour of their lost prince.

Within a few more days, Ardhu's warband reached the Harrow track, the Way of the Temple, and came at dusk within sight of Khor Ghor. Stark, eternal, it gleamed hazily in the purple of the twilight, the trilithons a faded red, like old blood, surrounded by the ever-circling black birds that made their homes beneath the lintels.

Ardhu drew rein, watching as night drew down its cloak, furling the Seven Kings on their high ridge and the Spirit-Path with its attendant barrows. All was silent, still, save for the distant yipping of a fox…

And then the lights began, twinkling in the gloom, myriad tongues of flame that leaped down the Avenue's parallel banks, over the rounded heads of the Seven Kings, and along the top of the Great Spirit-Path itself. A drum rolled, its sound awful and solemn, reverberating within the massive Stones that made up the holy circle, and the shrine itself came to life with fire. The darkened stones turned red once more, flickering torches moving between the archways, and suddenly the tops of the lintels were ablaze, as flames shot high into the air before dissipating in an instant, some magic wrought by the priests of Deroweth in tribute to Gal'havad and his passing from the world of men.

Dismounting his steed and passing the reins to Hwalchmai, Ardhu started down the Avenue, the urn heavy as stone in his arms, and the fires burning around him, blinding his eyes.

And so he came to Kham-El-Ard and found its people waiting for him, lining the path that led up the hill with torches burning in their hands, and on the top of the ramparts were fires so great it almost looked as if the entire wooden fort was alight. He could hear the flames roaring, and huge clouds of smoke and ash puffed into the night air, obscuring the stars.

As he ascended the path, men and women knelt before him, weeping and crying out, rending the earth with their hands. He passed them, stony-faced, and then, just within the great oaken gates, halted and placed Gal'havad's urn upon the ground.

Across the yard from him stood Fynavir, face daubed with chalk, as was customary in times of mourning, her unearthly whiteness and the thinness that had come upon her since the banishment of An'kelet making her look like a skeleton that walked. Upon her shoulders gleamed the golden shoulder-cape that she had worn to their marriage-feast, still as bright as the day it was made... though the linen that drooped from its eyelets hung in tattered grey shreds, a shroud that tangled around her gaunt limbs.

Ardhu went to her; he clasped her hands. She stared blankly at him, her fingers not enclosing his. He sank to one knee before her and suddenly he wept, for the first time since Gal'havad had died. "Forgive me," he said. "I have not brought him back to you."

"I know..." she said. "The whole land has mourned for him."

"The gods willed that he go to the Undying Realm..." Ardhu said feebly, brokenly.

"I know that too. But everything to me is lost, grey ash on the wind. If the spirits would take me away to be with him, I would gladly die this very instant."

She knelt in the dusty soil beside him, great sobs tearing from her chest, and he held her and wept with her, and it was as if, for a moment, the tears washed away some of the dark stain that blighted their marriage, joining them in purpose if only for a brief time. When their grief was at last spent, they both rose and walked, hands clasped, to Gal'havad's urn.

"Where shall we bury him?" asked Ardhu. "I leave it for you to choose, my Queen. We can build a new barrow on the Plain or inter him in the edge of one of the great mounds of the Tin-Lords that cluster in the fields."

"I do not want him far from me," She wiped her red-rimmed eyes. "I want to gaze out and see where he is, and think upon him until the end of my days. Can we not build him a fitting grave near us here at Kham-El-Ard?"

Ardhu inclined his head. "It will be done, Fynavir, my Queen,' and so the order was made—and a barrow raised below the ramparts of Kham-El-Ard the Crooked High Hill, a fine round tumulus overlooking the curves of bright Abona, which flowed between the stands of ash, and elm, and stout oak that grew behind the hill. Fires were kindled along the banks of the river from the fort all the way to Deroweth and drums were beaten and cattle slaughtered and eaten in a vast funeral celebration. Men and women danced with mad abandon, and leapt through the clouds of flame and smoke... and beside them Mordraed danced harder and longer than the rest, almost till exhaustion took him.

Then Gal'havad's urn was lowered into a central grave-pit and a vessel full of meat placed beside it, along with bronze pins and amber beads and worked flint. Earth and chalk was shovelled over the pit with a cow's scapula, and great wailing went up from Fynavir and the women of the tribe, who cast themselves into the barrow's newly-dug ditch, tearing at their hair and faces, their beauty turned to ugliness as death itself turned all that was fair to ash.

Mordraed sidled over to one of the slaughtered bulls and bathed his hands in the blood welling from its slashed neck; he rubbed it through his hair, painted it on his chest and arms and cheeks. His fair face took on a demonic scarlet hue, his dark blue eyes vivid against the crimson gore. He scarcely seemed human, more like a spirit of war, of death.

He was the Dark Moon.

He *was* Death.

The grief that had almost felled him in Ibherna had dissipated and a renewed anger had replaced it. Anger toward Ardhu Pendraec. It was *his* fault Gal'havad had to die. If Ardhu had acknowledged Mordraed and given him his rightful due, Gal'havad could have been allowed to live. Mordraed was wise. Mordraed could be merciful if he chose. He would have sent Gal'havad off to the priests at Deroweth; he would have been happy there, talking to spirits, with holy men to tend him in his illness...

Mordraed shot Ardhu a venomous glare through the haze of the burning. The Stone Lord, dancing with his warriors in a circle around Gal'havad's barrow, did not notice him. A cold, hard emptiness rose up in him, filling his belly like poison, mingling with the hatred of his heart.

Soon... let it be... Let there be an end!

Let him come into his birthright and take Ardhu's head in battle and give it to the Great Circle... before he destroyed the loathsome place forever, breaking its malign power with the breaking of its Stones.

*****

Mordraed left the funeral celebrations after Sunset, when most of the mourners were drunk and ill, glutted with the mead and meat they had wantonly consumed. Keeping to the bushes, he dashed along the riverbank, the wind ruffling his gore-clotted hair. Light was failing, but the twilight would be his friend, hiding him from any curious eyes, from the men of the Stone Lord, his enemies, who did not trust him.

He was doing his duty.

He was visiting his mother, Morigau, to tell of his victories.

She was waiting for him on Prophet's barrow, as if she knew he would come, her unbound tresses a dark foaming cloud like the smoke of Gal'havad's pyre. She sprang down the hill, lithe as girl, and hurled her wiry arms about him, kissing his cheeks and mouth. His lips stung with her assault and he yanked his head away, noticing his mouth was bleeding at the corner. "So you have done it... at last," she breathed, "You've killed the precious prince, Ardhu's boy. I wonder how my brother feels to lose what he holds most dear. A just punishment for him. Tell me, my darling Mordraed, was the death long, did he suffer as I have suffered..."

A wave of nausea crashed over Mordraed. Suddenly he felt pure, blinding hate toward Morigau... the same kind of hatred he felt towards Ardhu. "Shut up, your unnatural bitch!" he spat. "It is ill to gloat over the dead! He did not deserve to die, mother... and although he needed to be removed, I will regret

201

killing him until the day that I too fare across the Great Plain. One day the Spirits will sit in judgement on me for giving him that poison draught…"

Morigau's eyes narrowed angrily; but her voice dripped with sarcasm. "What is wrong with you, boy? I didn't bring you up to have such weak, womanish thoughts. What is the matter, why do you care so much for his fate… were you his lover?"

Mordraed whirled around and struck her so hard that she fell to the ground. "Never speak of such things to me again, women!" he snarled. "Or you may find yourself as dead as Gal'havad!"

Morigau laughed; a high crazy sound. She pressed her hand to her face, already swelling from his blow. "I am glad you have not completely lost your spirit. Don't forget, that although you may not approve of the things I make you do… it is for *you*, for all of your close kin. You will thank me one day when you are the most powerful chief in all Prydn!"

Mordraed grunted and turned from her. He could see Khyloq in the field, pressing on towards him through the long summer grasses. Although he knew he had only been away a few weeks, the swell of her belly seemed much bigger now, more obvious to his eyes. He thought of the child inside her dragged screaming into the world by Morigau when the time came—to be taken and used by her just as she had used him, to be moulded into her creature, her pet, maybe even the one who held the poison chalice for *him* if he displeased her. Fear ate at him, and hatred, deep hatred that expanded in his heart and consumed like fire…

Khyloq reached him and stood arms folded, red hair tumbling in burnished coils around her. Her face was dirty, her feet bare. "You've been a long time coming to us," she said curtly. "You've been back in Kham-El-Ard for days!"

"Gal'havad had to be buried with proper rites," he said shortly. "I could not leave without remark. And it was only right I honour him." He cast a fierce glance at Morigau as if daring her to disagree.

Khyloq pressed herself against him; she stunk of the pigsty and he guessed she had been mucking it out while Morigau waited for him. "I am glad you are back; I heard most of Ardhu's men were killed. Are you glad to see me? Do I look fair to your eyes after so long away?"

Mordraed's lip curled. "You look fat. And filthy. But I will be glad enough of your company when you are washed."

"Yes, go lie with her." Morigau stepped up to him, still rubbing her swelling cheek, though in an almost reverential way, as if his blow had been as soft and desirable as a kiss, perhaps even more desirable. "Maybe it will put you in a sweeter mood."

"I am not here for dalliance," Mordraed said dismissively. Khyloq looked furious, flushing as red as her hair. "I want to know what is to be done now. Gal'havad is gone, but Ardhu remains strong, with many loyal men around him. Now that his only heir is dead, he may well take another woman since the White One seems barren. He could beget more sons yet. I must move and move swiftly… but how can I, when he still has his warband, depleted though it is through his foolish Imram?"

"He must leave Kham-El-Ard." Morigau smiled. "He must fare abroad with his men, and leave you behind with those who are loyal to you. Then you will be free to make your move, with few to withstand you… and I will be free to leave this hovel of my exile, and help raise you to the position for which you were born."

"Leave Kham-El-Ard? Why would he? He is deep in grief, and has no reason to leave his home to go questing once more."

"The madness of his grief may be his undoing," she grinned. "I can turn the dagger of pain that is already in his heart. Believe me; I have not been idle in your absence, my son. I have travelled far and found out many things. My hands have not been idle. Wait and see. Watch the River, my son. Abona will bring you a gift."

*****

Night lay over Kham-El-Ard, uneasy, dreaming night. Torches on the stout earthworks twinkled like fallen stars, while the true stars, shining through tufts of fast-moving stratus, glimmered on the moving swell of Abona. Mist coiled from the temperate surface of the Sacred Pool and crept through the trees like a living thing.

Inside the fort, in his sleeping quarters at the back of the Great Hall, Ardhu tossed restlessly, as he had done every night since Gal'havad died. Coiled at his side but not touching him, Fynavir wept quietly in her sleep. He averted his face, unable to bear the sight of her tears.

In the hut assigned to youths in training, Mordraed too lay sleepless in the dark. Now that Gal'havad was dead, he had been excluded from the warband, thrust back into the quarters of the inferior young men who would never make warriors. He sprawled under a patchy old skin, listening to the chorus of snores around him, the rattle of mice in the rushes. He was not one of Ardhu's chosen men any longer, so this would be his band instead, a band where he was no follower, obeying orders, but where he was the unquestioned leader. His warband would have no old men like the king, no fools with high ideals and their endless prattle of honour. Killers, berserkers, the foolhardy and the vainglorious would serve Mordraed well.

He grinned, fingering his dagger blade in the dark. The new would sweep out the old; the fierce would put down those that had become tame as old dogs.

Suddenly his ears caught a sound, brought on the night-breeze… an alarmed shout from one of the night-watchmen on the ramparts. Mordraed sat up, head on one side, listening intently. Another shout came, louder than the first. Footsteps sounded across the dun and he heard the creaking of the gates of the fort as they were dragged open.

Something was happening, something abnormal.

Mordraed sprang up and kicked the shoulder of Wyzelo, who sprawled near him in the rushes, mouth hanging and snores emerging. "Quickly, up, up, Wyzelo... all of you!" he cried, glancing at the other supine shapes scattered across the floor. "The watchers have left their posts. Some ill is afoot."

The youths clambered up, bleary-eyed and yawning, and with much grumbling followed Mordraed from their hut like a flock of bad-tempered sheep. A stream of curious people hurried past them, heading toward the open gateway. Ardhu and Fynavir, dressed hastily in tunics and cloaks, strode through the middle of the crowd, surrounded protectively by the remaining members of the warband. Everyone looked disorientated and confused.

They proceeded to the riverbank, far below, led by the gate-guards with drawn bows. The Sun was just peeping above the eastern horizon, a streak of blood-red between the boles of the trees. Its rays stroked the flowing waters; caressing the hair of old River-Woman... and illuminating a strange craft that floated along Abona's swell.

A deep dug-out canoe was drifting aimlessly along the current. An old man sat in it, shoulders bowed, face chalked to reflect death and grief. Before him, in the prow of the boat lay a girl as fair as the sunrise, stretched out on her back, her hands holding pebbles of magic white quartz. Flowers were heaped around her, lilies and flags, foxgloves, red campion. Two pots stood by her head, one filled with milk, one with grain, and an awl and two scrapers had been placed at her side.

As beautiful as she looked, her features made rosy by the warm dawn-light, there was a livid hue marring the cheeks, the full mouth.

She was dead.

Ardhu pushed through the crowd of tribesfolk and warriors and reached the river bank first. His face looked haggard and strained and angry. "What do you here, bringing this strange burden to Kham-El-Ard?" he asked. "She should be taken to her people and buried in their rites."

The old man glanced up; tears had made snail's tracks through the white chalk paint on his cheeks. "I come here because I want vengeance, reparations... although nothing can bring my daughter back to me."

"What has this to do with the folk of Kham-El-Ard?" snapped Ardhu, irritation obvious in his voice.

"Everything!" The man poled the craft to the shore and clambered onto the bank. He marched up to Ardhu and stared into his face without flinching. "It was one of your warriors that brought this doom upon my daughter... my beautiful daughter who was more precious than the Sun and Moon to me."

Ardhu frowned. "I do not understand. How did she die? There is no mark upon her. What has happened here? Speak clearly, old one!"

"I am Phelas of Astolaht," said the man. "And my poor dead child..." he gestured to the body in the boat, "is Elian, known as the Maid of Lilies. I will tell you her tale and you will know why I have come here in my grief...

Several Moons ago Elian found a wounded warrior from Kham-El-Ard on the edges of our territory; she saved his life with her healing arts and nursed him back to health... and he repaid her by forcing himself upon her, then casting her aside like a broken beaker. Her heart may have healed from that wicked deed, but there was more... he left a child in her belly. The shame was too much for her to bear. She wished to rid herself of her burden but her simple remedies did not the job. So she went to another wise-woman in the valley and gave herself into her care... but the woman's arts failed and she died in my arms, in agony..." He stopped, his face crumpling.

Mordraed felt his heartbeat quicken at Phelas's words and he craned his head to see the dead Elian and her father. A 'wise woman'... could it have been his mother and her poisons? Morigau had told him to 'watch the river.'

Ardhu's lips tightened as he stared down at Elian's still countenance, the cheeks slightly speckled with livid stains.. "Who is the warrior of my band who has done this grave deed?"

Phelas's breath was a sob. "An'kelet Prince of Ar-morah."

Ardhu's breath whistled between his teeth; a muscle jumped in his jaw. "He is long gone from here... he may even be dead. I wounded him with Caladvolc..."

"He is not dead." Phelas shook his head. "Elian healed him. When he abandoned her to her fate, he told her he was heading back to his domain in Ar-morah, over the Narrow Sea."

Ardhu stood in silence. Indeed, it seemed the whole of the world had grown silent, save for the soughing of the breeze and the continual gurgle of the holy river.

Suddenly Fynavir, pale and sharp as a winter icicle at her husband's side, fell to her knees beside the riverbank and began to sob.

Ardhu whirled, an awful rage in his face. Even his oldest friends recoiled —none had seen such a terrible expression of anger, grief, and despair. "Cease your noise!" He grabbed Fynavir's arm, hauling her roughly to her feet. "Look! Look what he has done to this innocent girl! Look what evil he has wrought. What kind of a creature did you lie with, Fynavir of Ibherna?"

Fynavir struggled free of Ardhu's grip. Tears spattered from her eyes, but there was fire in her stare for the first time in months. "One who loved me... as you did not. One who valued me not because my mother was god-touched, because I am the White Phantom, but because I am Fynavir. Think on that, Stone Lord."

Tears still falling, she gazed down at Elian... this girl who An'kelet had taken in her stead, taken cruelly and thrown aside if the story was true. Taken and then killed as sure as if he had stabbed her with his Ar-moran dagger. It was beyond bearing... even the memory of their love was now tainted, mould upon the blossom. Choking back sobs, she picked her way back toward Kham-El-Ard in the chill dawn, while the crowd murmured and stared at her retreating back.

"What do you intend to do?" asked Phelas, facing Ardhu again with an air of defiance, as if daring him to do nothing. "This foul deed must not go unpunished. When you took power, ruling the Great Trilithon and assuming the mantle of that king of old, Samothos, you swore to defend Prydn from all evil. Instead, by taking the foreigner from Ar-morah into the fold, you brought it to us. My daughter has paid the price for your folly, Stone Lord."

Listening to his words, Mordraed jabbed Wyzelo in the back with a finger. "You... I need you to speak for me," he whispered in his ear. "Now. Shout out that Ardhu should take his warband and ride for Ar-morah to take vengeance on An'kelet for his crimes."

"Why me?" Wyzelo was still half-asleep, his hair sticking up in tufts around his bovine face. "Why not you? You're kin!"

"He won't listen to me; he no longer trusts me. But seeking An'kelet is the right thing to do; you know that, don't you, Wyzelo? Deceitful killers and adulterers cannot be allowed to live. He has murdered this girl with his lust and he has made a fool of the King. Ardhu *must* go forth across the seas and slay him..." His eyes narrowed. "And if he goes, that leaves our lot in charge at Kham-El-Ard, Wyzelo. His band is so depleted, he will need to take them all, leaving just us. Think of it. Something of merit to do, rather than waiting for scraps to be flung to us."

Wyzelo nodded, expression brightening at the thought of a Kham-El-Ard where he could have his say. "I did not think of the benefits to us. I will put in a word, Mordraed."

The warband had gathered in a circle around Ardhu and Phelas. "I counsel a cool head," Hwalchmai was saying. "A vile thing has happened, and I would not have expected it of An'kelet, but what can we do? He is far from here, hidden in his ancestral lands. It would be foolhardy to follow him."

Ardhu drew Caladvolc, holding it out before him. "But when men hear that he has escaped my justice, what will they think? That the sword of the Terrible Head is weak, that he allows treacherous men to go free."

"Who cares what others think?" said Hwalchmai, testily. "We know the truth..."

Ardhu slammed Caladvolc back into its sheath. "*I* care. For once rumours spread that I am not in control of this Land and all that is in it, then a darkness will spread, like a night that has no day following. Evil men will come as they did of old—raiders will burn the coasts and chieftains who dwell within our very midst will turn to bloodshed and plunder."

"You should go, lord!" Seeing his opportunity, Wyzelo shouted out, his voice booming amongst the trees. "Bring the miscreant to his knees! Take his head for your hut! Restore the glory of Kham-El-Ard!"

"Shut up, boy!" Bohrs looked Wyzelo up and down contemptuously. "Why do you speak, when you are not even a man of the warband but a useless ox who fails in his training?"

Wyzelo reddened and his teeth clenched but Ardhu held up his hand. "No, even such as he should speak, for he will have to fight should our borders ever fall. I have made a decision; when I saw the body of the Maid of Lilies, I knew it to be right. We will cross the Narrow Sea to Ar-morah. Every able man of the old company will come with me, even you, my brother." He patted the shoulder of Ka'hai, who stood with a worried frown at his shoulder. "It will be one final last flowering of our might, to make this Land safe forever."

CHAPTER SEVENTEEN
THE TIME OF BURNING

The journey across the Narrow Sea was surprisingly smooth, the winds favourable and the seas calm, though Ardhu was glad they had to go no farther South, for just beyond lay the Little Sea, Mar-Byhan with its many green islands, and then the vast curving expanse of the Great Bay, where the tides were always capricious, sending unwary Tin-men to watery graves for the last five hundred years.

The company sailed round the jagged tip of Ar-morah, so similar in appearance to the coast of Belerion, and set ashore below a headland crowned by a massive cairn made of many steps. It dominated the landscape, grey and brown, its pebbled layers rising towards the horizon and its summit surrounded by wheeling, screeching seabirds.

Climbing to the top of the cairn, Ardhu gazed out across a land of verdant fields and grey rock that shimmered under the watery sun. He sighed, wishing he had been able to bring the horses with him on this journey... but it would have been far too dangerous to take such animals in their relatively flimsy craft. Cattle and sheep, yes, if kept with careful handlers and tied well—horses, no.

Hwalchmai came up next to him, the daggers and axe in his belt jingling as he walked. "Where now, Ardhu? How do we find An'kelet in this great space?"

Ardhu waved his arm in an Easterly direction. "I suspect he has gone to ground in the forest of Bro-khelian, which lies in the territory of Ar-goad, the Land next the Wood, somewhere in the middle of Ar-morah. Within its depth he was born to Ailin, the Priestess of the Lake Maidens and King Bhan, and he claimed his kin still had holdings there amidst the trees."

Hwalchmai frowned, squinting into the distance. "We will be far from our ships... I do not like it, Ardhu."

"Nor do I, cousin." Ardhu placed a hand on the other's shoulder, leaning on him for a moment as if for support. Then he pulled away and drew himself up to his full height. "But my choice is made and whatever the spirits have destined for me, I will accept."

The warband trudged on amidst a landscape of golden gorse and speckled boulders, of fallen tombs and standing stones that seemed to point the way across Ar-morah, as well as to the Moon and Sun and stars. As they settled down to camp for the night in the lee of a bald hill, they heard the drum of hooves and saw a solitary rider on a stocky pony galloping over the terrain towards them. Immediately the archers raised their bows, and Hwalchmai and Bohrs readied their axes in case of attack.

But Ardhu, leaving Caladvolc sheathed, walked forward alone to meet the rider. It was a youth of about fourteen Sun-turnings, with honey-bronze hair and long limbs tanned golden from the sun. He reminded Ardhu of a younger An'kelet. "Who are you, boy?" he called out. "What is your business with us?"

"Are you Ardhu Pendraec, king of Prydn?" the boy shouted, leaning over his pony's neck.

"I am. Who asks?"

"I am Brandegor, kinsman to An'kelet of Ar-morah, who dwells in his ancestral holdings in Bro-khelian. He has given words to me that I may speak them to you."

"Speak, then, Brandegor kinsman of An'kelet. You have nothing to fear from me."

"An'kelet says that if you come in peace you may meet with him within the woods of Bro-khelian. But if you bring war to his door, you will never go home alive... the forest will have your bones, the moss will consume you, and you will pass from this earth as if you have never been."

Bohrs made a growling noise. "He presumes... We should cut the trees with our axes and then burn his blasted forest."

"Be silent Bohrs," frowned Ardhu. "Such talk does no good. Let me think..." He passed his hand across his brow. "Brandegor, bring An'kelet this message from me—I do not come in friendship, because there is much in Prydn that he must still be taken to task for. But I will not bring my warband into the forest. Instead I will come alone. We will meet one on one, as princes and warriors, and make a final end to what is bad between us."

Bohrs made a derisive noise. "Are you mad, Ardhu? He knows the forest!"

"And I know him," said Ardhu. "It is the only way." He nodded toward Brandegor. "Go now, with all haste, to announce me to your chief. I will follow as quickly as I may."

The youth bowed his bright head. "I will tell the Lord An'kelet of your decision." He struck heels to the pony's flanks and galloped toward the tree-furred hills on the horizon.

Bohrs stared moodily at Ardhu. "I pray you have done the right thing, Stone Lord," he murmured. "An'kelet is not the man who was once your friend, and how can you ever trust him?"

Ardhu shrugged. "I do not trust him. But I will face him, and let the Ancestors decide between us."

*****

In Kham-El-Ard Mordraed crouched on the ramparts, watching the river and the fields below and occasionally glancing over his shoulder at the inner bailey of the fort. Under a weak blue sky, pale and vapid after yet another summer rainstorm, people went about their daily business—herding beasts, weaving, making reed baskets, cutting wood, cooking. Dogs yapped and barked and children ran screaming amidst the huts. Lazily Mordraed counted the men folk, sizing them up—most were either very old, lame in some way, or very young, with the exception of his band of perennial ne'er do wells, who stalked about swilling beer from their beakers and brawling with each other.

It was as he had hoped. The only important member of Ardhu's warband left in the dun was Per-Adur, whose head-wound had never really healed and now suffered shaking fits similar to those of Gal'havad... Mordraed shuddered, lips curling into a snarl. He would *not* think of Gal'havad, would not let his foolish grief cloud the days leading up to his great glory.

Staring back out into the fields, he spotted a band of strangers coming from the direction of the ford. Straining his eyes into the bright midday light, he saw Wyzelo marching at their front, his expression one of self-satisfaction. He smiled to himself. The great oaf had done one thing right, at least—he had gone and collected all his kin and fellow malcontents from their villages on the edges of the Plain. They had dwelt too long in the shadow of Kham-El-Ard and now they wanted more.

As he did.

Wyzelo led the newcomers up the crooked hill to the wooden gates of the fortress. They came slowly, seemingly no threat to anyone, a crowd of stout lads with poorly-knapped axes and flint knives, little copper amongst them. In Kham-El-Ard the tribesfolk stopped their weaving, potting, and scraping skins and turned to stare at the newcomers. Women, sensing something amiss, called their children to them and bustled them inside their houses. The men came up from the fields and from the river, frowning, wishing they had their daggers, but they had not taken such weapons to their daily toil.

Only Mordraed's chosen, the unfit and the uncouth, seemed pleased to see the newcomers. Still slurping from their beakers, they grinned and nudged each other, obviously enjoying the discomfiture of the rest of the tribefolk.

At the gate, one youth with a spear stepped forward and barred their way. "I know you, Wyzelo," he said, "but these others have no right to be here, and you have no right to bring them in the Stone Lord's absence."

Wyzelo looked the youth up and down mockingly. "I think you'll find you are wrong," he drawled. "I think you'll find things are changing here, and that I can do as I bloody like."

"You've gone mad!" hissed the youth with the spear. "You've had too much sun!"

Mordraed stood up. He climbed gracefully down from the ramparts, and padded cat-like toward the stand-off at the gate. Smiling a dangerous smile that did not reach his eyes, he put his hand on the young guard's spear, pushing its sharp tip towards the ground. "Step aside, my friend, I would advise it."

The youth erupted in anger, though dawning fear was clear in his face. "Who are you to tell me what to do? Ardhu's nephew but a man disgraced, cast out of the war-band..."

Mordraed's hand shot out, catching him round the throat in a vicious grip. In an instant he was on the ground, helpless and gasping. Mordraed pulled his bow from his shoulder and fitted an arrow to the string, pointed toward the youth's chest. Women screamed inside the dun and old men flurried, too fearful to get involved but craning to see. Mordraed's fellows began to strut up and down in front of the tribefolk, smirking and swinging their axes, daring the people of Kham-El-Ard to come forward.

Mordraed lifted his head, his glance raking over the assembled villagers. "I will tell you and *this*..." he kicked the fallen guard, "who I really am and why I it is my right to command all within these walls. Listen well, you sheep, you worthless cattle! Ardhu Pendraec is no fit master for you; he is fit only for the grave. Not only have the land and crops failed, showing he is no longer rightful king... he is the breaker of taboos, a dealer in the forbidden. He has lied to you for years, pretending he had favour with the Spirits—but they had no love of him! The White Phantom was barren save for one sickly son, who the Ancestors have now taken. The Spirits cursed Ardhu and rightfully so!"

"How can you speak such treachery?" one elder cried, his voice tremulous. "Your tongue is that of an adder!"

"Is it, old man?" Mordraed's eyes crackled. "Look at me, all of you. What do you see? Am I not in the image of the Stone Lord himself and all his Ancestors before him in Belerion and Dwranon? Do I not look, more than nephew, but more as son? That is because, you fools, I *am* Ardhu Pendraec's son, born of his own sister, the Lady Morigau. He begot me in forbidden union and deceived you all, while robbing me of honour and birthright!"

A hush fell over the crowd, a horrified silence.

Mordraed's lips tightened to lines. "He has gone on his fool's quest to Armorah, leaving his lands yet again. He is no fit leader—may the sky fall on his head and the sea eat his bones! I will take his place here, as is my right by the strength of my arm, ruling over you in high Kham-El-Ard from this day forward."

"You cannot do this unjust deed!" a voice roared. Across the dun hobbled Per-Adur, leaning on a stick for support. Despite the injury that made his gait unstable and his limbs shake, he still managed to clutch a bronze axe in his free hand. "No one will follow you, son of a serpent-woman and witch! If what you say is true, you are cursed by your birth and by your actions."

Mordraed stared at the shambling figure of what had once been a proud warrior. He felt nothing but contempt. Per-Adur would be better off with the Ancestors. His eyes turned hard as diamonds, cold as winter. "Kill him!" he said to Wyzelo, and then, sweeping his gaze over the whole of the inner bailey. "In fact... kill them all. Only keep the White Woman... for me."

Wyzelo and several of his companions lunged forward toward Per-Adur as people shrieked and howled and ran about madly in panic. Drunkenly, Mordraed's followers drew their weapons and chased the villagers, baying for blood like mad dogs. The youth at Mordraed's feet recovered from the compression on his throat and tried to get a firm grip on his fallen spear. Seeing his arm reach out, Mordraed spat disdainfully on him and shot him through the heart with an arrow.

Wyzelo and his cronies now had hold of Per-Adur. He swung at them with his axe, knee-capping one and sending him rolling in the dirt in agony. Wyzelo kicked his staff from under him, and the injured warrior staggered forward, unbalanced. Mordraed ran over to him, striking him with many blows from his fists, before snatching the older man's streaming hair, worn, as customary, in an upswept style like a horse's mane. It was perfect to grab hold of.

Mordraed forced Per-Adur to his knees, dragging him around so that his face was toward the village... and the terrified people who ran screaming through the huts, falling to dagger, rapier, axe blow and arrow's flight. "Look your last on Kham-El-Ard!" he snarled. "Look your last on the Sun." He dragged Per-Adur's head back, forcing him to stare into the sky at the glowing disc of Bhel Sunface. "Now look at me... your lord, your death." He twisted Per-Adur's head again, until their eyes locked. "I am Mordraed, son of Morigau, son of Ardhu. I am the Dark Moon, and I am vengeful! Fear me and despair."

"I fear neither death nor you," Per-Adur croaked. "You are a deluded fool. By the gods, you will pay dearly for this act." And he spat at Mordraed, the spittle hitting the Moon-scar on his cheek.

Mordraed's dagger flashed in the sunlight. Per-Adur crumpled to the ground in a spreading pool of blood. The yellow mane of his hair turned red.

Mordraed took his dagger and licked it, bringing the essence of the dead man's power into himself, and then wiped the other side of the blade across his cheeks, painting himself with this symbol of victory. So it had begun... what he had been born to do...

Glancing around he saw bodies strewn, men, women, children, dogs... even a pony. His band was running wild throughout the dun, screeching like wild animals and destroying anything in their path, their distorted faces barely human and their arms red to the shoulder with gore. One took a brand from a fire and shoved it into the thatch of a hut; it exploded into flame as the youth shrieked with crazed laughter.

Mordraed cursed. He raised his own dagger and shouted a halt. Reluctantly his band ceased to chase the remaining villagers and came slowly towards him, grinning like the fools they were. "Enough!" Mordraed shouted, fixing them with a hard stare. "Put out that fire, you idiots! We don't want to destroy Kham-El-Ard; it is to be ours, the finest and most powerful settlement in all Prydn."

Wyzelo, Ic'ho and a few others hastened to beat out the flames. The fire died away as the hut collapsed inwards, walls and roof disintegrating. Mordraed gestured to the cowering survivors of the raid, a handful of terrified, ashen-faced women and girls, a dozen wailing young children. "I am merciful; these creatures have survived thus far, so I shall spare them. We need women to cook and mend our garments. You can have them for slaves or bedmates, if you desire any of them."

The youths of the band rushed towards the women, who screamed. Mordraed called his men back again, his voice taut with annoyance. "Later, you dogs. We have work to do! Where is Fynavir... has anyone found the wife of my father, the faithless whore they call White Phantom?"

"Here, Mordraed!" Two youths came forward, dragging Fynavir between them. She showed signs of having fought them and her gown hung in tatters, but she hardly resisted them now; in her thin face her eyes were dead, hopeless. Her cheeks as white as her hair, which hung down knotted and in disarray. She resembled one Moon-mad.

Mordraed stared at her and felt sick; he was to bed *that*... old, cold as snow, dead as a piece of bone? She... who was Gal'havad's mother? At the thought of the half-brother he had murdered, his sensation of sickness deepened; a cold ripple travelled up his spine, as if somewhere a man had stepped on the ground where his barrow would one day be raised. No, he would not think on it... Gal'havad was meant to die; his death was due to Ardhu's actions; Mordraed was only the agent, the one who struck the blow. The spirits surely had meant for it to end that way or they would have intervened.

Fynavir pulled away from her captors and stepped right up to him so that they were face to face. She was a tall woman, not much smaller than he. He could see her eyes beneath their pale gold lashes, green like Gal'havad's had been, and the lines that showed her age and suffering, marring what once had been a face of great beauty. She showed no fear, no hate, just a dull resignation. "Why have you done this terrible deed, Mordraed? Why? When Ardhu was so good to you, giving you a place in Kham-El-Ard, letting you befriend his only son? Gods, I wish he had never been so trusting... yes, I know what the warriors whisper about my son's death... and it is only because Ardhu is fair and would not accuse you without proof that you yourself do not lie dead!"

Mordraed's lips quirked up; more of a grimace than a smile. "Lady, I see no one has ever told you the truth... neither the Merlin nor Ardhu Pendraec himself. You say Ardhu is good to me? He has me here on sufferance! Humiliates me! He withholds deserved rank and respect!"

"Why do you think you deserve anything, as son of the woman who hated her brother and continually strove against him?"

"*Because I am Ardhu's son!*" Mordraed grabbed her roughly by the shoulders and shook her. Fynavir looked genuinely shocked; her hand flew to her mouth and her knees buckled and she fell to the ground.

"Yes, know the truth, woman. Know what you married." Mordraed clutched her wrists and yanked her roughly back onto her feet. "Know also that I will take you in his stead, make you my own woman. You are the White Woman, the Sovereignty of Prydn bound within you, and now you are mine... and the lordship of Prydn with you."

"You are mad! I would sooner slit my own throat that let you lay a hand on me!"

"That I cannot permit." He gestured to two of his men, who stood nearby, grinning. "Take her away and guard her well. Make sure no sharp objects come near her hands." Reaching out, he ran one thumb down the side of Fynavir's long pale neck, trying not to shudder... she felt as cold as the snow she resembled. Cold as a dead body. God, how he hated the thought of bedding her! "You will have a small reprieve to get used to the idea of being my woman... I have other things I must attend to before you, Lady of Kham-El-Ard."

Whirling on his heel, eager to put her from his sight, he motioned to Wyzelo and the rest of his warband. "Take any horses than remain in Ardhu's stables. Bring your weapons. We ride to Deroweth."

Fynavir, caught in the strong arms of her captors, stared at him with dawning horror.

"What are you planning, Mordraed?" she screamed.

White teeth flashed against his dark, handsome face. "I go to get a blessing from the priests, lady. For our marriage."

Mordraed's warriors began to laugh and make obscene jokes. Fynavir was dragged away, struggling furiously, screaming and begging Mordraed not to go to Deroweth.

He shut his ears to the noise and turned to Wyzelo and the others. "We must destroy all the priests, or they will turn their magics on us and kill us all. So show no mercy. You need feel no guilt, no fear of wrathful spirits—the priests have supported my corrupt sire for years, so they too are corrupt and deserve to die like dogs. Burn them out. Cleanse their evil with fire!"

The horses were brought and torches lit and passed out to every man. Mordraed swung up on the back of a black mare, one of Lamrai's foals and a favourite of Ardhu, and took up a brand in his left hand. Rising high in the saddle, like some vengeful young god, he thrust the flame toward the fading sky. "With fire," he cried, "we shall destroy our enemies. Fire... to burn away the darkness, to burn the sins of the world to ash!"

*****

The young acolyte Dru Bluecloak strolled between the stout, rectangular houses of Deroweth, carrying a beaker of mead for his master, the high-priest Gluinval. Behind him trundled two serving woman, hauling a huge cauldron-like pot of boiled meat. The Sun had just set, and a purple cloak of twilight lay over the sacred space and the Plain beyond, furling the stunted head of the Khu Stone, stone of Dogs, that pointed the way to Khor Ghor. Woodenheart was a black blot, its posts rising up like a forest of bare trees, and the causeway to the river shone pale dull silver. Night-loving insects made strange chirping and chuntering noises in the growing dark, while a fox yipped somewhere in a clump of bushes, a noise that sounded eerily human.

Dru Bluecloak cast a jaded glance at the two women struggling along behind him with the great cooking pot. They were spilling broth and scalding each other, and scolding each other too, in some sort of ludicrous rivalry of incompetence. "Come along," he said testily. "The High One will not wait much longer to take his meat and drink!"

Suddenly one of the women gave a cry. She dropped her end of the cooking pot, making her companion stagger forward and almost fall face first into the cauldron. "Oh, look, look both of you! Down by the Abona! The stars... the stars are falling to earth!

"What?" her companion shrieked, still trying to gain her equilibrium. "Where?"

Brow furrowed in annoyance, Dru Bluecloak turned sharply around, ready to lash both women with the sharpness of his tongue for their foolish imaginations. Instead, his tongue cleaved to the roof of his mouth, and his heart began to pound like a solstice drum. He stood transfixed for a moment, unable to move or speak, then released a great and terrible cry. The beaker tumbled from his hands, smashing on the ground.

"Those are not stars! They are torches! Torches born by men on horses! There is no reason why such men should come to Deroweth except for evil... Run, *run*!"

The first horse came into view, bursting through the night vapours sailing from the river. A warrior with a grinning, painted face sat astride it, torch in one hand, battle-axe clutched in the other. He paused for a moment, surveying the settlement, then hammered his heels into the horse's flanks, driving it forward into the enclosure. Waving his axe, he screamed a war-cry, and thrust the torch into the thatching of one of the many huts that clustered around the chalk banks. Flames leaped into the growing shadows.

The acolyte and the two women fled, screaming, the females bounding like hares across the field and into the shadows that furled the Khu Stone. Dru Bluecloak hoisted his robes around his knees and ran toward the High Priest's hut, with the timber trilithon standing proud and tall before its doorway, marking it as a place of high status. Gluinval emerged even as he reached the door, staring in wonder at the younger man's stricken face and breathlessness, his feebly waving arms.

"What is amiss?" he asked urgently. "Why do I hear screams and smell smoke? Have you set the cook-hut on fire?"

Dru Bluecloak's mouth opened and shut; no words would emerge. He shook his head weakly and pointed with a shaking hand into the gloom.

Gluinval let his gaze follow the trembling hand of the acolyte. Brightness was appearing all over Deroweth, the brightness of flames—flames that blossomed in the dark like hot orange flowers. Flames that ate and gnawed at huts with vicious incandescent teeth, twirling up and consuming walls, devouring thatched roofs with a terrifying hunger. In the direction of Woodenheart there was a groan and a crash so loud it sounded as if one of the mighty oak posts had been tipped from its pit. Screaming and shouting followed the sound, and course, drunken laughter.

Grasping his staff, the High Priest strode forward to defend his enclave. Acolytes and other priests could be seen fleeing through the smoke and fire, chased by men on horseback who swung at their skulls with honed axes of bronze. Some priests had robes aflame and screamed like terrible demons of darkness as they burned to death even while in flight.

"Who commits this act of sacrilege?" Gluinval thundered, glancing right and left. He wielded his staff like a weapon, held rigid across his body as a protection. "A curse be upon your head—you shall have no happiness from this hour forth, you shall not prosper in aught that you do. Whatever you touch will wither and die. Your blood will feed the earth in penance for your crimes, no barrow will hold your bones, and your name will be spat upon unto eternity…"

"Save your curses, greybeard." Mordraed rode out of the smoke on his stolen steed, ash on his cheeks and falling from the flowing darkness of his hair. In his lean face his eyes were blue cold stars. "I am cursed already by the circumstances of my birth. I care not for your curses."

The high-priest glanced up, recognising the young man instantly. "You! You are the Stone Lord's nephew!"

"No, priest," sneered Mordraed. "Not his nephew, his *son*. And soon I will be his bane!"

Mordraed forced his mount forward; it whickered and fought his control, frightened of the growing flames, the screams of the dying all across the settlement. Gluinval swung out with his staff but Mordraed struck out with a huge black basalt war-hammer and shattered it in the middle. Laughing, he herded the priest back towards his hut, through the arch of the wooden trilithon, and into the narrow doorway. Behind him his men rushed in, eager for sport, and he gestured to them to barricade the door from without.

"We have a rat in the trap," he said. "Put it to the torch."

Wyzelo thundered up to the hut and hurled his brand into the thatch; others joined him. Smoke spiralled, and there was a flicker as the thatching caught… and then the roof exploded, showering sparks into the night air. Watching the destruction, the young men roared in approval and dismounting their steeds, they began a war-dance, a victory dance fierce and terrible to behold with the firelight shining on polished weapons, and on glistening, sweating torsos and on the glassy surfaces of drink and blood-crazed eyes.

Behind the hut, hiding in the mud at the bottom of an animal pen, Dru Bluecloak wept in sorrow and terror. "My master, my master," he sobbed, but as he heard the roof cave in, he knew there was no hope of the High Priest's survival. "I will go to Ardhu Pendraec… I will bring him back to take his vengeance and right this wrong!"

216

Hauling himself over the fence of the pen, he ran for his life out past the Khu Stone and across the Plain, into the Deadlands where he prayed his enemies would not follow.

Mordraed saw a flash of blue heading West, but paid little heed. One lowly servant was of no interest to him. He turned his attention to the wooden trilithon before the High Priest's burning hut, lit luridly by the dancing flames.

"Wyzelo... come help me. We must bring this thing down."

Wyzelo and his fellows crowded around. They hacked at the huge oak posts with their axes, hammering at them in frenzy as if they were hated enemies. Other warriors joined in, scraping at the bases with picks and other implements they had found around the site, trying to undermine the structure. Yet others gathered kindling and stacked it around the bottom of the posts.

When the structure seemed sufficiently weakened, the two posts full of notches and rocking in their beds, Mordraed kindled two torches and thrust them into the pyres that had been built around their feet. The dry tinder caught instantly and flames darted up the sides of the trilithon, fanned by the nightwind blowing from the East. Higher and higher they roared, twisting around the posts in an all-consuming embrace, illuminating the underside of the wooden lintel. The old wood, already dry from untold years of exposure, crackled and began to glow as the flames burnt through the surface towards the core.

Up and up the conflagration rose, eating, consuming. Ashes started to fall through the showering sparks, and for a brief instant the entire shape of the trilithon was lit up, a stunning red-hot beacon against the starry sky. Then, with an unearthly groan, one leg of the structure slumped forward. The whole structure wavered back and forth, back and forth in unearthly motion.

"Get back!" shouted Mordraed, gesturing wildly to his celebrating warriors. "It's coming down."

The youths scattered in all directions, as the burning wooden trilithon seemed to dance in its pit. Wood crackled and snapped, and in a blazing flash of flame the whole structure collapsed, one post completely fallen, the other tilting at a disjointed angle. The blazing lintel was cast into the darkness, where it continued to burn.

Mordraed raised his axe to the sky in victory. "The priesthood of Deroweth is cast down! Next we will bring our vengeance to Khor Ghor. A Moon will rise there to replace the failing Sun. But not tonight!" He motioned for his men to take to their horses once more. "It is still an unsafe place in the dark, and I have more pressing matters. We ride to collect my mother, the esteemed Queen Morigau of Ynys Yrch, and take her in triumph to Kham-El-Ard."

*****

Morigau and Khyloq squatted amid the rushes in Ardhu's Great Hall

217

gleefully rummaging through Fynavir's personal possessions. Morigau had appropriated her golden shoulder-cape, ripping away the aged fabric and replacing it with weavings in her own colours. Khyloq was fingering a huge crescent-shaped jet necklace with shale spacer beads, holding it up to her throat and admiring her reflection in the blade of a ceremonial dagger.

Several feet away Mordraed sprawled across Ardhu's throne of antler tines, a beaker of mead clutched in his hand. He had washed the ash and blood from his face and was dressed simply in a close-fitting deerskin tunic and leggings, but on his head he wore a circlet given him by Morigau, wrought of two strands of gold from the rivers of her birthplace, Belerion, beaten into fine sheets and fastened by rivets. She had hidden it amongst her possessions for years, waiting for this day.

"Tonight you will bed the White Woman," Morigau said cheerfully, trying on coiled armlets and bronze finger rings, "so you will be wedded to the Land in the eyes of the people. You have sent men to Place-of-Light to tell them that you have taken Ardhu's throne?"

"Yes." Mordraed's voice was curt. "I have sent guards to make sure none of the villagers there try to take up arms or send messengers to Ardhu while he is in Ar-morah. The more time he is gone, the more resistance I can devise against him."

Morigau rose and went to her son. She kissed him on the cheek, twining her fingers in the long black silk of his hair. "Don't look so sullen, my beautiful child. We are attaining all that we have ever desired."

He gave her an inscrutable look. "Did you ever ask what it was I desired?"

She seemed surprised. "Surely this is it…"

He waved her away as the doors opened and one of the men came in leading two young boys—Gharith and Ga'haris. Although they were being brought to greet their own mother and brother, they looked terrified and clutched each other's hands as they were herded down the hall.

Morigau frowned to see them; she had almost forgotten they were in Kham-El-Ard. "The brats," she hissed under her breath.

The children were brought before Mordraed's seat. He leaned forward, placing his hands upon their shoulders with surprising gentleness. "Don't be afraid," he said, "I won't hurt you. Indeed, now that I am master of Kham-El-Ard, it will go better for you. I will make sure you rise in position, and have many heads of cattle and as many lands as I can spare. I only ask that when you are grown you do not raise hand against me, but serve me well. Will you, my small brothers?"

Looking from one to the other, the boys both nodded gravely. They did not understand what was going on… but they trusted Mordraed. Their older brother had always watched out for them, even while Morigau ignored them.

"Then go and sleep well, and do not fear. Any that wish you harm, will have me to contend with."

The children bowed and were led back out of the Hall. Morigau glanced at

218

Mordraed with a raised eyebrow. "They were terrified," he said testily. "I wanted them to know their lives and futures are safe with me."

Morigau's lip curled. "Mordraed, you must learn to be harder. If I were you I would have them drowned in the Sacred Pool like unwanted puppies! They have seen your actions today, what you have taken solely with the strength of your arm... What makes you think in a few years they will not do to you what you did to Ardhu? I counsel you to have them put to death"

His eyes were ice, and furious. "You unnatural bitch. You are their *mother*. Do not ever speak of such a thing to me again." He leaned forward, a vicious smile twisting his lips. "I have followed your orders long enough anyway. Now I have something I want from *you*..."

She frowned, twisting a coil of her hair with sudden nervousness. "And what is that?"

He nodded toward the end of the hall where Morigau's long-time companions, La'morak and Ack-olon, stood in the light of the flickering tallow-lamps, haggard-faced and out-of-place amidst the raucous youths of Mordraed's warband, who played games with coloured pebbles, drank copious amounts of beer and wrestled with each other in the rushes. "Those two... .your 'attendants.'"

"What of them?"

"I have always hated them. I want them dead."

Morigau straightened abruptly, high colour flaring into her cheeks. "They have served me since before you were born!"

Mordraed cast her a sharp glance. "I know how they have 'served' you! Listen, I have done your bidding in all things so far, even when I did not agree. I am not yours to move as you will, like the game-pieces my men play with. I am now your lord, mother, even if you are priestess here. Do what I command you!"

She looked furious, as if she would explode. But there was also resignation in her face; she knew Mordraed would not be moved. "Do what you will," she spat. "I can find other younger servants who interest me more anyway. Just do not expect me to watch the execution! Now I will go prepare for your union with the White Woman—I am sure you are looking forward to *that*."

Lips curved into a rigid sneer, she stormed from the Great Hall, striding straight past Ack-olon and La'morak without giving them even a glance. The two men moved to follow their mistress but Mordraed leapt up from his high seat, casting his beaker to the ground and drawing his dagger. "Halt, you!" he shouted down the hall. "Do not move!"

Ack-olon and La'morak stared at him and then at each other in growing fear and confusion. The young men of the warband ceased their gambling and brawling and set down their beakers. All eyes turned expectantly on to Mordraed. Tension grew in the room; the air crackled with it.

Smiling cruelly he glided down the hall, hair of shadow, eyes blue death, gold fire on his brow. His lips smiled but it was not a smile one wanted to see. He nodded to the warriors nearest to the two older men, who were already loosening the daggers at their belts.

"Kill them," he said softly.

*****

Mordraed stalked toward the hut where Fynavir was imprisoned, guarded by several warriors in case she attempted to escape. As he neared the entrance he saw that it had been decked out for the marriage-rite, the high door frame twined with flowers and greenery. Bowls of milk to please passing spirits and encourage fertility were laid out before the door. *Not much chance of that,* he thought sourly, his stomach suddenly churning. *She is a barren stalk...*

Morigau appeared, as if from nowhere, wearing a wreath of hawthorn and cloak dyed red with madder. In silence, she laid down chalk balls and phalli before the threshold while Mordraed watched. He noted that her eyes were red-rimmed ... had she wept for Ack-olon and La'morak, whose heads now adorned the gates of Kham-El-Ard? He hoped so with all his being ... it was time she felt some of the suffering that he had felt at Gal'havad's death.

Coming over to him, she took his hands and daubed them with life-affirming ochre, whispering spells to make him potent and Fynavir fertile... although *she* was nowhere to be seen, the unwilling bride held captive inside the hut. Mordraed resisted the urged to heave as Morigau finished her ministrations. He had never felt less like lying with a woman; in fact it was as if someone had tossed freezing river water over his loins.

"Mother," he whispered thickly. "I do not want to go through with this."

She cast him an evil look. "You must... even if only once. To make the marriage with the Land."

He gritted his teeth. "I do not think I can."

A mocking laugh left her lips. "Oh, so that is the problem. Fear not... I can brew you a potion that will make you like a bull with a herd of cows."

"No! I have had enough of your potions."

"Then let your anger fuel your lust, my son." She leaned against him, hand to his face, her nails caressing the scar she had placed on his cheek. "Think of all the injustices Ardhu has done to you and your people. Think of how this will be the ultimate vengeance! Think of this, and take his White Woman; fill her with your fury and make her scream for your mercy!"

Mordraed tore away from his mother in disgust and pushed his way into the hut. Inside were the guards and a gaggle of women who had been preparing the marriage-chamber for his arrival. Fynavir lay naked and motionless on a pallet of furs; she had been washed and painted with the customary designs. She almost looked dead; there was no resistance in her, her eyes closed and her legs drawn up in foetal position.

Mordraed gestured to the grinning men and the frightened, pale-cheeked women. "Get out."

They hurried from the hut, leaving him alone with his father's wife. He flung off his cloak and pulled off his leather tunic and trousers and knelt on the pallet, staring down at her, his breathing slow and heavy. So beautiful once, he knew that... but ruined now. He let his hands slide across her ribcage and hollow belly, feeling her shudder with revulsion at his touch. He tried to conjure up the anger that would bring the lust Morigau had spoken of, but he felt nothing except a vague sense of sickness. And guilt. This was Gal'havad's mother, and he had killed her son. Now he planned to destroy her further by dishonouring her.

He suddenly felt exhausted, his head heavy as a stone. He just wanted to lie in the dark, alone.

He must have made a small noise, a soft groan, for suddenly Fynavir opened her eyes and glanced up at him. Again, he was shocked by her eyes; green like Gal'havad's, bringing with them bitter memory... He recoiled, staggering back and falling onto the floor near the fire-pit.

"Are you ill?" her voice was heavy, dull. "I thought you had come to rape me, you, the strong conqueror who takes all!"

Anger rose in him and he leapt back onto the pallet, throwing his body over hers and pressing her down into the furs. "How dare you speak so to me!"

"If I displease you, kill me." She sounded as weary as he felt. "I would prefer it."

"I don't want to kill you. And, truth be known ... I don't want to bed you either."

She stared up at him. "I... I don't understand..."

He shook his head. "I don't want you to understand. I just want..." He picked up his discarded cloak and flung it at her. "I want you to leave. To go from Kham-El-Ard. Now. This night. The men are getting drunk; they will not notice, not if you go to the back route, the escape route that leads down from the rear of the fort to the Abona. Behind the goat pens. Can you manage it in the dark?"

"I... I, yes... I can."

"Then go."

She wriggled out from under him, dressing quickly in her discarded robes and wrapping the cloak he had given her around her shoulders. Going to the doorway, she glanced back at him, sitting on the furs, his shoulders slumped, a figure of gold and shadow in the fluttering, failing light of the tallow lamps.

"Why have you decided to free me?" she asked once more, softly.

He raised his head and his eyes met hers. Cold, dark blue eyes beneath lashes long and black that a girl would have been proud of. But there was something new in that sharp, uncompromising gaze, something she had not seen in Mordraed before tonight. It horrified her, because she guessed its meaning.

She gasped and staggered, clutching the doorframe for support. "You are freeing me because you feel guilty! It is in your eyes, your face! So it is true what men whisper ... you killed my son! You are suffering torment for his death!"

The solemn mask of Mordraed's face shattered, twisting as if she had drawn a blade and stabbed him. "Just go, get out!" he rasped. "Before I change my mind!"

She fled, and Mordraed curled up on the floor, his arms flung over his head, crying out in rage at the gods who had afflicted him with this madness.

CHAPTER EIGHTEEN
THE FOREST OF BRO-KHELIAN

The Forest of Bro-khelian gleamed golden in the late afternoon sun. A magical place it seemed, the leaves of the deciduous trees light-spangled, the scent of greenery and running water permeating the air. Ardhu walked silently along its mossy paths, past dolmen capstones long fallen and hidden by foliage, through tangled briar-thickets where blossoms masked sharp thorns, and over streamlets where mists coiled like shy water-spirits, touching his legs as he passed. His men waited at the forest's edge as promised and to leave them made him uneasy, but so far he had seen nothing of danger in the confines of the wood.

By the time the light had just started to fade, he reached a spring which bubbled up out of the ground and filled a basin half-natural and half-wrought by human hands, its bottom lined with water-rolled quartz pebbles. Kneeling, he laved his face and took a deep refreshing draught. The day had been hot—the climate in Ar-morah was warmer than that of Prydn—and he was growing weary of the long walk.

As he knelt on the lip of the basin, the cool spray descending on skin and hair, he suddenly caught sight of a reflection in the crystalline water behind his left shoulder. A wavering image of a face... a face he knew, a face he had once loved... Leaping up, his hand went to the hilt of Carnwennan and he dropped into a crouch.

An'kelet of the Lake, prince of Ar-morah and son of a priestess and a sacrificed king, stood on the edge of the clearing where the spring flowed, watching his former friend with sombre eyes.

Ardhu felt a slight stab of envy, just as he had when he first met An'kelet in Prydn when they were both young, himself little more than a boy. Despite the hardships of the years and the wound Ardhu had given him on their last meeting, An'kelet looked hale and hearty, his youth and vigour restored now that he was back in the land of his birth. Indeed, caught in the rose-glow of the dying sun, he almost seemed a god, his amber hair flowing from beneath a pin of polished bone; jadeite pendants around his neck; gold upon his arms and at his belt and upon his brow. He wore leather calfskin breeches and a fringed jerkin that was open to the waist; Ardhu suspected this choice was deliberate, for it showed the jagged white line of the scar from the injury he had dealt him with Caladvolc.

"Ardhu..." An'kelet stepped forward, unarmed, although Ardhu could see gold-hilted Ar-moran daggers at his waist. "So you have come chasing me. I suppose I should have expected it. Eventually it had to become known that you did not kill me."

"It became known, that is true," snarled Ardhu. "Along with the evil that you wrought upon the one that helped you escape my justice."

An'kelet's expression changed to puzzlement. "I know not of what you speak."

"Have you forgotten so soon? Ah well, your ignorance proves your baseness. I am here to finish what should have been done in Prydn... by the Ancestors I will feed your blood to the earth for all that you have done." Drawing Carnwennan, he flung himself with wild abandon at An'kelet. His sudden burst of rage clouded his aim, and An'kelet carefully sidestepped his headlong rush, and he went crashing into the foliage.

"Must it come to this, our troubles brought even to the green glades of Bro-khelian?" said An'kelet sadly.

"Yes, it must! Have you forgotten what has gone before? You escaped justice and wreaked more evil before your departure..." Ardhu crawled from the greenery, ripping vines and fronds away from his face. "Don't you remember?" he flung at his former friend with venom. "You begged me to kill you. I was the fool and did not smite off your head with Caladvolc. Now I will claim it, as I should have done back in Prydn."

An'kelet raised his hands; he still had not drawn blade. "I was ready to die for my sins at Kham-El-Ard... but the spirits spared me. None have survived the blade of Caladvolc save I. Does that not tell you, Ardhu, my old friend, that the Ancestors have some plan for me? I do not think we have come to the end of our tale as yet."

"You have come to the end of yours!" Ardhu spat, and he charged madly at his former friend once again. He halted, skidding on moss, as An'kelet folded his arms. "Draw blade, damn you. Do not make me kill you with dishonour."

"I will not draw weapon on you... you are still my lord. And despite all that has gone awry... I still think of you as my friend, my brother in heart if not in blood."

Ardhu stood spitting with rage, his face suffused with colour. "Curse you... curse you! If you will not draw weapons, fight me without! Fight me!"

An'kelet undid his belt and flung it aside with his golden-hilted daggers attached. "This I will do, though with a heavy heart."

The two chieftains lunged at each other, grappling. An'kelet was taller and in youth had been the stronger, but his belly-wound, though well-healed, was still tender and blood-loss had sapped his former strength. Ardhu, on the other hand, was fuelled by his anger, his grief, his loss, and his strength flourished until he was an even match to the man who once had been known as the most powerful warrior of the western world.

Grunting, they fell and rolled on the moss, rose again, struck out with fists and feet. Ardhu managed to hurl An'kelet against a tree, and An'kelet, recovering almost instantly, retaliated and flung Ardhu straight over his head, sending him crashing into the waters of the fountain.

Soaked to the skin, an oath on his lips, Ardhu sprang back up and attacked An'kelet with renewed fury, seeking to fling himself on his back and get his hands round his throat, to twist his head backwards and break the spinal column. But An'kelet guessed his intention and tucked his chin low, and grabbing Ardhu's legs by the calves he heaved him up high, throwing him into a nearby bramble bush.

And so it went on for many an hour, with neither man gaining the advantage. The glade and the waters near the fountain were trampled to mud, the bushes were rent and branches of the trees snapped. The daylight died in the West and the forest turned the hue of blood. An'kelet and Ardhu drew apart, seeking a moment's respite to regain their strength, and stood staring at each other across the waters of the spring. Both were muddy from head to toe, bruises blooming like dark flowers on their flesh, blood on cut mouths and on their battered hands.

"Do we go on?" said An'kelet softly. "Does this not show that we are equal before the spirits? Would it not be better if we put our strengths together and fought as one instead of fighting each other?"

"Have you forgotten? You dishonoured my marriage bed! You had my woman!"

"I know, Ardhu... it is the shame of my life... But, listen... I tell you, I did not take Fynavir to dishonour you or without thought or guilt for my action. Nor did she betray you lightly. It was as if—do not be angry at my words—we were fated to come together. It was as if the spirits and gods had decreed it so, and we could no more deny it than we could stop the rising of Bhel."

Ardhu hunkered down, suddenly weary. He did not want to hear these words... yet somehow knew he needed to. And to accept them. That was what tormented him the most; that Fynavir had wed him and he had been too blind to see that her heart was not with him but with another. Secretly, it had made him doubt his own kingship; the people thought the White Woman was the Land, the spirit of the chalk personified... and the man she bedded the rightful master over all. An'kelet had been her true choice of mate... Ardhu had been endured and no more, and had been too deluded and sure of his own claims to see it. Was he just a tool of the Merlin as many of his enemies had claimed? Maybe it should have been An'kelet who sat in Kham-El-Ard, the greatest warrior of all with his great barbed spear, the Balugaisa, and the White Phantom at his side...

Across the glade An'kelet was washing his bloody, swollen hands in the spring. The dying light turned his curling hair red, red as Gal'havad's. Ardhu felt his throat tighten. No... he could not allow himself doubt or grief at this moment, when he must steel himself against all weakness and summon his last vestiges of strength, and end this rivalry for once and for all. Hopefully, if the Ancestors willed, with his one-time friend dead at his feet.

"I was greatly grieved to hear of Gal'havad," An'kelet said suddenly.

"News of his death reached me here; all the traders on the coasts were abuzz with it. I went to the great stepped-cairn on the headland and stared across the sea that sunders us and wept for him. I imagined—it may have only been in dream—that I could see the beacons burning on Prydn's far shore all through the night."

"Fires burned on every hill." Ardhu's voice cracked. "The banks of Abona blazed with great pyres; the waters themselves looked to be aflame. No man has been so mourned in Prydn as Gal'havad, the Prince of Twilight. And now I am lost, my strength failing... and I have no heir."

Both men fell silent, staring at each other over the darkening water.

"I would throw in my lot with you again, Ardhu," said An'kelet softly. "If you can forgive me my sins against you. I cannot replace him... but I can fill one space at your side and firm your hand if it wavers."

"And the girl? What of the girl?"

"Girl?" An'kelet frowned in perplexity. "You speak in riddles, Ardhu! I know of no girl."

"Elian... the Lily-Maid. She died through your dishonouring of her, and her father begs for retribution. He brought her body to Kham-El-Ard and many of my men cried for your death when they heard she came to grief by your hand. And so I came here, to finish it... and you."

An'kelet passed his mud-splotched hand across his brow. "Elian! This is evil news you bring! She was a sweet and trusting girl. I behaved shamefully with her, that is true; my mind was not right, so ill and grieved was I, but I never wished her ill. I cannot bring her back, for no mortal can tread beyond the Great Plain and return a living man... but I will send restitution to her father, as poor a thing as that might be."

Ardhu was silent. The anger and the pain inside him was a tight knot. And yet, he wanted to trust in An'kelet's words, wanted things to be between them as they were of old. But, with Gal'havad dead, and Fynavir a creature in perennial mourning, a withered white flower that knew no spring, surely that could never be again.

Or perhaps there was a way... a sacrifice of pride, an acceptance of what was once unacceptable.

"An'kelet..." his words came in ragged pants. He did not know where they came from or how he managed to speak them. "I want you to ride with me again. I have never lied and will not lie now. If you return with me to Prydn and stand by me in all things and help me restore the Land to what it should be, I will not only forgive your sins against me but reward you above all men. Above anyone. I will take you and Fynavir before the priests at Deroweth and I will give her to you. If she is spirit-of-Earth, it was you she chose, not me, no matter how I wished otherwise... who am I to force her to remain at my side? I should praise her for her sense of duty! And you... if the White Woman has chosen you, and remained loyal throughout all these long years, then why should you not, as the greatest warrior in the Western World, be king of Prydn after me? In older times a King could choose his own successor; it need not be the heir of his body."

An'kelet stared at Ardhu in shock. "You would do that... even though many men would speak ill of you for it and even laugh behind their hands?"

"I care nothing for the laughter of fools," Ardhu said angrily. "For the first time in months it seems darkness is lifting from my eyes, and I see clearly what must be done. An'kelet, will you return with me? Will you be the heir to Kham-El-Ard should I fall to my enemy's daggers or to evil magic?"

An'kelet strode forward, through the spring and he grabbed Ardhu's hands in his own and went down on his knees in the mud and water. "Oh my friend," he said, and his cheeks were wet. "I had only hoped you would accept me at your side again. Yes, I will return to Prydn with you. And yes, I will be your heir if that is your wish... although you will live many years yet!"

Ardhu laid his hand upon the mane of waving amber hair. He felt strangely at peace. "I have missed your company, An'kelet," he said. "Can we not now go from this place of fruitless battle, and eat and feast as we did in the days of our youth?"

An'kelet leapt up, eyes warm honey-amber. "We can and we shall. I will take you to the settlement of my kin, and have your warband sent for, and we will dine on suckling pigs and fish of the sea. I look forward to seeing old familiar faces again... Hwalchmai, Bohrs, Betu'or, and hearing the tales they have to tell."

CHAPTER NINETEEN
DESECRATION

The Sun bled between the bruise-dark clouds tiered over the edges of Mo Mor, the Great Plain. Heat mingled with the promise of thunder and late rain. Heat waves shimmered above the soil; the first real heat in the long damp summer that had spoiled crops all across Prydn.

In the heart of Khor Ghor Mordraed stood staring at the sky. The Sun was coming out... surely that was a good omen for his reign? And yet, the sky behind was dark as if Tar-ahn the Thunderer was angry, and Bhel's Eye was a burning red slit, an evil eye watching him with scorn...

Shuddering he turned from the stormy sky to the activities taking place within the great circle. Morigau was there, dressed in the robes of a priestess, her face painted with Moons. Child crania clacked round her neck on a thong and her belt was full of fingerbones reddened with ochre. She had taken magic draughts and her eyes were wild and crazed; she swayed from side to side, staff in hand, mumbling gibberish then suddenly becoming lucid, shouting out to proclaim her son as rightful lord of all Prydn—Mordraed, the Dark Moon, who had wrest power from the waning son of Bhel and who would bring back the Old Ways of the Land, before the Tin-men came. The days when Moon with her skull-face was Mother of all, and even the mighty Sun was in her cold shadow.

She raised her arms, her tattered raven-feather cloak, patched many times, streaming out around her. "Hark now!" she howled like a mad woman. "Mordraed of Ynys Yrch has won the right of kingship in the Five Cantrevs. He will restore us to the glory we once knew. We will bring down the Stones of this tainted place, this haven for fools, this place where the true powers were forgotten and false ones venerated!"

Behind Morigau, Mordraed's men worked steadily, raising a great wooden cage around one stone of the Great Trilithon, the southern one nearest to the Throne of Kings with its axe and dagger carvings. Others were digging with antlers picks at the base, sweating profusely in the heat and white with chalk dust. Yet others were dragging bundles of kindling and pitch-lined buckets full of river water. They worked steadily, occasionally glancing up to listen to Morigau's proclamations, but many looked uneasy as if they hated and feared what they had been commanded to do.

Mordraed stalked back and forth between the bluestones. The red sun, glancing off his golden circlet, made the metal hot and his head pound like a drum. "Mother, the men look unhappy," he whispered testily in Morigau's ear. "It is not their wish to slight this place. What can I do? If they turn from me now, I have failed."

"Promise them the world." Her dark eyes gleamed. "They are stupid oafs, without the high ideals so beloved of my brother. You will not even have to keep your word, just throw them a few scraps and kill any who complain." She gave him a mocking glance. "You will have to work a bit harder to keep them, my son. I cannot believe you let the White Phantom slip away so easily when she was such a important symbol to the people."

Mordraed bridled; averting his head so she could not see the truth within his eyes. "She spent the hour in my bed; that was time enough for the deed to be done. Why endure her whey face beyond that? I would have to watch my back at every turn!"

Turning from Morigau, he stepped toward the working men, inspecting the woodwork circling the massive southern stone of the Door into Winter. "This is good," he said loudly. "You will all be blessed by Mother Moon and the Ancestors. Tonight we will all feast—you may bring all your families, and you will have the best of the pigs—Champions' Portions, for that is what you are: champions of Prydn, cleansing the old, evil ways to make way for the new. Gold I will give you, and amber for your women, and you may divide amongst you the weapons, cattle, sheep and women left by the men of the unclean and unworthy Ardhu Pendraec, whom the gods once favoured, but now is fallen in glory. The unnatural man who has left you in time of need to go to Ar-morah on a fool's quest!"

Leaning over, he inspected the crater that widened at the foot of the stone. The upright rose many feet above his head, casting a black shadow over him, its stone foot held in place only by the remains of ancient packing and the wooden supports constructed to stabilise it while the underminers worked.

It was time.

Backing away from the stone, its grey face a stern warning, he gestured to Wyzelo, who was directing the men in the slighting. "Let us begin," he said. "Light the fires."

Flushed with excitement, Wyzelo flung the dry kindling into the pit and lit it. Flames crackled and licked around the edge of the pit and the half-buried base of the stone. More kindling was dumped on and the flames sprang higher, blackening the face of the monolith. Earth began to give way, and the huge sarsen swayed dangerously, the wooden cage around it groaning as over forty tons of rock strained against it.

Morigau began to shriek and wail, dancing in circles and chanting, her eyes rolled back in her head as if she had gone mad. Spittle shone on her mouth, trailed down her chin. She writhed sinuously around the bluestones, a serpent-woman spitting out words of hatred and venom. "The Dark Moon is risen, beloved of old Moon Mother who was here before the Sun himself!" she cried, pointing with a clawed hand to the ghost of a Moon between the brooding tiers of cumulous. "The old ways will return with the rule of my son, Mordraed the Dark Moon! My brother has made you not-men, giving gifts only to his favourites. You will all live as men were meant to—making war, gaining cattle, earning glory. And Mordraed shall be your ruler, cruel and yet benevolent to those who follow his path."

The youths roared, calling out Mordraed's name in proclamation. They started to dance, weaving in and out of the Stones, striking them with hands, with axes, driving themselves into frenzy, all their frustrations and hatreds blazing out in this act of ultimate desecration. Mordraed stood near the base of the unstable stone, watching his men, sweat pouring down his forehead as the fire flared. He ripped off his smouldering jerkin and stood naked to the waist in the blistering heat, ash smearing face and body, his hair lifting and crackling in the updraft. "Today the first stone of Khor Ghor falls!" he cried. "Today the Dark Moon rises over Kham-El-Ard and my sire's evil reign is ended forever!"

He glanced up at the encased stone of the Great Trilithon. The wooden struts were beginning to ignite; flames licked the lowest rungs with harsh red tongues. "Get behind it!" he shouted to his men, waving his arms, his motions almost as frenzied as Morigau's. Fear and excitement shot through him like a spear. "Push it... push it into the pit!"

The youths ceased their victory-dance and rushed up to the great standing stone, some eager to bring it down, others more reticent. Not all in Mordraed's band believed the desecration of the temple was wise; they thought of eyeless skulls deep underground and fleshless mouths of Ancestors in rictus-screams of rage. Others, more practical than superstitious, thought on what might happen if the stone fell awkwardly, crushing or trapping them beneath its bulk. No man could survive being struck by such a weight.

Mordraed gestured again, a downwards motion with his arm. The young men pushed, trying to tip the mighty stone that had stood framing the south-western sky for over five hundred years. At first little happened. The flames licked higher, shooting up the front of the menhir, burning the wooden scaffolding away utterly and sending clouds of rank smoke and burning ash billowing high into the air.

With the wooden support completely engulfed in flame, the stone began to slowly lurch forward, straining towards the huge pit that had been dug at its foot. The intense fire that burned in the crater roared up to meet it, funnelling round it as the wind blew, and sending the men behind running for safety. One or two howled, burnt by the searing updraft, and ran out of the Circle onto the Great Plain where they fell into the long grasses, writhing in agony.

And then the earth began to buckle. A strange shriek filled the air, as if the stone itself was crying out, the spirits locked within its heart wailing in rage and despair, and with deadly speed it plunged forward into the fire-pit blazing at its foot. The huge stone bulb at its base pulled up from the ground as it descended, showering chalk and packing material, and sending men flying across the Circle as if they were no heavier than feathers.

Mordraed leapt back as the megalith came down, roaring like a giant creature that had taken on a life of its own. It struck the Stone of Adoration, ripping it from its socket and beating it into the earth with its enormous weight, then cracked through the middle as it rocked back and forth over the sandstone block that had been the heart of Khor Ghor. Instantaneously the giant lintel that spanned the top of the trilithon was thrown violently through the smoke-filled air and landed near the Guardian's Gate with a noise like a thunder-clap, leaving the remaining half of the Door into Winter standing alone with its naked tenon thrust like a dagger at the storm-laden sky.

"It is done!" screamed Morigau. She was half-white with chalk dust, half-black with ash. Her eyes were wild, ecstatic. "The Moon has smiled on us and felled the Sun!"

Mordraed approached the fallen stone. Fire was still licking it from the pit below, but the flames were beginning to go out, smothered by its fallen bulk. He should have been pleased; he had always hated this place of Stone Ancestors, of memories. But he felt strangely empty and afraid... the remaining Stones seemed to cluster about, the bluestones huddled like conspirators, a wall to hold him in. To pinion him, while punishment was meted out to him for all his evil deeds...

Overhead the ominous sky grumbled.

A storm was coming!

Moments later, the sky roared again, shouting the agony of the desecrated Stones, the angry Ancestors. Huge forks of lightning pierced the ebony clouds, spearing down amidst the barrows of the Seven Kings on their rise. Sulphurous smells filled the air; hair stood on end with static charge. Another boom sounded, the drum of a waking god, followed by the piercing crack of a thunderbolt. The sky turned a sickly yellow and suddenly the circle was filled with eerie ball-lightning, spinning and bouncing from stone to stone like a living entity, lighting up frowning faces and carvings from the days of old.

Mordraed's men screamed at the sight of the unnatural balls of light and they fled the ruined inner sanctum and cowered within the ditch. Even Morigau, her sanity returning, yelped in fear and ran from the circle dragging Mordraed behind her as torrential rain began to lash down.

"What have we done?" Mordraed gasped, huddled in the ditch beside his mother, rainwater streaming down his face, his bare chest. He shivered wildly although even with the storm it was not cold. "This is a sign! It is not good, not good at all." He held his head in his hands, his heavy, aching head that seemed to pound every waking hour and sometimes even woke him from sleep.

Morigau recovered her composure and sneered at him. "Don't be a fool. The storm-god Tar-ahn smites the Stones even as you did! He joins you in their destruction. Men will come to see this as a sign of his approval, even if they are frightened now. Men, especially the mindless dolts of your warband, are fearful of change, fearful of anything beyond their customary rutting and fighting. But they will adapt. Now, come... we must hasten to Kham-El-Ard and shower them all with food and riches! You must get out before the tribes and show yourself to be the most generous lord that ever walked beneath the Everlasting Sky!"

*****

Drums boomed within the high ramparts of Kham-El-Ard. Men danced and drank, chased the unwilling women who were the wives and daughters of those who had gone to Ar-morah with Ardhu. Gold was distributed, animals slaughtered and eaten, clothing divvied up, and weaponry and jewellery fought over. Drink-fuelled youths grew angry and tussled with their fellows; split eyebrows and bloody noses abounded and threats and curses rang out.

Mordraed watched for a while, face pinched with distaste. How he hated these quarrelsome and greedy fools! He could never trust them; one foot wrong and they would tear him to pieces...

He shuddered and walked away to the Great Hall, Khyloq trailing behind him like some lost sheep. She was wearing so much pilfered amber and jet jewellery he though her neck might bend and snap. It sickened him.

Without a word, he took off his dagger belt and cloak, flung himself onto his pallet and yanked a skin over him. Khyloq crawled under the fur, trying to rub seductively against her husband. He felt her growing belly press against the small of his back and to his horror, felt the thing inside her stir, just a little...

Cold terror ran through him; icy sweat broke out on his forehead despite the warmth of the night. This was a magic he did not understand—woman's magic. What if it, this unborn brat, was planning evil even when in the womb, eager to come forth so that it could steal all he had striven for... just as he had taken all that his father Ardhu Pendraec had attained?

Jerkily he tore himself out of Khyloq's embrace and stood up. He hoped she could not see in the smoky darkness that he trembled from head to foot.

"What is wrong?" she asked. "Come lie with me... you have paid me little attention of late."

"Nor shall I, if you continue to whine," he snapped. "Go to sleep. I need time... alone. I will return to you later."

He picked up his discarded belt, fastening it tight about his waist and strode back out of the Hall, feeling stupid and angry at the same time. Outside in the dun the fire-pits were starting to gutter, and inebriated men sprawled about, their drinking-vessels strewn around them. From the clustered huts came continual waves of irritating and disturbing noise; harsh laughter, a barking dog, a woman's screams.

Mordraed glanced towards the gate. A single guard stood there, leaning against a huge post, but he was obviously drunk, his head lolling onto his chest.

Anger flared inside Mordraed... at himself as much as anyone. What was he thinking to let these fools go mad like this? Ardhu was in Ar-morah... but he would be coming back, unless An'kelet killed him in battle. *He would be*

232

back! And even with his smaller forces, Ardhu would swiftly overwhelm these undisciplined idiots unless Mordraed established some kind of order... and swiftly. He had to find Wyzelo, the most receptive of that unruly bunch, and get him to try and drag his fellows from their mead and women and ready them for the conflict that was almost certain to come.

Approaching the fine, large roundhouse he had bestowed on Wyzelo, he heard a lot of groaning and panting coming through the open doorway. *He's got some slut in there...* Mordraed thought with a grimace, as he stepped over the threshold.

On the sleeping pallet he could see two figures writhing on a nest of skins, clawing at each other's flesh like beasts. The white moons of Wyzelo's fat, moving buttocks were an unwelcome sight to Mordraed's eyes.

And then it all got worse. As Mordraed took another step into the hut he could clearly see the female entangled with his prime warrior, her hair spread out across the skins like coiling snakes and her head arched back, her lean brown body slippery with sweat, her mouth drawn back in a taut grin that was almost deathly.

It was Morigau.

She had not seen Mordraed. She pulled Wyzelo down on top of her, curling her legs around his back. He groaned and rolled heavily onto her, while she laughed as if she had won some huge prize by taking him to her bed.

Mordraed stood and stared in shocked silence, unbelieving. He knew she had many lovers over the years, but other than Ack-olon and La'morak she had never mentioned names and he did not ask. But now, she was here, playing the slut with his warrior, his most trusted man, who was young enough to be her son, manipulating him and binding him to her will, just as she had done with Mordraed from childhood onwards...

He must have made a sound because Morigau's expression rapidly changed. She glanced over and saw him standing in the doorway, eyes feral, too bright in the taut white mask of his face, his breathing suddenly erratic, strangled. "Mordraed, why are you looking so stricken?" she taunted. "You killed my companions of many years... did you think I would live alone forever more like some dried-up crone? I found new flesh... as I warned you I would." She ran her nails down Wyzelo's broad back, laughing. Wyzelo jerked uncomfortably, all desire gone with a wave of embarrassment; still locked in her embrace, he looked both afraid and confused.

Mordraed felt his hands knot into fists. Strange rushes of hot and cold flashed through his head, his heart; he wondered if the spirits, the angry spirits from desecrated Khor Ghor, were coming to punish him. "You are a foul, wanton creature," he snarled, his voice thick; it felt as if his tongue would not move correctly to form words. "I think it is true what men say; your mind is possessed by evil spirits."

"You sound like your father, your oh so righteous father, Ardhu Pendraec.

And who are you to judge me? It is obvious to any with eyes that you loved that dead half-man, Gal'havad... a man and your own half-brother! If I am foul, you have wallowed in the filth with me." Morigau's eyes were blazing, mad, with too much white showing; her lips were drawn back almost in an animalistic snarl showing pointed white teeth.

Looking at the twisted countenance of his mother, something snapped in Mordraed's skull. The pounding in his head that had assailed him for days suddenly became a violent hammering. He said not a word but lunged towards the pallet where Wyzelo and Morigau lay, still entwined.

Wyzelo reacted first, trying to disentangle himself from both furs and Morigau. "Mordraed... my lord... no, no!" he squealed, sounding like a pig brought to the slaughter. He half-turned, trying to rise, one arm flung up defensively to shield himself. "It was nothing... I was drunk..."

It was too late. Mordraed's hands were lightning and his long Ar-moran rapier was in his hand. In deadly silence he thrust downward with the long, fire-red blade, piercing straight through Wyzelo's heart and driving the long, spiked tip into Morigau beneath him. Wyzelo had no chance to scream, but blood rushed from his mouth in a great burst and his body collapsed over Morigau's, twitching in death throes. Morigau started to shriek; the blade had entered her chest, but not deep enough to kill. She heaved at the heavy body of Wyzelo but could not move him.

"Mordraed, Mordraed!" she cried. "Why have you done this to me? I gave you the world... the world!"

He knelt beside her and viciously gripped her hair in his hand. His face was inches from hers. His blue eyes, death eyes, burned into hers. "You gave me ashes, mother... ashes and dust."

"Oh, let me go, take out the blade... *help me!*" She writhed in pain, her blood mingling with Wyzelo's on the pallet. "I won't speak more of Gal'havad; I swear to you... I won't try to tell you what to do..."

"Too late..." he said coldly, but he withdrew the Ar-moran danger from Wyzelo's corpse and from Morigau's chest.

She sighed and gasped with relief and pain, tried to stem the bleeding with her hands. "I knew you'd see sense. You are angry... that is good. It shows you are a man and not some tame creature. Call the healer now; I am losing much blood..."

"I told you, mother... *too late.*"

The dagger suddenly flashed down again, plunging into her ribs. The blade struck the floor on the other side of her body and snapped, leaving Mordraed with a useless horn hilt and fragment of bronze in his grip.

Morigau made a gurgling, gasping noise and clawed at the broken blade. "You... you have slain me. I... I am your mother."

"I know," he said, bending over her so that his lips almost touched her greying cheek. His breath blew hot against her ear. "I am indeed your son—you made me what I am and now you pay the price."

234

Mordraed walked out of the hut, the bloody broken rapier in his hand. A crowd had gathered; rough young men suddenly sobered by the screams and noises. Mordraed gazed around him and then flung the gory dagger-hilt to the ground before them. "Morigau is dead," he said defiantly, "and so too her leman, Wyzelo. She was a sorceress, a witch who had dread spirits in her head. She would bring only ill to the people of Kham-El-Ard. And to me, your chief."

The people in the dun were silent. Mordraed heard a faint whimpering and saw his two small brothers hiding behind taller members of the crowd. They clung to each other, as ever, two little dark birds huddled against the storm.

Going over to them, he sank to one knee and took them in his blood-stained arms. They shivered, as cold as winter ice, afraid to touch him in return. "Forgive me," he said. "It had to be done. For all of us."

"But... but she was our..." began Ga'haris in a tiny, tremulous voice.

"I know... But there is much you do not understand. She would have killed you one day, I swear it. With me, you will be safe as long as you are true to me."

He turned from the boys and gestured to his silent men. "The time of feasting is over. You have your gold, your bronze ... now you must work to keep it. Put down your beakers and lift your axes. A guard must be put on Kham-El-Ard and Place-of-Light at all times. No strangers must go in; no one must fare out, unless I give him leave. I want men in the woods, men on the Ridgeways and the Harrow track. I want others to fare to the coast and watch the movements of any ships across the Narrow Sea. For, unless the Ancestors smile on us, Ardhu Pendraec will be returning to Prydn. And he will want his fortress... and his revenge."

CHAPTER TWENTY
THE DARK MOON

Ardhu Pendraec sat with An'kelet of Ar-morah in the wood of Bro-khelian, two chieftains side by side, united in friendship once again after their bitter separation. Ardhu's warband was gathered around a fire, laughing and merry-making, as in old times. Joints of roast pork lay spread out before them, brought on wooden trenchers by members of An'kelet's fair-faced clan, and there were also shining silver fish from the nearby Little Sea, cooked in nests of sweet yet salty weeds gathered from the water's edge. Big, multi-handled beakers different in design from those in Prydn were passed through the group, brimming with thin, grape-based alcohol unlike anything the men of Albu had tasted before. Branches spread above the company like an enchanted, green canopy; and in the boughs the birds were singing without care. A golden haze hung over the whole of the haunted forest, enfolding it, embracing it, almost making Ardhu feel he was in a protected Otherworld where harm could never come, where grief could not find him.

But in his heart he knew that could never be.

Evil and sorrow would always find a path.

And so it was, while they feasted and the Sun faded and the stars came out, that Dru Bluecloak, one-time acolyte at Deroweth, arrived after a long and perilous journey at the forest's edge, seeking Ardhu Pendraec. He was met by the men of An'kelet's tribe who patrolled the edge of the woods with their man-high yew bows, and taken into the heart of the forest where An'kelet had his holdings away from the prying eyes of outsiders.

"My Chief, one is come from Prydn bearing news," said the leader of the patrol, bowing before An'kelet, who sat cross-legged on a sheepskin, holding a pork joint in his hand. "He wears the robes of a priest in training."

Ardhu and An'kelet both frowned and glanced at each other in consternation. "Bring him forward," ordered An'kelet, setting his food aside.

Dru Bluecloak stepped from behind the warriors of An'kelet's clan. He was maybe five and twenty Sun-turnings but looked ten years older, his hair knotted and his beard wild and dark lines underscoring haunted eyes. The blue cloak of his order was stained and torn, and his shoes were ragged flaps bound to bloodied and blistered feet with leather ties. "I... I come from Deroweth," he said, his voice high and wheezy, as if he struggled for breath. "I bear grave tidings."

Ardhu's visage became stone. He sat up straight, fingers on Caladvolc's hilt in an instinctive gesture. "Speak these tidings, holy man."

Dru's mouth worked; he licked his salt-cracked lips. "It... it... is Mordraed, Stone Lord, your kinsman of Ynys Yrch."

A chill rippled up Ardhu's spine, despite the balminess of the evening. "What of him? Speak!"

Dru bowed his head; tears stood in his eyes. He blinked them away. "He has… raised men against you and burned Deroweth to the ground. I saw him burn the High Priest alive; I survived only by fleeing like a coward. I made for the coast and heard more news while hiding there; the land is ablaze with it. Mordraed has desecrated the stones of Khor Ghor, toppling the Door into Winter… and he has also taken the dun of Kham-El-Ard as his own. When I heard those tidings, I knew I had to fare across the Narrow Sea to find you."

"And Fynavir… the Queen?" An'kelet leaned forward, a dangerous light in his eyes. "What news of her?"

Dru choked and coughed, staring at his feet. "Men say Mordraed swore to have her as his own Queen, because she is the White Woman. But it did not come to pass. She is gone."

"Gone?" There was a dangerous note in An'kelet's voice.

Dru shrugged. "That is what is whispered. None know where. Pray to the spirits she is safe in hiding."

Ardhu glanced at An'kelet, his look agonised. "I have been such a fool," he said hoarsely. "I came to Ar-morah seeking your death… and in my stupid need for vengeance, I left my realm open for evil to take hold. And now the worst has happened. Mordraed! I should have guessed!"

An'kelet was white as bone beneath his golden tan but he managed a tight-lipped smile. "Maybe it was meant to be, Ardhu. Maybe if you had stayed in Prydn he would have come at you at night, stabbed you while you slept. Maybe the Ancestors guided you here not for war that would solve nothing but for us to reconcile so that we can stand together against Mordraed." Reaching out he clasped Ardhu's hand in a tight, firm grip. "We will stand as brothers again, fighting side by side… and we will surely win."

"But your weapons… I took them from you, destroyed them. The Balugaisa…"

An'kelet shook his head. "Do not fret over their loss. More have been made for me by my people. Now…" He leapt to his feet, tall and imposing as a god under the swaying trees. "I must summon the tribes of Ar-morah to join me if they will. Your band is sadly depleted… but I will fill the ranks of your host from the Land of the Sea." Brow furrowed in concentration, he began to pace. "We have some ships, in which we sail the coasts of the West from here to Ibero, trading tin… and you have a few boats too—but not enough for our purposes. I will sacrifice some of the trees of Bro-khelian to build more, and will have the best wood-carvers employed upon this task. But preparations will take time, even if it is done in all haste and orders given today. Then we must look for the right auguries, divined in the entrails of a bull slain upon the strand, and for the turning of the tide."

Ardhu bowed his head, resigned, through frustration shone in his eyes. "Although time is doubtless against us, there is no choice in the matter unless we learn how to fly across the Narrow Sea like the gulls. I praise the Ancestors that you are here to help, An'kelet of Ar-morah, my brother in all things, lost to me through our mutual folly and blindness but now returned to me and to my cause."

Ardhu's warband began to shout and cheer, beating the hafts of their axes against the earth. *"Ardhu! Pendraec!"* they chanted over and over and then *"An'kelet!"* until the magic forest of Bro-khelian rang with the sound, echoing from crystalline spring to mossy dolmen, from solitary standing stone to spreading trees with their leaves aflutter in the night-wind.

Ardhu stood amongst his men with Caladvolc unsheathed and held up to the black vault of the sky, and An'kelet joined him with a new spear whose head burned like fire, raising the weapon until its tip joined with the blade of Hard-Cleft, and both knew in that moment that this was the hour that men must stand together or all they worked for would be lost, and that nothing must ever come between them again lest the Prydn they had striven for fell forever into decay and darkness.

*****

The Feast of the Rage of Trogran had just ended and the earth of Prydn baked in the hot sun. The constant drenching rains that had afflicted the country for so long had ceased, but this was not the normal heat of summer. It was humid warmth, thick and sticky; the wind hot and burning to the eyes and throat of man and beast. The skies were not clear summer-blue but massed with storm-clouds that unleashed their fury every evening, then rolled back to brood on the edges of the horizon like strange, megalithic formations of the heavens. The Sun was a dim blob amid the frowning, twisting trilithons of the clouds, a bleeding and baleful eye that cast lurid light over the Great Plain with both rising and setting.

Mordraed shifted uneasily under the gaze of that dwindling red eye as he stood upon the ramparts of Kham-El-Ard. Crackles of lightning began over Magic and Harrow Hill and a low wind moaned in the trees down by the great river. Mordraed shivered, despite the stormy heat; he felt troubled and alone. Bron Trogran was a celebration of fertility, when the crops were gathered in and thanks given to the Ancestors for the bounty of the earth... but the time it took place was also the month of death, when, in the days of Samothos the first Tin-Lord, the Corn-King would die with the last cut sheaf, a gift to the Corn-Woman whose body incubated the wheat. He did not know why this old rite, now reduced to a play of men and women in masks, wielding sickles that cut only sheaves and not flesh, bothered him so, for it was always the Old King who would fall, be taken back into the earth, his blood and bones feeding the crops for seven Sun-Turnings, while a young newcomer took his place to restore the Land.

The young Challenger never failed, never died...

Nor would Mordraed fail...

Another shudder gripped him and, despite the heat of the day, he felt cold to the bone. At the start of Bron Trogran, Nin-Aeifa the Priestess of the Lake, had left her watery dwellings and made the journey to Kham-El-Ard. Men had stopped and stared and prostrated themselves on the ground, for despite her great age, she was still very fearsome... painted blue and white, her kirtle shining like fish scales, her hair matted with lime and decorated with shells. She had walked into the dun, bold as a she-wolf, and stood before Mordraed's seat, unafraid, although a naked axe-blade lay across his knee. "I have a message for you from the High Priestess of Suilven and the Nine Ladies of the Lake," she had intoned, fixing him with her terrible single blind eye, milky and blue, that saw into the Otherworld as well as the hearts of men. "News has reached Suilven and Glas-duin of the murder of the priests of Deroweth and the slighting of Khor Ghor. These deaths, these desecrations, are abhorrent to us and to the Spirits. Neither you nor any of your people may attend—or celebrate—the Feast of Bron Trogran, lest your sins blight the earth and the crops and anger the Ancestors. This Ban, spoken at the Full Moon, in the Great Cove of Suilven, will be for your lifetime and three men's lifetimes beyond. So it shall be." She then spat at his feet, and slammed her wizened hawthorn staff on the ground three times to seal the ban.

"I care not," he had snapped back, half minded to kill the loathsome woman and throw her body into the pig-pens where the perennially hungry swine would devour her stringy frame to the bone.

But he had held back from touching her, as her horrid, damaged eye fixed on him again, unblinking like the eye of a corpse. "Where lie the bones of wise Merlin?" she breathed, so quietly that only he could hear, and he realised that she, half in trance-state, exhaled damning words torn from some unknown realm. "He who had the triple Death that was forbidden to him. Maybe nowhere, maybe everywhere—in the air that surrounds you, the earth below your feet, in the flame that burns, in the water where he was drowned..."

Mordraed had leapt from his seat in alarm at these last words. *She knew*! Nin-Aeifa and the priestesses of Suilven knew he had killed the Merlin! "Men!" he had shouted, in frenzy "Get this creature from my sight before I kill her with my own hands and feed her to the pigs!"

But Nin-Aeifa had cast him a contemptuous glare and turned and walked proudly away of her own accord, and none, even Mordraed, had been brave enough to touch her as she descended the hill of Kham-El-Ard and headed for the Old Henge and the river. "Remember, Mordraed of Ynys Yrch," she had called back over her shoulder. "Three lifetimes beyond your own... though I daresay your own life will be a short one. I do not foresee your days being long and fruitful, for darkness is within you."

Mordraed rubbed his arms at the memory and scowled into the thunderous late afternoon. She had cursed him... or maybe it was just empty words meant to frighten, to take the resolve from his sword-arm. He did not believe in curses, at least when the fires were bright and weapons close to hand. What was wrong with these fools, why were they so against him? Yes, perhaps he had been harsh in his punishment of the priests of Khor Ghor, but they were corrupt, pawns of Ardhu—surely the Priestesses, who were deemed to be wise, could see that the Priests had lost their way? Surely they were aware that the realm was falling into ruin because Ardhu was old, weak, unfit... no true king.

He began to pace, high on the rampart, walking with the ill-controlled tension of a caged beast. He had hardly slept... since *she* had died, impaled on his dagger. Hardly slept as he waited for news to come from the South. News of Ardhu... was he dead in Ar-morah, fighting An'kelet for lost honour, or was he on his way back to Prydn with anger and vengeance in his heart?

Down by the Abona he caught a slight movement in the trees and saw several of his men running to ascertain the cause of the disturbance. His heart began to hammer against his ribs as he saw a dishevelled rider loom out of the murk, half-falling from his horse in exhaustion. He could see the man gesticulating wildly as the warriors surrounded him and he heard raised voices, though he could not make out the words.

A second later one of the men broke away from the horseman, and ran haphazardly toward the gate. As he approached, legs pumping, Mordraed could see the scaly pallor of his face, the terror in his eyes.

He knew what news he would bring.

Ardhu, his father and his bitter enemy, was on his way back to Kham-El-Ard.

*****

Mordraed gathered his bow and strapped on his quiver of arrows. He lifted his new dagger, which the smith had forged for him after he broke his rapier in Morigau's body, examining it for balance and sharpness. It was good... he had asked that it be made longer and broader than was the fashion; now it looked almost a twin of Ardhu's Caladvolc the Hard-Cleft.

He called it King-killer, in hope.

All around him the people of Kham-El-Ard milled; the air was crackling with fear, with tension. Women wept outside their huts; even though they were Ardhu's people they feared they would be caught between the two opposing forces and killed by either blade or fire. Even Mordraed's own sworn men looked fearful, their bravado leaving them as they realised they would truly have to face the wrath of the Stone Lord, wielder of Caladvolc, and his sworn companions, who had years of battle experience and an innate discipline and purpose that they lacked.

Khyloq came running, her flame-hued mane a tangle, and flung her arms around Mordraed's waist. "I hear the cursed one comes! Kill him, my dark Lord. Let me be set up as a true queen of Prydn, with none left to question my right!"

"Get off me!" Mordraed grabbed her wrists and pushed her away from him. "I do not have time to think of you and your wants…" Yet as he looked at her, with her swelling belly and her eyes full of both desire and fear, he suddenly thought, *She must go from here… If the day goes wrong, anything could happen. Ardhu would not kill a woman, but I do not trust the motives of my own men… And my brothers, would any spare them?*

"Look…" His voice was kinder and his hands slid to her shoulders, squeezing gently. "I am going to send you from here, and I want you to take Ga'haris and Gharith with you. It is not safe in Kham-El-Ard for a woman… particularly my woman. Go down the Abona, into the valley, and seek the Priestesses of the Lake. They are my enemies, but they would not harm or turn away another woman, I think, and I pray they will not turn away innocent children either."

"I do not like this idea!" Khyloq gasped, clutching his leather jerkin. "It is as if you prepare for your death!"

"I do *not* prepare for my death," he said, a dangerous edge in his voice, "but I leave nothing to chance… I am not a fool. Now get my brothers and go, and do not tarry upon the path!"

She left him, tears running down her cheeks, and soon he saw her, wrapped in a woven shawl that covered her bright head, picking her way down the hillside toward the Abona, clutching the hands of his young kinsmen tightly in her own.

Turning from the sight, he cast his gaze over his own men—the stupid, the violent, the malcontent, the idle who only spoke of great deeds and did none. They seemed completely dwindled in his vision, hardly a warband, just a rag-tag bunch of brawling and boastful boys; even if their numbers surpassed his father's, they would never be able to withstand an onslaught from Ardhu's experienced warriors for long. If hatred and blood-lust spurred them on at first, their ardour would soon diminish and they would break and scatter, to be hunted down and slaughtered.

Something within him bent, twisted. There had been so much death already. Why needless slaughter, even of such cattle as these? He raised his hand, gesturing for their attention. "Listen, listen, I have made a decision! I will fare to Khor Ghor… on my own. You must all stay here, holding the dun. When Ardhu Pendraec arrives, tell him to stay his hand and swear that you will do the same. Then tell him that I am on the Great Plain, at the Stones, and that I await him there. He must come alone, bringing none of his followers. We will do battle, one on one, as men and chiefs, and the Spirits will decide between us. If I should fall…" he took a deep breath, "I would council you surrender to him, and pray to the Ancestors he gives you mercy. If I win… then you may strike at his men with all your fury, for their spirit will be broken."

The youths of the warband reacted with horror and an angry murmur went up. They had long wished to engage in battle with their sworn enemy,

241

and had filled the fort with round stones to cast down at their opponents. Their blades were freshly sharpened and their arrows tipped with venom. The idea of hiding behind stout oak walls and waiting for an outcome held no appeal.

Mordraed glared at them, staring them down with eyes of bitter ice. "I do this to save your skins, you brainless fools!" he snarled. "Do you understand nothing? I have given you gold, amber, axes and status as men of the tribe. Now grant me this one bit of loyalty in return, damn you all to Ahn-un!"

They recoiled from him, fearful of his wrath, their anger hidden if not truly quelled. Mordraed turned scornfully from them, almost hating the sight of their hard, stupid faces... "Remember what I have told you," he said icily, and he strode forward into the storm-laden afternoon seeking the Sacred Avenue that would lead him to his destiny.

*****

Ardhu and An'kelet and their men reached Kham-El-Ard late the next day. The woods and fields were quiet, brooding under the hot sky; it was strange to see no harvesters, no washer-women, no children playing in the river. The landscape seemed almost empty, part of the Deadlands... except for the fort of Kham-El-Ard on the crooked hill, its gates shut and barred, its ditches full of newly-honed wooden stakes, and trails of wood smoke seeping from its many hearths to darken the skies above it.

Ardhu stared at the barricaded dun, his lips thin lines and his jaw tight. Deep anger flooded him, and he longed to charge up the hill and set a great tree trunk against those gates, *his* gates, but he knew such an action would be counterproductive. Those holed up within his dun would heave rocks upon his head, or boiling water, or animal dung, and with the height and the protection of the stout oak walls, the defenders had the clear advantage.

Seeing his friend's expression, An'kelet laid a steadying hand on his shoulder. "It would not be wise to act in haste. "I will go up to the gate and speak with them."

Ardhu nodded. "Take care, An'kelet. They may shoot at you before you speak. These are not true warriors; they are rabble corrupted by Mordraed."

An'kelet raised his round shield of leather and wood. "I will take no risks." He trudged towards the fort, his spear carried on his back in its sling rather than in his hand. Raising a clenched fist, he pounded on the great wooden gates. He could hear voices muttering behind. "Open the gates!" he shouted. "I am An'kelet, prince of Ar-morah, companion of the Stone Lord. How dare you bar entrance to the King of the West, the lord and builder of this dun?"

A coarse red face popped over the breastwork. "Kham-El-Ard is Ardhu Pendraec's no longer. Now it is held by Mordraed, lord of the Dark Moon."

"If that is so, tell Mordraed to come forth and speak to us—if he dares!"

"He is not here," replied the man.

"Well, where is he?"

242

"Gone to the Stones," the warrior shot back. "He has asked that we pass a message on to his adversary, Ardhu Pendraec."

Hearing these words from his position at the bottom of the hill, Ardhu quickly rode up beside An'kelet. "What message is this? Speak!"

"He says he will fight you man to man in the Stones. Whoever wins will be king of Prydn... the other will be in his barrow. He says that if it is settled in such a manner, we can avoid bloodshed; he has ordered us not to attack you unless you do not agree to these terms. "

An'kelet glanced uneasily at Ardhu. "I do not like this overmuch."

Ardhu took a deep breath. "I would not have the people inside Kham-El-Ard harmed, nor do I even greatly desire the heads of the dolts who bar our way. I will do as Mordraed asks; maybe it is the best way to settle this forever..."

"I do not trust Mordraed; he is a snake." An'kelet shook his head darkly. "I will come with you to Khor Ghor."

Overhead, the gateman leaned further from the parapet, shaking his head. "You must go alone, Pendraec. That is the order of Lord Mordraed. If you try to take men with you, we will ride down from the hill and join battle. Then we will fire this place and burn it to the ground."

Ardhu took a deep breath, thinking of all the men and women he knew who were captive in the dun. Ka'hai's wife and children, close as kin... he knew the big ugly man was fretting at the bottom of the hill, thinking of what their fate might be. "I will go alone. I am not afraid."

An'kelet paced uneasily. "If it is your wish. But let me have my say, since we are friends again and you have named me heir. It is late in the day and although the nights are light, still it will not be overlong before the Sun sets; it is not good to fight in the dark."

Ardhu laughed darkly and unsheathed Caladvolc. "I do not intend to fight at night. Before the Sun is down, it will be finished."

"If you are not back here by Moonrise, grant me permission to send men to find you," said An'kelet grimly. "Grant me that much, at least."

The Pendraec inclined his head. "It is granted."

He swung down from his steed and handed the reins to An'kelet. The taller man raised a quizzical eyebrow.

"I will go on foot," said Ardhu, "following the Sacred Avenue from the River. Khor Ghor has already suffered at Mordraed's hands; I would not disrespect it further by riding a beast beyond its banks, even on this day... this day of reckoning."

He turned from the fortress gate, the late afternoon sun flashing on his breastplate and buckle of gold and on the surface of the Face of Evening, his shield. He raised Caladvolc and he raised his copper axe, saluting bright-faced Bhel as He soared through the skyway on his journey to the West. He embraced An'kelet, kissing him on either cheek, and then his kinsman Hwalchmai, and also Betu'or, Ka'hai and Bohrs, who stood with his jaw

243

agape, for the Stone Lord had never behaved thus before when battle was imminent. It was almost like a farewell...

Then, his leave taken, Ardhu strode down the hill toward the chalk banks of the Avenue. He did not look back.

*****

Mordraed sat inside the circle of Khor Ghor on the fallen lintel of the Door into Winter. Moodily he stared out across the Great Plain, where the long grasses rippled in the late Sun like waves on a strange green sea. Every now and then he took a sip of water from a small clay flask or chewed on a strip of dried beef. He would not eat more, for he wanted his belly to be empty when the time for battle came; he did not want his body to be sluggish from consuming excess food or drink.

After a while he got up and started to pace. Ash from the destruction of the trilithon eddied around him, small black whirlwinds against the wrenched chalk. The bluestones frowned, close as conspirators, while beyond them the arches of the outer circle grinned, as if mocking him. Maybe Ardhu would not come. Maybe he was too afraid, or had some other plan...

He grimaced. He *had* to come; an ending had to be made. Overhead the westering Sun beat heavily on his head, increasing the throbbing in his temples that had gripped him for days... no, weeks. He hated it, both the pain in his skull and the relentless heat of Bhel; but not to worry, soon the Sun would fall from heaven and the Moon would rise, and it would be his time, the time of the Dark Moon...

A sudden noise, scarcely more noticeable than a breath of wind in leaves, made his spine prickle.

He was not alone.

Limbs tense, adrenaline rushing, he pivoted around, bow in his hands and an arrow to the string.

Ardhu Pendraec, father and uncle, chief and rival, stood in the gap that led to the Southern causeway, the reddish light of late afternoon flaming on his regalia, turning the unsheathed blade of Caladvolc to bronze flame.

Mordraed fired two arrows in quick succession. Ardhu flung up Wyngurthachar and the swan-feathered shafts bounced harmlessly aside, skittering in the dirt. He then sprang at his opponent, faster than one who was not in full bloom of youth had a right to be, and crashed his full weight into Mordraed before he could release another arrow, striking him in the belly with his shield and throwing him back onto the shattered block of the Great Trilithon.

Mordraed landed heavily, his bow tearing from his fingers, breath forced from his lungs with the force of impact. Almost immediately he recovered, thrusting himself up on his elbows and flinging himself forward against Ardhu's shield and trying to wrest it from his father's arm.

Grappling together, they staggered across the circle, bashing into bluestones and tripping over chunks of wreckage from the broken trilithon.

Mordraed gave one vicious wrench and twisted Ardhu's wrist, near breaking the bones, and Wyngurthachar tore loose and clattered to the ground. Grinning, Mordraed snatched it up and flung it outside of the circle. Now Ardhu's left hand side was open to attack, vulnerable.

Ardhu stared at the man before him... this thing he had made in one night of folly so long ago it seemed like a terrible, twisted dream. So alike in face and form, but Mordraed with a prettiness about him that contrasted with the ice in his eyes, the cruel and uncompromising set of his mouth. The downing Sun shone on the black river of his unbound hair and warmed his cold features. His skin was unadorned, with no sacred marks upon him for protection, nor were any talismans bound to his deerskin jerkin or belt; it was obvious he believed he needed no help from the Spirits to win this fight.

"I should have killed you as a child," Ardhu said harshly.

Mordraed smiled and drew his new long sword from his belt, the blade fashioned just for his hand. *King-killer.* "But you did not and now I shall kill you."

They engaged in the centre of the circle before the fallen half of the Great Trilithon and the crushed, half-buried Stone of Adoration. Bronze smote against bronze with metallic clangour and sparks flew into the air. In the West, through the towering arch of the Gate of the Guardian, the Sun was rapidly descending, spraying out spokes of incarnadine light like gore from a fatal wound. Above the Stones, the vault of the Everlasting Sky resembled a blood-stained shield. Sullen clouds towering on the horizon turned crimson and broke apart, burning like a thousand heavenly funeral pyres, a thousand fallen monuments. Nearing the edge of the horizon, the lurid, watchful red eye of Bhel looked distorted and huge, black cloud-streamers darting over its surface as it began its final descent into the Land of the Dead. Trapped in its last bloody rays, the stones of Khor Ghor burned out against the failing twilight sky—red, gold, green, beacons lit in a final blaze of glory before night fell forever.

Ardhu and Mordraed did not speak, nor meet each other's eyes as they slashed and parried and hacked at each other with their keen bronze blades, seeking to wound and then bring down. Mordraed fought like a wild animal, obviously hoping his youthful strength and the rage in his heart would carry the day; but Ardhu was more experienced and patient, his blows less frenetic and more accurate, and he countered every move the younger man made with consummate skill, stepping aside and around when Mordraed lunged in his direction, hoping to bring blade to flesh.. He was aware that his shield arm was unguarded and his left flank open to attack, but as Mordraed bore no shield himself, Ardhu did not greatly worry about it. They were equal, like the Days when Light and Shadow balanced in the great Circle...

Mordraed's face was pallid, sweat streaming into his eyes as he struggled to get in under Ardhu's guard. He had not expected the old fool to be so sprightly still, to have such an arm of stone. He had underestimated his father

245

sorely. But if he could not best him by swift blows and sheer force, other forces could and would come into play...

Stabbing and parrying with his long sword, he gradually managed to work Ardhu around in a semi-circle until the last hot piercing beams of Sunlight flared on the older man's helmet and breastplate... and shot into his face, making him squint against the harsh burning glow in the farthest West.

"Fool!" shouted Mordraed as he saw Ardhu try to shade his tearing eyes with his left hand, an instinctive gesture. He gave a great leap forward, throwing himself onto Ardhu, trying to smash his knee into his groin or belly and render him helpless. Ardhu staggered back under his son's weight, Caladvolc lowered to waist-level in defence of his lower body, and Mordraed's blow went wide, his kneecap meeting with force against Ardhu's hip bone. It was not what Mordraed had hoped for but a violent impact nonetheless, which made Ardhu's leg crumple beneath him, pins and needles rippling down his thigh.

Mordraed saw the agony in his father's face and rushed him again. Off-balance, Ardhu was hurled backwards, slamming into one of the mighty grey pillars of Throne of Kings on the Southern side of the circle. Anger flared in his eyes, and he swung Caladvolc in a shining arc towards Mordraed's head, eager now to end this in the only way it could end... in blood and death.

Grinning now, sensing that the tide might be turning in his direction, Mordraed threw his blade up to meet that of his father. The Hard-Cleft was like a tongue of burning flame in the dusk and, gleaming, King-killer leapt forth to answer its challenge. The two swords smote against each other with force, sparking and sawing. Aware that Ardhu had nowhere to go with the massive trilithon at his back, Mordraed relentlessly pushed his advantage, drawing in closer and closer till they were almost touching, hip to hip, shoulder to shoulder. Upwards he forced Ardhu's hand, a move he had learned from An'kelet whilst in training at Kham-El-Ard. He saw Ardhu grimace, and try to twist Caladvolc for a sharp downward thrust.

Mordraed used his last reserve of strength to slam his own sword heavily against Caladvolc, a blow violent as a thunderclap. Ardhu's hand snapped back and the blade of Hard-Cleft struck the face of the trilithon behind him, smote the stern grey sarsen that was one of the hardest stones on earth.

And shattered...

Glittering in the embers of Sunset, shards of the sword from the Sacred Pool, gift of Nin-Aeifa of the Lake, spun across the circle and came to land amidst the ashes left by Mordraed's destruction. Stunned, Ardhu stared at the hilt and jagged fragment in his right hand. The useless stump... his broken kingship.

At that moment Mordraed struck. Lowering his sword-arm, he grasped Ardhu's shoulder and yanked him close, almost as if he would embrace him. But it was no tender moment of forgiveness. Lips curved in a triumphant leer, he thrust King-killer into Ardhu's unprotected left side and twisted the blade.

246

Ardhu's face whitened with shock. Mordraed began to laugh, driving the blade deeper. "I knew I would prevail, " he gasped. "The Old King always dies at the hand of the new in the month of Death!"

Behind Mordraed's shoulder, the uppermost rim of the Sun was finally sinking under the horizon. The sky and the Circle were the colour of old blood. Real, fresh blood poured from Ardhu's side and reddened his pale and draining lips as his knees gave out from under him and he slumped to the ground at the foot of Throne of Kings, the inlaid daggers and axes shining out above his dark head.

Mordraed withdrew King-killer and raised it in triumph, red rivulets from the gutter of the blade streaking down his arms, his face, his chest.

And then... there it was. A soft sound, a faint movement in the deepening twilight near the Gate of the Guardian, no more substantial that the beating wings of a moth...

Afraid of new attackers, Mordraed whirled on his heel, weapon at the ready. The remaining fragments of brightness in the West briefly dazzled his eyes...and then, as he struggled to adjust his vision, he spied a figure gazing through the arch of the trilithon. Red blood-ruby hair, long robes wrought of twilight and eventide mist, a sad, solemn face he knew so well—object of love and hatred. Eyes green as the grass on a barrow-hill and deep as death caught his and held him in a reproachful stare.

"*No!*" he screamed, the word wrenched from his constricting throat.

Unwillingly he staggered in the direction of the vision, the apparition.

It changed.

The Merlin stood before him, not the old feeble man crippled by elf-shot whom he had dispatched to the Otherworld, but a strong youthful shaman in a great ceremonial headdress of horns and bone. His visage was dark and saturnine, strong lines running from nose to mouth, lips curved in mockery and deep dislike. His robes frothed around his ankles, blending with darkness; on his breast his hawk talisman gleamed, its eyes shining like molten bronze and its open beak dripping the blood of the sacrifice...

No words came from his lips but Mordraed heard cold, familiar words echo inside his head, first spoken Moons ago, *"You will never be king in Ardhu's stead... if I have to fight Hwynn and Nud themselves, I will return from the Otherworld to stop you!"*

"You won't stop me!" he shrieked, waving his sword like a madman. "My reign is destined!"

His back was turned to the crouched, wounded form of his father. He did not see Ardhu move, crawling on his knees, one hand pressed to his bleeding side, the other stretching toward his lower leg.

Mordraed had forgotten, in his moment of triumph, his moment of terror...

He had forgotten Little White Hilt, the Sword from beneath the Stone, the dagger that had given Ardhu his right to rule the tribes of Prydn...

Until it bit deep within his lower belly, tearing into his entrails, a fatal blow from which no man could recover.

Mordraed dropped to the ground, the pain, the fear, making the shadows and spectres that assailed him flee from his mind. There was no Merlin, no Gal'havad within the circle of Khor Ghor. Only him, with the horn-hilted dagger protruding from his side, and Ardhu Pendraec, bleeding from a similar wound beside him, their blood co-mingling, pooling on the ash and chalk. "This... cannot... be..." Mordraed gasped, disbelieving. "I... was... destined..."

He was clutching Ardhu's shoulders, trying to keep from collapsing; it almost looked as if they embraced as kinsmen, not as bitter enemies struggling against each other till the last. Ardhu glanced up at him, and his pinched, grey face was twisted with sorrow. "You... my son... were deceived..."

As Ardhu spoke, a horn suddenly sounded outside Khor Ghor, its notes bouncing eerily from stone to stone. Hoof beats made the earth tremble.

Ardhu glanced with swimming vision to the East, where a round, pale Moon-ghost floated in the sky. The Moon had risen. His men were here.

Mordraed craned his head toward the noise of the horses. He could see the dim shapes of men entering the stones... saw daggers drawn and bows with barbed arrows on the string. Ardhu's warriors!

Releasing Ardhu, he started to crawl on all fours toward the entrance of Khor Ghor, toward the Watchers and the Stone of Summer... toward the ghost Moon, the blessed Mother Moon to which he was sworn, as it soared higher into the night-time sky.

Instinctively his hand went to the hilt of Carnwennan, pulling it free of his flesh; blood flowed with renewed intensity and he stared at it, streaking down his legs, covering his hands, shining in the bitter Moon-light.

His life, slipping away, feeding chalk and stones and Ancestral bones buried deep beneath him.

Coldness seeped through his limbs, a strange tingling; he struggled to breathe. An iron taste hung in his mouth and he felt something wet on his lips that was not saliva.

Behind him he could hear shouts from Ardhu's warriors, knew that they were preparing to leap upon him, to rend him limb from limb with their axes and daggers. They would take his head, they would take his heart; his pieces would be scattered on the plain and his spirit would never rest. An ignominious death, devoid of honour. A traitor's death.

He heard Ardhu's voice rise, shaking, hoarse, as if from a great distance. "Men... finish him! But not with your blades. Give him to the Circle in the old way of our ancient forebears, to atone for his crimes against the Ancestors. Give him to the Circle that his spirit might be trapped here for eternity, guarding what he has tried to destroy."

Mordraed halted, mid-crawl. Behind him he could hear footsteps, heavy breathing.

He knew what his fate would be now... both relief and a curse.

Drawing himself up onto his knees through his pain, he flung his arms open wide in token of his submission and looked up toward the ascending Moon, the bone-white eye of She-Who-Guards, the Protectress of the Dead. On the pitted surface he swore he could see the face of Morigau gazing down at him, filled with love and hate and pride and mockery...

Three arrows flew. Three arrows struck.

One hit Mordraed's breastbone and then glanced aside into his heart.

Mordraed fell face first on the ground, arms still outstretched, and the men of Ardhu's warband took his body by the arms and dragged it to the terminal of the henge-ditch near Heulstone, where they dug a hasty pit. They threw the corpse in with little care, taking his weapons as trophies but leaving his archer's wristguard because he was a man of high status. They placed shards of bluestone around him, to bind his spirit with the power of the sacred Stones, then covered the crouched body with chalk and spoil and debris.

Done, the warriors returned to the inner sanctum of Khor Ghor. Ardhu had propped himself up against the Stone of Adoration; his breathing was shallow and laboured, a cold sweat gleaming on his brow. His mouth shone dark red. Hwalchmai, Bohrs, Ka'hai and Betu'or flung themselves down at his side, trying to staunch the wound in his belly with torn shreds from their cloaks but the bleeding would not stop.

Hwalchmai leaned over and laved his cousin's forehead with water, while Ka'hai steadied him. Ardhu swallowed, and reached out to clasp the hands of both Hwalchmai and his foster-brother, who was weeping openly. "I am glad you are here with me... at the end," he whispered. "And Bohrs too." He glanced at Bohrs who had got up and stood miserably beside the Door into Winter, his shoulders shaking. He wept freely, though in silence.

"It is not the end, lord," said Betu'or brokenly.

"In this life, it is." Ardhu closed his eyes. "I can see the long house of my Fathers across the Plain of Honey. Its doors lie open for me, in a land where falls not the rain, nor the snow, nor any tears; where there is no sorrow and no life's ending. I can see Gal'havad there, on shores awash with crystals and dragonstones, with the wind in his hair and light in his eyes... and the Merlin is with him... They wait for me..."

"Betu'or..." his voice was fading; his fingers, cold, touched Betu'or's arm. "Long ago I spared your life... now it is time you did something for me in return. The sword... the sword Lady Nin-Aeifa gave me... It must go back whence it came. Back into the Sacred Pool, into the holy waters. Will you take it there and return it to the spirits? I ask you because you are Betu'or, Knower of the Graves... Will you find the watery resting place for this thing of power?"

"I will, lord," said Betu'or, and he picked up the broken shards of Caladvolc, held them to his face and wept.

Ardhu gazed up at the sky; the clouds had suddenly rolled away and the heavens were bright with a thousand stars. The Cloak of Nud, the Milky Way, stretched above the Stones and into infinity. He smiled. He could hear the Hounds of Hwynn the Fire-White, god of the Mortuary, baying faintly and then louder, as they sallied forth from Hwynn's stronghold at the Tor and came towards him.

And then he was away with them, over the Great Plain and into the ultimate West.

CHAPTER TWENTY ONE
INTO ETERNITY

An'kelet camped before the gates of Kham-El-Ard with his men around him in hastily thrown-up tents and shelters. Every now and then, he glanced into the shadows by the banks of Abona. The Moon had long risen and Ardhu had not returned from Khor Ghor; he had sent Ardhu's most trusted warriors after him as agreed... but they had not returned either.

A knot of dread had settled in his belly, cold as the bone-white Moon floating in the sky.

Where could they be?

Suddenly, he heard the hammering of a horse's hooves. Grasping his spear, he raced in the direction of the noise. A pale grey horse was flying down the Avenue, heedless of any missiles fired from the ramparts of Kham-El-Ard, where Mordraed's warriors foamed and fretted like mad dogs bound on the lead.

The horse wheeled to a halt near An'kelet's encampment and the Armoran prince saw Hwalchmai, Hawk of the Plain, drop from the saddle-pad, his knees almost giving way as his feet struck the ground. He staggered toward An'kelet, footsteps so laboured and heavy that An'kelet thought he might be wounded.

"Hwalchmai, what has happened?" he shouted, hurrying towards the shambling figure.

Hwalchmai said no word. He glanced up at An'kelet, his eyes shining and wet, star-silvered. Reaching under his short fringed cloak, he drew out Ardhu's Lightning Mace, symbol of the Stone Lord's authority in Prydn. Its fossil head was smeared with blood.

Kneeling on the ground, he bowed his head and proffered the Mace to An'kelet.

And above him, the men waiting in the fort of Kham-El-Ard, seeing this as a token of Mordraed's victory, went wild.

*****

Dawn broke, sullen and red. Blood and fire everywhere, in the sky, on the river, on the ground. The Sun was a hot ball of flame over the horizon, while beneath its rays Kham-El-Ard burned, the greatest fortress in that age of the world, gone forever. Great oak posts toppled and tumbled into the defensive ditches, while gouts of flame shot heavenward and black smoke curled, a shroud that blocked half the morning sky.

An'kelet leaned on his spear, breathing heavily, his heart a stone. He had tried to avert such a disaster but Mordraed's men, believing their master was victorious, had acted in berserker fury, flooding down the Crooked Hill like a hive of angry bees, breaking the truce between the two warbands in their madness. An'kelet's more experienced warriors had taken them on in one great wave, driving them back up to the gates, killing half of them with arrowfire alone... Upon sensing imminent and utter defeat, Mordraed's band had acted with rashness, firing the dun around them as they retreated into its interior. The dry posts and the thatched huts and Hall had ignited almost instantly.

Everything lay in ruins... and yet An'kelet had won.

"Look." At his side Hwalchmai pointed to the Sacred Avenue. "He comes. Ardhu comes home... one last time."

An'kelet shaded his gaze against the brightness in the heavens. On the Avenue he could see figures moving slowly, heads bowed in mourning. A supine figure lay across their shoulders, raised up toward the strengthening face of Bhel.

"We will go to the River," he said. "And wait. Then we will prepare him for his last journey and do what must be done."

*****

Betu'or the Knower of the Graves stood beside the Sacred Pool at the foot of Kham-El-Ard, the place where the Old Hunters had gathered millennia past to hunt the great cats, the antlered deer, the mighty aurochs that could feed a whole tribe for a whole Moon. Coils of mist twisted from the waters; below the greenish surface, amidst moving weeds, bubbles streamed to the surface and burst.

Betu'or stood on the pool's edge, one foot in the holy spring, one on dry land—standing between the worlds of men and the watery Otherworld. In his hands he held the two shards of Caladvolc Hard-Cleft, shattered against the stony flank of Throne of Kings. He held up the pieces to catch the light, to let all those assembled in the woods behind see that they were truly broken, their spirits released forever and sent from the domains of mortal men.

A sigh went through the assembly, flowing out into the bright morning, and with that Betu'or flung the shards high into the air over the Sacred Pool. They spun in mid-air, shining like gold, like fire, like the tears of the Sun, and then, still whirling, they tumbled into the heart of the waters and were consumed, swallowed into the deep depths whence they came.

An'kelet, holding the Lightning Mace before him, led the mourning party from the Pool down to the fords of Abona. There, on a huge oak plank, lay Ardhu Pendraec in splendour, extended on his back, rather than in the usual crouched burial position of his people, signifying that he was more than mortal man, that he, alone of men, walked with the Great Spirits, the Gods and Ancestors. His face had been painted with ochre, giving him the semblance of life, his hair had been washed and combed down; he looked as if he merely slept, waiting for the right hour to rise. The Breastplate of Heaven gleamed on his chest, reflecting the moving clouds, and Wyngurthachar lay above his head, and all around him the folk of the Lake

Valley and Kham-El-Ard placed armfuls of meadowsweet and campion, the red flower of champions.

Beside him, guarding the bier was his sister Mhor-gan in her priestess's robes of death-green. Her hair was unbound in mourning and her face drawn with grief. Nin-Aeifa stood next to her, a very old woman now, but still tall and straight, her grey braids clattering with quartz beads and shells. Seven women circled them, priestesses with moon-collars and necklets of faience beads shaped like tiny blue stars.

The Nine Ladies of the Lake, drawn together on this day to honour the Stone Lord, to bear his earthly remains away on his final journey.

As An'kelet, the warband and the villagers watched, the holy women took up the oak plank with Ardhu's body and placed it reverently on a wide wooden raft anchored within Abona's swell.

"Where will you take him?" An'kelet breathed, sinking to his knees at the water's edge. "Where can I go to place offerings to the spirit of my friend?"

Mhor-gan looked at him solemnly. "He will have no known grave, prince of Ar-morah. Dark times will come to Prydn with his death; and warfare... I think you, as his successor, know that. There can be no risk of his bones being disturbed. Let it be thought he is everywhere and nowhere, like the noble Merlin... his grave and ultimate fate unknown. Maybe he will lie in a deep cave, under the protection of the Great Spirits; or maybe he will merely lie atop a hill in a coffin carved into the form of a boat, sailing the seas of time toward the Tor of Hwynn and beyond. Maybe some men will even believe he is not truly dead but has been taken by the Nine Maidens for healing in the Garth of Afallan, ready to return when he is needed again by his people."

She turned from An'kelet and gestured to Nin-Aeifa to join her. They boarded the raft with the Maidens gathered around them, and knelt in a ring around Ardhu's body, singing and chanting and keening. Then the ropes mooring the raft were cut and they slipped slowly, mournfully, down the breast of Mother Abona, the Holy River, the Cleanser, away past the grieving people, past the Old Henge, away into the wilds of the lake valleys, away into eternity.

EPILOGUE
DAWN

For the next eighteen turns of the Moon An'kelet of Ar-morah, heir to the legacy of Ardhu Pendraec, strove to build a new settlement to replace fair, doomed Kham-El-Ard; he chose a place on the hither side of the Plain, not far from the charred remains of Deroweth, but not so close that the angry ghosts of slain priests might disturb the slumber of the inhabitants. Between bushes and sylph-like trees, the ravaged stones of Khor Ghor frowned in the distance, shimmering in sunlight, standing bleak as skeleton bones in the morning mist.

Men seldom went there anymore. Some still visited, curious as much as worshipful, and carved axes on the stones, in imitation of those graven on the Throne of Kings but the days of the Great Feasts at Midsummer and Midwinter were over; the people now lit fires within their own home villages and jumped the flames among folk they knew. Once An'kelet had tried to rouse enthusiasm for a rebuilding of the shrine, and he took the tribe's holy man and a force of ardent youths, and they dug pits all around the Stones, hoping, perhaps, to add more monoliths, to rebuild the structure anew.

His plan did not work. Men drifted away, putting up single stones near their hamlets and worshipping at cult-barrows; after what had happened at Khor Ghor, the death and the destruction, it had become little more than a haunt. Only the ever-present birds remained, nesting under the lintels, squabbling over long-dried bones in the ditch.

It was the way of time... felling and changing.

An'kelet sighed. He could not resurrect what the spirits had doomed to die. Khor Ghor was meant to go. So instead he turned his thoughts to other things pressed to the back of his mind through the long painful months after Ardhu's death.

Fynavir.

He had asked the folk of Place-of-Light, the Valley, and the Plain if they knew of her fate after the night of her forced marriage to Mordraed. They knew nothing, only that she was gone... but many hinted she must be dead, maybe even by her own hand, through shame and bitterness.

An'kelet could not bring himself to believe it.

And one bright day of sunshine and showers he found himself walking down the river to the House of the Ladies of the Lake. If any would know Fynavir's fate, it would be those wise women who saw all, in both the realms of the living and the dead. He pondered why he had not sought them out earlier, and hung his head in shame—it had been too painful to see them,

254

those women who had borne his friend on his final journey, carrying him to a resting place they would not even reveal to him.

He spied their hut ahead, standing on its long spindly legs in the river's swell; ancient Nin-Aeifa squatted outside the door, dandling a raven-haired infant on her knee and singing to it as it gurgled and wriggled, while two young, brown-haired boys splashed in the water nearby, trying to spear the fish that darted below the surface. An'kelet did not know whose the baby might be, but with a jolt he recognised the boys...Gharith and Ga'haris of Ynys Yrch. Ardhu's nephews... and half-brothers of Mordraed.

As he drew closer, the boys glanced up and fell silent, their harpoons clutched in their hands. The elder sprang from the river and dashed inside the house and brought back Mhor-gan of the Korrig-han, leading her by the hand.

She walked toward An'kelet and gave him the kiss of peace on either cheek, and he felt his heart near break again for she looked so much like her dead brother... the same smile, set of cheekbone and jaw, the dark eyes mixed with forest green. "I knew you would come," she said softly. "I am only surprised it took you this long."

An'kelet nodded toward Ga'haris and Gharith, who had resumed their play in the water of Abona. "It seems you have made the House of the Lake something of a refuge."

Her white teeth flashed. "Indeed. Many have been under the care of the Ladies of the Lake; some shall stay with us as servants... others must find their own path in the world."

He was silent a moment, an awful thought filling his mind. "That infant... Surely it is not..."

"No. Not hers. His. Mordraed's. But do not look unkindly on it because of its parentage. Remember, it is still Ardhu's grand-child, no matter what evil its father did."

He leaned over her, a good head and shoulders taller and gently took her arm. "Where?"

Mhor-gan nodded toward the vale-side, overlooking the old barrowfields of the early Kings. "Beyond. She goes there often, to look and to remember."

"Should I seek?" His eyes were weary, tired. He pushed his amber hair from his brow. "Or is it too late? Is it tearing open an old wound, making it bleed again?"

Mhor-gan touched his face with her fingertips. "Go to her. There are some wounds that cannot be healed... but many that can."

He turned from the river and headed over the hillside toward Khor Ghor. He could see it in the distance, with the barrows of the old kings lying before it like supplicants, dappled by Sun and by cloud shadows. The skylarks were dipping and swirling in the grass, and a small, fierce hawk soared against the Sun, reminding him poignantly of the Merlin.

And then he saw a woman, kneeling in the long waving grass, simply dressed in a woven kirtle, with a large basket of plaited river-reeds at her side. He frowned at first for the hair that coiled on her shoulders was an earthy brown, not the white mist he had expected, but as she moved, hands seeking in the grasses, he recognised the curve of cheek, her sweet long neck, that he had kissed, that he had loved. She had used dyes to disguise herself, so none would suspect.

He began to run, unable to help himself... though he felt an eager fool, he who was now Ardhu's heir. Fynavir shifted in the grass and stood up, her face calm and her eyes shaded by her fair lashes, so incongruous with her dye-stained hair. "An'kelet. Or should I now speak of you as Stone Lord?"

He halted, hands dropping to his sides. "You know then that Ardhu passed the mantle on to me."

She nodded. "I was surprised to hear such news... but I am glad you were reconciled. And that you were with him at the end." She pressed her knuckles to her mouth, her voice faltering. "What was it all for, I ask you? I ask the spirits day and night. We ruined it, An'kelet... between us, we made the great thing he wrought fall to ashes."

He went to her then and held her, and she wept against him for a while, and he wept too against the darkness of hair that had been white as snow.

"He will never die," he then said quietly. "He is legend now, Fynavir. In a thousand years or more they will still tell his tale, though it will be changed by many tongues and many retellings."

"That is some small comfort."

"Sometimes..." he clasped her hand, twining his fingers with hers, "a small comfort is all we have."

Together they turned and faced the Stones, distant on the Plain, the remaining half of the Door into Winter a barren stick with its naked tenon stabbing the sky, and An'kelet took his axe from his belt and saluted the temple three times with blade upraised—for Sun, for Moon, for Ancestors. Then he gathered Fynavir beneath his cloak and led her from that place of loss and memory, from the realm of the Dead to the realm of the Living.

To start anew.

To live in the new age that must come.

MOON LORD
HISTORICAL NOTES

As ever, my thanks for help and support with this novel to my partner Dan, mapmaker and blogmaster, cover artist Frances Quinn http://echdhu.deviantart.com/, my proof reader Simon Banton, and the Stonehenge team. Thanks too to all those who purchased copies of book one, enabling me to produce the second. A special mention must go to Andy Rhind Tutt of the Amesbury Museum, who showed me the 'magic' colour changing stones from the 'sacred pool' at Blick Mead, which inspired an important character in this book. (If any of you visit Amesbury, do go to the museum, and see the history of the area PRE-Stonehenge!)

As with STONE LORD, nearly all the places in MOON LORD are real, as is the archaeology, although I have played around with dating sequences to a certain extent... .some things are just too good to leave out! The characters fare farther afield in this book than in part one, just as King Arthur's knights quested far and wide in traditional legend on their trek to attain the Holy Grail. In Moon Lord, this meant a trip to the Wastelands of the East (Seahenge), a sacred journey to Ireland where they visit the Bronze Age ritual monuments built around Newgrange while seeking the Cup of Plenty, and they even travel to An'kelet/Lancelot's homeland in the forest of Broceliande in Brittany. Mordraed, Arthur's illegitimate son and nemesis, comes down to his father's holdings on the Great Plain from Ynys Yrch, the Isle of Pigs—Orkney—and recent findings from the complex discovered at the Ness of Brodgar are featured in the early part of the book. Closer to home, there is a ritual pit based on the Wilsford shaft, and also a cave in the side of Khal-El-Ard... this is Gay's Cave on the Antrobus estate and a place we feel needs further investigation. It is thought to be a folly of approximately the 17th or 18th century, but there has been some suggestion that some of its stone is sarsen and a local legend says that it was there at the time of the Romans. It was also rumoured to be used as a cell by the Dark Age Guinevere after Ardthur's death and her retreat to Amesbury Abbey!

Later in MOON LORD, there is a sequence showing some destruction at Stonehenge itself. Although it is unlikely it was slighted in prehistoric times, there is some evidence that one or two stones had fallen even before it ceased to be used. We don't exactly know when one stone of the Great Trilithon fell, only that it was before any realistic drawings of the monument were made. I have incorporated its collapse into my fiction.

I have also endeavoured to show a changing Bronze Age world at the end of the novel, a veering away from the building and use of big ceremonial centres due to climate deterioration (perhaps caused by the eruptions of Thera and Hekla) and other social factors. This is of course is a deliberate anachronism for, although this change did happen, it was not till several hundred years after the period MOON LORD is set in.

As many readers have requested a map, there now is one, showing the main sites in the Stonehenge landscape.

I have also had requests for a list of character names. I have included the main ones and a complete list will be appearing on my blog in the next few months. As for pronunciation, most names sound roughly how they are spelt. C is always hard, never an 'S' sound and 'ch' is as in the Scottish 'loch' and never as in 'change.' A single F is pronounced V. Ardhu can be pronounced in two ways, however—Ar-dee (as in Welsh) or Ar-doo (as in Irish.) Take your pick!

For further discussions of Stonehenge, King Arthur, folklore, myth, linguistics, archaeology and more, visit stone.lord.blogspot.com

STONE LORD and MOON LORD

Names of main characters and places

Abona—The River Avon. One of the great sacred rivers of Britain and also its tutelary goddess.

Ack-olon—lover and servant of Morigau

Afallan— The Apple Garden. Avalon

Agravaen—son of Morigau, half brother to Mordraed

Ahn-ann—a shadowy mother goddess figure. Also known as Ahn-u

Ahn-is—priestess witch slain by Ardhu

Ahn-un—The Not World or Un-world. The Otherworld.

Ailin of the Lake of Maidens—Priestess and mother of An'kelet

Albu—The White. Name of the lower part of the British Isles encompassing the White Cliffs of Dover. Roughly England

Ambris—high priest of Stonehenge, mentor of Merlin, kinsman of U'thyr

Amhar— Child name of Gal'havad, son of Ardhu and Fynavir

An-fortas—The Maimed King, king of the Wasteland

An'kelet— Equivalent to Lancelot. From an older form of the name. In Stone Lord, the suffix or prefix 'An/ahn' refers to a goddess/god or supernatural place.

Ardhu—Dark Bear, Merlin's protégée who becomes the Stone Lord of Khor Ghor.

Ar-morah—Land of the Sea. Brittany in France, which was once known as Armorica. Homeland of An'kelet

Arondyt—one of An'kelet's daggers

Art'igen—The Bear-that-is-to-Be. Ardhu's childhood name

Astolaht—village of Elian the Lily Maid

Bal-in and Bal-ahn—twin warriors who are followers of Ardhu

Balugaisa—barbed spear of An'kelet. Spear-of-Mortal-Pain

Belerion—Cornwall

Betu'or—Knower of Graves. First a combatant then friend to Ardhu. Bedwyr in Arthurian legend

Bhel Sunface—'Shining' spirit of the Sun.

Boann—spirit of the River of the White Cow in Ibherna-the Boyne

Bohrs—One of Ardhu's prime men after an initial clash

Boneman, the—priest of the stones of Stenness

Breastplate of the Sky—Golden lozenge worn by Ardhu. Similar to that found in Bush barrow near Stonehenge

Bresalek—the name of the Green Man of Lud's Hole-the Green Knight

Brig-ahn—priestess of Brygyndo.

Brig—high, royal

Bro-khelian—the forest of Broceliande in Brittany

Brygyndo. Fiery Arrow. High One-3 faced goddess Equivalent to the goddess Brigit.

Buan-ann—the real name of the Old Woman of No name, Merlin's first mentor

Caladvolc the Hard-Cleft— Ardhu's blade, equivalent to Caliburn. The name seems to derive ultimately from Caladbolg, sword of an Irish mythological hero

Carnwennan- Little White Hilt. Ardhu's dagger,taken from a burial cist-the sword from beneath the stone

Crossroads-of-the-World—another name for Avebury, given by later traders

Dag—father god in Ibherna

Deadlands, The —the West where spirits went; also referred to liminal areas like the fields around the Cursus in Dorset and at Stonehenge

Deroweth—settlement at Durrington Walls

Din-Amnon—the stone circle where the young Merlin saw the red and white dragons

Dindagol—Gorlas's holding on the headland in North Cornwall. Birth place of Ardhu. Modern Tintagel

Dragon Path of Dwr—the Dorest Cursus

Drem—brave youth and messenger from Kham-el-Ard

Dru Bluecloak—acolyte at Deroweth

Duvnon—Devon. Land of Dark Valleys.

Dwr, Dwranon Dwri—Dorset and the folk who live in it. The People-from-across-the-Water

Eckhy—priest of Stonehenge; his ghost speaks to Merlin

Ech-tor— father of Ka'hai, foster father of Ardhu. First element of name means Horse

Elian—healer who finds An'kelet wounded. Her love for him ends in tragedy

The Feast of the Rage of Trogran—another name for the Feast of the Corn—Lord in August

Fhir-Vhan—the Man-Woman-Cross dressing figure at the Sanctuary, considered sacred. Curses Ardhu. A skeleton of mixed male/female parts was found buried at the Sanctuary

Fragarak the Answerer—dagger of An'kelet

Fynavir— The White Phantom. Daughter of Queen Mevva of Ibherna, becomes Ardhu's wife. Name is equivalent to Irish Findabhair, daughter of Queen Meadbh and of course Gwynhwyfar/Guinevere

Ga-haris— son of Morigau, half brother to Mordraed

Gal'havad—Son of Ardhu and Fynavir, Hawk of Summer, Prince of the Twilight. Mystic and warrior, attainer of the Golden Cup

Gharith—son of Morigau, half brother to Mordraed

Gleyn—river where Ardhu's first battle takes place page

Gluinval— priest who takes over from Merlin at Khor Ghor

God-of-bronze—the Holy Mountain in Wales. Carn Menyn in the Preselis

God's Peak—a name for the ritual complex at Newgrange

Gorlas—an obnoxious and war like petty chief of Cornwall. Husband to Y'gerna, mother of Ardhu

Great Barrowhill—mound that once stood inside Marden henge-the Hatfield barrow. Now destroyed

Great Trilithon, The—as it is today… the Great Trilithon. Also known as the Portal of Ghosts and the Door into Winter, and Door of the Setting Sun

Ha-bren— The Severn River and its tutelary goddess

Hill of Suil—Silbury Hill. Hill of the Wise Eye

Hwalchmai— Hawk of the Plain, Ardhu's kin and one of his chief companions. Defeater of the Green Man/Green Knight

Hwynn the White Fire—god of the Mortuary. Equivalent to Gwynn Ap Nudd, the Faerie king who lives in Glastonbury Tor

Ibherna—Ireland.Ireland was known as Hibernia by the Romans, perhaps NOT land of Winter but from land of the Iverni, who were a tribe. The bh here is pronounced as V

Ickenholt—The Icknield Way

Ivormyth—tragic daughter of Metheloas, briefly betrothed to Gal'havad

Ka'hai—Ardhu's foster brother and close friend

Kaladhon—a name for what is now Scotland

Kar Sarlog— hill encampment. Old Sarum

Kein-Mother of Merlin. Takes from the Saint Keyne, but interestingly means 'nothing' in German

Kham-el-Ard-Crooked High Place— Equivalent to Camelot. Vespasian's camp hillfort in West Amesbury

Khaw—a rebel chieftain

Khiltarna— The Land Beyond the Hills. The Chilterns

Khyloq—Mordraed's wife

Khen the Head River—the river Kennett near Avebury

Khelynnen—Fynavir's serving woman

Khor Ghor—Dance of Spirits of Great Ones—Based on the recorded named Choir Gawr, the Giant's Dance.Choir hear is related to the word 'chorea' not 'choir.'

Khu Stone, The— Stone of Hounds or dogs. The Cuckoo stone in the field by Woodhenge. A Romano British shrine with child burial/dog skull was unearthed here

Kichol of the Red Eye— priest of Ibherna who serves a blood thirsty solar god

Kon-khenn—sea monster whose bones were said to be the spikes on An'kelet's spear

Krom the Bloody Crescent—dark god of the grain in Ireland. Received human sacrifice every seven years

Lamps of Uffern—two stone lamps outside of Gods Peak

Lailoq—'friend' Child name of Merlin.

La'morak—lover and servant of Morigau

Loth—King of Ynys Yrch, the Orkneys. Enemy to Ardhu

Lud's Hole—abode of the Green Knight. Lud's Chapel

Maedh'an na Marah—Maids of the Waves, mermaids

Maheloas—priest and tribal headman at Gods Peak

Mahn-ann— sea—spirit. Equivalent to the Irish Mannanan

Maigh Dhun—Fort of the Plain. Maiden castle in Dorset

Mako'sa— priestess of Silven, Odharna's successor

Marthodunu—enclosure of the Plain. The ceremonial site of Marden in Wiltshire

Melwas of the Summerlands—King who abducts Fynavir

Merlin. Also the Merlin— Adopted name of Lailoq taken from his totem animal

Mevva— Irish tribal Queen known for her fierceness and lust. Name refers to mead—hence 'the Intoxicator'. Mother of Fynavir

Mhon—Anglesey, still known as Mona. The Mother Isle

Mhor-gan of the Korrig-han—sister of Ardhu, friend to him, and priestess

Mineth Beddun— mountain of the Graves. Scene of a battle

Mordraed—illegitimate son of Ardhu and his half-sister Morigau. Ardhu's greatest enemy and his bane. Name means 'judgement'; equivalent to Irish Midir and later Moderatus.

Morigau—half sister to Ardhu, his bitter enemy, mother of his son Mordraed

Moy Mell, the Plain of Honey—Where dead warriors go after death

Moy Mor, The Great Plain—Salisbury Plain..and also the Plain the spirits of the dead travel over

Nin-Aeifa—Priestess of Afallan. Equivalent to Vivian/Niniane

Nud Cloudmaker— Hwynn's father. Also known as Snarer and Snatcher. Also God of the Milky Way. Equivalent to Nuada/ Nodens

Odharna—high priestess of Suilven-Avebury

Ogg—a god of eleoquence, hill name after him

Old Circle—the henge at the end of the Stonehenge Avenue, recently

Palomides—a slave of the Sea-pirates, freed by Ardhu. A Greek from Delos, long said to have ancient ties to Britain

Pelehan—the Fisher King, son of the Maimed King

Per-Adur—One of Arthur's chief warriors

Phelas—father of Elian

Rhagnell—wife of the Green Man/Knight; takes up with Hwalchmai

Rhyttah—gigantic warrior, slain by Ardhu.

Rhom-gom— Ardhu's ceremonial mace/sceptre. The Lightning Mace. Similar to that found in Bush Barrow

Sacred Dragon Mound—Dorset Cursus

Sacred Pool, The— spring and pool behind Vespasian's camp. Has been used for feasting and ritual deposition since Mesolithic times

Samothos—one of the first of the Tin-lords or kings. One of the beaker people and a metal prospector, now seen as semi-mythical

Sanctuary, The—timber and stone circle attached to the Avenue of Avebury. Called the Sanctuary in 'real life'

Seven Kings, The—Very large barrows on the ridge to the east of Stonehenge. They are called the Seven Kings in modern times as well as in STONE LORD and MOON LORD

She-Who-Guards—death goddess, watcher of the dead.

Sherdan—Palomides' name for the Sea-pirates

Sovahn—feast, equivalent to Samhain

Spiralfort—another name for Gods Peak-Newgrange

Suilven—Place of the Eye. Avebury Stone circles

Tarn Wethelen—the site of Mount Pleasant in Dorset. Both real and fictional places were burned in a great fire.

Tirre—brother to Elian

T'orc—a giant boar trained by Ardhu's evil sister Morigau

U'thyr Pendraec-a chief of the Dwri, father of Ardhu. Ardhu the Chief Dragon or the Terrible Head

Urienz—cousin to Loth, Ardhu's enemy

Vhortiern— Great Lord. Merlin's chief

Wastelands, The—eastern lands hit by plague and famine. Norfolk.

Woodenheart—Woodhenge

Wyngurthachar—Ardhu's shield. The Face of Evening. Carved with representation of the Watcher of the Dead

Wyzelo—the Weasel. Companion of Mordraed

Y'gerna—mother of Ardhu, Mor-ghan, Morigau

Ynys Yrch—Isle of Pigs, the Orkneys

Y'melc—feast of Lambing, Feb 1

Zhel—aspect of the Winter Sun, said to be buried in Silbury in a golden coffin

Lightning Source UK Ltd.
Milton Keynes UK
UKOW04f1242190913

217510UK00002B/58/P